Witchfinder

Also by Andrew Williams

# Witchfinder

## ANDREW WILLIAMS

HODDER

First published in Great Britain in 2019 by Hodder & Stoughton
An Hachette UK company

This paperback edition published in 2020

1

A CIP catalogue record for this title is available from the British Library

Paperback ISBN 978 1 473 63178 6
eBook ISBN 978 1 473 63177 9

Typeset in Celeste by Palimpsest Book Production Limited,
Falkirk, Stirlingshire

Printed and bound in Great Britain by Clays Ltd, Elcograf S.p.A.

Hodder & Stoughton policy is to use papers that are natural, renewable and
recyclable products and made from wood grown in sustainable forests. The
logging and manufacturing processes are expected to conform to the
environmental regulations of the country of origin.

Hodder & Stoughton Ltd
Carmelite House
50 Victoria Embankment
London EC4Y 0DZ

www.hodder.co.uk

Things said or done long years ago,
Or things I did not do or say
But thought that I might say or do,
Weigh me down, and not a day
But something is recalled,
My conscience or my vanity appalled.

From 'Vacillation', W. B. Yeats

For Kate, Lachlan and Finn.

# DRAMATIS PERSONAE

## THE SECRET INTELLIGENCE SERVICE [MI6]

**Sir Dick White**, *chief of SIS, known as C, formerly director general of MI5*

**Harry Vaughan**, *fictional officer assigned to the PETERS investigation, then a member of the joint MI5 and MI6 FLUENCY working party on the penetration of both services; former head of station, Vienna*

**Maurice Oldfield**, *chief liaison officer in Washington, then deputy chief of SIS*

**Nicholas Elliott**, *director for Africa based in London, then director for Requirements, former head of station in Berne, London, Beirut*

**Terence Lecky**, *counter-intelligence officer and a member of the joint MI5 and MI6 FLUENCY working party on the penetration of both services*

**Christopher Phillpotts**, *Oldfield's successor in Washington then director of Counter-intelligence and Security*

**Stephen de Mowbray**, *officer assigned to the PETERS investigation*

**Clive Johnson**, *fictional 'watcher', then A Branch MI5, formerly Special Branch*

## THE SECURITY SERVICE [MI5]

**Sir Roger Hollis**, *director general of MI5*

**Graham Mitchell**, *deputy director general*

**Martin Furnival Jones**, *director D Branch, assistant director general and from 1965 director general of MI5*

**Arthur Martin**, *head of D1 (Investigations), then MI6 Counter-intelligence*

**Peter Wright**, *scientific officer, then head of D3 (Research) and chair of joint MI5 and MI6 FLUENCY working party on the penetration of both services*

**Evelyn McBarnet**, *D1 research officer, then D3 (Research) and a member of joint MI5 and MI6 FLUENCY working party*

**Patrick Stewart**, *acting head of D3 (Research), then D1 (Investigations) and a member of joint MI5 and MI6 FLUENCY working party*

**Jane Archer**, *formerly MI5's principal Soviet expert and MI6 Section IX Soviet and Communist Counter-intelligence*

## THE CIVIL SERVANTS

**Elsa Frankl Spears**, *fictional permanent under-secretary at the War Office, formerly of MI5 and MI6*

**Sir Burke Trend**, *cabinet secretary*

## THE CENTRAL INTELLIGENCE AGENCY (CIA)

**James Jesus Angleton**, *chief of Counter-intelligence*

**Raymond Rocca**, *deputy chief of Counter-intelligence*

**William 'Bill' Harvey**, *CIA clandestine operations specialist*

**Jack Ellis**, *a fictional officer in Soviet Division*

**Anatoli Golitsyn**, *formerly KGB major, defected 1961*

## THE FEDERAL BUREAU OF INVESTIGATION (FBI)

**J. Edgar Hoover**, *director of FBI*

## ROYAL CANADIAN MOUNTED POLICE COUNTER-INTELLIGENCE

**James Bennett**, *assistant chief of Counter-intelligence*

## THE ACADEMICS

**Sir Anthony Blunt,** *Surveyor of The Queen's Pictures and director of the Courtauld Institute of Art, formerly MI5 officer*

**Sir Isaiah Berlin,** *professor of social and political theory and a fellow of All Souls College, Oxford*

**Goronwy Rees,** *journalist and fellow of All Souls College, Oxford, formerly the principal of Aberystwyth University and an MI6 officer*

## THE POLITICIAN

**Tom Driberg,** *a Member of Parliament and of the Labour Party's National Executive Committee*

## THE JOURNALIST

**Huw Watkins,** *a fictional* Daily Mirror *reporter and friend of the poet, Dylan Thomas*

## THE DOCTORS

**Sir John Nicolson,** *senior resident surgeon at Manor House Hospital, London*

**Dr Walter Somerville,** *consultant at the Middlesex Hospital, London*

# Author's Note

*Witchfinder* is an imaginary account of the turbulent years in the British intelligence services that followed the defection of master spy Kim Philby to the Soviet Union. The story is based on real events and the role played in them by prominent figures in British and American intelligence. A brief chronology of significant dates leading to the defection of Philby can be found on page 457.

1963

# 1

## 6 March 1963

M Y NEIGHBOUR SAYS his name is Roger and he works for Jaguar Cars. I think he's telling the truth.

'I'm Vienna,' he says, 'I used to be Rome.' Planting his forearm on the rest between us, he leans close enough for me to smell the in-flight brandy on his breath. 'Ah, Rome, what a city,' and he gives me a man-to-man smile.

To be sure he's the off-the-peg salesman he appears to be, I ask him about his business. Growth at last, he says. Jaguar didn't sell with the Soviets occupying the city, but Austria has been independent for seven years now and people are ready to spend: the new model E-type is proving a sensation.

'Have you driven one?' He pauses for my name.

'Harry. Harry Vaughan. I've seen pictures.'

'Beautiful, isn't she, Harry?'

Then he asks what I drive. He would love to take me for the price of a car in the two hours we're obliged to spend together flying from Vienna to London. I don't mind. I'm relieved, because Roger is Roger. He isn't a policeman, he isn't a spy: he's a burly car salesman in his late forties.

'What do I drive? Nothing special,' I say, which is his oppor- tunity to convince me that I'd like to. Then he asks me what I do, how long I've lived in Vienna, and if I'm Welsh. I don't want to answer his questions. Roger, it's over and out. I fold away my table, settle my chair back and pretend to take forty

3

winks. I won't sleep. I can't sleep. I can only teeter at the edge. When I feel I'm falling, a shadow thought of what may await me when we land in London is enough to set my heart racing. The cause I date precisely to ten minutes to nine on 30 January.

I was shaking snow from my coat when the station duty officer scuttled from the cipher room with a MOST IMMEDIATE message.

'It's in two parts,' he said, and thrust the first at me. THE FOLLOWING NAME IS A TRAITOR. Printed out carefully in bold on the second were the letters P-H-I-L-B-Y. 'Did you know Kim Philby?' he said, consigning him to the past already.

'Doesn't everyone in the Service?' I replied. 'His name was all over the papers a few years ago.'

Roger touches my arm. 'Are you all right, Harry?'

'Fine, Roger. Why?'

He shrugs. 'You must be pleased to be home,' and he leans across me to gaze down at the countryside shrouded in snow. 'It's colder than Vienna. Colder than Moscow, I shouldn't wonder. Worst winter for two hundred years, the weathermen say. How can they tell?'

Windsor Castle is at the tip of the wing and the air hostesses are preparing the cabin for landing. We're dropping over the skirts of London, over a chequer-board of black villages and frozen reservoirs, ahead of us the runway lights and a thick coil of yellow smoke rising from somewhere in the suburbs.

'The big freeze must end soon. It's March, for God's sake.' The plane's engines roar and Roger slumps back in his chair. 'I hate flying,' he says. 'Please, please me, Mr Pilot, a soft landing, please.'

So, I'm back in London to face the music. Briefcase from the overhead and Roger twittering at my shoulder, I shuffle towards a hostess with an airline smile. 'Be careful,' she says. 'The steps are slippery.' This hazard I manage without difficulty, but in the luggage hall there's a young man in a Marks & Spencer raincoat who may be one of London's finest – until he rescues his luggage from the carousel and leaves. I have time as I wait for mine to reflect that the word *paranoia* comes from the Greek for madness. I remember Kim Philby used to say, 'Just because I'm paranoid doesn't mean that everyone isn't out to get me.' He stole the joke from his friend Guy Burgess, who stole it from Marx – Groucho, not Karl. I expect it will go down well in Russia.

From the luggage hall I push my trolley to a newsstand on the concourse where I buy a copy of *The Times*. I know it's foolish but while I'm there I run through an old routine just to be sure no one is following me. It doesn't make sense. I'm home and on my way to see the head of the Secret Intelligence Service, but after twenty years of looking over my shoulder I can't stop.

'The Reform Club.'

'In Pall Mall?' the cabbie enquires.

'Is there another?'

The verge is hard packed with ice, the road awash with melt-water. Winter is retreating at last. Filthy London, this is my birthday. The date on the front page of *The Times* is 6 March 1963. I am just a year short of grisly five zero. There are no felicitations from my ex-wife and our children in the paper's notices, but Philby is on page ten. 'He isn't missing,' says Mrs Philby, 'he's on an assignment for a newspaper,' and there's a photograph of her showing a cable to jackals from the press. 'All going well,' imaginary Kim writes. 'I promise to send a letter and explain soon.' No one is ready for the truth.

My cab sweeps round Piccadilly into Haymarket and pauses in the matronly shadow of Honour, her bronze arms outstretched to garland the fallen. Ahead of us, the white granite column of the grand old duke who marched men up and down a hill in another war. We turn on to Pall Mall and pass the classical front of the Athenaeum Club. St James's Square is on the right – the home of the Army and Navy – the Carlton Club a few hundred yards further. Buck's, Brooks's and Boodle's are in the streets to the north, White's, Pratt's, and the Oxford and Cambridge Club, too. Princes and grand old dukes are dozing in their libraries, soldiers, sailors and the civil servants of a decaying Empire sip tea or gin, while in their smoking rooms businessmen are twisting the arms of clients-to-be. In an hour or so chaps from Parliament will show their guests to tables for dinner, and in the course of the evening any one of these clubbable gentlemen may rub shoulders with a spy, because we belong here, too. In a country of circles this is the one closest to the centre. Philby loved this circle, it was just the temptation to belong to an even smaller and more exclusive one was too great.

'Here we are, sir.' The cabbie has my suitcase on the pavement. 'The Reform.'

I pay him and climb the steps to the door where the porter takes my bag and follows me into the atrium.

'Haven't seen you in a while, Mr Vaughan,' he says. 'Still refusing to wear a tie, sir?'

'Only at the club. It's been six months, Mason. The Cuban crisis, remember? The world on the brink of nuclear annihilation.'

'Was it, sir?' he says. 'Well, glad to have you back.'

Mason disappears to fetch a key and my post. I take a few steps across the mosaic floor to stand inside the Reform's famous ring of marble statesmen. The atrium is like the courtyard of an Italian palazzo. Above me there's a gallery and a lead crystal pavilion that, on a bright day, refracts light into even the darkest corners of the club. Today is not a bright day but gazing up at the gallery I see Philby and Burgess step from the shadows to lean over the rail. Guy Burgess is drunk, of course, and fills the atrium with noise. Philby is trying to quieten him: members don't mind a chap blowing off a little steam but there are limits. Only Burgess doesn't give a fig for rules. He stands shoulder to shoulder with Philby in that secret circle within the country's inner circle, sneering and yet relishing its pretensions. Fitting that Burgess chose to spend his last day in London here at the Reform. It was poor Mason he asked to rent the car for him: the police recovered it from the docks at Southampton a day later. By then he was well on his way to Moscow.

Mason returns with my letters. I can tell from the envelopes that there's one from the bank and three from my ex-wife. I thank him, ask him to keep them for me, and, no, I won't require a table for dinner.

I walk to 'the office'. The cold helps clear my mind: why did I work myself into a state? But turning into Broadway my chest tightens again and I have to stand in the doorway of the Old Star pub to smoke a cigarette. Six o'clock. There's a steady stream of office workers pouring into the Underground station opposite. Most of them have come from the vast art-deco head-quarters of London buses and trains – it dominates the Broadway – but I recognise some Service faces, too. The cigarette isn't helping; I drop it into a drain. Best get this over.

From the pavement, number 54 Broadway Buildings looks like the smart headquarters of an international corporation; inside it's a dirty burrow. Stevenson is still behind the security glass in the lobby. He peers at me through National Health spectacles, then asks me to take a seat while he rings the fourth floor. I choose the bench against the wall, opposite the security barrier. I scratched my initials on the arm twenty-three years ago and they're still there. Same cheap furniture, same dirty cream paint on the walls, same closed and dusty blinds through which daylight struggles to penetrate. Friends can't imagine it any other way. It's a hole-in-the-corner sort of business, after all. From the lobby a single iron lift squeaks and grinds to the fourth and seventh floors; friends must climb the staircase to the rest. Office wags say the stair is white-tiled like a urinal because only shits would think to work here.

Stevenson beckons – 'Miss Edwards' – and hands me an in-house phone. 'How are you, Mr Vaughan?' she says, with a warmth she reserves for only a few.

It is written that no man can approach the chief of the Secret Intelligence Service – MI6 – except through Dora Edwards. Twinset and pearls, precise, private, and rich, they say.

'*Noswaith dda*, Dora.'

'I'm afraid C can't see you, Mr Vaughan.'

'Now or ever?'

'If you don't mind waiting . . . I believe there's a little do for Mr Fulton in the basement. I'll ring down and let you know when C is free.'

Stevenson has already written a chit for me. Stated purpose of my visit: security check.

The basement bar is crowded. Most evenings it's haunted by the small self-regarding circle of old-school-ties and scraped-a-university-third officers, who think of themselves as the Service's 'robber barons', and entry is by invitation only. But tonight they're hosting a farewell bash for 'Soapy' Sid Fulton and his chums. He's standing at the bar with a couple of secretaries.

'Harry Lime, as I live and breathe. Gin? Two more, Linda,' he says. 'You've come all this way for me, Harry? I'm flattered.'

'We've always been such good friends, Soapy.'

Fulton laughs. 'Well, I quite like you, Harry.'

He is pink with gin and bonhomie, so it would be churlish of me to call him a liar.

'Really, Harry, why are you here? Something to do with PEACH?'

I hold my hands open wide.

'PEACH? That's what we're calling the Philby investigation,' he explains. 'You know how it is when something like this happens. Remember Burgess in 'fifty?'

''Fifty-one.'

'Well, it's the same.' He sips his gin. 'Nick's the one I feel most sorry for because they were best friends for years – for ever.'

I follow his gaze to where Nicholas Elliott is perched on the arm of an old leather couch. The deputy head of the Service is telling him a joke. They look more like boarding-school housemasters than robber barons in their tortoiseshell spectacles and three-piece suits. Nick is one of many in the Service who fought his first battles on the playing fields of Eton and became a spy because it promised even greater sport. 'They sent him out to Beirut to confront Philby,' says Soapy. 'Nick was sure Kim was ready to confess – cough it all up – then poof! Gone. Didn't even tell his wife. The shit. The funny thing . . . he'll hate Moscow. Everyone does. You know how he loved cricket.'

Soapy knocks back his gin in one great gulp. 'Never thought I'd say this, Harry, but this business with Kim, well, I'm bloody glad to be going. Really I am.'

His declaration drops into a sudden silence like a cymbal crashing on a flagstone floor.

'Cheer up,' says one of the secretaries.

'Yes, old man,' says someone else.

'I will, I will,' he says, without conviction.

In an hour or so he'll be under the table – and why not? He's grieving. They're all grieving for how the Service used to be. It's a wake. All we're missing is music and a body. The body has gone, but there will be music.

'Remember this one, Soapy?' I say, settling at the bar's old piano.

> Though now and then, di di ah
> The world may seem so blue
> A song will see you through
> Let's sing again.

It's one of the 'keep buggering on' songs we were so fond of during the war, because most of us are of the finest-hour generation, the officers anyway. My song is well sung. I'm a respectable baritone – a matter of national pride, really. And to lift the gloom a little more I stride through my Fats Waller repertoire. Soapy is tearful with gratitude. A sentimental song or two and the past washes through him again.

'I *will* miss this place,' he says, and offers to buy me another drink. When it comes I raise my glass in a secret toast to the late Mrs Bugs, who used to slap my knuckles with a ruler when I played a wrong note. If only Mrs Bugs could have walked with me through life.

'Good for you,' Nicholas Elliott says, his hand on my shoulder. 'Cheered us all up.' His hand slips to my elbow and he steers me away from the group about the piano. 'How's Vienna?'

'Same as usual.'

'Soapy says you're here for PEACH?'

'I don't know why I'm here.'

'Ah. Well, you heard about Beirut?'

'Just now.'

He nods and tries to smile.

'Sorry, Nick,' I say. 'I know you and Kim were close.'

'Everybody seems to,' he says gloomily. 'He isn't a Communist, you know. Doesn't have a political bone in his body. It was a game. A nasty little game of lies that he played with all of us, his wives too.'

'I don't know him, really.'

Nick laughs.

'No, really, I don't,' I say.

'Nobody does except me, apparently,' he drawls, in the nasal way they learned at Eton. 'It doesn't matter. I'm finished here. I'll always be the one who let our greatest traitor slip away. The thing is, I think that's what the chief wanted to happen. He could have picked up Philby in Beirut – he sent me to show him the evidence instead. The chief gave Kim a chance to escape and he took it – I was just a dupe.'

'Why would he want Kim to run?'

'Imagine the embarrassment of a treason trial?' He shakes his head. 'Better to have Philby out of sight and mind in Moscow.'

I gaze at my drink, rattle the ice, until Nick realises I have nothing more to say and he's standing too close to me.

'How's Elsa?' He takes a step away. 'Still at the War Office?'

# 2

'I RANG THE MOMENT I heard the chief wasn't going to see me,' I say.

Elsa is standing with a hand on her hip at the door of her Dolphin Square flat. 'You're drunk.'

I say,

> 'My birthday began with the water –
> Birds and the birds of the winged trees flying my name
> Above . . . Above . . .'

'Too drunk to remember. He wouldn't have forgiven you.'

'He would, and I have it anyway. It's "I rose in rainy autumn and walked abroad in a shower of all my days." A shower of all my days. I love that line. He was a genius.'

She lifts her chin a little, the better to look down her nose at me. 'You think you can charm your way in here with a few lines of Dylan Thomas?'

'Elsa, I'm just a year from fifty.'

She pulls a face – 'Oh, disgusting' – and pretends to shudder. 'Self-pity!' Quicksilver she moves, like a sparrow taking flight.

I've drunk too much to catch her. My ears are ringing, my left cheek is stinging. 'What was that for?'

'For not telling me you were back.' Then she reaches for my

coat lapels and rising to tiptoe she kisses me. 'And *that* is for your birthday.'

I put an arm round her waist and stroke a strand of chestnut brown hair from her face. There are voices around the corner of the corridor. 'What *will* your neighbours think?' I say, though I know she doesn't care for what others think of her. 'Going to let me in?'

She frowns, as if the matter is still in doubt. 'No sex. I'm not ready to forgive you.'

'It's my birthday.'

She pulls free with a sly smile. 'You should have thought of that before.'

'I've had a lot on my mind. Fix me a gin and I'll tell you.'

She is a step ahead in the hall but I reach for the waistband of her skirt.

'Hey. Let me go.'

I draw her back and she turns to kiss me. I want her so much and she is ready to have me, and because I'm still a year from fifty, and because she loves adventure, I know we won't make it as far as the bedroom.

Elsa Frankl Spears. Frankl from her Austrian Jewish mother, Spears from her English Protestant father: the most unlikely of matches. London boarding school, then Oxford University, where she dropped the name Spears to protest her father's support for appeasing the Nazis. By the 1930s the soldier spy who fell for the feisty student from Vienna was a most solid Conservative backbench MP. Poor man. His clever wife and daughter must have led him a merry dance. But when the war came it was Papa Spears who helped Elsa play her part by introducing her to one of his chums in MI5.

I was working for Five then too, helping to turn Nazi spies

into double agents. We met for the first time at Guy Burgess's flat in Bentinck Street. He liked to draw the pretty boys and girls of Five and Six into his own special circle. Bugger the bombs, we'll party, was his approach to the war. He was working for Five, and so was his flatmate, Anthony Blunt. Their old Cambridge University chum, Philby, was a Bentinck Street regular, too. But it was *my* friend Goronwy Rees who introduced Elsa to the party. I'm sure he wanted to sleep with her, because that is what one does in war, and that was the way Guy Burgess wished it to be. The bedroom doors in Bentinck Street opened and closed with the frequency of a French farce. You never knew who you would pass on the stairs. Rees was a newly-wed, Philby a father of three, and I was married then too. We were an egocentric and faithless bunch. Did Elsa sleep with Goronwy Rees? She didn't sleep with me, although she says she wanted to. She was twenty-four and I was twenty-eight.

Elsa's forty-five now, a senior civil servant at the War Office. She hasn't married and she says she doesn't want to, that having it off is enough. We finish on her couch. 'Nice,' she says, as casually as she can. She visits the bathroom and pads back with the dressing-gown I left in her wardrobe. Who has worn it in the months that have passed since I was here? She bought it for me in Vienna seventeen years ago and paid more than she should have because we'd made love for the first time just a few hours before.

Both of us moved from Five at the end of the war and were working for Six. Elsa was sent to Vienna to file and type but was too capable to do that for long, and by the time I arrived from Berlin she was running agents in and out of the Soviet zone of occupation. She was electric, she was tireless, driven by grief and anger that, so soon after the death of her mother's people in the gas chambers, a new totalitarian order was taking the place of the old in Europe.

In those days we were clinging to the rubble of Vienna by our fingertips. The city was a shooting gallery. Its people did what they needed to do to get by; everything was for sale, everyone a tart or a tout, and Fräulein Frankl was ready to crawl through shit for their secrets. You pay a price for living in those sorts of dark corners.

Friends love a good spy story. I remember a showing of *The Third Man* at the barracks we were using as Six's station headquarters. 'This is me,' she said, as Harry Lime escaped through the sewers, 'or it could be.' She could see clearer than most of us who work for the Firm that the lies we tell and the people we hurt in pursuit of our greater good will turn us in time into someone we hate. Our colours bleed. The image of who we were is washed from the page. SUBALTERN. 1948. It came to a head for Elsa when we lost SUBALTERN and dozens of our most successful agents.

She's standing at the drinks tray in a lamb's wool jumper that barely covers her nakedness and her hair is falling in tight brown curls about her face. Watching her, I *know* I'm happy, and I can't remember the last time I felt that way. I think of her as my little Jewess, although she would slap me if I said so, because she isn't mine and she's small only in stature. Petite and dark, like her mother, she has an elfin face with thick eyebrows and charming little laugh lines at the corners of her mouth. 'No ice, I'm afraid,' she says, turning with the bottle. 'Sure you still want some?'

After the failure of the SUBALTERN operation she left the Service for the War Office. I stayed but moved to London with her. Then the fourth floor thought it a clever thing to send me back to Vienna as station chief, and I made the mistake of going.

'You have your drink now,' she says, as she walks towards me with two glasses. 'What is it you want to tell me?' She settles beside me, her legs curled beneath her on the couch. 'Let me guess: they're looking for someone to blame.'

'Is that what they're saying at the War Office?'

'No, it's what I say. The government's still hoping, praying, Philby will turn up. One security scandal is unfortunate. Two is going to look like carelessness.'

'There's another?'

Her glass hovers at her lips while she considers whether she should say more. 'You'll read about it soon enough. The secretary of state for war was sleeping with a prostitute. She's nineteen and he's about your age.'

'Profumo? The one with the actress wife?'

'Take that smile off your face. What have you got to smile about? First Burgess and Maclean, then Blake and Vassall, and now the man in Six who used to be responsible for catching spies turns out to be one too. And you knew Philby was a spy, didn't you? After Burgess and Maclean, you knew.'

I turn too quickly and slop gin on her legs. 'Not true.'

'You suspected, Harry. You did. We discussed it. You said there were people in Five who thought the same.'

'Not enough. He was too popular to accuse anyway.'

She gives me a withering look. 'He was sly – that corner-of-the-mouth smile and something dead in his eyes. But he was "one of the chaps", one of your robber barons.'

'Not mine.'

'And the chaps came to his rescue time and again, even when it was as plain as the nose on your face that he helped Burgess and Maclean to escape.'

I sip my drink and say nothing: it's time to be humble.

'The Service won't be able to sweep it under the carpet this time,' she says. 'Philby took the Americans too, and they'll want heads to roll.'

'*Yes*. Thank you.'

She pulls my head down and kisses me. 'Yours will be all right, my sweet.'

'Have they spoken to you?'

'Me? I hardly knew Philby.'

I nod slowly. 'He was a great collector of women. I thought perhaps . . . Ow!' She has nipped my ear.

'Not funny,' she says. 'Philby was only half a human being. I prefer your rough sincerity.'

I hold her face in my hands. 'Can I just say . . .' and I kiss her again, because we love each other, but circumstances . . . Well, we hardly ever say so.

Later, I stand at her bedroom curtains and watch the last lights go out in the blocks on the opposite side of Dolphin Square. Elsa lives on the fourth floor of Beatty. There's a garden below with a few frostbitten saplings, and three bronze dolphins are leaping from a floodlit fountain, but the square is little more than a fortress for the well-to-do, with ten floors of red brick on all sides, as bleak as the blocks they've built in Moscow for heroes of the Soviet Union. I expect Philby will be given a flat just like this one.

Soapy says Kim's old pal Tony Milne is on the way home from Buenos Aires station for questioning. They were at Westminster School together. Tony slept with Kim's first wife. In just a few hours I'll meet the chief and my head may drop into the same basket. Perhaps it's time: the best 'friends' left years ago. I have my daughters – they're still young enough to be polite – and I send Christmas cards to a brother and an aunt in Wales, but it's Elsa who matters most to me. I should climb back into bed beside her and ask her to marry me. Pin her wrists to the pillow until she says, 'All right, you fool.'

There's a pinprick of orange light beneath one of the trees. Someone is drawing deeply on a cigarette. It must have been his final drag because he steps from the shadow and stubs it out on the low wall round the fountain. He's about five feet seven or eight, broad shoulders, broad chest, and he's wearing a black mac and trilby, like one of MI5's ex-coppers. It's after midnight and the temperature must be close to freezing, but he's in no hurry. He glances up at Beatty block and reaches into his coat for his gloves. He can't see me at the curtain, but he knows where I am, and he doesn't care to hide it.

# 3

'WHAT ABOUT THIS evening?' Elsa asks, at the bedroom door. She's wearing a black dress and pearls and an imperial-purple coat: what a figure she must cut in Whitehall.

'I'll ring you if I can, *cariad*.'

She rolls her eyes. 'You're older than I remember, Harry. What on earth do you expect to happen?'

I reach behind my head for the pillow. She's too quick – it smacks against the door.

The chief lives in an elegant eighteenth-century red-brick house in Queen Anne's Gate. A private bridge connects home to the 'the office' where Security waits with the lift door open. He barely sets foot on any floor but the fourth. To the junior officers working on the other floors he is no more than a single letter in green ink on confidential papers: he is C – our very own Wizard of Oz. The curtains in his personal office are always drawn against Russian spies with long lenses. I'm sure they would be in any circumstance, because secrecy is his life – all our lives – and secrecy is a narcotic.

The front door in Queen Anne's Gate has been buffed to a mirror sheen. I use it to straighten my tie. On this day and every day, the basement and ground-floor windows are half shuttered. I ring the bell, and before I can step back the door opens. It's the chief himself, Sir Dick White – 'Hello, Harry' –

and he shakes my hand with what feels like genuine warmth. 'Long time . . . Come in, come in.' I follow him into the oak-panelled hall.

I've known Sir Dick White a long time, in the hail-fellow way one knows most people in the Service. We turned German agents together during the war, and he would sometimes fetch up at Bentinck Street parties, but I sensed even then that he didn't think much of Burgess and some of his set. Guy used to call him 'the Schoolmaster' – he was for a time – and it's true that he seems too solid and trusting to be a spy. But Guy meant bourgeois and boring, because Guy was one of the Service's old-school-ties, and Dick had gone to nowhere. That much we have in common, and it's no small thing.

'I think we'll talk in my study, Harry.' He gestures to the stair. 'Sorry about the short notice. What is it the Americans say? "We have a difficult situation here."' He's dressed casually in an open-neck shirt and moleskin trousers, as if he's just stepped in from the garden. 'You're wearing well,' he says, as we climb.

'Not as well as you, sir.'

Dick had been a university athlete and, a couple of years short of sixty, he still has something of the physique. Not bad for a man who has spent the last ten behind a desk as director general of MI5 and then as the chief of MI6. Whitehall loves him as much as the robber barons despise him because he doesn't like to rock the boat. Well, it's rocking now.

Our meetings have always taken place behind the green baize door of his office in Broadway, curtains drawn, a mile of desk between us. This is the first in his home. I half expect to find an interrogator in his study, but instead of a grilling he seems to have arranged for a cosy fireside chat. The room is lined with calf-bound books and paintings of quiet landscapes that he's borrowed from the National Gallery. We sit in burgundy silk armchairs on either side of the fire and he asks after Elsa and my two daughters. He may even be interested in my answers, because he's a family man with chapel views on sex and marriage. Lies *are* excusable but only in the line of duty.

'You know why you're here, Harry?' he says, at last. 'When did you last speak to him?'

"Fifty-one, sir. I haven't seen him since Burgess and Maclean went over.'

'But you knew him. You got on with his crowd.'

'Court jester and musician. In, but not of.'

'If I remember, you were introduced to Burgess by Goronwy Rees.'

He doesn't have to remember because he's read my file. 'That's right, sir.'

'Spoken to Rees recently?'

He's watching me intently, yet contrives to look completely at ease. I meet his gaze and am struck for the umpteenth time by the sun-bright blue of his eyes.

'Not recently.'

'Rees knew Burgess was working for the Russians but didn't think to say so.'

'Did I know? No, I told the investigation at the time. Same with Philby.'

He inclines his head slightly and looks down his very large nose at me. His expression . . . Well, he wants to believe me. That's the trouble, the barons say. Dick wants to believe everyone. 'Oh, come on, Harry. Not even when Burgess and Maclean slipped away?'

'I wondered. But *you* interrogated him, sir. If he was guilty . . .'

He smiles ruefully. 'I knew he was lying. But my predecessor here . . . You know how well connected Philby was, and when I took over here . . .' He slaps his knees with both hands and rises. He's the chief: he doesn't have to make excuses. 'It's what we do *now* I want to talk about.'

I breathe deeply again. Dick must have studied my file and made up his mind before he ordered me home.

'Coffee?' he says, pushing the servant's bell to the right of the chimneypiece. 'The damage that shit has done to the Service. The men and women he's sent to their deaths.' Selecting a poker from the hearth tree, he stirs the embers of the fire with unnecessary vigour. 'The Americans are hopping mad. Have you met Jim Angleton? Head honcho at CIA counter-intelligence. He was devoted to Philby. They used to get drunk together. Philby has compromised more than a score of the CIA's most important operations.' Dick turns back to face me with the poker at forty-five degrees. 'The thing is, who tipped him off, Harry? We know he warned Burgess and Maclean. Well, who did the same for Philby?'

There's a polite knock and a young fellow enters with a tray.

'Thank you, Brown,' says Dick. 'Milk, Harry?'

Brown has brought us three bone china cups.

'Why do you think Philby was tipped off, sir? I understand you sent Elliott to confront him.'

'Sugar? I've read a transcript of their conversation, Harry. He wasn't surprised to see Elliott. He knew we were on to him.'

'Then he would have escaped before the meeting.'

Dick hands me a cup then steps over to his desk – 'I'd like someone to join us' – and picks up a phone. 'Ask Arthur to come up, would you?' I watch him put the receiver back and pour more coffee. He knows the 'someone' well enough to slide two spoons of sugar into his cup.

'You see, Harry, this goes deep – deeper than we thought possible. First Burgess and Maclean, now Philby, and it isn't the end of it, because there are five of them.'

'Five?'

'A Ring of Five.' He sits back in the armchair opposite with a sigh. 'On my watch.'

I can see in a quiet 'Dick way' he's in a bit of a funk. Perhaps he's imagining the visit he will have to make to Number 10. The prime minister hasn't even come clean to the country about the third man yet. If there's a fourth and a fifth . . . Well, Dick was supposed to keep that sort of stink from Downing Street.

'Do you have any idea who, sir?' I say. 'And what's it got to do with me?'

# 4

'D O YOU KNOW Arthur?' says Dick.

Arthur Martin. The head of Soviet Counter-espionage at MI5. Spycatcher in chief. The scalps Martin has taken and tried to take are the stuff of Service legend.

'I haven't had the pleasure.'

'Actually, you have,' says Martin, offering me his hand. 'We met at a party in 'fifty-one. Perhaps you remember my wife, Joan. Joan Russell King.'

I apologise and ask after her, and while he speaks of their life together in Surrey, I beat back the memory of a drunken pass I made when she was still Dick White's secretary at Five.

Martin is about my age. He's scrubbed and polished in a sergeant-major sort of way. It's easy to imagine he's fastidious about everything. Dick speaks and he leans forward to listen, with a smile that's tight enough to play, as if he's having to concentrate unnaturally hard on being amiable. I think, Ex-copper, and when he speaks, I hear grammar-school boy from the shires. He's a Roundhead. Six has always belonged to Cavaliers. A few of us are tolerated on both sides of the House.

'Arthur knows more about this business than anyone,' says Dick. 'Tell Harry why you think we still have a cuckoo in the nest.'

'I've been going through the files,' Martin says, a thick one open across his knees. 'The leads are there. Remember Gouzenko? Defected September 1945. He walked out of the Soviet Embassy in Canada with its secrets stuffed down his trousers. We rounded up dozens of their agents. But there was one – codename ELLI – we couldn't identify. There was a chance . . . A few days before Gouzenko came across, our people in Istanbul were approached by a KGB agent: Konstantin Dmitrievich Volkov. He'd worked at Moscow Centre and he was ready to sell us its secrets, only he was betrayed before he had a chance to.'

'That shit Philby,' says Dick. 'He tipped off his KGB controller here and Moscow's hitmen managed the rest.'

'But we did learn something,' says Martin. 'Volkov told us the KGB was running agents in our Foreign Office and the intelligence services, and that one of them was the head of a counter-espionage section. With this . . . well . . .' He glances down at his file, and something in his manner . . . I sense there's a piece of intelligence he isn't ready to share with me.

Dick clears his throat, then says, 'We did have some success. The Americans identified Donald Maclean as the agent in the Foreign Office. Of course, Philby was our man in Washington at the time, and he arranged for Moscow to exfiltrate him from London – Burgess too. We were pretty sure it was Philby who tipped them off.'

'Not old Kim,' says Martin, bitterly. 'Good old Kim. His friends at Six wouldn't believe us. He went to Westminster School and Cambridge University, you know. I pushed for a full investigation – open all the files . . .'

Dick is twitching.

'. . . and now Philby's gone and the damage is done!'

There's an embarrassed silence. 'Yes.' Dick clears his throat again. 'Thank you, Arthur,' and to me, 'Arthur has been struggling with this for a long time. Would you like some more coffee?'

But Martin is ready to turn another page. December 1961, defector number three. KGB officer Anatoli Golitsyn rolled up at the American Embassy in Helsinki with his wife and child and offered his secrets in return for asylum. Golitsyn claimed the KGB's most valuable assets in Britain belonged to a Ring of Five spies who were at university together in the 1930s. 'The first two were Burgess and Maclean, and we were pretty sure the third was Philby. Then one of his women came forward: Flora Solomon.'

Dick slaps the arm of his chair. 'Know what she said? "Oh, Sir Richard, I *do* wish I'd come to you earlier." She was twenty-five years late.'

Kim had asked Solomon to join him in his 'work for peace' in the thirties. Maybe they were lovers, maybe she was a little in love with the memory of that time, but she had kept his secret for twenty-five years. The cat out of the bag at last, Five and Six agreed that Arthur Martin should confront Philby with the evidence. But a switch was made at the last minute and it was Elliott who flew out to Beirut. Philby confessed to his old chum and promised to co-operate in return for immunity. The following day he ran to Moscow.

'He was ready. He was expecting us. You hear it on the interrogation tape,' says Martin. 'The very first thing he says to Elliott is "I thought it would be you." How did he know? How?'

His gaze slides sideways to Dick, and I sense he's reluctant to tell me more. But Dick has made up his mind. 'Arthur thinks we still have a cuckoo in the nest. Arthur?'

'Yes. Yes, I do. Kim was tipped off by someone. Only five of us saw the new evidence. Only five of us knew the plan to confront him.'

'Go on.'

'Well, it's one of two people. In my view only two of us fit the profile of an enemy penetration agent.' He leans forward a little to place his cup on a table. 'Yes. It's either the director general of the Security Service or his deputy.'

'The director general?' I want to laugh. 'You think Sir Roger is working for Moscow?'

'That's right,' says Martin.

Dick looks embarrassed, as well he might – 'Not the DG.' Roger Hollis was his deputy at MI5 and anointed successor. 'No. We're not investigating the DG,' he says again. 'There's no question of that – but his deputy, Mitchell, Graham Mitchell . . . Arthur's been through the files. He's spoken to the Americans . . .' The thought of the Americans drives Dick from his fireside. 'The Americans are furious. Too many leaks, they say. They don't trust us. The British can't be trusted – that's what they say, Arthur?'

'That's right, sir.'

'No, Harry, it sickens me, but we can't ignore the evidence. There may be a penetration agent – what do the KGB call them?'

'A mole.'

'A mole – at the very top of the service.'

I nod thoughtfully. 'Mitchell? It's been a while, but he doesn't strike me . . .' The Graham Mitchell I knew during the war would have had neither the imagination nor the courage to be a traitor. 'Why?'

'Opportunity,' says Martin. He's the deputy director general. He's been with Five since 1939. He had Communist sympathies at university.'

I pull a face.

'It's a piece of evidence,' he says belligerently.

'Or is it hearsay?'

'*And* his record – the leads that Five ignored while Mitchell was head of Counter-espionage . . . Look, I've been through what we have on paper – there's a good case. We can't sweep this under the carpet, not this time, not after Philby. If it isn't the DG, it's his deputy. Believe me, we'll find the bloody evidence – only, for God's sake, let's get on with it!'

Martin is glowing indignation. I think of Joan, his wife, who used to be fun. 'It's instinctive with Arthur,' Dick says to me, by way of apology. 'There's no one better at ferreting the truth from the files.'

'But this time we need phone taps, surveillance – the works,' he says.

'So,' I say to Dick, 'you're going to investigate the deputy director general of MI5? Does the DG know?'

Dick sits slowly back in his chair with the air of someone who has just run a marathon. 'He's given the go-ahead.'

'Sir Roger's agreed to investigate his own deputy?'

'Didn't I just say so? No more nasty surprises. We need to be sure he's clean. That's what Roger's going to tell the prime minister and the Americans. He recognises what's at stake here. If there's a mole at the top, well, how many enemy agents is he protecting?'

'Dick wants me to be part of the investigation,' I explain to Elsa later. 'He doesn't want this blowing up in his face.'

It's after nine o'clock at night and we've drunk a bottle of wine and made love on her living-room floor.

'Do you know Mitchell?' she says.

'Not as well as you do. My job is to keep an eye on Martin.'

'You said Martin was Dick's man.'

I lean forward to kiss the gap between her breasts and mutter, 'But he's combustible.'

'Sounds as if Martin's the one in charge,' she says, pulling me back by my hair.

Dick White's parting shot to me was 'Tell no one,' and he

was thinking of Elsa. But she's sitting naked on my knee. I'm her prisoner. What can I do? Secrecy is the currency of our lives in the Service, and because we can't share some things it's easier to share none, even with colleagues. But secrets are a burden and always will be; that's why the Service is such a great user of people. I tell Elsa more than I should but there are some secrets I hope I'll take to the grave.

'Arthur Martin's driving it, yes. That's the trouble. That's why Dick's brought me back,' I say.

'Arthur bullies Dick, and Dick bullies Roger into investigating Graham,' she says. 'Sounds very messy.'

There's a trickle of perspiration at the top of her cleavage I want to kiss, but she still has me by the hair. 'It's late,' she says, rolling away from me. 'We've got to stop doing this.'

'Day two and you're exhausted already? Sorry, but you can see that time's been kind to me.'

'Ha.' She stares pointedly at the fold of my midriff. 'That's the trouble with old spies. They can't even be honest with themselves.'

'What?' I follow her gaze. 'That's nothing, girl.'

But there's a well-lit mirror in her bathroom that catches me in inglorious profile as I pee. True, I'm not the matinee idol I used to be. Elsa used to call me her Welsh Dirk Bogarde. Older by a few years, certainly, and taller by a few inches – five feet ten – but with the same wiry physique, the same mahogany brown eyes and hair – a little grey at the temples now – the same ironic smile, and with Bogarde's way of viewing the world from the corner of his eye. I'm an actor too. It became a necessity at eight when guileless Harry Vaughan was taken from his father's home in a pit village to be turned into a sly young gentleman. Aunt Elen and her bank-manager husband paid the boarding fees at Llandovery, and in a matter of months I wasn't one boy, I was two.

But we may be many people in a lifetime. Most of us try to hide from ourselves most of the time. Sometimes we hide from others. Some of us can't remember much about who we were when we began our journey, or quite believe who we have become. Who we are – who we *truly* are – is concealed in a confusion of colour, like a drip painting by Mr Jackson Pollock. We're all liars and spies in our own way, it's just that for some of us it's a duty. The war didn't turn me into a spy, it was you, Aunt Elen.

I step out of the bathroom and Elsa shouts from the kitchen, 'Cover yourself up.'

'Now you're hurting my feelings.'

It's almost midnight but she's trying to make an omelette.

'Let me,' I say, because we both know I'll cook a better one. 'Cheese and ham?' But her fridge is bare. 'You need a good husband.'

'You?' She pats my bottom. 'There's nothing good about you, darling.'

*Well, I love you* is on the tip of my tongue. As I break and whisk the eggs our conversation turns once more to Philby. Elsa says she can't understand why a cautious man like Dick White doesn't just let sleeping dogs lie. The prime minister won't thank him for stirring up a hornet's nest in the intelligence services.

I say I expect she's right but it's too late to sweep things under the carpet. 'The Americans think the Service has more holes than a Swiss cheese. Here,' I say, turning her omelette on to a plate.

Elsa carries it back to the sitting-room couch and asks between mouthfuls for my impressions of Arthur Martin. 'He doesn't suffer fools,' I say, 'and he thinks there are too many of them in Six – too many chinless wonders. He's the sort of bloke who tells you he's a patriot.'

'Is that a criticism?'

'The funny thing is' – I catch her arm to prevent her rising from the couch with her empty plate – 'it was Philby who talent-spotted him for the Security Service.'

She laughs. 'Then why aren't you investigating *him*?'

'You're not serious?'

'Well, you say, Harry' – she shakes free and gets to her feet – 'but if Philby chose him . . .'

'You mean Martin is our master spy – the mysterious agent ELLI.'

'Scoff, if you like, she says, turning at the kitchen door, 'but you're still underestimating Kim Philby. He's one of nature's cavemen. He was brilliant at deceiving everyone – goodness knows how many important secrets he must have passed to the Russians – and he was committed enough to his cause to run to Moscow. So why would he recruit someone to MI5 who might threaten that cause? He wouldn't. He fooled everyone because he reads people, and I imagine he saw something in Martin to his advantage.'

I smile, and she rolls her eyes. 'No, you should remember that, Harry.'

# 5

## May 1963

CLIVE AND TONY are waiting on a meter in Curzon Street. At five thirty sharp the deputy DG will clear his desk and return his papers to a combination safe. He'll double-lock his door, then wait for the lift that's reserved for senior officers. *The Times* will be in his briefcase. He will have polished off the crossword with his morning coffee – seniors at Five seem to. He won't make eye contact with the policeman in Reception because he's shy in a boarding-school way that is easy to mistake for arrogance.

It's a warm spring afternoon and the hawthorn and cherry in Green Park are white and pink. Graham Mitchell will walk. Clive and Tony will follow. They won't have any difficulty. Deputy DG is an office spy. He doesn't have that sixth sense of danger that comes with experience of working a street. He suffered from polio as a boy and has limped through most of his life, but he walks to Waterloo station because he has time. Time aplenty. He's fifty-eight now and winding down to the gold watch. Four months to go before he hangs up his old pinstripe suit, kicks off his office brogues and retires to the golf course – and I haven't found anything in his past to suggest that isn't the way it should be.

I'm waiting for Clive's report in a café beneath the railway arches on Waterloo Road. I can almost stand my spoon in the tea. I drink it for the memory of a chocolate brown pot on an oak table in a smoky kitchen, Father calling from a tub in the yard. I read in the *Mirror* that the miners have accepted an increase of fourteen shillings a week, but the railwaymen are preparing to strike. A British spy called Wynne is about to go on trial in Moscow. He's pushed Philby from the front page; he'll be back there soon enough. We're still pretending we don't know where he's gone, which is only possible because the KGB is saving him for a big show. When the time is ripe to create maximum confusion, it will return its star defector to the stage to twist the knife. I understand the home secretary is preparing a statement, and at Six we tread softly while we wait. This is the eye of the hurricane.

I have a tiny office in the Broadway warren with two telephones and a filing cabinet. My radiator leaks, my blind is broken. To the question, 'What are you doing here, Harry?' I say, 'Vetting review for C.' It's a cast-iron alibi because everyone knows we need one. The ship is holed and Harry Vaughan is back from Vienna to bail. I can flit between Six and Five without arousing suspicion, because it was Graham Mitchell who wrote the old procedure. In the last six weeks, I've wasted hours in his office discussing its failure to pick out Philby and the rest, and he is the same clever, shy, almost sly man I met at MI5 during the war, still barely capable of looking me in the eye.

The café door jingles and in walks Clive with a face as long as a fiddle. He eases his weary frame into the seat opposite to make his report. Subject left at the usual time and took the usual route. Subject didn't execute a brush-pass exchange with a thickset Slav or leave a package on a park bench. No pick-up, no dead drop, no phone-box call, no attempt to play it by Moscow Rules. Subject took the usual train home to his wife Pat in Chobham. Clive says we're wasting our time, and Clive's one of the best in the business – ex-army, ex-Special Branch.

We're nothing without numbers, he grumbles, and if MI6 is serious about this man it should have watchers on him round the clock. 'Someone who plays golf would be useful,' I say. Clive's too footsore to smile. I summon the waitress and order him tea and a bun, and I warn him that it's the same routine tomorrow, but it's forecast to rain.

With time to kill I take a cab back to Dolphin Square where I've rented a furnished flat on the opposite side of the court from Elsa. 'Until you're sure you're here to stay,' she said – but I can count on the fingers of one hand the nights I've spent in the place. It belongs to an MP who's on good terms with the Service. Elsa says it smells of his cigar smoke, of whisky and damp wool.

My neighbour to the left works at the Treasury, my neighbour to the right in the City. The Firm has fitted a disc tumbler to the door, so the Firm has a duplicate key, but everything seems the same. There's a fox head on the wall in the hall and a photograph of the Honourable Member in hunting pink. I've added touches of my own: some pans, an old upright piano, and a pair of binoculars. I pick them up now to check the square below. Street, park, club, a greasy spoon beneath a railway arch – I'm always looking for someone who's trying too hard not to look at me. Clive says Mitchell never goes through this routine, that he's either a brilliant double agent or no sort of agent at all.

As for Dolphin Square, I can breathe easy. I haven't seen Mr Black Mac and Trilby since my first night here. There may be someone, there may always be someone, but if there is he has the decency to keep his distance.

I raise the glasses to Beatty block to be sure there are no lights in Elsa's flat. She's expecting to work late at the War Office. A tidal wave of shit is rolling up Whitehall and in the next few weeks it will break over her minister. Jack Profumo was sharing his call-girl lover with a Soviet intelligence officer. A personal crisis has become a matter of national security. His blood is in the water. The sharks are circling. They'll splash it all over the country's front pages. And the public will enjoy one of its periodic fits of morality. Churchmen will pray for more probity in political life. But Elsa says Jack Profumo's a decent and courageous man, a soldier who fought on D-Day. I know he will feel more frightened and helpless now than he has ever done. Because he's lied to Parliament, he's lied to his wife, he's told all the lies he can tell, and the only thing he can do is crawl under a stone and hide. And if that's no longer possible, well, then they have you.

A couple of hours later I'm standing in one of the streets near the rubble of what used to be Euston station. The monumental stone arch that was built with hope and confidence at the dawn of the new railway age and through which millions of passengers passed has gone: work is beginning on a timid glass box that I suppose we must believe is someone's vision for the future. Arthur Martin lives close enough to the new station to be woken by the pile-drivers. He isn't expecting me and I'm not expecting a warm welcome, but one of his neighbours is leaving the block, so I draw the last comfort I can from my cigarette, kick the stub into the gutter and march across the street to catch the door from him before it closes.

Martin's flat is on the second floor, second on the right. He takes his time to answer and I sense him looking at me through the spy-hole. 'Vaughan. What on earth . . .'

I show him a bottle of whisky. 'We must talk, Arthur.'

He frowns, and I guess he's wondering if we absolutely must talk. But the doorstep isn't the place for 'friends' to argue, so he leads me into his hall. 'What is it you want?'

'To talk about Mitchell.'

'Why can't it wait? I'm not alone.' He looks embarrassed, and I wonder fleetingly if a young thing is lying naked by the fire in his sitting room. Ridiculous, of course.

'He's one of us,' he says. 'Our principal scientific officer. All things technical and more.' He pauses. 'He knows about Mitchell.'

I want to ask him why, because Hollis and White have instructed us to tell no one, but Martin has made up his mind to introduce me and is holding the sitting-room door open.

His friend is at a small dining table with what looks like a file from MI5's Registry. Perhaps things have changed but removing files from Leconfield House used to be a hanging offence. He smiles and rises, and as he steps forward to greet me the fingers of his left hand trail surreptitiously across the table and he flips the file shut. His name is Peter Wright. I haven't heard of him, but he seems to know about me. He speaks with a stutter, like Philby, and must be in his late forties, bald, with just a sad fringe of grey at the back and at the sides. As we exchange fatuous pleasantries, an image comes to mind of a stone grotesque at my old Oxford college, a lined, weather-beaten face, with a large nose and a stern brow.

'Peter has come to me with his concerns,' says Martin.

'P-p-putting two and two together,' he says, 'jobs that have gone down suddenly, the failure of some of our double agents, I've been worrying about it for . . . er . . . years.'

I shrug off my mac and throw it over the back of the couch. 'You've spoken to Roger Hollis?'

'I told him I'd spoken to Arthur – let my hair down about my worries,' he says, without irony. 'Do you know R-Roger?'

'Not well.'

'Roger's a bit aloof.'

Martin grunts contemptuously. He must be resigned to my presence because he has found some whisky tumblers in a sideboard. The room is small and crowded with cheap furniture, but neat and spotless, in keeping with his fastidious nature.

'Peter thinks it's Mitchell, too,' he says, handing us our drinks.

'And what did Hollis say?' I ask.

Wright spreads his hands upon the table. 'Well, he d-d-didn't seem surprised, actually. I think he was expecting me to come to him. He said, "Graham Mitchell's retiring in six months. That's how long you have to prove it." Oh, and "I don't have to tell you I don't like it Peter. I don't like it one bit."'

'So . . .' I raise my glass. 'Welcome to our wild-goose chase.'

'If that's what you think, Vaughan . . .' Martin is twitching with anger.

'Hold on, this isn't an investigation, it's a farce!' I say. 'Turn on the tap. Twenty-four-hour surveillance of Mitchell or we're wasting our time.' I pick up a corner of the Registry file. 'Unless you think you'll stumble across the truth in these.'

'I've told Hollis,' says Martin, 'but he's refusing to let us bug a deputy director general.'

'Then we don't have—'

'But I'll take this to the prime minister if necessary.'

I want to laugh, but that wouldn't be wise. 'Right, Arthur,' I say instead. 'Fine.'

Martin is wringing his cut-glass tumbler. I hope he's imagining them around Roger Hollis's neck and not mine. Wright says something about Dick White: they went to the same minor public school in Hertfordshire. Perhaps he's giving his friend time to recover his composure.

'Dick White says we have to be seen to do this properly,' says Martin. His gaze flits to my face and away. 'He's going to speak to Roger.' Reaching into the pocket of his fawn cardigan for his cigarettes, he shakes one free from the packet. 'You think this is a wild-goose chase? You're wrong.'

He lights his cigarette with a match and shakes out the flame. 'We're sure we have a mole now.'

'You seemed pretty convinced before.'

'Well, now we know,' he says coolly. 'The Americans can place a KGB officer called Modin in Beirut. He hasn't left Moscow for years, then out of the blue Beirut. Why?' Leaning across the table, he draws the Registry file towards him and flips it open. 'Our old friend Yuri Modin.' A photo is clipped to the first page: he's forty something with a fleshy face, high forehead, and an Asiatic look about the eyes. 'That was taken here a few years ago. He was Burgess's controller in London – Philby's too.'

'Philby's?'

'Oh, yes. Old comrades. The Soviets knew we were on to Philby, so they dusted off Yuri Modin and sent him out to Beirut to arrange his exfiltration.'

Martin sits back and draws on his cigarette with a challenge-me-if-you-dare look in his eyes, and I don't care to because he does seem to be on to something.

'Who tipped off the Soviets?' he says. 'I think it was Mitchell, and so does Peter.'

I nod slowly. 'You've made that very clear.'

My glass is empty. Philby would have finished a bottle by now; Burgess would be halfway through the next. I reach across the table for the whisky. Martin refuses more, Wright takes a little, and as I fill my own glass I talk about surveillance and of the many hours I've spent with Mitchell pretending to review our vetting procedure. 'Graham doesn't give much away,' I say, 'and after a working life at MI5 that's how it should be. Yes, he's distant and an intellectual, but only our Soviet enemy would consider that a crime. He's more interested in chess and sailing than in our great game and those who break its rules. Within sight of the finishing post, who can blame him? I have watched Mitchell on the golf course and sailing on the Solent, and in Oxford I spoke to the few who remember the student scholar, and I've found nothing to arouse suspicion.'

Martin protests. He repeats his assertion that Mitchell was known to have Communist Party sympathies in his youth. Well, fine, but no one I've met has said so. The only Party on his curriculum vitae is the Conservative Party because he worked in its research department before the war.

'You were at Oxford, weren't you?' says Martin. 'Did you find that helpful?'

'Helpful?'

'In persuading people to talk to you?'

'Of course, Arthur. I wore my New College tie.'

He smiles his tense smile and grinds his cigarette out in an ashtray painted with a picture of the Kremlin. 'Goronwy Rees was at your college.'

'Before me.'

'Did you catch up with him when you went down there?'

I sigh heavily, then finish my whisky in one fiery mouthful. 'Up, Arthur. One goes up to Oxford.' Slapping my hands on my knees, I rise. 'As Marx – Groucho – would say, "I've had a perfectly wonderful evening, only this wasn't it,"' and reach for my coat. 'If you can't work with me, you'd better tell Sir Dick – or I will. It's about trust, see.'

Wright's on his feet, too. 'I should go as well, Arthur.'

Martin has thrust his hands into his cardigan pockets like a bolshie schoolboy. 'Trust has to be earned,' he mutters.

'Then I've no more reason to trust you than you to trust me,' I reply.

# 6

WRIGHT FOLLOWS ME into the street. He says he lives somewhere in Essex but he's going to spend the night at the Oxford and Cambridge Club. As we walk towards Euston Road he tells me of the chart he's drawn up of operations that have gone wrong and the probability they were compromised by a Russian spy. He's going to put his case to Dick White in the morning, spread the chart on his table so he can see the scale of things. I nod and grunt and wonder why a technical bod with no experience of investigations is caught up in the hunt for a mole. But I don't want to ruffle his feathers because he seems a reasonable bloke and anxious for my good opinion. We pause at the entrance to Euston station.

'You're living in Dolphin Square, aren't you?' He seems reluctant to say goodbye.

I raise an eyebrow.

'Arthur told me. That's where we picked up last year's traitor – Vassall. A p-poof – so many seem to be.'

'I'll be careful.'

Wright smiles. 'Expensive.'

'Oh, not that bad. Right' – I offer him my hand – 'I'm walking back.'

'Are you?' he says. 'Mind if I join you? I'm going that way.'

We cross Euston Road and walk into soot-stained yellow-stock Fitzrovia, where the papers say the new London bohemians are playing their guitar music, smoking marijuana and reading Jean-Paul Sartre in translation. We click-click in step, pass a pavement café where students are debating with too much passion what is worth saving and what of the past should be swept away, and their raised voices follow us into the next street, with their angry talk of *isms*: *imperialism* and *colonialism* and the old *cultural Fascism*. I wonder if we look like the past to them in our macs, dark suits and brogues; Wright is wearing a trilby and swinging an umbrella.

As we walk he begins to talk of Martin, who is, he assures me, a 'solid chap', a voice in the wilderness until now. He was right about Philby all along, and right about the penetration of both services. Dick White was a good head of MI5, he says. When it blew up in the fifties with Burgess and Maclean, Dick was one of the first to realise the enemy's best spies weren't hogs in the parlour, they were clubbable chaps who had gone to good public schools and Cambridge – a tight little Communist circle festering at the heart of the establishment. Dick was ready to fight the good fight – 'think the unthinkable' his refrain.

Five was prepared to root out traitors in high places, only it didn't, it couldn't, because the enemy was in and of the upper classes, but the upper classes knew him not. The Cavaliers at Six dismissed Five's claims as service rivalry and reds-under-the-beds nonsense, and when push came to shove, Dick White didn't have the guts to take them on after all. Martin was hung out to dry. He'd made enemies at Six and in Whitehall, so to keep the peace Dick sent him to Coventry for a few years or, to be more precise, to the police service in Malaya.

We scuttle between Oxford Street buses and walk on into Soho. Dean Street doors and windows are open even on this cool evening, and from a house where I know Karl Marx lived and three of his children died, there's the jingle-jangle of pop. As I walk along the street there are memories of evenings with

Rees and Burgess at the Flamingo Club, of too much wine and cruel laughter, of girls in the blackout, the smell of hot fat at the Super Fry, and the poems of Dylan Thomas read by Thomas in the York Minster pub; and if I thought Wright was a companion to enjoy such things I would ask him to share a memory at our old table in the corner of the lounge bar, beneath the cracked mirror stuck with theatre bills and photos of dead musical-hall performers. But Wright is still talking of his friend Martin and the years he's spent hunting for spies. 'All those years, while your country's enemies collect a good salary for selling its secrets, no one will believe you because you didn't go to the right public school or to Cambridge University.'

'Arthur has some old scores to settle.'

'Unfinished b-b-business,' he says. 'Arthur's impatient to put things right. You know, he was over in the United States briefing the CIA? Have you met Angleton and Harvey? Angleton's the prep school sort. Harvey's a cowboy. They used to respect us, but now they think we're untrustworthy motherfuckers – that's what Harvey said to Arthur, "untrustworthy motherfuckers".' Wright swings his umbrella at an empty cigarette packet, which slides from the pavement into the gutter. 'Arthur says we're treated like beggars in Washington and the only way to change that is to deal with our problem. That's why he's impatient.'

The curtain has fallen at the theatres on Shaftesbury Avenue and we have to weave our way along the crowded pavement in silence. The people I pass are smarter and more at leisure. For all the bleak headlines of spies and strikes in the newspapers this is a brighter city than the one I left for Vienna. 'Swingin',' they say. There's a new American musical on at the Queens. 'Remember this place in the war?' I shout, above the babble of excited voices. 'A bomb took off the front.' I was there just the night before. Burgess got so drunk Goronwy Rees and

I had to carry him from the theatre. Guy was a clever man, but he only really cared about his own performance.

It's quieter in Whitcomb Street, quiet enough for Wright to tell me he could see Arthur was rubbing me up the wrong way and he wanted to tell me why. 'Don't take it personally. You have to make allowances for him,' he says. 'He doesn't trust the management.'

I say it *is* a matter of trust and that I'm not the management. 'I'm either in or I'm out, Peter.'

'If Dick White says you're in you are.'

I nod. 'We say in Welsh, "*Wrth gicio a brathu mae cariad yn magu.*" While kicking and biting, love grows.'

He laughs. 'Well, you can expect some scars. We all can.'

'And there's nothing else Arthur isn't telling me?'

Wright stops and turns, lifting the brim of his hat a little to catch my eye, no doubt to prove his sincerity. 'Not that I know of, Harry.'

I walk as far as the Oxford and Cambridge but turn down an invitation to join him inside for a nightcap. He shakes my hand warmly and assures me he's looking forward to working with me on the PETERS investigation.

'PETERS?' I ask.

'Arthur didn't say?'

'No, he didn't.'

'The code name for Mitchell.' He pulls a face. 'Sorry.'

The porter has hailed me a cab. 'No need to be,' I say, as I climb into the back. 'An oversight, I'm sure.'

In the court at Dolphin Square Elsa's flat is dark and the curtains are open. I stand by the fountain with a cigarette in the vain hope she'll return before I finish it. Someone in a ground-floor apartment is playing a blues favourite of mine on the piano, but badly. In a cigarette haze I try to imagine Elsa sitting at a big desk in the War Office, twisting a strand of hair about her forefinger, her blouse open a button lower than civil-service serious; when she crosses her legs her stockings make a sound like rushes in the wind. Someone bursts through her door – it's Jack Profumo – and I hear myself say, 'In the name of God, go, Minister!' Then the cigarette burns my fingers.

The trace splints have gone from my door and there are tiny scratches on both locks. Someone has broken in and may still be there, someone who's clever enough to pick a lock but too stupid to replace the splints. Or does the someone want me to notice? I take a deep breath. I'm too old for rough stuff. I unlock and open the door very quietly, and the first thing I see is Elsa's purple coat lying in a heap in the hall. She has left a trail for me to follow: cardigan on the couch in the sitting room, shoes kicked on to the polished oak floor; her dress is hanging on the back of the bathroom door, and the rest of her things are at the foot of my bed, where she lies curled like a fern beneath the covers.

'I've seen this in a film,' I say. She groans sleepily, and I reach under the goose feathers for her thigh. 'Didn't I give you a key? I was going to shoot you.'

'Don't touch me!' she shouts, because my hand's cold, and she rises to her elbow to repel me. 'Impressed I managed to break in? I can still do it!'

She wants to know why I'm late, so I tell her about Tweedledum and Tweedledee, that I left half a bottle of whisky on Dum's table, that Dee is joining the investigation, and that they're both quite certain there's a mole at the top of MI5.

'Are *you* certain?' she says.

'It looks like it. Martin and Wright think it's Mitchell. I don't know. Maybe there's more than one spy. We're all untrustworthy motherfuckers, apparently.'

'Did Martin say that?'

'His American friends. Arthur doesn't use bad language.'

'Will Dick let him keep digging?'

'Don't you think he should?'

'I don't know,' she says, sweeping a loose strand of hair behind her ear. 'How would I?'

I insinuate my hand under the covers again. 'Don't worry.'

'I'm not,' she says. 'Why should I?'

'You shouldn't but it sounds as if you are.'

'No! Stop,' she snaps, and clamps my hand between her thighs. I lean forward to kiss her, but she pushes my face away. 'Hurry up and come to bed.'

'Bad day? I blame Profumo. I want to be one of the first to do so.'

While I'm undressing she asks me about Wright. First impressions, generally positive. He's a technical bod with no experience of this sort of investigation, and he feels he has something to prove. He couldn't wait to tell me he'd left school without any qualifications and worked for years on a farm, and when he got a place at Oxford, the best he could do was a short course in rural economy.

'Snob,' she says.

'Not me. As Marx says, I am free from all prejudice: I hate everyone equally.'

'Wasn't that W. C. Fields?'

'Was it?' I'm standing on one leg, pulling at a sock and losing my balance. 'There.' I hold it up in triumph.

Elsa asks: 'Do they know about me?'

'By "they", I assume you mean Martin and Wright.'

'Do they know you tell me everything?'

'Do I?'

'Don't you?'

'To answer your first question, not unless they have a warrant from the home secretary to bug me. And to answer one you haven't asked, Wright seems to want to get on with me, which is refreshing. I expect he knows I'm just an ordinary boy from the South Wales Valleys.'

'Humph. If you say so.'

'But with a foot in both camps.' I've finished undressing and stand naked before her.

'A sight for sore eyes,' she says.

'Do you think so?'

As she sits up, the covers slide, and she opens her arms to me. 'More like a Cheshire Cat.' Then she drops them again. 'Ah. Almost forgot. There's a letter for you on the piano – it's marked "urgent".'

Elsa has propped it on the music rack in front of a jazz piece by Peterson I'm learning. My name and address are written on the envelope and I know the hand very well. My skin prickles with anger as I gaze at the loops and curls. It's seven years since he was in touch with me, and ten years more would be ten years too soon.

'Who is it?' Elsa shouts from the bedroom.

'My aunt Brenda,' I lie. 'One of my cousins is unwell . . . dying, she says.'

I walk through to the kitchen and pick up the matches I keep by the stove. The letter catches at once and I drop it flaming into the sink. Then I scoop up the burned flakes and drop them into the bin with the peelings and bones from the roast I cooked for Elsa on Sunday.

'Were you close to your cousin?' Elsa says, as I climb into bed beside her. 'Why don't you visit him? I'll come with you.'

'Not him – her,' I say. 'No. We lost touch a long time ago.'

# 7

# *June 1963*

PROFUMO HAS GONE, the Pope too, and the President of the United States has visited the new wall between East and West to boast *Ich bin ein Berliner!* In the spirit of this June madness the PETERS investigation has moved to an MI6 safe house in a tatty little mews flat above a garage in Pavilion Road, five minutes from Harrods and Harvey Nichols, and five minutes the other way from the long-hair, suited and booted youth of the King's Road, where I swear hemlines have risen a couple of inches in just the few weeks we've been here.

Clive comes in from his shift in the observation post opposite Leconfield House, flumps into an old armchair, shuts his eyes and pinches the bridge of his nose. 'PETERS is still at his desk,' he mutters, behind his hand. 'Jean from Administration has taken over the OP, with Bill from Training in the car.' This is a job for streetwise ex-coppers from Five – but the man who makes surveillance operations like this happen is our target: Graham Mitchell. To make matters worse Martin is at daggers drawn with the director general. Hollis is a sceptic and he's only agreed to a full investigation of his deputy on Dick White's say-so. That means we have no choice but to bumble on with a makeshift team of office juniors and secretaries from Six.

A new boy, de Mowbray, is handling the day-to-day street work for me. He puts his head round the door and says, 'I'm picking up PETERS at Waterloo, Harry.' He's fresh from South America and as keen as mustard. 'Team of three – Jean, Maureen and me – all the way to Chobham. His house is about twenty minutes from the village. An acre of grounds, a tennis court . . .'

'He plays a lot.'

'It's all rather lovely, but damnably difficult keeping an eye on him. If we could set up an observation point nearby . . .' But he knows we can't, that Hollis won't wear it.

'I've said it before, Stephen . . .' I lift my feet off the desk and push back the chair '. . . no risks. Tell the girls.' Too close on the street, too slow, too casual, and the entire operation will be blown.

For some reason lost to memory the transcription centre at Leconfield House is on the same corridor as the staff canteen. There's no name on the door, but everyone in the lunch queue knows it's where the Security Service eavesdrops on enemies of the state. 'Our Tower of Babel,' says Wright. He rings the bell and steps back to allow the assistant duty officer to view him through the grille. 'They don't like visitors, but in the circumstances, they'll make an exception for you.'

A plate slides open and I can see small dark eyes. Wright holds up his badge and slides a permission slip through for me. The hutch closes and an automatic lock turns. On the other side of the door we're met by the new head of A2A. Nothing is said because he knows we've come about PETERS. He leads us across a large room, where technical types are recording telephone intercepts on reel-to-reels, and into a corridor with blue doors left and right.

These are the box rooms where the section's secretaries transcribe the tapes. A member of our little magic circle is sitting in one of them with a closed-circuit television and a recording machine. 'Hugh' has spent hours hunched over his large stomach watching the feed from the camera behind the two-way in Graham Mitchell's office. He has a pen in one hand, a cigarette in the other, and the air is thick with smoke. Someone coughs and it takes me a moment to realise it's the deputy DG. Bending closer to the screen I can see a noisy black-and-white image of him at his desk. The two-way mirror is only ten feet from him but it's difficult to gauge his expression because the camera lens is wide open. But I've spent enough time in his office to know his face and voice will betray nothing more than the careful reserve of a Winchester College schoolboy.

Wright asks Hugh: 'Anything?'

'Nothing,' Hugh replies. 'Still chuntering to himself. I can't make sense of it, but I've got a transcriber working on the tape.' He runs a fat finger down the log. 'He had a meeting at eleven with the director of D Branch and with someone from the Home Office at three. Mrs Mitchell says she's roasting a chicken for his dinner. Golf and drinks with guests unknown on Saturday. As I say . . .' He shrugs and shows us his palms. 'Sorry, Peter.'

Wright checks his watch. 'Almost five thirty. You go, we'll hold the fort.'

Hugh eases his heavy frame out from behind the table and picks up his jacket to leave. 'PETERS will be on his way soon,' he says.

PETERS is already tidying his desk. As I watch him straightening the picture of his wife I wonder at how much is invested in a name. No one knows this man called PETERS. A deputy DG known to colleagues as Graham Mitchell used to do the same thing at about this time. Graham was a stiff colleague but decent enough, and he did some useful work during the war. But that was Graham, this is PETERS. What loyalty do we owe this stranger called PETERS?

He limps to his safe with a file and we watch him close it

and turn the dials. Then he walks over to the mirror, and the fisheye distortion of his face is so unnerving I'm convinced he's guilty. He mutters something like, *What? I couldn't*, and *If you say so.*

Wright smirks. 'First sign of madness.'

'Twenty-five years in the Service: who can blame him?' I say.

'You know, he picks his teeth in this mirror.'

'You don't like him, do you, Peter?'

'Not much,' he says. 'Actually, not at all. I wouldn't let that cloud my judgement, though.'

I would like to quote Marx (Groucho) but for once I bite my tongue.

Mitchell picks up his briefcase and *The Times*, pauses at the door to check everything's in order, and he's away. I take the radio from my coat pocket and warn de Mowbray.

'We should wait a few minutes,' says Wright. So, we sit and smoke and talk, and I ask him if he's convinced we have the right man. He's been checking the log, but now he looks at me over his large steel-framed glasses. 'You don't think so?'

'I'd like to see something more concrete.'

'That's why we're here,' he says. 'You know we've interviewed Philby's wife?'

'You?'

'Arthur. She says Kim suddenly became very anxious last summer, began drinking even more heavily than usual. Arthur thinks that was when he heard we were investigating him again. Tipped off by someone here, Harry, in this building.'

He can't be sure of that, but I don't say so. I say, 'Arthur should have told me. What the hell's he doing?'

'Sweating the files, I think.'

'Want to tell me what he's looking for?'

There's a deep frown between his eyes that not even a large pair of glasses can hide, and once again he reminds me of the sternest of the stone heads in the quad at my old college. 'Believe me, Arthur knows what he's doing,' he says. 'You – we – have to trust him.'

'Do you use that word often?' I ask. He has the good grace to smile.

A few minutes later we step out of the lift on the fifth floor and walk swiftly along the corridor and into the director general's Secretariat. The desks have been cleared for the day, but the DG's Secretary, Val, is still at her post. She knows why we're here – she knows everything because she's Hollis's mistress and has been for years. He has asked her to rescue the contents of Mitchell's wastepaper basket and his ink blotter at the end of every working day. The blotter's treated with some sort of chemical solution so we can develop it and check what he's writing. It's the sort of thing a technical bod like Wright relishes. To date we've learned nothing more than answers to *The Times* crossword puzzle and a chess move or two. Val walks towards me with today's wastepaper and the key to the DDG's door. She's holding the basket at arm's length, as if it's full of shit. I don't expect she thought she would ever be called upon to do something at the sharp end of the Service.

I've visited Mitchell's office many times in recent weeks. I'm always struck by how little he's made of the place in his seven years as deputy DG. It belongs to Whitehall. There's just a single photograph of his wife. I don't know Pat Mitchell, but I worked with her brother during the war, when the people here were still a family.

'Graham's a very private person,' I say.

'Secretive.' Wright is fiddling with the combination of the safe.

'What's the difference? Do you know him well enough to say?'

'Does anyone?' he says, glancing over his shoulder at me. 'Ah. Here we are.'

He has the safe open. 'D Branch files – Communist Party of

Great Britain – and what do we have here? A personal file. Well I never!' He holds up the buff cover to show me. 'Your file.'

'Mine? How the hell did he get his hands on that?'

'You joined MI5 in 1940?'

'Is that any of your business?'

He eases his glasses down his nose and looks over them at me. 'The question isn't how but why does PETERS have your file?' He offers a weak smile. 'But I don't think it should concern us now.'

It concerns *me*. I take a step towards him, then stop because the connecting door to the DG's office is opening.

'Hello, Peter.'

Wright shuts the safe and turns to greet Sir Roger Hollis. 'Do you know Harry Vaughan, sir?'

'Of course.' Hollis shakes my hand. 'Back here after all these years.'

He doesn't seem happy about it, although it's difficult to be sure because his voice always sounds flat. It's been a while, but I remember a shy man, who used to tell a lot of filthy jokes, which is perhaps what you do if you want to forget you're the son of a bishop. He was a bottom-pincher too. I don't suppose he bothers any more, with his mistress in the house. The funny thing is, he looks a little like Sean Connery. Twenty-five years older and *without* the charm certainly, but the same strong face, the same dark eyes and thick black eyebrows. Hollis's hair is silvery and receding now, and no one would mistake him for a man of action, but it's easy to imagine why Service ladies of a certain age consider him handsome.

'You know Graham Mitchell's retiring in September?' he says.

I say that I do.

'And I'm sure Peter's told you that I don't like this one bit.'

'None of us do, sir.' I'm quite sincere.

'All right,' he says, and turns to Wright. 'This is the transcript of Graham's mutterings – or transcripts, because there are two versions, both incomprehensible.'

Wright thanks him and takes the envelope. 'Harry's going to look in his desk, sir.'

'If you must.'

Hollis stands over me as I wedge the lock with a small wrench, feel the pins with the pick, then push the springs back one by one until they set. I glance up and he has the sourest expression. I don't suppose he's ever got his hands dirty in this way. I'm tempted to say, 'Yes, this *is* what we do, Bishop.' But the drawers are open already. *'Voilà!'*

We work our way through his deputy's papers in silence. They're full of other people's secrets, which makes our dirty business even dirtier. An officer in D Branch is asking for leave to settle a messy divorce, and one of the 'ladies' in Registry has breast cancer: there's nothing out of the ordinary.

Wright has found some photographs and is busy arranging them beneath the desk lamp. 'I'll take copies and we can run checks,' he says, pulling a mini camera from his jacket.

Hollis is losing patience. 'Let me see.' He picks up a picture of Mitchell with a bluff-looking fellow in his late fifties – 'Graham's brother-in-law' – drops it back on the table and picks up another. 'Son and daughter.' Then another: 'Oxford friend. A gaudy, I shouldn't wonder. Do you have those at your college, Peter?'

Wright looks stony.

'Graham took a first,' says Hollis. 'He isn't going to keep incriminating photographs in his office.'

'Agents b-b-become complacent,' says Wright.

But it's the bottom drawer of Mitchell's desk that interests him most, which is strange because it's empty. 'See these,' he says, pointing to four small marks in the dust.

Hollis bends closer. 'What do you mean?'

'Drag marks. Something small on legs. He's taken something from here.'

'What are you driving at?' Hollis snaps.

'Perhaps a c-copying camera, sir.'

Hollis stares and I know what he's thinking. 'You can finish up here, Peter, can't you?' he says at last, and nodding to me, 'Harry,' he steps back through the connecting door into his office.

'Roger isn't interested in evidence,' Wright observes later. 'He's made up his mind Mitchell is innocent.'

Wright has persuaded me to join him for a Scotch at the Oxford and Cambridge. 'You saw how he dismissed the marks in Mitchell's drawer?'

I sip my whisky.

'They would fit the base of a KGB camera like the one we found in Vassall's flat last year.' He lifts his briefcase on to his knee and takes out the transcripts the DG gave him in Mitchell's office.

'These relate to a barium-meal story we fed PETERS. I must say the results are very interesting.'

He explains: Arthur Martin has cooked up a fake surveillance operation against two Soviet security officers in London and passed the details to Mitchell to see if he'll bite. It's just the sort of information a top-level mole in MI5 would slip to his KGB controller.

'And it looks as if he might have. Here,' Wright passes me the transcript. 'Something he was muttering to his mirror.'

The transcriber has offered two typed versions of the same sentence.

*(i) Well I must tell? Yu-Yuri that they are. I am sure – (slight laugh) – he'll laugh if the Russians (??have booked).*

And:

*(ii) Well I am most terribly curious if they are. I am sure – (slight laugh) – he'll laugh if the Russians (??have booked).*

I look over the top of the transcript and Wright is suppressing a smile.

'I was thinking about your file in *his* safe.'

'You didn't mention it to Roger.'

'Do you w-want me to? He doesn't need to know everything at this stage,' he says, inspecting his fingers. 'Not if it doesn't help the investigation.'

He's making me feel extremely uncomfortable. He, we, will decide what the DG needs to know.

'Explain what these mean,' I wave the transcript at him, 'or are you feeding me a barium meal too?'

'The first version is the most likely. You will note the mention of Yuri. P-P-PETERS is going to tell Yuri about the surveillance operation. I know we can't be sure it's entirely accurate, but small pieces of evidence like this may be all we will have to go on. PETERS is clever. You heard Roger – he took a first!'

I smile. 'I didn't, did you?'

'I don't think it would make Roger think more highly of me. I didn't go to a famous public school, you see.' Before I can think of a reply he's on his feet with his arm raised. 'You will have another, won't you?'

The steward takes our order, then Wright makes his way to the lavatory, and while I wait, I smoke and gaze about the room in search of a familiar face. The members near me are sober middle-ranking civil servants. The Oxford and Cambridge is that sort of place. Burgess would have wanted to kick up a fuss in here, just for the hell of it. I imagine him sprawling on burgundy leather beneath one of the room's two enormous crystal chandeliers, twinkling like an old matinee idol as he sings a dirty ditty. Civil servants tut, civil servants remonstrate, and Burgess sings even louder.

'Penny for your thoughts,' Wright says, resuming his place.

'I'm trying to remember a filthy song.'

'You can share it with Hollis. It's the sort of thing he likes.' He watches me with a wry smile as the steward serves our drinks.

'Penny for *yours*,' I ask, when the steward has gone.

'Something Mitchell said to me two years ago. He said, "They're not ten feet tall, you know, Peter!" He meant the Russians. I was pretty sure someone was shitting on our doorstep then, and I told Hollis and Mitchell so, but Hollis let Mitchell tear into me.' He sips his Scotch. 'He said I had n-n-no proof and it was speculation, that I was just hypothesising. "Not ten feet tall, Peter." Patronising shits.'

I've heard enough. 'Sorry, Peter.' I finish my drink and lean forward to rise. 'Promised to cook supper for someone.'

He nods slowly. 'Miss Frankl Spears?'

'Do you know her?' I haven't spoken of Elsa and wouldn't choose to. 'She doesn't use the name Spears.'

'You were in Vienna together?'

'That's right.' I slap my hands on my knees – 'OK' – and stand up. 'And you're still moving the television feed from Mitchell's office to Pavilion Road?'

'I am. Hollis has got a warrant for a tap at his home, too.'

'Good.'

He's looking up at me, but I can't see his eyes for the chandelier in his glasses. 'I *would* like to talk to you about Vienna,' he says. 'You were both there when the SUBALTERN operation went down, weren't you?'

'Yes.'

'A terrible business. And Miss Frankl left the Service. Terrible. Did they ever get to the bottom of it, how the Russians . . .?'

'Doesn't it say in my file?'

He smiles. 'You'll have to ask PETERS,' he says, which is nonsense, because I know now that he's read it too – and, what's more, he knows I know.

# 8

## 1 July 1963

THE CURTAINS ARE drawn in C's office and the air is thick with smoke.

'In the circumstances, the minister made a decent fist of it, sir.'

'Ted Heath's a sound fellow,' Dick replies.

A bead of sweat trickles down my spine. On my way to Broadway I passed a party of young women in bright dresses, with an ice bucket and a hamper for the park.

I've come from the gallery in the House of Commons where I listened to the minister cough up as much of the truth about Philby as we're ready to share with the people. Gazing down at the green benches below me I thought, If only you knew. The lives and secrets he betrayed: if only you knew. The many apologies made for him by his friends over the years: if only you knew. But we tell ministers what they need to know, and ministers tell MPs even less.

'A Labour MP asked if Philby was tipped off by someone in the Service,' I say, consulting my notes. 'He said, "Now the country knows there's a third man, can it be sure there isn't a fourth?"'

Dick sighs. 'The prime minister blames us for opening this up. He says when his gamekeeper shoots a fox he doesn't hang it at the drawing-room door, he buries it out of sight, and that's what the Service should have done with Philby.' He closes his eyes a moment. 'And now we're at his door with another fox.'

I find it hard to judge. Are we on the trail? Martin tells me nothing. Dick says he's a good chap, just needs careful handling. 'That's why I've given the job to you, Harry.'

Ah, the old Dick White charm. I don't argue because I have no wish to return to Vienna. Life with Elsa . . . Well, I couldn't be happier.

'You will bring her to dinner, won't you?' Nick Elliott says, when we meet in my office an hour later. 'Elizabeth is cross with me for not asking, only you're never here.' I thank him and enquire after his sainted wife. But he isn't listening. He has stepped over to the window I share with the corridor and is forcing the blind shut.

'What's going on, Harry?'

'New vetting procedures, Nick,' I say, shaking a cigarette free from a packet.

'Can't tell me, right? May be a traitor. This place is full of 'em.'

He sounds hysterical. I say so.

'If you spent any time here . . .' he says, gesturing to the warren on the other side of the blind. 'We're treading on eggshells.'

This is the first time I've seen him lose his old Etonian sangfroid. 'Things settle down, Nick. It was the same when Burgess left in 'fifty-one.'

'It's not the same. Some people want to use this to break the old Service. Come on, Harry.' He runs a hand through what's left of his hair. 'What's going on?'

'What do *you* think is going on?'

He stares at me while he considers what he's prepared to say. 'It's anyone from the old days, Harry. They're lifting all our files – yours too, I shouldn't wonder.'

I draw deeply on my cigarette, then grind the butt into the ashtray. 'Peter Wright?'

'Who?'

'Doesn't matter.'

'Quine from Counter-intelligence here. Martin at Five. But I hear Jim Angleton at the CIA is running the show. He wants to tear our house down and Martin is ready to help him. Spends half his time in America.'

I shake my head.

'You don't know?' He sighs with exasperation. 'Come on, Harry.'

'Say "Come on, Harry" one more time, Nick, and I'll punch you.'

'Ah.' He pushes his glasses back up his nose with his index finger. 'Sorry, old boy.'

There are voices in the corridor and one is C's secretary's. A moment later, an impatient knock at the door and in she sails, filling my box with lavender perfume. 'Glad I caught you, Mr Vaughan. Ah, and Mr Elliott.'

He holds up his hands. 'Just leaving, Miss Edwards.'

Dora inclines her head and smiles just like the Queen.

Elliott pats my arm. 'Take care now.' I sense he leaves a happier man for turning me into a suspect, too.

'Polly Garter, we're alone,' I say. But Dora Edwards is in no mood for teasing and no lover of Dylan Thomas in any case.

'C asked me to give you this,' she says, presenting me with a note, 'and Mr de Mowbray is trying to contact you.'

It's just a couple of lines: *PETERS has broken cover. Intensive surveillance. Your presence requested at safe house. C.*

Dora fingers her pearls. 'A reply?'

'No, Miss Edwards. As Marx says: "Please go, and never darken my towels again."'

I take a cab to Sloane Square, and dash between cars to the white stone island in the middle, where fashionable young sit at the edge of the Venus fountain, trailing their fingers in the water, laughing, flirting and smoking, and I pause to light one, too. There's a soggy copy of the *Evening News* at its base with the report of Ted Heath's statement to the Commons on the front page. I'm the only one in the square who cares. You'd have to live in Wonderland to care on a balmy evening like this one. No one crosses the road after me, so I carry on to the opposite side, pausing again to check the reflection in the window of the Peter Jones department store.

Clive's little team is kicking its heels in the makeshift sitting room of the safe house.

'On standby,' he says, when I ask him why. He looks thoroughly pissed off. I expect he's thinking of the summer evening he might be spending in the garden at his local pub or with that little minx on the Transport desk at the Battersea garage.

'Get someone to clear those plates off the floor,' I say grumpily. I had plans for the evening too.

Martin, Wright and young Stephen de Mowbray from Six are upstairs in the office. No one has opened a window or emptied the ashtrays in days. Even by the standards of a Service safe house it is a kind of summer hell. But as good as his word, Wright has moved the closed-circuit television feed here and now it's my people from Six who are watching Mitchell on the other side of the looking glass, noting any word or activity that might be suspicious. I'm here, it seems, because Wright is convinced he's identified one.

At about four o'clock in the afternoon PETERS was observed writing on a scrap of paper. At half past four he changed his mind and tore it into small pieces. When he left for home, Hollis's secretary fished the pieces from the burn bag used for classified waste and Wright has pasted them together. The paper is on the table in front of them, weighted by an ashtray, and it must be important because Wright is grinning like the cat that got the cream.

'It's a map of the common land near PETERS's home. Here,'

he says, sliding it towards me. 'Your man Clive says it's to the north of the village.'

The sketch is in Mitchell's fine hand, certainly. He's drawn arrows and dotted footpaths, including one across the Common with the letters RV between. I don't need Wright to tell me that it's the sort of map you make for someone if you're planning a rendezvous in the middle of nowhere. He tells me all the same because he's excited, and so are Martin and de Mowbray. They want me to agree to round-the-clock surveillance on the Common at once. I have doubts. A good agent doesn't meet his handler on his own doorstep – not in my experience. Neither would I expect him to be foolish enough to sketch his intentions, then throw them into a Security Service bin. But if I say so Martin will counter, 'Even good agents make mistakes,' and he's right, we do. But if Graham Mitchell *is* a Soviet spy he has been one of the best in the game for twenty years. So, yes, I have doubts and questions. If I ask them, Martin will judge me a non-believer and he'll lose his temper, and I'll be no closer to finding out what the hell he's doing behind my back.

'We've sent Bill to the Common with a couple of the girls,' says de Mowbray. 'It's open heathland so it isn't going to be easy.'

'All hands on deck, then,' I say. 'We need eyes on Mitchell's house, on both of the car parks marked on the map, someone at the rendezvous point and a couple of dogwalkers on the Common. Do any of the girls have pets?'

'He knows we're looking for someone,' says Martin. 'He may be meeting his controller. I don't think he'll run – not yet. He'll want an exfiltration plan to be put in place.' He takes a step to the table and picks up the map. 'Anyway, keep me posted, won't you?'

By the time I've made the arrangements it's midnight. In a few hours I will be on the Common. My head is thick with fatigue, with the details of the operation, with intrigue and stale smoke, and although I'm weary I must walk if I am to sleep. This time I pass the windows of Peter Jones without a glance and follow the road from the Underground station into Holbein Place. All I can hear as I walk beside the yellow-brick wall that runs the length of the street is my footfall and the song of a solitary bird confused by the big city night.

When my mind is clear and I can think of something else, I think of my girls whom I've seen just once in the five months I've been home. They live with their mother and stepfather near Virginia Water. He's an insurance broker and a golfer; I haven't the foggiest idea what she does with her days. She isn't reading *War and Peace*. I'm paying the fees for the school she chose. She must be happy it's money well spent because the girls are beginning to sound just like her.

I want them to visit their other family, to see the pit where their grandfather and his father cut coal, and their house in the middle of the terrace at the head of the Rhondda. I want them to aspire to more than Susan, who loves them, I'm sure, and whose great misfortune it was to fall for a man she didn't understand and couldn't trust. I want the girls to make better choices. I want them to know more of life than Surrey. I want them to meet Elsa. I want them to have a better father – if it isn't too late. Graham Mitchell is a good father.

# 9

S TEPHEN DE MOWBRAY rings me from the chess tournament in Brighton. Mitchell drove down in his Morris, watched and played and ate a round of egg sandwiches, and now he's on his way home. He made no attempt to pass a message to any of the Russian competitors. The investigation draws another blank and de Mowbray is lucky to be alive and at liberty after racing red lights all the way to the south coast to be there in time.

Here, in a rented house in Sunningdale, I work my way through the overtime sheets and wait for the next shift change on Chobham Common. It's just a couple of miles away. Our watchers walk back, eat, sleep, grumble and fart, and, if they're not on an overnight, catch a train back into London – except Jean, who drives home with the poodle. The bright lights have never seemed brighter. They're bored and losing patience because we've nothing to show for our summer break from the city but sore feet and red faces. Mitchell's little sketch map has sent us on a wild-goose chase, and I'm beginning to suspect it was drawn and tossed in the full knowledge that someone would fish it out of his wastepaper basket.

I ring Pavilion Road and speak to Wright. 'Oh, come on, Harry,' he says, and uses his favourite line of Mitchell on me: 'He's not ten feet tall, you know.'

I trump him with Hollis's: 'No, Peter, but he did take a first at Oxford.'

He has the grace to laugh.

But when I ask if Martin is with him the answer is 'No,' and to the question, 'Where can I find him?' there is no answer. So, I tell him to warn Martin that if nothing happens on the Common this weekend I'm pulling our watchers out.

Clive is briefing the night shift and he'll handle things on the radio from the safe house. I leave them to their pie and beans and beer, and set off for home in a pool car. My ex-wife and daughters live a short distance away. I'm not expected and an awkward hour with the girls in the golfer's sitting room would be worse than no time at all. But I drive past their house and admire the front garden, cut and rolled like a green, and on my way into London I resolve to persuade Susan to let me take them for a couple of days' re-education before they go back to school.

Elsa is dressing for dinner. I telephone her. 'Draw your curtains if you're going to walk around in your underwear – I'm not the only Peeping Tom in Dolphin Square.' She threatens to have me arrested and I remind her I do this for a living and on Her Majesty's behalf.

'Pick me up in half an hour,' she says. I change into a clean shirt, pour myself a drink and have time to settle at the piano to run through some favourites. I'm struggling to remember 'Lullaby of Birdland' when the telephone rings. The porter in Reception is with a 'gentleman' called Watkins, who would like a word.

''Arry! Surprise. How are you, mate? Been a while . . .'

'It'd better be important, Watkins,' I say. 'Wait for me at the King William – it's on Grosvenor Road.'

Watkins is one of the last people in the world I would welcome on my doorstep. I met him at Dylan Thomas's table in the York Minster many moons ago. He's something on the news desk at the *Daily Mirror*. A former Communist, 'former' by his own report. He's waiting in a discreet corner of the pub, which is empty in any case, and he has bought me a pint of bitter. 'Or would you prefer a Scotch, 'Arry?'

'Who gave you my address, Huw?'

'I promise it will go no further than here,' he says, tapping his head with his forefinger. 'Wouldn't have come, only the story's breaking, see, and I thought for old times' sake . . .'

I gaze at the sags and bags of a face ravaged by years of dissolution and feel a great urge to punch it very hard, then walk away. First, I must be sure there's nothing that will hurt me or embarrass the Service.

'The *Telegraph* got the story but we're all going to carry it,' he says. 'The Soviet defector – Dolnytsin. I know you know about these things.'

'Who?'

'Anatoli Dolnytsin.'

'Never heard of him.'

'The *Telegraph* will say ex-KGB – American property – and he's warned them we're as leaky as an old boat, that Philby was responsible for a network of spies. Come on, 'Arry. Dolnytsin? There was a Dolnytsin at their embassy here?'

'Was there?' I get to my feet. 'I didn't know.'

He leans forward to whisper: 'The paper's goin' to pay.'

I push back the pint he bought. 'Not me. I look forward to reading your story.'

'Hang on, 'Arry, you owe me.' He's struggling to release his gut from the table. 'Remember when Goronwy Rees wrote those pieces on Burgess for the *People*?'

'Goodbye, Huw.'

'I knew you were close to Burgess, too, but did I say anything?' He steps between me and the door, close enough for me to feel his malodorous breath on my cheek. His beer-shot eyes chase

about my face. 'I told them, "'Arry couldn't have known Burgess
was a spy . . ."'

That's enough. I grab the lapels of his jacket and drag him
to tiptoes. 'Threaten me, Watkins, and I'll finish you. Understand?
I'll finish you.'

I hear him protesting his innocence as I walk to the door.

'I wish you'd punched him,' says Elsa, a little later. 'He may
have punched you back.' She's impatient with me because we're
late for drinks at Nick Elliott's home in Belgravia. 'This was
your idea,' she reminds me, as our cab turns into Eaton Square.

I squeeze her hand, 'Thanks,' and she gives me a resigned
smile. 'Watkins offered me money. They're like that, aren't
they?'

'What do you mean?'

'His newspaper preaches hell fire for Philby because he gave
away secrets, and yet here he is, offering me *money* to betray
some more. Damn fool threatened me too.'

She frowns. 'What did he say?'

I smile and kiss her cheek because a cab isn't the place to
talk of such things, and we're in Wilton Street with the driver
to pay.

My conversation with Watkins rolls around the back of my
mind throughout the evening. Nick and Elizabeth Elliott have
invited old friends from Six and their wives. Some have left
the Service, some are ready to, and because they're decent and
loyal friends, they've invited Eleanor Philby too. Elliott introduces me to her and we try to make polite conversation that
dances round her husband's presence in Moscow. She's about
my age, a west-coast American, slim, elegant, engaging, and
very drunk. She can't be still for a moment, fluttering like a
small bird or an enchantress casting a spell that will help us

all forget she's married to Kim. We can't talk about that scandal, so we talk about the other, the one involving Jack Profumo. The room wishes to hear from Elsa. I try to draw Elliott to one side but he's listening too.

Someone asks if the government can survive and if Butler will replace Macmillan. 'Hailsham for prime minister,' says someone else, 'because he'll strike the right moral tone.'

'You knew Kim, didn't you?' Eleanor Philby has me by the buttonhole. She's drunk so much she has the staggers. Lifting her finely manicured fingers from my jacket, I steer her to a chair.

'You know, Kim's the most interesting man I've ever met,' she says, when she's seated with her glass. 'And so soft-hearted. When his pet fox died he was quite inconsolable.' I shake out a cigarette and say nothing: her kind husband abandoned his last wife to the bottle and she died alone in penury. I listen to Eleanor rattle on, until she says, 'Kim won't stay there, you know.'

Then I feel sorry for her. 'I'm afraid he won't have a choice, Eleanor,' I say. 'They won't let him go.' But I can see she isn't listening.

Elsa smiles graciously, like the good civil servant she has become, and whispers through her smile, 'Get me out of here,' and I'm ready with one of the best of my many excuses 'to oblige. We breathe more easily on the Elliotts' steps. She asks me what I'm going to do to thank her for her efforts, and flowers won't be enough. 'I love you,' I say, 'but I must leave you too. I have to speak to C.'

'Is this about Watkins? What did he say, Harry?'

She's worried, and I'd like to confide in her, but there isn't time before the papers hit the streets.

Number 54 Broadway is as empty and dark as the London Transport headquarters at 55, and the international property company at 29, because office spies like to keep office hours. I don't know the senior duty officer, and I'm obliged to bully him into surrendering the emergency number. Dick is dining with the foreign secretary and is grumpy with me on the phone.

'The newspapers are running a story about a defector working for the Americans – and us, sir. Anatoli Dolnytsin, they say.' I pause to make him feel uncomfortable. 'They're making some wild claims.'

'All right, Harry.'

'The British can't be trusted – that sort of thing. A network of spies . . .'

'All right,' he snaps at me again. 'Wait there, will you.'

The line goes dead.

I wait in his outer office. I smoke and, in a reflective haze, consider quite calmly just how angry I want to be. I'll make it personal. 'All about trust,' I might say (isn't it always?) and 'You left me out of the circle, sir.'

Who came up with this masterstroke? Martin? Angleton? Can't kill the story, so feed the sharks the name *Dolnytsin*. Change a couple of letters and you have the CIA's favourite defector and the man who really set the PETERS ball rolling, with his talk of a Ring of Five: Anatoli Golitsyn.

Dick greets me with a warm handshake and a smile, neat and trim in his well-cut dinner suit. We are to enjoy another fireside chat at his home in Queen Anne's Gate. 'You think you're owed an explanation?' he says, gesturing to an armchair.

'Yes.' I want him to tell me everything *and* apologise, and because he's Dick White I expect he will.

'The story must have come from the Americans.' He lifts the crystal decanter from his drinks tray. 'Scotch? You like ice, don't you?' He places a glass on a table at the arm of my chair. 'Golitsyn is helping us with a general security review.'

'Helping Arthur Martin?'

'Yes.'

'Wright knows?'

'Because it's a Security Service operation,' he says, taking the seat opposite, 'you didn't need to know, and Golitsyn insisted on the smallest possible circle. He says it's common knowledge in Moscow Centre that the KGB has a source at the very top of Five, and that makes him very jumpy.'

'Common knowledge?'

'That's what he says, and he's convinced the Americans. They think we've completely underestimated Soviet penetration of the Service.'

'Jim Angleton?'

'And others. And this leak to the newspapers, it's come from Angleton – or one of his people – a crude attempt to put pressure on us to order a full security review.'

Dick gets to his feet to signal he has nothing more to say. 'We'll speak to our friends in Fleet Street, issue a denial.'

'And Mitchell?'

He looks uncomfortable. 'Golitsyn says he has the right profile.'

'The right profile?'

Dick's colour rises. 'Your scepticism is noted.'

I finish my drink and rise. What happened to cautious Dick, the safe pair of hands, the politician's favourite? Worst case, Golitsyn is still Moscow's creature; best case – still bad – he belongs to the CIA and dances to 'Yankee Doodle Dandy'.

Dick's gazing at me. 'Look, Harry, he understands how Moscow Centre operates. He's a great resource . . . This time we're going to get it right. We need to eliminate the possibility of a systematic infiltration.'

'I don't doubt it, sir, but perhaps someone else,' I take a step towards the door, 'someone with a taste for this sort of thing . . .'

'No. You have the field craft. Arthur's a good chap, but . . . excitable. I need a clear and steady eye, a cool head – I need you.'

'Then why did I have to get my intelligence from a *Daily Mirror* hack?'

'That was a mistake,' he says. 'Sit down, would you, please? Another?' He picks up my glass. 'There's something else you should know.' He turns with the decanter in his hand and stares at me as if caught in two minds whether to say more. For once slim, fit Peter Pan looks something like his age. 'What I'm going to tell you . . . Well, you know the spiel, but we're talking about *our* crown jewels or, to be precise, Uncle Sam's. We call it VENONA, and it changed everything after the war – everything.'

There's a twinkle in his eye now because he knows I relish a good secret – we all do. But there are bad secrets too, and Dick can't see but my skin is pricking with apprehension as I imagine for a moment what this one will lead to.

'We keep it to a small circle here and in Washington,' he says, placing the whisky on the table beside me. 'For eight years – the war years and after – we managed to intercept intelligence signals between Moscow and its embassies in Washington and London. We can't decode them all, but enough to know they had – may still *have* – an army of agents in America. Two hundred so far. And at the heart of government. Two hundred! How many they have here in Blighty isn't as clear. We have code names – a score or more. We know the Russians were running an inner circle with access to grade-one intelligence – a Ring of Five. Burgess, Maclean and Philby belonged to that circle; two of the Five are still in place. We've barely begun to work on agents in the outer circle.'

Dick shuffles to the edge of his chair to look me in the eye. 'Golitsyn says the KGB has moles in senior positions in MI5 and MI6, and there's enough in VENONA to suggest he's right. Honestly, it puts the fear of God into me.'

He pauses. 'I'll arrange for you to view VENONA. Wright would be a good guide.

'Wright?'

'Yes, Peter has been indoctrinated,' says Dick, tetchily. 'Please. No temper tantrum.'

I laugh, and he's pleased to hear me.

A clock strikes the witching hour, and we rise. As we walk towards the door he puts his right hand on my shoulder. 'Glad we had this talk.'

'And Graham Mitchell?'

Dick touches his brow. 'Arthur's convinced he's ELLI. He's the mole. I haven't seen the evidence yet.'

'*Is* there any?'

'We'll make that call soon.' His hand falls from my shoulder to the door handle. 'We should have listened to Arthur sooner . . . I should have. Which of the ancients was it who said, "A nation can survive its fools but not its traitors, because the traitor appeals to the foulness that lies deep in the hearts of all men"?'

# 10

## *12 August 1963*

I WATCH THE rain rolling down the safe-house windows and imagine my girls on their holiday in Devon. Do they have a bedroom with a view across the sea to Wales? I promised to take them there. Daddy is spending the summer on his backside in front of a television monitor. Mitchell coughs, and I glance at the screen. He's scribbling quietly at his desk and has been for an hour.

My sometime girlfriend Nina writes that Vienna is enjoying temperatures in the nineties, that she has left the city for her family home on a Riesling slope in the Tyrol. 'Bring your new girlfriend,' she says, but my new old girlfriend is tired of waiting for me, tired of summer rain, tired of spoon-feeding the new minister at the War Office, and has taken refuge at her godmother's house in France. There's a respectable chance he'll have gone by the time she gets back, because the government is rocking. There's too much news, too many bad headlines, here and in America. *The Times* correspondent in Washington says our closest ally is beginning to wonder if we're an ally at all. He writes:

> To an American public already mystified by the Profumo scandal, the Philby case, and a long list of other security troubles, the Dolnytsin affair is another shock. Political and security scandals are turning Britain into the Latin America of Europe and causing great pain in the American intelligence community.

Someone in that 'community' has taken the trouble to tell *The Times* so, perhaps the same someone who gave the *Dolnytsin* story to the papers in the first place.

So, I yawn and hum a tune and imagine the mop-head boys and the girls in cotton dresses tearing up and down the King's Road on their scooters; and the man who hawks newspapers at Sloane Square tube, who told me he left a leg in the desert; and Arthur Martin getting tight in the Duke of Wellington, around the corner. We see a good deal more of each other now and I can tell from his face he's drinking too much. But he's making an effort to be agreeable. Perhaps he hopes to win me round before he goes into battle with Hollis. He seems quite certain the director general will do his damnedest to kick the PETERS investigation into the long grass. I think Arthur needs a holiday, that we should all go on holiday.

Mitchell gets to his feet and walks round his desk to the mirror. The transcription girls say he spends part of each day muttering to his reflection. I've noticed him fidgeting, scratching, bouncing his knee under the table. Why is he so anxious? He hasn't long to go before he retires. His secretary has begun to organise his leaving do in the Pig and Eye Club at the top of MI5.

'Picking his teeth again?' Peter Wright settles into a chair beside me. 'He needs a dentist.'

'Yes.'

He reaches across the table for the ashtray. 'Anything?'

'Nothing.'

'Arthur thinks we've enough to interrogate him and we should d-d-do it now. Do you agree?'

I say, 'I do,' and that it's the only way to put this to bed. I've read the VENONA signals and I don't doubt there's a Fourth Man and a Fifth, but it's going to take more than dust marks at the bottom of a drawer to convince me it's Graham Mitchell.

We've crawled all over him for months, bugged, burgled, rifled his belongings, and his wife Pat's stuff too. We've listened to their cooing, chased them from golf course to golf course and even down the Solent in a yacht. In short, we've done all we can with the resources available.

'It was PETERS who recommended we stop work on the VENONA,' Wright said, when he was acting as my guide to the signals. 'Suspicious, don't you think?'

'Deeply,' I said, 'but what about Dick?'

'Dick?'

'Well, Dick was director general at the time and it says here in the file' – I had it open in front of me – 'that he agreed to suspend the decoding operation because it was getting nowhere. Too much effort for too little in the way of solid leads. It was his decision, not Graham's.'

Wright pursed his lips, hummed, pushed his glasses up his nose then said, 'Dick was persuaded.'

He says the Americans have a powerful computer working on the old VENONA signals now and it has thrown up new information that *proves* Philby was a traitor during and after the war.

'That's good,' I said. 'When he comes back from Moscow we can have a public hanging.'

Mitchell has a visitor. His brother-in-law, James Robertson from D Branch, has popped his head round the door and begs a few minutes. 'It's about that bloody man Wright,' we hear him say. 'Can't you clip his wings, Graham? He's a law unto himself.'

I turn to Wright with a sympathetic face. 'Doesn't like you, Peter.'

'I don't like *him*,' he says coolly.

Mitchell waves Robertson to a chair. 'What is it?'

'He's supposed to be working for me but I hardly see him,'

he says, 'and when I do he's evasive. Is he doing something for the DG?'

Mitchell picks up a pen and puts it back again.

'The thing is, Graham,' his son-in-law continues, 'this fellow Wright thinks he knows everything about counter-espionage. Honestly, I don't know what's happening to this place.' He leans forward to clutch the edge of Mitchell's desk. 'We're becoming second rate. The calibre of people since the war . . . He's a bloody technician. Time you put him in his place!'

Mitchell is on his feet encouraging Robertson to rise. Can they talk about this later? His manner, the slight tremor in his voice . . . I lean closer to the monitor. But his head is bent – I can't see his face. When he raises it he is bonhomie again. 'Pat is very well, thank you,' and 'Can you make lunch on the fifteenth?' They leave his office together, closing the door on their conversation.

Wright's face is as hard as stone. 'Christ, he's still fighting the last war.' Robertson's technician jibe has cut deep. 'And Mitchell said nothing.'

'You're right,' I say. 'He was determined not to. That's surprising, isn't it?'

'Mitchell's lazy, he's going in three weeks . . .'

'No, think about it for a minute. Mitchell's anxious – we've seen plenty of evidence of that – and he's careful. He doesn't want to talk about you in his office – even to Robertson. Why? Too busy, he said, but he hasn't come back.' I tap the top of the monitor. 'Where is he?'

'Meeting someone else?'

'Perhaps,' I say. I don't believe it for a minute.

Then Mitchell sends me a note. He wants to share his last thoughts with me before I circulate my recommendations for a new vetting procedure, and he suggests the following Monday.

I'm surprised because he was struggling for something to say at our last meeting. But the transcription ladies have heard nothing suspicious, our watchers seen nothing out of the ordinary. I run into Arthur Martin on the Friday before the Monday. He's taking a turn in front of the monitor, and I can tell he's straight from the pub. 'It's just like before,' he says, glumly. 'They're closing rank.'

'Who?'

'The old guard, the public-school boys. It was like that with Kim and now . . . Mitchell went to Winchester, you know.'

When I press Martin to say more, he accuses Roger Hollis of doing his best to kill the investigation. 'But I won't let him this time.'

I leave him slumped over the monitor, a cigarette trembling in his fingers. Sunlight is streaming through windows into the mirror camera. Mitchell is no more than a shadow.


'Is he guilty?' Elsa asks on Sunday. She's unpacking her holiday clothes and I'm watching from the bed, jealous of her tan and her breezy humour.

'Did you miss me?'

'Come on,' she says, pressing me for an answer.

I tell her an officer from D1 investigations at Five is pulling the evidence together for Hollis and White. 'Ronnie Symonds – was he there in your time?'

'But you've seen the evidence already. Do *you* think he's guilty?' she says.

'Martin and Wright seem certain.'

She punches my arm. 'Come on. If you don't want to talk about it, just say so.'

'I don't want to talk at all,' I say, pulling her on to the bed beside me.

# 11

# *19 August 1963*

GRAHAM MITCHELL'S SECRETARY rings on Monday morning to tell me to meet him at his club.

'Couldn't you dissuade him?' Martin grumbles, when I telephone Pavilion Road with the news.

'He's the DDG,' I reply.

Wright talks some nonsense about rigging a wire. Where? No, I'm glad they won't be breathing down my neck.

The Royal Thames Yacht Club is next to the French Embassy, just along from the Hyde Park Hotel in Knightsbridge. Mitchell's waiting in the entrance hall, his coat over his arm. It's been a while since I've seen him in person and I'm surprised by the change in his appearance. He's lost so much weight his Savile Row suit is hanging from his shoulders as if it was off the peg. Do I mind if we take some air?

'I was going to show you my draft of the vetting report,' and I lift my briefcase.

'Later,' he says.

We walk into Hyde Park, heading north towards the Serpentine. It's another grey day in a summer of such days, with a dense front of cloud rolling in from the west. Conscious that Mitchell is dragging his foot on the gravel path as he limps, I shorten my stride. 'Terrible summer,' I say, to draw him into conversation. He offers a wan smile.

A few yards further, and I try again. 'You wanted to talk, Graham?'

'Let's sit down first,' he says, gesturing towards one of the benches at the edge of the Serpentine. 'Do you mind?'

There are spots of rain in the wind now and the promise of more is driving rowing boats from the water and mothers with small children towards the buses at Hyde Park Corner. Mitchell steps in some of the duck shit that speckles the path but seems not to notice. 'You sail, don't you, Harry?' he says, wiping the bench with his handkerchief.

'Not me. I'm uncomfortable aboard anything smaller than the *Queen Mary.*'

'Ah. I thought you were a sailor.' He's pulling at a loose button on the cuff of his jacket, his chin almost on his chest. 'I've always admired you, Harry. You're good at things I've never been good at – you make people like you. I remember during the war when you were thick with Rees and Burgess . . . You were great clowns.'

I reach into my jacket for a packet of cigarettes. 'I'm not sure I appreciate the comparison.'

'I mean you make people laugh. But you're a decent chap too. Rees is arrogant and lazy, and Burgess is . . . Burgess. *You* don't tear down people for sport.'

'There were times,' I pull a face, 'and I'm sorry for them.' He ignores this and the cigarette I offer him.

'Look, Harry, I've made mistakes – we all have – but I love this country. We both do – you know my wife, Pat, worked for the Service?'

'Yes.'

'Of course you do. Of course. I can't understand a man like Philby, can you? I would *never* turn my back on my friends and my country. Never.'

'No.'

'Look, I know it's time to go – yesterday's man, and all

that . . .' He closes his eyes a moment. 'But not like this, Harry. Tell Dick and Roger, "Not like this."'

'I don't understand . . .'

'Yes, you do.' He stares at me, very angry in a quiet way.

I nod once. 'Right, Graham. Noted.' Then, to avoid his gaze, I lean forward to rescue his cuff button from the gravel. 'And this is yours.' I drop it into the palm of his hand, dry and calloused by ropes and the sea. 'I don't suppose Pat will need to sew it back. Not now.'

He tries to smile. 'I don't suppose she will.'

The wind is whisking the surface of the Serpentine into short, white-tipped waves and rolling the chained boats on the opposite bank. We have only gone a few yards when it begins to rain hard and straight, soaking my linen jacket and speckling the thin summer dress of a young woman, who scurries past in search of shelter. Mitchell holds his umbrella over us but in seconds my slacks are soaking. I glimpse Clive from my watcher team between the trees and wonder if Mitchell has seen him too. He doesn't say much as we walk, although we couldn't be much closer beneath his umbrella. At the door of his club he offers his hand and another sad smile, then calls me back to remind me of his farewell drinks party.

'And Elsa? I'd love to see her,' he says. 'Such a shame she left us after SUBALTERN.'

'You think so?' How can he say so now?

'The Service is that sort of place, isn't it? If you want to take the blame, everyone is happy to oblige you.' He takes a deep breath. 'I don't want it to be like that for me. I'll always wonder if there was any point to my life.'

At Pavilion Road the officers and foot-soldiers are gathered in the transcription room on the first floor. There has been a most unholy row. Heads turn to look at me as if *I'm* responsible for the poisonous atmosphere.

'Who died?'

Martin is slouching against the wall by the window, de Mowbray hunched over a monitor, and Wright presents a stony face.

'Well, who died?'

No one replies. So, I address my watchers, 'Show's over, boys,' and, glancing down the staircase behind me, 'What are you waiting for?' It's the cue for everyone below officer rank to troop out of the door.

Wright explains: 'Roger has been here. He's spoken to the prime minister and the PETERS interrogation is out of the question.'

'The useless bastard! But the bottom line is, the bottom . . .' Martin is so incensed he has to pause for breath. 'We have to make him. Threaten to resign – all of us.'

I catch Wright's eye. 'It was the prime minister's decision?'

'R-Roger says Harold Macmillan believes another scandal would be calamitous, but I expect Roger encouraged the PM to think so.'

Martin bangs his fist on the window ledge and curses. In the difficult silence that follows, I watch him twitching with anger. His certainty is troubling, and why is it so personal? Revenge, perhaps, for old-school-tie putdowns and the years he was passed over for promotion. He's turning PETERS into a feud with Hollis and the old Service.

'If the prime minister has spoken . . .' I venture.

'What about the Americans?' Martin barks back. 'We must tell them – they'll insist on interrogation. PETERS has compromised joint operations.'

'*If* he's a traitor.'

'You don't think we have enough to justify it?'

'Steady, Arthur.' I smile with all the sincerity of the old Maerdy minister, who preached love and forgiveness to our parents in chapel, then martyred us boys in his Bible class with a stick. 'If you want to shout at someone, shout at the prime minister.'

Martin gestures with his arms in frustration. 'You don't know James Angleton. If the deputy director general of the Security Service turns out to be a traitor and we've kept the evidence from him . . .' He catches my eye; his are tired and bloodshot. 'After Philby, it will be a complete disaster.'

'All right,' I agree. 'We show the Americans all the evidence.'

Martin's shoulders sag, Wright puffs out his cheeks, and de Mowbray . . . Well, no one gives a fart for his opinion.

'I'll tell Roger we think the same,' says Martin.

'On the Americans,' I say cautiously. 'And just the evidence, because we haven't proved Graham Mitchell's guilty. I don't think we will.'

Martin opens his mouth to argue. 'Hold on, Arthur,' I say. 'There's something you need to hear. Mitchell knows we're investigating him. And I think he's close to a breakdown. That's what I'm going to tell Dick White. As far as I'm concerned, PETERS is over. We've nothing. It's over.'

I know they don't agree but that's all I have to say, and now I want to go, with a silent prayer to whatever God there may be to spare me from another day on PETERS. At the bottom of the stairs I pause to pinch my wet trousers from my knees, and hear Martin ranting and stamping round the room above. I hear my name and a chair crashing to the floor, and so do the watchers waiting in the room below. Clive's back from foot patrol and greets me with a wry smile.

'All right, boys,' I say. 'Anyone fancy a pint?'

# 12

## 27 August 1963

THE MAERDY MINISTER was a liar. I realised that when I was seven and Mum was dying but God wasn't listening. *I* could hear her pain: why couldn't he? We were mid-terrace, so our neighbours on either side could hear it too. A few months later I moved to my aunt Elen's home where it was possible to scream blue murder and no one would take the slightest notice. I think I understood even then that it was the minister's job to make excuses for God. Mum was the believer, and Dad was something called a Communist. 'Opiate of the people,' he used to say, quoting Marx (Karl) on religion. Someone must have told him because I never saw him read anything more challenging than a paper. But I read Marx. Window-seat over-looking the quad, the college choir processing to chapel, and I thought of Marx and Mum and her minister and the miners and their families in Maerdy. 'To call on them to give up their illusions,' Karl Marx wrote, 'is to call on them to give up a condition that requires illusions. The criticism of religion is, therefore, in embryo, the criticism of that vale of tears of which religion is the halo.'

So, I return to the safe house the following day, where Dick White says I must stay for as long as it takes to read PETERS the last rites. My watchers go out in the rain again, the tran-scription ladies sit in front of the monitor. Martin is distant, Wright conciliatory, and at half past six in the evening de

Mowbray comes in off the street to say Mitchell's rumbled him too. 'He just turned and stared at me,' he says. 'London passing by, and he stood and stared.'

Perhaps he twigged when his name was dropped from the 'Most Secret' circulation list, or perhaps it was our street work, because we were never good enough. I expect him to storm into Hollis's office, but he gives nothing away. 'Because he's guilty,' says Martin. It is hurt and bewilderment I see in his eyes. Then, on the Thursday after his Tuesday encounter with de Mowbray, he approaches the mirror in his office and mutters, 'Why are you doing this to me? Why?'

Jill, the transcription girl, drops her pen, and I swear in Welsh.

'He's cracking up,' I say, and Jill begins to cry.

Later I tell Wright, and he dismisses it casually as 'good acting'. 'I've no scruples about this, Harry,' he says.

'You've no scruples because you've no empathy,' I reply.

We're all trying to pretend we're as worldly and insouciant as James Bond, but deep down we're the same resentful school-boys, cripples and orphans we were before we joined the Service, even the tough guys, the hard men who enjoy the nastiness, like my watcher Clive, who grew up pulling wings off flies and boasts of losing his virginity at fourteen.

'I think he's goin' mental,' says Jill (she isn't a brigadier's daughter).

I look up from her legs to the calendar on the wall behind the monitor. 'He has to survive one more week, then he's gone. Free.' I tell her this because she's a sweet-hearted thing and there's no need for her to know that the stink will follow him home when he retires, that he won't be clear of it until D1 finishes its review of the evidence, and that Martin is demanding a full interrogation.

'I feel sorry for him, 'Arry,' she says. (I encourage informality.)

'Do you, love?' I reply, and pat her knee affectionately. 'Me too. Fancy a drink after this?'

Late Friday afternoon, and the chief is at his desk in Broadway Buildings. For once the blinds are open and sunlight is pouring into the dusty corners of his room – and they *are* dusty. He's sitting with his back to the window – I can barely see his face – and there's a blinding halo about his white hair: Sir Dick White, martyr to his subordinates. I tell him one thing and Arthur Martin tells him another. My turn now. We're meeting to review PETERS before the big showdown. Martin and Wright are preparing to confront Hollis. Officially, it's an MI5 affair – so I won't be there – but Roger listens to Dick and Dick is listening to me.

I don't waste time with the mistakes we've made: we all know there isn't enough evidence for a prosecution. What about the KGB camera? Dick says, and it takes me a moment to realise he's talking about the marks at the bottom of Mitchell's desk drawer. 'Really, sir?'

I'm quite sure Mitchell is in the clear and should be allowed to retire to the golf course. But we should show the Americans the evidence and if they insist on an interrogation . . . The PETERS investigation team is of one mind on this, and we'll resign if Sir Roger doesn't agree. Dick makes a note, then glances at his watch. I guess he's impatient to escape to Sussex to be with Kate and the boys.

'What next for me, sir?'

'Let's see what the D1 review of PETERS comes up with, shall we?'

I *want* to say we're dancing on eggshells, that Mitchell's in danger of losing his mind and Martin's a casualty, too; that I hear from Nick Elliott and others that the scent of treachery lingers in every corridor of this building, that 'friends' are going about their everyday business on tiptoe; that we've spent months and thousands of pounds on surveillance but we're still looking for proof in the dust at the bottom of a drawer, and we're no closer to proving there's a master spy than we were eight months ago. Instead I nod and grip the arms of my chair to rise.

Dick checks me with a gesture. 'From Moscow station.' He leans across his desk to present me with a signal flimsy.

Beneath the usual security and circulation codes there is a single line of type in capitals. I gaze at it for a few seconds and try not to show that it hurts me: BURGESS DIED BOTIN HOSPITAL THIS MORNING.

Guy Burgess, formerly of this parish.

'Drank himself to death,' says Dick.

'I don't doubt it,' I reply, with faux nonchalance. 'Was he alone?'

'I don't think Philby was at his bedside, if that's what you mean, and his mother lives in London. I don't like to speak ill of the dead, but I'll make an exception for Burgess: he didn't have one redeeming quality. He was a bugger and a shit. Good riddance.'

'I wonder if the Russians will bury him in his Old Etonian tie. That's what he would want.'

'After putting two fingers up to us all?' He snorts with derision. 'I suppose I should tell Anthony Blunt. Do you think he knew Burgess was a traitor?'

'You know Blunt better than I do, sir.'

I remember the two of them were thick before Blunt left Five for finer things. He's Sir Anthony Art Expert now, director of the Courtauld Institute, Surveyor of The Queen's Pictures.

'They were at Cambridge together,' says Dick. 'I'll drop him a note. Everyone else can read it in *The Times*.'

I wonder if by 'everyone' he means Rees in particular, because

Rees was Guy's closest friend for years, and mine, until he betrayed us both.

Dick is shepherding me to his door. 'Take a few days off, Harry. Go somewhere with your girls.'

'They're going back to school, sir.'

'Take a week. The smoke will have cleared by the time you get back.'

'I'll miss Mitchell's leaving do.'

Dick grunts. 'Seriously?'

Guy Francis de Moncy Burgess: he claimed his family was Huguenot many moons ago and that Burgess used to be 'Bourgeois', which is funny, because bourgeois is everything he used to despise. He went from his posh school to Cambridge and was immensely proud of both, and so was Philby. He was a book Communist. The only members of the proletariat he was truly interested in were the young men he used to forage for in the blackout during the war. That isn't quite true, because he did like me, even when I refused to let him suck my cock.

'What do you feel?' Elsa says, when we're together with wine.

'Mostly relief.'

She lifts her head from my shoulder and turns to look at me. 'Why?'

'He was trouble – always.'

'He couldn't harm you, could he?'

'Besides, can you imagine what it was like for him in Moscow? They're terrible Puritans there.'

Elsa pinches my chin between her thumb and forefinger. 'Hey, you're worrying me.'

'Why?'

'Answer! Could he hurt you?'

'From the grave?'

'Harry! You know what I mean.'

'Ow!' She's pushing her nails into my cheek. 'Of course not.' I smirk at her. 'I'm just teasing.'

Can Burgess hurt me? I lie awake in the early hours, Elsa breathing softly beside me, and wonder. There wasn't an appetite for blame when Burgess and Maclean defected all those years ago. Dick was at MI5 then, and I remember him saying, 'No witch hunt! It's bad for morale,' but he's forgotten, and he's willing to start one now. These things gather a terrible momentum. We must be ready.

I roll on my side to stroke Elsa's cheek lightly with my fingertips, and whisper, '*I could tell you my adventures . . . but it's no use going back to yesterday, because I was a different person then.*'

'What?' she moans.

'*Alice's Adventures in Wonderland.*'

'No,' she moans, 'go to sleep,' and turns to snuffle her pillow, like the Dormouse.

But these are the witching hours. Trouble staggers towards me in an Old Etonian tie, with a vindictive smile. And Dick has an eye for his legacy. He listens to me, but to Martin more closely.

'We're going to clean up the Service, Harry,' he said to me at his office door. 'We have to – we're losing. We're going to turn over every stone this time. This is about more than one man. You see that, don't you?'

Goronwy Rees is hiding under one of those stones.

# 13

## 1 September 1963

M Y EX-WIFE RINGS me on Sunday morning. Our eldest is refusing to go back to school and, for some reason, she thinks I can persuade her. I roll out of bed with the covers and say, 'I want to make love to you, but I have to be a father.' Elsa laughs. She's naked and truly a sight for my sore, sleepless eyes.

'Hey, don't laugh,' I say. 'You're coming too.'

I expect her to refuse but she swings her legs round to get up. 'Why not?'

We motor down the A3 to Virginia Water in her smart little Sprite. She looks young and attractive in a pink pleated skirt made of lamb's wool and matching sweater, her chestnut hair blowing about her face. God, I love her, I really do. I'm wearing the polo-neck she bought me on holiday in France, 'because Dirk Bogarde wears them too'. We pull up in front of the house and she stays behind the wheel while I negotiate. Susan's frazzled and worried about our daughter, too worried to blame me. 'Talk to her, will you? I can't.'

My Bethan is small and hippy, and when her face is set in a determined expression, as it is now, I remember the same face in the kitchen at home in Maerdy. '*Ble buoch chi?*' Mam would say. 'Where have you been, Harry?' the pitch and timbre of her voice the music of the Valleys.

But when Bethan speaks I hear flat commuter London. She's sixteen now and clever enough for university, if she has the confidence, but when I introduce her to Elsa she appears sullen and shy.

'Back seat, Harry,' says Elsa. 'Bethan's in the front beside me.' And soon we're bowling along country lanes at a speed that would shock both her mother and the new secretary of state for war. Bethan turns to look at me and her green eyes – my mother's eyes – are shining, and I know she's thinking, Do middle-aged women really do things like this? We stop in a village for sandwiches and pop, and Elsa and Bethan talk about Cliff Richard, Adam Faith, the Beatles, boys and clothes. And when my daughter is sure she likes my crazy, beautiful friend she speaks of home and her troubles at school. I listen and nod and touch her hand, but I may as well not be there. Elsa coaxes, she charms; she hated school too, and was always falling out with her mother and father. 'I still do.'

Bethan says she doesn't argue with *her* father because she never sees him.

'He was in Vienna,' is my feeble defence, 'but he's home.'

At five o'clock I walk her back to the house. Stepfather is raking leaves on the far side of the garden and he's careful not to catch my eye. Real father is resolved to make a better fist of things. She's going to visit us in London, *if* she goes back to school and *if* her mother agrees. Elsa has convinced her it's worth the trouble and it's Elsa she wants to see again soon.

On the doorstep she asks, 'Are you going to marry?'

I say, 'Maybe.'

I tell my ex-wife we've made a deal and Bethan is returning to school, and I'm naive enough to assume she'll be grateful the heartache is over.

'Without consulting me?' she says. 'Don't get her hopes up. You've broken too many promises.'

I hold my daughter's face in my hands and kiss her forehead. 'See you soon, *cariad.*'

'I'm serious,' I shout, on our way into London. 'Marry me!'

Elsa can't hear over the roar of the Sprite's engine. I shout louder: 'Marry me!'

She glances sideways. 'You're serious!'

'Of course.'

A few minutes later we slow for the lights on Wandsworth High Street and she turns to me with a wry smile. 'Ask me nicely and I'll think about it.'

'What's "nicely"?'

'Harry! You used to have some imagination.'

'All right, I'll surprise you,' I say, 'on one knee.'

The porter at Dolphin Square has a message that takes a little of the gloss off my day. Watkins of the *Mirror* wants to talk about Burgess. 'Non-attributable,' he writes, 'for the obituary – the view from inside.' I scrunch his note into a ball and put it into my pocket.

'You know, the girls will want to be bridesmaids,' I tease in the lift to Elsa's flat, 'and we can't live here when we're respectable. It's full of tarts and spies and . . .'

'Civil servants.'

'And civil servants.'

She laughs. 'Hark at you, the master of the house.'

Guy's death is reported in *The Times* the following morning – but only on page ten. That would have hurt. '*More than either Philby or Maclean, Burgess owed his place in the public notice to the single act of defection. His career before 1951 was one of dissipated talents and disorderly private life.*'

'Is that true?' Elsa asks, between mouthfuls of toast. She's dressed in black for work, with a string of antique pearls.

'Not entirely. "Our diplomatic correspondent"' – I show her the newspaper – 'makes the mistake of underestimating the late Mr Burgess. He collected secrets. Not just the ones that crossed his desk at Five and Six, but gossip and the confidences of the powerful. It was his hobby.'

She lowers the finger of toast at her lips to the plate. 'Did you share any, Harry?'

'He believed the struggle between capitalism and Communism was the great struggle of our times,' I say, ignoring her question. 'Choose America or choose Russia. Choose once and for all. You remember how it was before the war . . . it wasn't a crime. But Guy wanted to be important – spoilt rotten by his mother. It always comes down to something like that, doesn't it?'

She considers this for a moment, then leans forward on her elbows to consider *me*. 'Did *you* confide in him too?'

'No,' I say indignantly, 'no. No more than anyone else. He was just there . . . But not after the war, not when I left Five for the Firm.'

'Good.'

'No, you're the one I talk to – that's my big mistake.'

She laughs – 'Ha! Don't you worry, dear' – then, rising with knife and plate, she steps over to the sink. 'I'm late. The minister wants the Service chiefs to . . .' Her voice tails to nothing. Frozen she stands, plate still in hand, as stiff as poor Lot's wife, who saw more than she should.

'Elsa?' I push my chair from the table, but before I reach her she turns. 'The letter from your aunt. What happened to your sick cousin?'

'What on earth made you think . . .?'

The plate clatters on the tiles by the sink. She moves quickly towards the door, and her face . . . She's furious with me in her cold, controlled way.

'Hey!' In the hall now. I hear the cloakroom cupboard open and guess she's going to leave for work without speaking to me again.

I shout, 'What the hell's the matter?' and sound puzzled, aggrieved, but in the few seconds it takes me to follow her into the hall I recognise only the truth will do. Coat on her arm and she's slipping on her shoes, black leather civil-service brief-case against the wall.

'Sorry.'

'You lied to me,' she says.

'Don't you want to know why?'

'To *me*!' And snatching up her briefcase she rustles down the hall. I have my weight against the door before she can turn the latch. 'Elsa, let me explain.'

'Too angry to talk,' she says, stepping very deliberately on my bare foot.

The next thing I know she's in the corridor and I'm hobbling after her in my pyjama bottoms. 'Will you listen!'

Thankfully, the lift is on the ground floor. 'You're right, there isn't a dying cousin.' The lift machinery whirs, the floor indicator flickers at 1 then at 2, and somewhere in my mind too. 'Burgess? You think the letter . . .' I laugh. 'It wasn't from Burgess. *Not* Guy.'

The lift opens, Elsa steps inside, and so do I. 'Come on! Let me explain.'

'No.'

'It was from Rees.'

She turns to study my face.

'Yes. Rees.'

Ping. Ground floor, and the doors open on an elderly gentleman. His wrinkled liver-spotted skin suggests a working life in a hot part of the Empire. A stickler for proprieties, no doubt, because he looks quite disgusted at my state of undress, and Elsa can't suppress a smile.

'Which floor?' she asks him. 'We're taking the lift back up.'
The old fellow decides to wait for the next.

'Explain,' she says, the second the flat door closes.

I sigh. 'Can we sit down?'

'No.'

'Here in the hall?' But the look on her face . . . 'All right, all right,' I hold up my hands. 'I haven't spoken to Rees for – oh, seven years, 1956, not since those bloody awful pieces he wrote for the newspaper . . .'

'I know that.'

'It wasn't just the lies he told about Guy but our other friends – university people, senior civil servants. He turned them into Communists and degenerates who couldn't be trusted . . .'

'Yes, Harry,' she says impatiently. 'What about the letter?'

'You remember, it was the sort of thing the Americans were doing at the time. A reds-under-the-beds scare – Commie traitors in high places – and we were this close' – thumb and forefinger almost together – 'to a witch-hunt for anyone who made the mistake of having something to do with the Party before the war.'

'The letter . . .'

'Well, it's the same again, *cariad*. Rees is covering his arse. Rees knew Guy was spying for the Soviet Union but he said nothing. He'd known for years. He knew about Maclean too, and perhaps Philby. Those pieces for the *People* were a disreputable attempt to save his own skin by ruining the reputation of others. Only Dick White saw it then for what it was.'

'I don't understand.'

'Rees is afraid the Philby defection has started it up again – that the Security Service is pursuing him. He's panicking: *Am I a suspect? Is my phone tapped? Am I under surveillance?*'

'Can you show me?'

'I destroyed it.'

'Did you reply?'

'No.'

'You'd know if Goronwy's phone was tapped . . .'

'Not necessarily. Dick is talking about widening the scope of the investigation – to convince the Americans we're putting our house in order.'

Elsa folds her arms across her chest like an angry school-marm. 'Then why lie to me?'

I shrug. 'Because it's Rees, and Rees is trouble. Better you don't know.'

'You're being stupid,' she says. 'You always are when it comes to Rees.'

'Safer for you not to know.'

'What *are* you talking about? Are you hiding something?'

'You know how it is, *cariad*.' I try to touch her face, and she brushes my hand aside.

'No lies, Harry. Not to *me*. You hear?'

I hear. I hear. But I'm standing in her hall in my pyjama bottoms, and she's late for a meeting at the ministry, and if she wants the truth and nothing but, it will take time after so many years of silence . . . so I say nothing.

When she's gone I sit at the kitchen table with another cup of coffee and consider how to protect us both. Because truth has sides and colours: a different time, the thirties; a different place, Oxford; the story of a broken friendship. Elsa knows some of it because she knows Goronwy Rees, the brilliant, charming, funny academic who took me under his wing all those years ago.

He was a university fellow, and I was just an undergraduate, but Welsh, like Rees, and proud to be, and we shared the same sort of upbringing, the same interests. He introduced me to his circle of friends – journalists, writers, philosophers – and to

Guy Burgess. They were hard-drinking, quick-thinking, principled friendships, united by a love of ideas and a conviction that things must change for the better, not least in the coal valleys of our native Wales: we were socialists.

Our friendship should have lasted – I'd stuck with him even when I was tired of his ego and his drinking – but in a piece of madness, an act of self-immolation, Rees went into print about those times. *His* truth was self-serving – he was careful not to mention me – but he lit a fuse that is burning seven years later, and now we have Philby, we have PETERS, and Dick is talking of a purge. They'll go back to Rees and they'll use him. Is he strong enough? The flame is inches from the powder.

Thursday, 5 September. *The Times*:

> *Guy Burgess, the runaway diplomatist, was cremated yesterday as a Soviet brass band crashed out the Internationale. His ashes will probably be taken to England by his brother. His body was carried into the crematorium by Mr Donald Maclean, who fled to Russia with him, Mr Nigel Burgess, three Russians and a British correspondent. In one of the two brief funeral orations to the fifteen people present, Mr Maclean said that Burgess was a 'gifted and courageous man who devoted his life to the cause of making a better world'. Mr H. A. R. Philby, the former British diplomatist, was not present at the funeral.*

'Because he blames Burgess for running,' Sir Dick White says, folding his newspaper. 'Burgess didn't need to disappear with Maclean, we didn't have enough on him, but for some reason he chose to. Perhaps it was to *make a better world*!'

We're meeting at Dick's club and, because he likes to be a little different, it's the Garrick. Dickens and Trollope are hanging on a wall somewhere, and I passed the actor Laurence Olivier on the stair. I'm here because MI5 has had its showdown. Martin and Wright threatened to resign if Hollis kept their suspicions from the Americans and it seems that was enough: Roger's going to Washington tomorrow and he's taking D1's preliminary report on a penetration of Five with him.

'No surprises. The evidence points to a mole at the top of the Service,' says Dick. 'Arthur says Mitchell, but the jury's still out.'

He sips his coffee. Decent Dick who tries to believe the best of people. He's looking very dapper today in the sort of light summer suit none of his predecessors would have been seen dead wearing but it goes down well at the Garrick.

'I'm sending you to America too,' he says, marrying his cup and saucer. 'We can't leave it all to Five. We have to make our own mark on this with the CIA, convince them we're serious about cleaning up our bit of the Service.'

'Martin has a relationship with Angleton,' I say.

'He doesn't work for me. Come on, Harry, Washington's lovely in the fall.'

The following morning Peter Wright joins me at the Pavilion Road safe house to read the last rites. My team from Six is moving the furniture and the recording gear in a Morris van, but the camera feed we keep until Mitchell has taken the combination boxes from his safe, shredded his diary into a burn bag, and signed away clearance for his case files.

Midday, he sits alone at an empty desk, and as I watch him staring into space I remember our first meeting in blackout London during the Blitz, when both of us were turning Nazi agents into doubles, and when, for all the darkness and danger, things were incredibly simple. We were fighting for freedom and decency and no price was too much to pay. Now we fight for small advantage in a world threatened by nuclear holocaust, and I try not to consider whether there is a moral case for mutually assured destruction. I do know most of what we do is completely futile. Mitchell may be thinking fondly of the war too, and of twenty more years in the Service he says he loves but may have chosen to betray. Perhaps he is considering the final words he will deliver to his colleagues at his send-off in the Pig and Eye Club this afternoon. Martin and Wright are staying away; I'm going to show faith in his innocence.

'What now for you?' asks Wright, when my men have carried his monitor away.

'America.'

'Ah, I w-wondered if Dick was sending you there.'

'And you?'

'Back to Science for now,' he says, 'but I'm going to ask R-R-Roger for a transfer to D Branch. I like this work and there's plenty to do.' He pauses. 'I can tell you for free, the CIA will want to push ahead with a full investigation. Hollis can look forward to a hot reception. By the by, give Jim Angleton my regards, won't you?'

'Right,' I say.


A cab drops me in Piccadilly and I walk the short distance to Curzon Street to be sure I'm not among the first at Mitchell's party. Five o'clock in the foyer and a gang of debs from the Registry is hurrying for a train to the country. I give my name at the desk, and while I wait for the usual security chit, the duty copper talks about football. Then I take the lift to the top, because the Pig and Eye is many floors and a cut above the basement bar at MI6. The Security Service opened it as a watering-hole after the war so that officers could drink and ramble on without fear of being overheard by a Russian spy. We didn't realise in those days that he was sitting on the plush bench beside us, making a mental note for his real comrades.

Thankfully, there's a decent turnout of officers from both

Services this evening. The spirit of Vera Lynn hovers in the room, and I'm moved to order a gin and It for old times' sake. Mitchell looks terrible. I catch his eye and smile, but he looks away at once.

Then Hollis brings us to order with a knife and a glass, and I'm reminded, by the cadence of his voice, that he's the son of a bishop, and even the filthy joke he works into his peroration is delivered like a gospel reading. Graham Mitchell will always be a respected member of this club, he says. Someone in the congregation says, 'Hear, hear,' and someone else says the same. There's no doubting the goodwill in the room, but I sense some awkwardness too. Heads are bowed and the brethren shuffle their feet, because they know Graham is leaving under a cloud. What's more, he can feel their embarrassment. The PETERS investigation was supposed to be a secret but we don't seem to be able to keep them any more. The DG's praise is turning to ashes in his mouth. Mercifully, his speech is short, Mitchell's reply even shorter: it's plain in his face that he doesn't trust himself to mutter more than a few platitudes without breaking down. There was a collection, there's a presentation, more applause, and a few minutes later he's gone.

When Hollis has left us too, a party of sorts begins. By popular demand, Harry Vaughan and another badly tuned piano. He feels a hypocrite because he has played his part in making Graham Mitchell's life a misery, and now he's laughing, joking and drinking gin. But old Harry's an entertainer who must sing to be loved and to forget. A few songs, a few drinks – easy, until the following morning when he wakes with the sort of hangover a man a year from fifty should never inflict on his body and his mind.

I'm alone in my own flat so I must have had the sense not to disturb Elsa. My sheets are damp, I feel cold sweat on my skin and I think I'm going to be sick. The ghost of a memory is troubling me too, but my brain is so fuddled it takes a while to conjure it up. I remember I was making my way home through Pimlico when I heard something. I heard something, and I turned in time to see a man disappear into a doorway. Mac and trilby, I think, like the gnome with a cigarette I saw in Dolphin Square on my first night home. It was a glimpse, a gin-soaked second, and in the blinding light of day I can't be sure mac-and-trilby man wasn't just a shadow of my mind, my evil Russian fairy. We are old acquaintances. I meet him in my cups. He is Koschei the Deathless, because he hides his soul from his body. Now I'm going to be sick.

# 14

## 11 October 1963

I N A PLEASANT three-gin haze over the Atlantic I read in *The Times* that Burgess's ashes have been interred in a churchyard in Hampshire. Was it his choice to come home? There must be dozens of plots for socialist heroes in Moscow. That his brother Nigel has insinuated him into consecrated ground makes me smile. I think of it as a final fitting contradiction to the end of a life made up of them, because he was the most dogmatic of atheists.

Slipping the newspaper into the seat pocket, I lean back to feel the cool jet from the air vent on my face. Some will say Burgess's determination to avoid a corner of a foreign field implies an admission at the last that he'd got it wrong. Some will say so because it's comforting to believe so. I don't see it that way. Guy honestly thought he was doing his bit for a fairer classless country. But he was always the Eton schoolboy, Cambridge college club-bable Burgess too, a sentimental mother-loving homosexual, who would weep at the music of a chapel choir. That's the Burgess who wished to fetch up in the family plot in a honey-stone, dove-cooing, bell-tolling English country churchyard: the sort of place his Communist comrades would like to level and sweep away. His heart ruled his head at the last, and those inclined to judge him only with the head will think him a hypocrite. But I say we're all guilty of the same hypocrisy in some degree, and that such contradictions of the heart are what it is to be human.

I touch the elbow of a passing stewardess. 'Same again, please.'

'Certainly, sir,' she says, with a smile I won't forget in a hurry.

Our flight is due into Washington in about four hours. Maurice Oldfield is going to meet me and brief me, then take me to CIA headquarters at Langley, so this gin will be my last.

Maurice is at the wheel and we're heading east on the interstate through Arlington. The meeting at Langley is off. Harry Vaughan, you're a beggar in this town. 'The British aren't that welcome,' says Maurice, 'not since Philby made us look like clowns.'

I have a lot in common with Moulders, and that's a good reason for liking anyone. He's wartime and scruffy and baggy and effeminate, and he plays the organ and drinks whisky, and after a few of those he'll tell a good story of growing up on a sheep farm in Derbyshire. I hear he's homosexual, but if that's true he has the good sense to deny it. He is Charles Laughton to my Dirk Bogarde.

We cross the Potomac and turn towards the heart of white imperial Washington, where he describes the scene a few weeks ago when a quarter of a million people – most of them Negroes – marched for jobs and freedom, and a civil-rights leader called Martin Luther King spoke of his dream that one day America will end segregation and offer blacks the rights the country's founding fathers promised whites. I like the sound of King's dream and say so, and Maurice agrees. 'We must be a beacon of freedom – and of course we are,' he says, without irony. 'We're the free world.' I tell him to save it for his next Washington dinner party.

Then left on to 17th, and as we drive towards the White House, he says, 'They have President Kennedy, we have Harold Macmillan. Doesn't that tell you all you need to know about

America and Britain? By the way, Jim Angleton says he's briefed the president on PETERS.'

'And did Kennedy have a view?'

'Jim didn't say. I expect it was information only. The president has plenty on his plate, what with the civil-rights unrest and the war in Vietnam . . . You're at the Mayflower? Jim prefers La Niçoise on Wisconsin Avenue – if he decides to meet you for lunch.'

'You speak with such reverence, Maurice. Don't call him Jim, call him Jesus.'

'I would if it would help,' he says coolly, 'but he's touchy about the Jesus. He doesn't like people to know his mother was Mexican.'

I've come back to the Mayflower for the memories. January 1946. Room 235. We had tracked the Nazi beast to his lair and where better to celebrate than in the land of plenty? There was a girl, of course, because the best memories are the ones you share. We're on Connecticut now and I can see the Stars and Stripes over the hotel entrance, but Maurice is changing down and parks his big Chevy short.

'I like you, Harry.' He blinks at me through his glasses.

I raise my eyebrows. 'But?'

'A word to the wise. Jim Angleton is the best contact we have at the CIA. He has more reason than most to cut the Service loose, but he's still a believer. So, be nice. Be very nice. Don't fuck things up!'

Room 235 is nothing like the room I remember after the war. The first thing I do is telephone almost my only friend in the CIA. I worked with Jack Ellis in the forties, he knows Elsa and we were both at his wedding in Washington. Jack's in the Soviet Division at Langley now, and at this hour he'll be at his desk, but I ring his home and speak to his wife, Michelle. She's delighted and wants me to come over for drinks this evening. Half an hour later the phone rings and Jack is on the line from Langley, and his voice . . . I know something's wrong. Not at the house, he says, not in a bar, it has to be somewhere private: the park near his home in the Georgetown district. Do I remember the bridge? 'This is crazy, Jack,' I say. 'Are we going to play this by Moscow Rules?' The line goes dead.

The taxi drops me in Lover's Lane and, after consulting the map at the gates, I pick up the path along the stream towards the old pump house and the bridge. It's a balmy evening and the park is a picture of deep maple reds and browns and golden tulip-tree yellows. A young couple are canoodling on a bench, a middle-aged man in university corduroy strolls by, and there's laughter and children's voices somewhere over the hill, but the sun is blinking through the trees and will be gone altogether in an hour. The park is almost deserted on the pleasantest of evenings.

Jack Ellis is on the other side of the stream and lumbers across the bridge to greet me with a big Texan smile.

'What's this about, Jack?'

'Counter-intelligence has us by the balls!'

We embrace – he's put on weight – then he takes my arm and we walk on slowly. 'Karlow was the first. I didn't know the guy: he was a specialist in Technical Services. Lost a foot fighting for his country. They don't have a shred of evidence, but he's gone all the same. If sacrificing a foot isn't enough to prove you love your country . . .'

'Angleton?'

'Guess you're here to see him. Well, I can tell you, he's slicker than a boiled onion.'

I offer him a cigarette. 'You're watching your back?'

'Damn right. Sounds silly, but you sent us Philby. It isn't safe to be seen with a Brit.'

'Come on!'

'No, seriously, Harry. Have you met Anatoli yet?'

'Anatoli Golitsyn? No, I haven't had the pleasure.'

'So vain he can strut sitting down. Won't talk to anyone at the Agency who speaks Russian in case we're Commies. He's managed to convince Angleton the Russians have an agent at the top of the CIA – more than one.'

'He may be right.'

'Well, maybe,' he drawls.

We amble into a glade with a last patch of sun and stop to smoke our cigarettes.

'They've suspended the head of our division,' he says. 'Angleton's convinced he's one of them.'

'Is it possible?'

'How the hell do I know? His Russian's good, he was in Berlin a few years, and the way things are . . .'

'That's all it takes.'

'Yep.' He drops his cigarette butt and grinds it into the gravel with the toe of his shoe. 'That's all it takes.'

# 15

## 12 October 1963

S ECURITY SAYS TO Maurice, 'How are you today, sir?' and
waves us through the gate to the parking lot in front of
the main building. The Company moved headquarters from
the city to leafy Langley in Fairfax County a year ago and I
remember *Spies in the Suburbs* was a headline in one of the
newspapers. My first impression is of a new concrete university
or Mormon tabernacle, where students wear the same crisp
white shirts, dark suits and shiny black shoes. We're here to
visit the Faculty of Counter-intelligence, and I admit, I'm as
anxious as a tart in church.

'That's the conference bubble.' Maurice points to a large
domelike building opposite the car park. 'The statue in front
of it commemorates the first spy to die for America – hanged
by us during their war of independence.'

A member of Angleton's staff is waiting in the lobby.
'Welcome to the CIA,' he says, gesturing to the large marble
representation of its seal set into the floor. The walls and pillars
are dressed in the same black and white marble, the space too
bright and clinical to be welcoming. Our young guide leads us
to the security desk to arrange passes, and while he talks, I
gaze about the lobby and am struck by the synchrony of suits
and shirts and marble, like a chequerboard with black and
white pieces. Because this is America, and these are American
spies, a verse from the Bible is carved into the wall opposite

the entrance: 'And Ye Shall Know the Truth and the Truth Shall Make You Free.'

Maurice follows my gaze. 'That verse begins, "Continue in my word then are ye my disciples,"' he says. 'Well, here we are!'

James Jesus Angleton rises but doesn't step out from his desk to greet me. He's more than six feet tall and as thin as a rake. I shake his hand firmly and feel his skin slide over his knuckles. His face is pinched and seems the more so because he's wearing a very large pair of black-framed spectacles. His mouth is unusually wide and straight, his eyes hazel, and he has a good head of dark brown hair, with a little more grey at the temples than me. I know he's a couple of years younger, and that he has his complexion from his Mexican mother. His suit looks expensive, and I guess from his appearance and the neat columns of paper on his king-size desk that he is a fastidious man – counter-intelligence officers should be. He sits with his back to a window and the blinds are drawn even on this dull day. I expect he shuts the light from the room the better to see. I picture him poring over files in the smoky circle of his desk lamp, his imagination roaming corridors, continents, time for patterns that will reveal America's enemies within. Maybe. But he's also an actor – we all are – and this is his stage, and in the swirling smoke and gloom, his face almost hidden by those glasses, he is the wise and inscrutable spycatcher.

'Mr Vaughan,' he says, offering me a cigarette, 'I'm afraid you've had a wasted trip. There's nothing you can tell me I don't already know.'

'Harry, please. I don't know what you know.'

'Everything, and from the director general of MI5.'

'And Arthur Martin, of course. But Sir Dick wants the CIA to hear from our side of the Service. You know, he's taken a personal interest in PETERS.'

Angleton leans forward to tap the ash from his cigarette.

'Didn't I say? I know everything. For instance, you used to be friends with Guy Burgess.'

Maurice shifts in the chair beside me. 'Jim, I don't think that's quite fair.'

'No, Maurice.' I touch his arm. 'Jim's right, but not friends like *you* and Kim Philby were friends, Jim.'

Angleton pushes his glasses to the bridge of his nose. I meet his gaze, and the silence grows.

'We've had our fingers badly burned, it's true,' says Maurice, coming to our rescue. 'C is determined it isn't going to happen again.'

'That's why I'm here,' I say. 'To ask for your help.'

Angleton considers this for a moment. 'All right, let's hear it.'

So I tell him what we know for certain (nothing), but there's some evidence to suggest a Soviet agent at the top of Five (circumstantial), that the mole may be former DDG Graham Mitchell (unlikely), but in any case there will be no repeat of the cock-up with Philby, and the investigation team is authorised to do whatever it considers necessary to clean up the Service.

'But it isn't, is it?' he replies. 'You didn't interrogate Mitchell.'

'That was Sir Roger Hollis's decision. But if there's more evidence?'

He stares at me. He hasn't stopped staring. That he should so devoutly wish to make me feel uncomfortable is unsettling and at the same time amusing.

'We're reviewing all our joint operations with you British,' he says at last, 'and we'll be sure to let Sir Dick know if we find something.' Then he spreads his bony hands on top of his desk signalling his intention to rise.

'That's very reassuring, Jim,' I say. 'Don't you think so, Maurice? Graham Mitchell was working so closely with the Agency and the FBI. If there's nothing obvious to suggest he was leaking intelligence . . .'

'This isn't your field, is it, Mr Vaughan? These things take time. So . . .'

He gets to his feet and we must follow. We are followers. Our audience is over and old Harry didn't manage to charm. Not even the faintest crack in the ice. He likes orchids – Maurice says so – but I know nothing about them. So, as we shuffle to his door, I say, 'You're right, this isn't my area of expertise, but I *have* been in this game a long time and intelligence is about people and a study of people. I know Graham Mitchell isn't our mole.'

'You *know*?' Angleton stops and turns to gaze at me again. 'Let me tell you, *History has many cunning passages*, Mr Vaughan, it *deceives with whispering ambitions, /Guides us by vanities.* Who knows what we'll find when we investigate those joint operations?'

'*We would see a sign!*' I fire back. 'Only signs are so often *taken for wonders* when they are nothing of the sort, and when they fail us we can find ourselves trapped in a *wilderness of mirrors.*'

He claps his hands. '*Touché!* Mr Harry Vaughan, *touché!*' He takes off his glasses and examines them. 'Well, well . . . Shall we say twelve thirty? I have a table at La Niçoise. Maurice, you can come too.'

'What on earth happened there?' says Maurice when we're walking to his car.

'I'm not entirely sure, but I think we have Mr T. S. Eliot to thank for a sudden change of fortune.'

Upon such small things . . . At lunch we learn that Angleton corresponds with Eliot and counts him as a friend, and that he's on good terms with a number of poets. He says Mr Eliot is a genius, and in the next breath that they have a great deal in common: brought up in the Midwest of America, students at Oxford University, 'and great Anglophiles – although *my* faith is being tested,' he says. I ask him if he reads the poetry of Dylan Thomas. Yes, he says, but Thomas doesn't have the intellectual rigour and depth of Mr Eliot. Dylan has passion, I counter, and Eliot's so deep it's impossible to see the bottom – and so on, and so on, for three martinis.

By the fourth we have moved on to politics. Removing Fidel Castro from Cuba is a priority and holding the line against the Commies in Vietnam and everywhere. More money and energy must be spent, not least by 'our British allies'. We are too complacent, he says, too slow to realise the Soviets have agents of influence everywhere, in Britain's political parties, in the civil service and universities – everywhere. I ask him why he believes that is the case, and he says he has his sources.

By the fifth martini my head is spinning. Angleton is still talking and seems to be making sense. Moulders is beaten and slumps into silence. We eat with wine, and then our host insists on bourbon. I join him because that is my mission. He holds his glass in his right hand, a cigarette burning between his fingers, and gazes over the top of his spectacles at me. 'Are you sorry Burgess is dead?'

Even in a bourbon fog that's an easy one. 'I'm sorry he was a traitor,' I say, 'but I hear his life in Moscow was some sort of punishment.' He takes a moment to gauge my sincerity, then leans forward, grinds out his cigarette in an ashtray, and, with a stone-cold-sober passion that makes my flesh creep, he tells me he isn't the sort to commit murder, but he would happily make a very bloody exception for Kim Philby. I am still imagining Angleton rudely covered with gore when a smiling waiter delivers the check on a silver plate for him to sign.

'That's that, then,' says Maurice, as we watch Angleton's car pull away from the sidewalk a few minutes later. 'Welcome to Washington.'

# 16

## *14 October 1963*

I BREAK BREAD with Angleton alone. We sit at his table against the back wall with a view of everyone in the restaurant. He pays again but this time he makes me do the talking. What do I think of Sir Roger Hollis? (Too safe, a time-server, I say.) Can I work with Arthur Martin? (I'm diplomatic.) Peter Wright, do I trust his judgement? (Diplomatic again.) He presses me; I praise. Then I tempt him to offer an opinion of his own by raising a small doubt: I wonder whether a scientific officer has the necessary experience to take on the role of spycatcher. Angleton sips his bourbon and says nothing. I back away.

The following day I'm granted a short audience at Langley with the deputy director in charge of Clandestine Operations. He isn't interested in the details of the PETERS investigation or in my assurance that C will leave no stone unturned in the hunt for the mole. 'That's bull,' he shouts at me. 'You're losing your friends in this town. Put that in your report to Sir Dick.'

'Richard Helms gave me a roasting,' I tell Maurice later.

'That was probably Jim Angleton's doing,' he replies.

It's a Tuesday afternoon, and we're sitting in his small office at the British Embassy on Massachusetts Avenue. 'I can tell you, most people here think Philby was too hot for us to handle so we just let him escape,' he says, 'and now they look at us and ask, "What's the point?"'

'Angleton too?'

'He's relieved no one will know just how much he let slip to Kim during their boozy lunches.'

I say I have a friend at the Agency who thinks Philby's defection has changed Angleton, that he's going a little crazy. Maurice raises an eyebrow. 'A friend with something to hide?'

'We all have something to hide, Moulders.'

'Yes,' he offers me a wry smile, 'we do. Is Jim paranoid? I expect so. He's head of Counter-intelligence: he's paid to be the most suspicious man in the CIA.'

I nod slowly. 'But is he running the show?'

Maurice leans back with his podgy fingers laced across his stomach. 'You're referring to Golitsyn? Odious man. But he was at Moscow Centre for years. If he says the KGB has agents at the top of the CIA and in our own dear Service we have to take it seriously.'

'I don't suppose it's occurred to anyone that it suits Golitsyn very well to say so because it's his meal ticket, and very much in his interests to string it out for as long as he possibly can!'

'Really, Harry!' Maurice shakes his head in wonder. 'I expect it's occurred to everyone.' He takes off his spectacles and pinches the bridge of his nose. 'What do you expect Jim to do? Sweep it under the carpet again? I hope we've learned from Philby that that isn't the way to go about things.' He looks at me sternly. 'I worry about you. I thought you were here to convince the Americans we can be trusted to put our house in order.'

'Of course I am,' I say, 'and we are.'

*

'Gutless and godless,' says Maurice, as we wait to brief the director of the FBI. 'He says we're dregs of a once great Empire. He hates us.'

'Hates?'

'I don't think that's too strong a word.'

We approach J. Edgar Hoover through four interconnecting rooms as one might a great potentate, and just like one he wastes no time on civilities. 'We're fighting an evil and relentless enemy,' he says, 'and you British keep messing up.'

I've heard stories over the years, of course, but I'm still amazed that he presumes to denounce our politicians – especially the Labour Party – in the most intemperate language. The pouches of loose skin on his face are quivering with passion and his eyes are as dark as pebbles of lignite. I don't protest because that would be unfair on Maurice, and I can't forget – no one will let me – that we're beggars in this town. So, rattle on, J. Edgar Hoover, street bruiser, I don't expect you've had this much fun since you took on Dillinger, Ma Baker and Al Capone all those years ago. His charge sheet ends with our greatest crime and the name Kim Philby.

'Let me warn you, I'm going to ask the president to review our security relationship with you British.'

He pauses and I manage a few words at last: would he permit me to brief him on PETERS?

'Heard all about that,' he snaps. 'Don't believe it. Graham Mitchell is as timid as a mail-order bride. Useless, but not a Commie.'

I don't quite believe what I'm hearing. 'You seem very sure, sir?'

'Your Arthur Martin showed us the evidence.' He spits the word. 'Pitiful. We've run checks on our joint operations with you and we've come up with nothing. You're barking up the wrong tree.'

And with that the lesson endeth. Hoover picks up his pen and we are marched back through his marble halls to the street.

'Hoover can't stand the British,' says Angleton. 'What's the point of them?'

Dinner's over and we've retired to Maurice's lounge upstairs for brandy and cigars. I'm sitting on a couch beside the picture window. The curtains are closed but I can hear rain tapping at the glass. The room is dim and smoky, perhaps to please Angleton. Maurice has no eye for furniture or pictures, but there are many good books, piles of British and American newspapers, ashtrays full of stubs, a record player and an old upright joanna. A modern house in a tidy Washington suburb that Moulders has turned into a home for everyone's favourite bachelor uncle, and tonight for a male-only soirée. Angleton's chief analyst, Raymond Rocca, is of the company, Harvey from Clandestine Operations, and Bennett from Canadian Counter-intelligence is here too. Strong drink has been taken, Rocca and Harvey are talking politics with Bennett, and tempers are fraying, but Angleton and I sit apart on our couch by the window.

'What's the point of the British?' I say. 'We're here to make you feel smug about being American, to remind you of the decline and fall of great empires.'

'I'm not the one you need to convince,' he says, between puffs of a cigar. 'It's Mr Hoover – and just about everyone else in Washington.'

'Well, at least one of us can be trusted,' I say, with satisfaction. 'Graham Mitchell. He's quite sure Mitchell isn't working for the Russians.'

The right side of Angleton's face twitches once. 'I know. But, Harry . . .' He leans so close that all I can concentrate on are his glasses and the smoke from his fat Cuban cigar, curling between us like an offering to the God of Moses who first sent spies into the land of Canaan. 'Mitchell isn't the only officer at the top of MI5 who fits the profile of a Soviet mole.'

'You have another name?'

To this, he doesn't reply. I want to press him and he knows

it because he makes a point of turning to the others. Their conversation is now at boiling point. The Canadian, Bennett, has lost patience, trying to explain to Americans why a democratic socialist isn't a 'Commie', and he has charged Angleton's chief analyst, Rocca, with being dumb enough for twins. Maurice is on his feet, trying to keep the peace.

Angleton whispers sibilantly in my ear: 'You know Maurice is a homo, don't you? Damn fool tried to seduce the son of one of our agents.'

I lie. 'I had no idea, Jim.'

'It was a tricky business to tidy up.'

'I can imagine,' I say. 'Good of you, Jim.'

I expect he's tucked his report of the incident into a file 'for future use'.

'You bastard!' Bennett struggles to his feet, a cushion to his nose. Rocca has taken a swing at him and Harvey is urging him to take another. Maurice is waving his arms around ineffectually, and if something isn't done Bennett's going to take a beating. I can't let that happen: Bennett is a Canadian from Wales.

'Come on, guys, cool it!' Angleton is on his feet beside me. 'What the hell's this about anyway?'

What's it all about? It's about drink and politics and testosterone. It's about the world according to Langley: for us or against us? No ifs and buts now, we're at war! The Soviet octopus sits astride the globe: its tentacles reach across oceans and continents. That's Communism: it's been the plan for more than a generation. Senator Joe McCarthy was right about that, see. And the enemy has slipped inside the gate in the guise of a socialist or a social democrat. Senator Joe was a prophet. And still Europe sleeps.

Angleton stares Rocca down; Maurice puts an arm round Bennett. 'Harvey! Stop hogging the bottle!' And I sit at the piano to soothe their troubled minds. *No one to talk with, all by myself,* I sing, *No one to walk with but I'm happy on the shelf. 'Ain't Misbehavin', I'm savin' my love for you.* Then I play my own version of 'The Star Spangled Banner' and Miller's 'In the Mood', and for a time the great Western alliance appears as one again. But when the music stops Bennett makes his excuses and leaves, and we all breathe a sigh when Rocca follows suit a few minutes later.

Come the dawn's early light, Maurice and Harvey are snoozing, and my head's spinning, but Angleton is still wide awake with things to say, and once again I marvel at his capacity. A disc is ticking on the gramophone, like the in-out pulse of a respirator, the last rhythm of life when the singing and the dancing are done. Angleton has me at an advantage. I should lift the needle and go, but here I am with my glass and my cigarette.

Smoke seems to swirl around him like a luminous fog, and in my bourbon haze I fancy he is Myrddin – Merlin – and he has cast a spell on us all. He leans forward to pour us another, and because I'm caught in his spell I don't seem able to refuse.

He was talking Kennedy and Cuba but now he steers the conversation back across the Atlantic. 'Rocca's right,' he says. 'The KGB has insinuated hundreds of spies into political parties, trade unions, universities, the arts – anywhere and everywhere they serve the cause of Communism. Let there be no doubt, if the West does not root out this evil and consign it to the ash heap of history, then it must fall.'

I nod and draw on my cigarette in the hope its sharp taste will bring me to my senses. Angleton needs no more encouragement. He's flushed with bourbon and conviction and it has loosed his tongue. What do I know about the new 'left wing' leader of 'your Labour Party'?

'Harold Wilson? Bit of a reputation for shiftiness. Other than that . . . Why?'

Angleton swills the ice in his drink, then takes a nip. 'You're right, Harry. Sly. He's sly. Want to know why?'

'Why, Jim?'

He places his glass carefully on the low table in front of us and leans forward to touch my knee. 'Because Harold Wilson is an enemy agent.'

'I beg your pardon?' I stare at him to be certain he's serious and he stares back, challenging me to protest, to laugh.

'Guess you think I'm drunk,' he says.

'Or I am.'

'No, you heard. Harold Wilson is an agent of the Soviets. It was the KGB who made it possible for him to become the leader of your Labour Party.'

'Right.' My voice cracks. I say it again more firmly: 'Right. You'd better explain, Jim.'

He tries to. 'We've been watching Wilson for a while,' he says, 'not just because he's a left-winger. We know he has close links with Moscow. And now a trusted source has confirmed it: Wilson is working as an agent of influence.'

'I see. The source . . . Anatoli Golitsyn?'

Angleton doesn't answer. He turns instead to the death of Wilson's predecessor a few months ago. Hugh Gaitskell was a moderate, a champion of a strong British nuclear defence, ready to work with MI5 to root out Labour Members of Parliament who took their orders from Moscow. He clicks his bony fingers – gone! Suddenly, at only fifty-six. 'Convenient, wasn't it?'

'Not for Mr Gaitskell.'

'You've heard of Department Thirteen? It handles the KGB's wet affairs. Our source says it was planning a hit on the leader of a major political party so it could put its own man in place. General Rodin's in charge of Thirteen, and Rodin cut his teeth at the Soviet Embassy in London.'

'And you think Gaitskell . . . ?'

'Let me finish, Harry. Gaitskell's doctor contacted MI5. He was suspicious . . . Gaitskell died from a blood disease called lupus, which attacks the organs of the body. It's incredibly rare in the West, and the doctor was worried because he couldn't understand where Gaitskell could have picked it up.'

'This is from Five?'

'From Arthur Martin.'

'Right.' I can't look him in the eye, not while I'm trying to make sense of what sounds like a fairy tale. 'Arthur believes Hugh Gaitskell was infected by the Russians?' I reach for what's left of my drink but think twice about more alcohol and take another cigarette. 'And, just to be clear, Gaitskell was murdered so Harold Wilson could become the new leader of the Labour Party?'

'That's right.'

'Because Wilson is a . . . Hard to believe, Jim!'

'Not if you know what I know about the way they operate,' he says, flicking a speck of ash from the knee of his perfectly creased trousers. 'We ran a check on all Russian scientific papers to find out what they're saying about lupus. There's one paper, written a few years ago. That's all. No one in the Soviet Union has anything to say about lupus.'

I don't understand the triumph in his voice.

'Standard practice,' he says. 'They won't let their scientists write papers on lupus because they don't want us to know they've found a way to infect people. It's the perfect weapon because it's deniable. I expect they've been working on it for years and were just waiting for a high-value target to use it. Well, with this and the intelligence from our source . . .'

'From Golitsyn?'

'From our source,' he says firmly.

'Can I meet your source?'

'No.'

'Can I meet Golitsyn?'

He takes off his glasses and rubs his eyes with his knuckles. 'That may be possible,' he says, so casually I know it won't it be. 'I'll ask him.'

I want to say, 'Come on, Jim, he doesn't fart without your say-so,' but what's the point if he's made up his mind to keep dear Anatoli away from me? So, I settle for a smile. He knows what I'm thinking, of course, and perhaps he's already regretting that drink and poetry have tempted him to share so much with me because he says, 'Sir Dick White has approved the investigation. OATSHEAF, that's what we're calling it. Just a small group here and at MI5. I don't need to remind you . . .'

He slips his specs back on and stares at me. I try to meet his gaze. What can I say? My head is thick with the stale smoke and heat of the room. I know I should say something because he's spun me such a tale . . . the leader of the Labour Party, who may well be our next prime minister, for Christ's sake. I can see a faint reflection of the room in his glasses and a dark outline that must be me, and a line of T. S. Eliot's that I spoke with little thought at our first meeting slips back into my mind because his spell is drawing me into a *wilderness of mirrors*.

I say, 'Jim, if the Russians published dozens, scores, of papers on lupus wouldn't that be proof they murdered the leader of the Labour Party, too?'

A little colour rises to his cheeks but he doesn't flinch. He stares at me for a few more seconds, then gathers his cigarettes and lighter from the table. 'Good to have had this opportunity to get to know you, Harry.'

Maurice is stirring. He's groaning and rubbing his eyes, like an old ham in a Whitehall farce. Was he sleeping or merely pretending to? 'Christ, it's almost six,' he says, 'I left you for so long.'

'Jim has been entertaining me.'

'Jim' has slipped on his jacket and is making for the stairs.

I follow him to the door and thank him for his hospitality and his confidence, but his mood has changed completely: he's as cool and aloof as he was at our first meeting.

'You're flying home tomorrow?'

'I'll postpone if there's any possibility of that meeting with Golitsyn.'

'I was meaning to ask,' he says, as he reaches for the front door, 'you were in Vienna when SUBALTERN was blown, right?'

'I'm afraid so. Why do you . . .?'

'Anatoli was there too. KGB British section.'

'Then we can swap old stories.'

Angleton's smile has all the warmth of a stab in the back. 'He remembers SUBALTERN well,' he says. 'I wonder if he remembers you, Harry.'

'Yes, I wonder.'


Maurice is tottering about the lounge, collecting the empties and the ashtrays. He's drawn the curtains and opened a window for a breath of fresh air. Myrddin has gone and his fog is clearing. Friend Harvey is in the bathroom and may be for some time. I collapse in a chair, close my eyes, and an image of our old Maerdy chapel springs into my thoughts, its polished-wood pews and gallery, the minister's hell-fire pulpit, and the Ten Commandments painted on boards at either side of the organ. The gold lettering is hard to read in the grey light of a Sunday evening a long time ago, but I remember number nine: *Thou shalt not bear false witness*. I was small enough to swing my legs under the bench then, and too small to understand what the God of Moses meant by false witness.

I'm not God-fearing, I've probably broken all the Commandments over the years, but if I were invited to preach to my black and folded town now I would say, 'Do you know your neighbour? Can you trust him?'

# Witchfinder

In the last few hours I have been taken to a place where nothing is what it is because everything is what it isn't. I know my head is thick with drink and fatigue, but Philby, you bastard, what have you unleashed on us all?

1964

# 17

## 6 March 1964

A ND NOW I *am* fifty I'm surprised by how little it bothers me. I have a new wife, a new home, and a table this evening at Kettner's to celebrate both, and my birthday. We will meet at the York Minster first, where I'll attempt a recital of a Dylan Thomas poem from memory and fail, and Elsa will tease me about my declining powers. Perhaps I'll promise to prove my youthful vigour later, and she will scoff that I'm vain and deluded, which is perfectly true.

I proposed to her again on a windy heather top in Wales a month after my visit to Washington, and with enough *élan* to secure her acceptance. Two days later, on 18 October, Macmillan stood down as prime minister and another Old Etonian took his place. We broke the news of our engagement to Elsa's parents and to my daughters on 21 November. The following day President Kennedy was assassinated in Dallas. (Is his killer a Communist or a madman? Angleton is in charge of the CIA investigation.) We married at Christmas – a simple register office ceremony – and the girls returned to their mother a little tipsy. Honeymoon in France, and on 1 February we moved into a red-brick terrace house in Gayfere Street, just a stone's throw from Parliament and Whitehall. One of my juniors in Vienna has ruffled a few feathers at Six by writing a spy thriller; Bethan says the Beatles are the best popular music group ever; and Cassius Clay knocked out Sonny Liston on the twenty-fifth and has announced to the world that he's 'the greatest'.

Peter Wright rang me on the twenty-sixth and we met to catch up. For some reason Hollis has made him head of Counter-intelligence Research at Five. He should know his people better. 'It's a chance to b-blow the dust off the files,' Peter said, with relish. 'Nothing official, you understand. Ch-check we haven't missed anything. Any money you care to wager, the spies we catch in the next ten years are in there already – we just have to look for them.' His D3 team is sifting through old Gestapo records because 'The Nazis knew how to run a counter-espionage service. There are thousands of old C-C-Communists in their files.' He claims to have the names of forty suspects on this side of the English Channel already.

His new role will give him carte blanche to grub about in all our pasts. That is real power. 'The Cavaliers have had their day, Harry,' he declared, as we were leaving the pub. 'The old-school-ties are beaten, or will be – soon.' The tone of his voice and his sly glance suggested a great storm over the Service. When I pressed him to say more he lied: 'No, no, you've g-got the wrong end of the stick.'

In the same spirit of frankness, I have made no mention of my conversation with Angleton. Peter will have heard the Gaitskell murder story from Arthur Martin, but neither of them has spoken of the OATSHEAF investigation to me. I was ready to challenge Dick White with it when I came back from Washington, but at the last minute I backed away. I think he trusts me and I want it to stay that way. The climate, my situation, it isn't the time, and for the same reason I've decided to keep it from Elsa. If I tell her we're investigating the leader of Her Majesty's Official Opposition, that he may be a Communist agent of influence, she will laugh at me and call me a liar, then take it to her minister at the expense of what's left of my career. For now OATSHEAF is filed in my imaginary drawer, *Self-preservation, for the use of,* while I walk abroad on my birthday in a happy shower of all my days, grateful for the new order of my life.

'The chief wants to see you.'

His secretary, Miss Dora Edwards is on the telephone.

'It's my birthday.'

'*Penblwydd hapus,*' she says. 'At once, Mr Vaughan. At once.'

'Am I in trouble, *cariad?*'

Sir Dick is at the window smoking one of his Senior Service cigarettes. He turns to greet me with a funeral face. 'Your birthday, Harry . . .'

'Yes, sir.'

'Happy birthday.'

'Thank you.' I'm going to joke about fifty, but think better of it: he's in a black mood.

'It's Anthony Blunt. He was their man inside the Security Service – or one of them.' He pulls on his cigarette as if he's trying to suck the nicotine from it in a single drag, then waves what's left at a chair. 'Blunt! The duplicitous shit.'

'There's no doubt?'

'None whatsoever.'

I can see he expects me to be as shocked as he is, but the instant I know for sure it seems obvious, and strange that we didn't unmask him years ago. Awkward and embarrassing too, and I say so, because Sir Dick used to be very thick with Sir Anthony.

The FBI came by the truth, he says. An American called Straight claims Blunt recruited him at Cambridge University in the thirties. He was a member of the same Cambridge ring as Philby, Burgess and Maclean, and as a senior officer in MI5 during the war he passed intelligence to the Soviet controller they shared.

'And Goronwy Rees warned me,' says Dick. 'Rees! I should have . . . but you know what a hopeless liar he is, and we questioned Blunt eleven times but we couldn't make anything stick, so . . .'

So, arise Sir Anthony, Surveyor of Her Majesty's Pictures, director of the Courtauld Institute of Art; notable expert on Poussin; notable aesthete; notable homosexual; and now a notable traitor.

'I don't know him well,' I say. 'He was part of the furniture in Bentinck Street during the war. The sober one. Very protective of Guy.'

'So it seems,' Dick observes. 'They were members of one of those elite Cambridge societies – the Apostles.'

'Yes.'

I remember Guy telling me it used to have its own liturgy, and I expect it still does. Members in waiting were known as 'embryos' and they were sponsored by a 'father'. When they took their oath of allegiance they joined the other 'brothers'. It was another of those circles beloved of the most privileged in this damned country of ours.

'Has anyone spoken to Blunt?'

'Not yet,' says Dick. 'There's the question of who needs to know first. The prime minister's a stickler for proprieties and would insist on telling the Queen. Roger wants to offer Blunt a deal – sweep it under the carpet.'

There's a light knock at the door and Dora Edwards ushers in a girl from the Secretariat with some coffee. I light one of my cigarettes, Dick lights one of his, and we wait in silence until she glides out again. 'Burgess, Maclean, Philby, and Blunt make four.' Dick dabs the ash from his cigarette. 'Golitsyn says there are five – a Ring of Five. Blunt left us after the war, so who's inside? Who tipped off Philby?'

I want to say, 'It isn't clear he was tipped off.' I want to say, 'Not Graham Mitchell,' but he isn't in the mood to debate with me. I watch him rise and step over to the fireplace, where he shows his hands to a bar heater. For the first time I'm struck by the shadow of his age and not the old athlete.

'Arthur's going to do the approach to Blunt – best man for the job – but I want you to keep across things for us. This has happened on our watch, Harry, so it's our responsibility to clean it up.'

'Of course, sir.'

Poor Dick, what will they say in Whitehall? He used to be their favourite, now he's fighting for his good name.

The interview is over and he shepherds me to his door, but as he's reaching for its shiny brass handle he checks and turns with an expression of hurt and bewilderment, like a small boy smacked by his father for the first time. 'Is it because he's homosexual? Is that why? You knew Burgess?'

'I imagine it was a number of things.'

Dick leans closer, his clear blue gaze fixed on my face. 'Tell me.'

'Before the war, before we knew what Stalin was like, it would have been an adventure.'

'We knew by 'thirty-nine. We *knew*, and Blunt persisted.'

'Loyalty to a tight circle of comrades? He must have believed in the dictatorship of the proletariat, too.'

Dick looks so incredulous I want to laugh. The Party cares nothing for the painter Poussin, and the monumental art of the proletariat is shit. Blunt must know. Well, Dick, I expect he does, but turning his back on Communism would be to acknowledge the last thirty years a lie. I don't know Blunt well (does anyone?), but I know his type. He is intellectually pure enough to justify the murder of millions. I have seen the shadow of the fanatic. But he has paintings to consider too, in particular his Poussins, and in the interests of his art he might be willing to forget the proletariat and come to an understanding with the Service.

'I'll be glad to leave this place.' Dick steps back from the door to let me pass. 'I want to blow away the cobwebs.'

For just a moment I wonder if he's telling me he's going to retire. But, no, he means the impending move to the wilderness he's chosen for the Secret Intelligence Service south of the river where, in the spirit of the age, we are to occupy a new twenty-two-storey concrete and glass box. Those who know predict it will be stifling in summer and freezing in winter, very like life in the gulag.

'It's about restoring trust,' he says. 'A junior minister had the damn cheek to ask me yesterday if we're all drunks and traitors – he's been reading John le Carré. I told him, "Fewer traitors than adulterers in your government, Minister." The trouble is, Harry, I'm not sure that's true any more, not now, not after Blunt.'

So, dinner isn't quite what I hoped it would be. Anthony Blunt is the ghost at our feast. Elsa says, 'Cheer up or I'll divorce you.'

I say, 'Then I'm keeping the house.'

We've drained the bottle and coffee is on the way when I decide the time is right to ask her if she is still in touch with Phoebe Pool. She wants to know why, of course: she knows me so well she can detect the berg of meaning beneath the surface. I say that someone mentioned Anthony Blunt at the office, and I remembered he's a friend of Phoebe's, too. Elsa's cup hovers at her lips. 'I'm not going to ask you again,' she says, 'in case you're tempted to tell another lie.'

'*Cariad*, really . . .'

She lowers her chin and gazes up at me from beneath her dark brow. 'You might *try* to.'

I look pained. 'We've spoken of this. You know how it is in the Service.'

'Yes, I do.'

Phoebe Pool, it seems, is recovering from another nervous breakdown. Elsa says she haunts the Courtauld Institute of Art, a bundle of bags and rags, teetering on the edge of despair. Blunt has taken her under his wing. She loves him, he's decent to her, and they've written a book on Picasso together. 'But I haven't seen her for a while. It's Jenifer who keeps in touch.'

'Right,' I say, signalling to a waiter for the bill. 'Jenifer who?'

'Jenifer Hart. Another friend from Oxford days.'

'Somerville College coven?'

'I wouldn't put it like that.' Elsa picks up her cup again and inspects the dregs of her coffee. 'We've kept in touch. I used to see Jenifer in Whitehall – she worked at the Home Office.'

The waiter comes with our reckoning and because I didn't manage a poem I must pay. 'I still have time to prove I'm a good husband,' I say, helping her into her coat. I expect her to smile but she isn't listening. I know she's turning our conversation over in her mind, and as we walk towards the restaurant door I hear a sharp intake of breath and her step falters, but I don't look back to find her until we're standing in the rain-drenched street.

'All right, go on.'

'Blunt!' she whispers. 'It's him!'

It would be futile to deny it now. I thought she would get there but not so quickly. 'I'll be shot.'

She touches my arm. 'I know how to keep a secret – I'm your wife.'

# 18

## 10 March 1964

I'M TO HAVE an office in Leconfield House, the better to carry out my charge. A pompous old soldier who's working out his pension in Personnel shows me to a stuffy box three floors above Arthur Martin's team in D Branch. 'It won't do, Major,' I say, and threaten to pick up the phone to the DG.

In the end, he finds me something more suitable on the third floor, with a view into Curzon Street and of the flat we used as an OP for surveillance of Graham Mitchell. Two junior officers are obliged to make way for me, and a large green combination safe. Wright and his D3 research team are along the corridor and Martin is round the next corner in Soviet Counter-espionage. He's set up an investigation room there, with his research officer and oldest ally in charge.

'Our little Welsh boy,' she says, when I put my head round the door. 'I suppose you're here to spy on us.'

'To bring a smile to your face, Evelyn,' I reply. 'Young Harry Vaughan never walks away from a challenge.'

Who is Evelyn? What is she, if not the dowdy and malevolent queen of the files? Maude Evelyn Pierrepont McBarnet. Evelyn haunts this place day and night and I'm sure she'll continue to do so when they've driven a stake through her heart and pronounced her dead at last. I guess she's in her late fifties, although it's hard to tell because she's just as I remember her at our first encounter thirteen years ago. Purple birthmark from a temple to her chin, small almond-shaped eyes (like all the children of the night) and she's wearing a navy suit jacket with what must be the same tatty crocheted shawl about her shoulders. She sits with a neat stack of duck-egg-blue files on the desk in front of her and a lockable Y Box open in her plump lap. The name on the label is Anthony Blunt, and I guess it's the new evidence from the FBI.

'You were a member of the Bentinck Street gang too, weren't you, dear?' she says, following my gaze. 'You, Guy and Kim, Anthony, Donald Maclean and that handsome Welsh friend of yours, Goronwy Rees.'

I raise my hands to confess. 'The fifth man! Or is it the sixth, or even the seventh now?'

She squints at me suspiciously. 'Do you think it's funny?'

'I think you said the same at my interrogation, Evelyn. And I said, "There is nothing . . ."'

'". . . you can't laugh about,"' she says, recalling my words from thirteen years ago precisely. 'You had that in common with Guy, didn't you, dear?'

I sigh. 'He's gone, Evelyn, *cariad*. But I'm here, your still small voice of calm.'

'Poor Dick is such a terrible judge of character,' she says.

And on we go, shuffling about the ring, like old sparring partners. Did I know Blunt was working for Moscow Centre? Did she? Yes, she says, but only Arthur Martin would listen to her. Blunt did the housekeeping when Burgess ran away with Maclean in '51. The DDG, in his wisdom, sent good old Anthony to check on his friend Guy, presenting him with the perfect opportunity to bag and burn any evidence that might incriminate the other three members of the ring. 'And I was called home for a grilling by you,' I say, and for once I do raise a small smile.

'Silly boy.' Her reply. 'That wasn't a grilling.'

'No?'

I'll never forget Evelyn watching me from across the table that day with a face like granite. I used to think she was the most morbidly suspicious person I knew – until I met Angleton. For now we can pretend it's a game.

'You've come for the FBI files.' She hands me the Y Box then turns to pinch more from the pile on her desk, and I wonder whether there's a buff one there with my name on the cover. 'You will bring them back, won't you, dear?' she says.

I sign for the files and carry them to my office, where the major's maintenance man is fixing my nameplate to the door. I protest I'm passing through but I have no more say in the matter than I'll have when they screw the plate down on my coffin. So, I light a cigarette, plonk my feet on the desk and open the FBI file.

It's a sorry tale, and painfully familiar. The hero is an impressionable young man from the New World who goes by the Dickensian name of Michael Straight. He's New York patrician and a student at Cambridge, so naturally he thinks very well of himself. It's the 1930s, Communists are at war with Fascists in Spain, and our hero's best friend dies fighting the good socialist fight. Grief-stricken and hungry for meaning, he turns to his lover, a university don called Anthony Blunt, who introduces him to a social circle, the Apostles, then to a political one, the Communist Party, and finally to the most exclusive circle of all: a ring of spies. Poor old Straight, by the time he leaves Cambridge he's bent completely out of shape.

Back at home, he takes tea with the president and the first lady, and because he's a sincere and patriotic young man a post is found for him at the heart of government. There is great rejoicing in Moscow, because young Michael is now able to slip secret papers to his controller. But with the coming of war he turns his back on Communism to fight the Nazis. 'Are you still with us?' Guy Burgess enquires, at an Apostles Club reunion in 1947.

'You know I'm not,' our hero replies.

Nevertheless, he kept your secret for twenty years, Guy. Guy's dead, Kim and Donald have fled, and Tony Blunt is the one left without a refuge when the music stops.

The following morning, I meet Martin and Wright to discuss just how the approach to Blunt will be done. It's Martin's show so he does most of the talking. I watch him crawl about his office and wonder at the change that has come over him in a year. He is full of righteous anger and so certain, he would pick a fight with the Queen. The management is doing everything it can to bury the truth, and if proof were needed, he says, the new report into the PETERS inquiry will conclude Mitchell is more likely to be innocent than guilty.

'That's the whitewash Hollis wants. You see, don't you?' he says, with pulpit fervour. 'But he isn't going to slip out of this one – Blunt changes everything. We will have our proof.'

I don't *see* and I say so, even though I know that owning to doubt is perilously close to heresy. Martin sighs with exasperation and wipes a hand across his brow, as a priest might with a simple sinner he is guiding to the light. Michael Straight's confession blows open the Soviet network, he says. Blunt and his Cambridge comrades were recruited in the thirties, and they recruited men like Straight in turn, creating a series of concentric spy rings, just like the ones that were revealed by the VENONA decrypts in the United States.

'Can we talk about Blunt?' I say. 'If he's the fourth man, is it possible that Straight is the fifth?'

Martin reaches down to a drawer, takes out a case file and tosses it across the desk to me. 'Small fry – and here's another.'

The name on the cover is John Cairncross.

'Cairncross was at Cambridge, he knew the others, but in

my view he isn't important enough to be one of the five. We're looking for a special sort of agent, someone so highly placed in Counter-espionage he's able to protect all the others.'

Wright chips in, 'Code name ELLI.'

'Why the hell didn't you tell me about Cairncross?' I say.

Martin shrugs. 'I'm telling you now. We've just forced a confession.'

'I'll keep this,' I say, rising from my chair with the file.

I carry it back to my office, slam the door and kick the wastepaper basket so hard I manage to split the side. The sense I have of this ending badly is back with a vengeance. So I light a cigarette. I smoke it, and when I feel calmer I flip open the file.

John Cairncross was picked up by a KGB talent-spotter when he joined the Foreign Office in 1936, and what a mine of information he turned out to be. He was with the code people at Bletchley Park during the war and for a time at MI6; after the war he was a senior civil servant at the Treasury. It was Burgess who finished him as an agent. Careless, drunken old Guy left a note in Cairncross's hand in his flat when he defected in '51, and Evelyn, the Queen of the Files, recognised his handwriting. No one with an iota of sense can have taken his cock-and-bull excuse seriously, yet he was permitted to walk. So, perhaps Martin has a case. Perhaps Cairncross was sheltered by a guardian angel in the Service, a red one, Blunt and Philby, too.

Two things strike me about Cairncross's history. The first, that he wasn't born with a silver spoon like the others. He's a clever poor boy from somewhere outside Glasgow, a people's champion from the people. The second is that, with his curriculum vitae, it is reasonable to assume he was a grade-one source of intelligence for the other side, and that he may be a much bigger fish than Arthur Martin imagines.

Wright puts his head around my door. 'What d-do you think?'

he says, nodding to the file. I say I want to know why Martin is keeping this sort of thing from me. I don't expect a straight answer and I don't get one, just the line about Arthur flying solo on an old case.

'They're all old cases,' I say. 'It's history until it isn't. You should know that, Peter. Bleaching old bones is your business in research, isn't it?'

'Look, you're back on board,' he says, 'and we haven't st-started on Blunt yet. When we shake the tree, who knows what will fall out? It's too soon to give up on PETERS.'

I'm about to remind him the FBI is as sure as it can be that Graham Mitchell is in the clear when he says, almost as an afterthought, 'Let's not forget, he isn't the only one who fits the profile.' He gazes at me with a slight smile: I don't think I've met anyone who takes more obvious pleasure in being conspiratorial.

'You want to investigate Hollis?'

'Of course not!'

'Come on, Peter, that's what you're trying to tell me. Don't be sly. You've almost finished with Mitchell and now you're after the director general of MI5.'

'That's nonsense,' he says defensively, 'and I'll thank you to keep your voice down. Sir Dick ruled that out. I'm just flying a kite. We know someone tipped off Philby, so who?'

I'm not sure we do know, but I'm not going to fight that battle now. I watch his fingers trail across the corner of my desk as he takes a step back to the door.

'Don't you think we should consider other possibilities?' he says, glancing up at me from beneath his Old Testament eyebrows.

'Do you want me to talk to Dick?'

Wright considers this a moment. 'I expect things to become clearer when Arthur has spoken to Blunt.'

'So, that's no.'

'It isn't the time,' he says, reaching for the door. 'I just w-want to let you know where we are. You want that, don't you?'

'Of course. Thanks.' I can't afford to be at war with both of them.

When he's gone I sit on the desk with my feet on a chair and consider how much of what he says I believe. He denies he wants to investigate Hollis: that's a lie. He says he's going to wait for Dick's approval: I guess that's another. I remember Angleton floating the same possibility on a haze of smoke and whisky: *Mitchell isn't the only one who fits the profile, you know.*

I guess Anatoli Golitsyn is pointing the finger at Hollis now, and Wright is sounding me out to see if I can be trusted to keep my mouth shut while he investigates.

And I wonder at my naivety, at my stupidity. This is more than a mole hunt: they're going to take possession of the house, or they'll bring it down trying to, and Sir Dick White is too confused and feeble-minded to stop them.

Out, Harry. Get out. Elsa would like me to – it's time. She knows someone who knows someone who works for the *Economist*. 'It would suit you, Harry.' Well, maybe. Maybe.

# 19

## *16 March 1964*

THE FOLLOWING MONDAY we meet to discuss PETERS. Hollis makes the mistake of summoning us too early, and while we wait in silence in his outer office, the temperature steadily rises. Martin is a caged bear. I catch his eye momentarily and I see confidence, close to arrogance. I watch him flick through his copy of D1's report, like an actor rehearsing for the last time before taking the stage. He's marked some of its pages: those will be his big scenes.

A green light flashes above the door and we all troop into the DG's office. He rises from his desk beneath the bay window to greet us, then takes his place at the head of the conference table. I find myself sitting opposite a photograph of Dick White on the wall reserved for the former heads of MI5, which is fitting because I am his holy ghost.

D1 Investigations – young Ronnie Symonds – has pulled the evidence together for Hollis and is invited to speak on his report. He has time for only a short summary before Martin launches his assault. 'The unthinkable turns out to be true,' he says. 'Blunt changes everything. We now know there *was* a spy inside MI5, that the KGB has penetrated both Services, and the conspiracy is bigger than any of us could imagine. But we can nail the truth if we act quickly, and we must begin in the 1930s.' Lifting the report by its cover, like rotten fish, he drops it back on the table with a smack. 'This exercise has achieved nothing,' he says. 'We will only discover the identity of the mole at the very top of MI5 today if we take a giant step back to when our enemy was actively recruiting at Cambridge and elsewhere.'

And with that, all hell breaks loose. Cumming, the new head of D Branch, loses his temper, mild-mannered Symonds, too. The PETERS investigation team has barely managed to lay a glove on Mitchell, they say, and yet it has the temerity to call for a knockout count. PETERS is a dead case and pressing ahead will only do more damage to the morale of the Service. The DG asks for my opinion, so I speak for Martin and a broader, deeper investigation, because I know that's what Dick White wants me to do.

Martin thanks me later. I'm picking up a file from the Registry and he's returning one, and as he sways forward to whisper in my ear I catch the whisky on his breath. 'Symonds is a coward,' he says, 'Cumming is a fool, and Hollis is a coward and a fool.' We're standing at the desk in the central hall where the indexes and most of the files are stored on shelves. Registry queens are loading files on to trolleys and pushing them on tracks to the box lifts that carry them to case officers on the floors above.

Martin is curious. 'The Klugmann file,' I say. 'Thought I'd take a look before you make the approach to Blunt.'

Klugmann was at Cambridge with Blunt and the others; he's been on the Service's radar for years. It's a safe thing to say.

'Talent-spotter for the Party,' says Martin. 'A posh romantic – makes no effort to disguise his sympathies.' He hands a file back to one of the girls and watches me fill in a request form for mine.

'Actually, I'm glad I've met you, Harry,' he says, and as we walk to the lifts he instructs me on the report I must make to Dick. A lift door opens and he steps inside, and it's only then that I remember my fountain pen in the Registry.

'And make sure you return the Cairncross file to Peter!' he shouts through the grille.

My pen is in the requests box where I made a point of leaving it, and I use it to fill in forms for two more names. The central hall is a little quieter but there are no short-cuts and it will be half an hour before I'll know if they're in the index. So I leave my number with the duty officer's assistant and ask him to ring me. I have time to run Cairncross along the corridor and be back at my desk for his call.

A tea trolley is passing the third-floor lifts and, with Chinese steps, I balance a cup on Cairncross as far as Counter-intelligence Research, which, to my surprise, has been deserted by its crew. In the war years there was always someone at the helm. A phone's ringing and I'm about to pick it up when I realise D3's door is ajar.

'Hey, Peter, where is everyone?'

No reply.

I knock – 'Peter?' – and push. His door is open, his safe is open. The housekeepers would throw the book at him. I'm a spy so I do what spies do – I pull the door shut behind me. Inside the safe, there's a copying camera, two buff personal files and some analysis of Russian radio traffic in London. I don't have time to examine the files but note the names ZAEHNER and HAMPSHIRE. I know them a little. Rees was the connection, the Service and Oxford, too. They're professors of something at the university now. Back they go, with the Cairncross file I've brought with me. Then I close the safe and spin the combination.

Wright's desk is locked but his diary is in his tray. I check this week and next, and an entry on the twenty-fourth catches my eye: 11 *at the Bodleian*, then *Franks at 3*. The Bodleian is the university library where I daydreamed my way through a history degree. What does he want with Oxford? There's nothing else of note. I see Peter's birthday is on 9 August, the day our allies dropped their A-bomb on Nagasaki. I return the diary to the top of his tray and take a deep breath. But there's no one to offer an excuse to: D3 sails on without its captain and crew.

The second I step into my own office one of the queens rings to let me know I can pick up the files. The duty officer's charmless assistant is picking his nose at the front desk. 'No record of a Phoebe Pool,' he says, 'but there's a Jenifer Hart in the index – one *n*. Married to Herbert.'

'Formerly of this parish?'

'The very same,' he says, and slides the file across to me.

I sign for Hart and Klugmann and am turning to leave with both when I notice *Who's Who* on a shelf of reference books behind the duty officer's desk. Spies are official nobodies until they retire, when the Service's senior officers slip into its pages as War Office civil servants. Herbert Hart is there. Another of the old boys who became a professor at Oxford University; married to Jenifer, the daughter of Sir John Fischer Williams. Address: Banbury Road, Oxford. I make a note. Then I flick back through the pages in search of a Franks. The only one who matters in Oxford is the civil-service Franks, our ambassador in Washington after the war. Baron Franks now – his peerage the most recent of his many honours – philosopher, businessman, consummate diplomat, and for the last year or so provost of Worcester College, Oxford. What business does Wright have with Franks?

I walk back up the stairs and I'm still blowing hard when I run into him a few yards from my office.

'What the h-h-hell are you playing at?'

I give a slight smile that must look like a grimace. 'A key,' is all I have the breath to say.

'D-d-did you go through my safe?'

'Tried to spare your blushes.' I imagine he marked the position of the files in his safe because that's what I do. 'We don't have secrets, do we?'

'That isn't the point.'

'I'm sick of being kept in the dark.'

We stare at each other belligerently for a moment. Then he shrugs and smiles his thin smile. 'My fault. L-l-left that silly bitch Phyllis to hold the fort, and she buggered off to the canteen.'

I don't know Phyllis; I don't expect I'll get a chance to now.

'But the files,' he says, 'we're running a few routine checks. Nothing to do with that other matter, the PETERS investigation.'

'Didn't look. You can rest easy.' I could challenge him with his visit to Franks but that isn't how we're going to play this game: while he was staring at me stony-faced, I was turning possibilities over in my mind, and I'm quite sure there's a connection with the mole hunt. I'm just waiting for the vital spark.

He nods – 'Okay, Harry' – and turns as if to leave but changes his mind. 'By the way, how do you think R-R-Roger handled the meeting?'

Is it the twitching of his lips? Perhaps his trouble with Roger? Doesn't matter. Everything falls into place in an instant.

'What do *you* think, Peter?' I say as cover.

'It's Arthur. I think he's close to snapping. He can't understand why Roger's determined to throw our investigation.'

'We don't know that.'

'We d-do.'

'The new report doesn't exonerate Mitchell entirely, it recommends we consider other candidates.'

'But is R-R-Roger ready to? We'll see.' He pauses. 'We can count on your support when the balloon goes up?'

'I'll do my job, Peter,' I say.

# Andrew Williams

I used to like Wright – at least, I didn't actively dislike him. When he's gone I dig out a copy of the Western Region timetable. There's a nine o'clock from Paddington that will allow him time to walk from the station to the Bodleian Library for eleven. I expect he'll spend a few hours with cuttings books from the twenties, student papers, reports of political meetings, and then he'll makes his way to Worcester College, and that's where his real business will be. I don't know what I can do, but if he's turning the clock back that far I must too, because Oxford is where it all began.

144

# 20

# 24 March 1964

R AIN IS BEATING the pavement and staining the heads of the emperors at the gates of the Sheldonian Theatre mustard-yellow. A little further along the street, a posse of undergraduates in short black Commoners' gowns shelters in the portico of the Bodleian Library, even though college lunch bells are calling. Broad Street is deserted but for a porter in a bowler hat, who sails past the shop window on his bike, head bent close to the handlebars. I watch him with a token book open in my hands and I'm jostled by so many boisterous memories I wonder the sales assistant doesn't accuse me of causing a disturbance and ask me to leave.

Among the group of undergrads on the steps of the Bodleian I see the shadow of the boy Harry. He clings to the stone like soot, or like dust on a calf-bound copy of something so obscure it's kept to dress the shelves above the honours board that bears the names of those who are supposed to live for evermore, the shelves beyond the reach of even serious students because the library ladder is six rungs too short.

Oxford belonged to middle-class Englishmen, like Mitchell and Hollis. It was just one more step along a time-honoured path from a boarding-school cloister to government and the professions, and, yes, the intelligence services too. At dinner under a high oak-beamed medieval roof in Hall, I listened to their displays of self-assurance, shouted the length of long tables. They knew they were going to rule the Empire, but their speech and manners were as foreign to me as those of its humblest Indian coolies.

'Do you know the Angleseys?' a New College aristocrat asked me once.

'There's only one,' I said.

I understood later that he was talking about a titled family, and that a duke or marquess or earl somewhere could take the dark isle of Wales we call Ynys Môn for his name.

Most Welsh students went to Jesus, their own little college colony on Turl Street. I knew a few of them in my first year, and they viewed their time at Oxford as a sabatical abroad. 'Stay away from Jesus or you may as well have stayed at home,' Goronwy Rees said at our first meeting – and I did. That was in 1933. Rees was just back from Berlin and someone – I forget whom – asked him to address our Labour Club. He spoke with the chapel eloquence of his preacher father, and even now, here in this bookshop, the memory of his passion and his poetry brings a little lump to my throat.

Rees spoke of how socialism was dying as Hitler and the Nazis tightened their grip on Germany, and that what had been just a nightmare had become the everyday. Sixty million people were proud to be governed by 'a gang of murderous animals', he said. It was 'the betrayal and death of every human virtue'. No mercy; no pity; no peace; madness shouted every day on the wireless and in the newspapers. Germany would be saved only if right-thinking people everywhere were prepared to stand up to Fascism, he said – and so it was to be, from that night, in student papers and political clubs, in college beer cellars and butteries, egged on by my new friend and all his clever friends, for the rest of my time at Oxford and after.

But that was the thirties. Roger Hollis was at Oxford in the twenties when students on the left – there were only a few –

were too busy condemning the last world war to imagine the next. They saw Berlin as the free-thinking capital of Europe, where – as Rees liked to put it – one could be on the right political side, the proletarian side, and where sex was encouraged because morals were viewed as simply a bourgeois prejudice. No one imagined the monster lurking at the bottom of the swamp.

I don't know if Hollis was a student radical (I doubt it very much). I *do* know he was a contemporary and acquaintance of Dick White, and that Wright is flying solo on this one. I imagine he's hoping to find enough in the Bodleian Library to justify this fishing trip, and that if he doesn't, no one will be the wiser. I watched him scuttle across the Old Schools Quadrangle under an umbrella, shake it dry and disappear into the library, where he will be flicking through volumes of the student newspaper, club minutes, and the debating records of the Oxford Union. 'R. H. Hollis spoke in praise of Lenin,' would do nicely, I'm sure. If he finds it I'll eat his trilby hat. If he doesn't, who knows? He may just conjure something from thin air, or even from a drawer full of dust.

Wright doesn't reappear until five past two. From a bench in the King's Arms I watch him turn left out of the library on to Broad Street. I finish my pint and follow. Ten minutes to Worcester College, and his appointment is at half past, so he may drop into a café at Gloucester Green for a cup of tea and a roll. The new baron provost of Worcester and his fellows will be very familiar with the story of the wine-and-roses student who was rusticated by the college before final exams yet rose to become guardian of the nation's security. Hollis will be a regular at high table. I expect MI5 has a talent-spotter and contact at the college (it was the bursar at mine). If so, Wright will have flattered him with false confidences in the usual way.

Something like 'Mum's the word, but one of Sir Roger's contemporaries may be talking to the Russians. Can you help?'

The rain's stopped and students and trippers have come out to play. There's cover enough for me to use in Broad Street and Wright is taking none of the precautions against being followed that become second nature in the field. He looks distracted, caught in two minds, pausing at the gates of Exeter College, touching his lips, glancing at his watch. I follow him a little further and he stops again. Thirty yards ahead of me now, opposite side of the street, shop window with reflections on his left, parked cars on his right, and if he turns towards them he may see me. I sense that's what he's going to do and drop to my shoelaces in front of the iron gates of Trinity. Sure enough he has turned and is retracing his steps. I do the same.

Right at the bottom of Broad Street and the majestic circular, domed reading rooms of the Radcliffe Camera are in front of us, and to its left, the high wall and gate of the graduate college, All Souls, where all the members are fellows and as wise as Solomon.

He walks towards the cut between the college and the University Church, then left on to the High, and I follow. But I'm too slow, too careful, and I've lost his fawn trilby among the hats and bobbing heads on the pavement. Is he in the Lodge at All Souls? Yes, it will be All Souls. I'm still considering whether to wait for him in the café opposite when he steps on to the street again. Ten yards, fifteen at most, and if he glances sideways he will certainly see me. Thank God for his hat because in the time he takes to adjust it I turn to seek the sanctuary of the University Church.

The porter at All Souls greets me by name. 'To see Mr Rees, sir?' he says, as if it were only yesterday. 'Afraid we haven't seen him in a while.'

'Did the last gentleman ask for Mr Rees?'

The porter hesitates. 'I can't say, sir.' Wright has shown him a police ID and told him to say nothing.

'That's all right,' I say. 'Is Professor Berlin in college?'

His rooms were on the other side of the quad thirty years ago. I sit on a bench beside a postgraduate student with mop hair and appalling acne and wait for him to emerge. Rees recommended Berlin to me and, I suppose, me to him. Berlin, the first Jew to be elected to a prize fellowship at All Souls, Rees, the first Welshman. Berlin was the cleverer, Rees the more entertaining, or so it seemed to this poor undergraduate. I was a guest sometimes at their gatherings, invited to admire their wit and erudition, and now Isaiah Berlin is a professor knight and international *éminence grise*, while Goronwy inhabits a wilderness of his own making.

The door opens, a young man scurries out with Berlin's new book on liberty under his arm, and I slip inside before my spotty companion can take his place. Isaiah is standing on the rug in front of his electric fire, a cigarette at the corner of his mouth. He appears lost in a thought, as philosophers should always be. Then he turns and sees me, and his thick eyebrows lift over the frame of his glasses. ''Arry,' he says, with a broad smile, 'come in, come in,' and he puts out his cigarette and steps forward to shake my hand. 'What an unexpected pleasure. Sit down. What have you done with Mr Jeffries?'

I gather that is the name of the postgrad waiting so patiently at the great man's door for his hour of warmth and light: *Mr Jeffries, please can you come back at the same time tomorrow.*

Then Isaiah telephones for tea. I listen to his precise Russian-accented English, and for the second time today I feel a lump in my throat, which is unconscionably weak-minded of me. He's dressed in an expensive dark wool three-piece suit that was probably cut on Savile Row, yet isn't quite the English gentleman. But I'm sure he doesn't care to be. Mid-fifties now. The fine lines that arched between his cheek and jaw have become creases and the little that's left of his hair is grey at the temple. But what do these things matter to a philosopher with eyes that always seem to sparkle with empathy and wit. He says I don't look a day older, which is gratifying, of course. I'm sure he remembers how vain I am, because he remembers everything.

In an old armchair and a fireside glow of books and art, it is possible to believe once again that man is progressing to perfection. A scout brings the tea and Isaiah pours, and we speak of nothing that might threaten his pretty bone-china cups. Naturally he knows I work for the Service and that Rees was there for a time too, because people at Oxford of Isaiah's sort do. He's on good terms with our old-boy professors, Hart and Zaehner, and another philosopher knight, Hampshire, is a friend and collaborator. He knew Burgess and was engaged to dine with him the week he fled to Moscow. So, he grasps my meaning at once when I say, 'There was another of us here today, a man called Wright, and he was asking for Rees.'

Isaiah takes off his glasses and touches them to his lips. 'Isn't that over?'

'I'm afraid it isn't.'

'You have nothing to do with him, I suppose, or you wouldn't have taken the trouble to visit me.'

I smile ruefully. 'I read his pieces for *Encounter* magazine. Do you think he knows it's bankrolled by the CIA?'

Berlin raises his eyebrows. 'I don't expect he does.'

'He's living in London?'

Isaiah rises from his chair and takes a thick address book from his desk. 'Have you a pen? South Terrace, Thurloe Square, South Kensington. I don't seem to have the number but that won't be difficult for a man in your line of work, will it?' He snaps the book shut. 'He was in a hospital, you know. A nervous breakdown. He's still quite fragile, and still drinking too much. Penniless, of course. Poor . . . ?'

'His wife? Margaret. Margie.'

'Is that her name? Poor Margaret. Cigarette?' He offers me an elegant silver box. 'You remember Maurice Bowra? The warden at Wadham. Maurice says Goronwy just wanted to stab someone. Simple as that. He didn't care who he hurt when he denounced innocent people in his newspaper pieces.'

One of those 'innocents' was Anthony Blunt, but I don't say so because I know they're on excellent terms.

'Is it too much to suggest it's something Welsh in him?' he says. 'Goronwy reminds me of your prime minister, Lloyd George. Delightful, affectionate, vain, a source of great vitality, but petulant and impetuous, too. A prisoner of his upbringing and of other people's expectations. Always the *enfant terrible*, and so was poor Guy.' He pauses. 'But you knew them better than I did.'

'I don't know that I did.'

Glasses back on, he leans forward and peers at me. 'What is it you want, 'Arry?'

'Does there have to be something?'

'No, but there is, isn't there? This man, Wright . . . You want me to speak to Rees before he does.'

'That's right.'

'And tell him to keep his mouth shut?'

'Tell him to think twice before he stabs anyone else.'

'You?'

I smile. 'His friends and yours at this university.'

'I see. Because you have reason to believe . . .?'

'Yes, I do. It would be a mistake for Rees to offer Wright anything. *Pryfed at cachu.* Flies to shit, Isaiah.'

'May I enquire whether this has *anything* to do with protecting our country?'

'I think so. Our values, certainly. The things we fought for in the war. Our independence – your view of liberty and mine. At the risk of sounding hackneyed, *Quis custodiet* . . . I forget the Latin, I'm sure you have it – who guards the guards?'

'*Quis custodiet ipsos custodes.* But Juvenal was writing about fidelity in marriage.' He gazes at me long enough to be sure I feel uncomfortable, then places his hands on his knees to rise. 'Why don't you tell Rees yourself, 'Arry? Is it pride? Is it fear? I don't think I want to be involved. I hope you understand.'

'Of course.'

I know I won't persuade him, and when he rises I follow suit, and we shuffle across his polished floor to the door. I'm about to offer my hand when he asks, 'Do you think Wright will wish to speak to me?'

'I'm afraid so.'

He nods. 'Goronwy wasn't much of a Communist. He was more interested in drama and women. He found Guy's badness attractive, and Guy knew how to manipulate him . . . It's ruined him.'

In the cold, hard, wet stone world beyond Isaiah's study, I seek shelter again. Rain is cascading from gargoyles and gutters and droning in the All Souls cloister, like a choir of elderly monks at their office. As I listen in something like a trance, the music changes and I hear an echo of this college in the thirties, irreverent, provocative, atonal, the voices of Rees and Bowra, Berlin and Burgess, from whom I learned that there were only two unpardonable sins: ignorance and boredom. (Explain that to the man in the fawn trilby hat, will you?) We didn't have much time for saints then or ever, but I do remember the words of an old prayer to St Peter I used to hear in the All Souls chapel: 'O glorious apostle, who can bind and loose sinners as you will, forgive those of us who chose the progressive way, especially those who were more active than others – we were very green in judgement.' Amen.

# 21

# 23 April 1964

THE GLASS OF water Arthur Martin lifts to his lips is shaking. He sips once, he sips twice, then places it carefully on the director general's conference table beside his notebook and his tape recorder. He has offered us an *entrée*, now the *plat*, served cold, naturally. He'll take his time, to be sure we savour his triumph: grammar-school boy who couldn't go to university tackles Blunt, professor knight and palace favourite. After eleven interview rounds in almost as many years, a knockout in the twelfth.

'I told him Cairncross confessed a few weeks ago, that he thanked me for making him do so. Then Blunt asked me to give him five minutes to wrestle with his conscience, and I let him step out of his office. He returned with a drink — whisky, I think – and stood by the window, and he said, "It's true." And, well, that was that: he sat down in his chair and confessed.'

Martin sits back with a smile that reminds me of the sickly piety of a plaster saint. He thinks Blunt's confession is his apotheosis, after years of martyrdom at the hands of the Service's Cavaliers – its non-believers. 'Well done, Arthur,' we chorus.

'He isn't sorry,' says Martin, and he switches on the tape so we can hear Sir Anthony speak some 'why I did it' stuff about the thirties and Fascism and his vision of a better way. His voice is deep and mellifluous, his accent expensive, his language cultivated, his manner charming. He is the perfect English gentleman of the clever metropolitan sort – only he isn't, because he's a secret homosexual and a spy. I don't like him but I feel sorry for him, and anxious too, because the tape we're listening to is just a beginning. Martin is promising to wring him dry.

The following morning, I take a cab to MI6's new headquarters south of the river to brief Sir Dick. Century House is just as ugly as Six's bar sages predicted it would be, and although we've moved only a short distance from our old home it feels like a great divide. Perhaps Dick is hoping government will forget we're here. A little further, and we may drop off the edge of the known world, and then the transformation will be complete. Instead of spying on our enemy we will be able to devote all our grey concrete days to investigating our own people.

Dick tells me before my backside has hit his leather that he 'always hated Blunt' and that his 'hauteur is irritating', which is not how I remember their relationship at all. And I tell him that Blunt has named another of his associates at Cambridge – Leo Long – as a Russian agent. Dick nods as if he knows this already, which he may well do.

'Does he know the name of his replacement at Five?' he says. 'Moscow would only have let him retire after the war if they could count on an even better-placed source.'

'You're right, sir,' I say, because he wants to be. There must be a bigger traitor than Blunt, someone to blame for the mistakes of the fifties, the clues missed, the interrogations that came to nothing, the failure of the Dick White years.

'You know, I supported Leo Long's application to join the Service,' he says, as I rise to leave. 'Christ! What a mess.'

Over the next few days we crawl over Anthony Blunt's life. Wright and McBarnet are preparing research briefs and I chip in with material from Six. Martin meets with Blunt at night and the following morning we go over the tapes and check for evasions and lies. He says he was recruited by Burgess, that their first controller was a Hungarian – 'Theo' – that he was replaced in 1937 by a controller called 'Otto' from somewhere else in middle Europe. They were both cultured middle-class men who knew how to make the proletariat appealing to Cambridge graduates. 'I don't think I would have become a spy if the approach had come from a Russian rather than a European,' he says. But 'Otto' was recalled to Moscow in '38 in one of Uncle Joe Stalin's purges, and for months the ring was without a controller. Contact was made again through the first of Philby's many wives. 'Because Kim had only one ambition in life and that was to be a spy.'

The spools turn through another few feet of tape and into the forties, and soon it's time to lace up the fifties, and there are names, but only of people who are known to the Service or don't really matter. Martin is losing patience.

I hear him say: 'Who replaced you in Five?'

And Blunt replies, 'I was quite tempted to stay. But they didn't need me. Kim was rising to the top of the Service. I know what you want, but I can't help you.'

But still we go on.

On the second Sunday in May, I take a few hours for lunch to celebrate Elsa's birthday. Bethan and Mary join us at the Ritz. Bethan is swotting for her final exams before university and has somehow contrived to fall out with her mother again. She says she wants to live with me, and glances shyly at Elsa in the hope of some encouragement. My clever, attractive, funny wife has them both eating from the palm of her hand, and I'm very grateful because I like being a father again.

We window-shop in Piccadilly and wander across Trafalgar Square, where the nuclear-disarmament people are campaigning for the country to set an example. The Honourable Labour Member for Barking is waiting to speak.

Elsa nudges me. 'Driberg.'

'The very same.'

Old Tom Driberg used to bugger about Bentinck Street with Guy, and he had the foresight to visit him in Moscow to write the book of why he went over to the other side.

'Let's not hang about,' I say, 'or we might end up in the Special Branch photos.'

Elsa laughs. 'Worse for you or for someone in Defence like me?'

'You, because I'm working under cover.'

We walk the girls along Whitehall and show them where Elsa works in the new Ministry of Defence. The War Office is no more; she has moved to the bleak white neoclassical monstrosity that someone without imagination christened 'MOD Main', and might very well be mistaken for a Communist Party block in Moscow. And Daddy – the girls want to know – where does Daddy work? 'Daddy works across the road in the Foreign Office,' I say, 'and poor Daddy must go there now.' I listen to them laughing with Elsa as they walk away, then cross into Downing Street. The Queen of the Files is waiting for me in her shawl of many colours. 'Not run off to Moscow?' she'll say – she always does. I'll tell her I've been putting on the Ritz and ask her to dance.

Monday morning, and an unholy row is taking place along the corridor in Soviet Counter-espionage. Peter Wright knows why. 'Arthur and Malcolm,' he says, with a wry smile. 'Malcolm wants to move some of our people to other duties.'

Poor Malcolm Cumming is the head of D Branch (Counter-espionage) and, in theory, the man in charge of both Martin's D1 Soviet section and Wright's D3 Research. In practice Arthur writes his own rules. As far as he's concerned, Cumming is good for counting paperclips and nothing else.

'It's unforgivable,' says Wright, 'just when things are running our way. M-M-Malcolm is so old school.' He means Cumming is an old Etonian Cavalier and non-believer who thinks Martin is obsessed with proving the PETERS case (he is), and that he's hiding evidence from the DG (he's right about that, too); and that the hunt for a mole is doing terrible damage to the Service (it may be). I'm still in D3 when Martin flings the door open with such force it crashes against one of Evelyn's precious filing cabinets.

'Suspended!' He's white and trembling. 'Cumming took it to Hollis, and he's suspended me for indiscipline. You'll have to take over the Blunt debrief, Peter. We can't let up now.'

And that's what happens, only Wright has ideas of his own about how to go about it, and one of them is to put someone from the old Bentinck Street set in front of Blunt: me.

'Are you going to do it?' Elsa asks, when I tell her sometime around midnight.

'I'm afraid it will muddy the water.'

'Then don't do it, Harry,' she says.

But Wright is insistent in a calculating way. 'B-B-Blunt knows we're groping in the dark,' he says, on the first day of Martin's gardening leave. 'We need to shake him up a bit. I'll play nasty, and you can be his friend.'

Evelyn looks up from the papers she's studying. 'That won't be difficult, will it, dear?'

'Evelyn, *cariad*, Anthony and I have never been close – you must be confusing me with Sir Dick White.'

The following evening, we are greeted at the door of the Court-auld by Brian, an effete young protégé of the director. Brian is wonderfully supercilious, as fine artists often are. We must look like old housebreakers in our raincoats, because he insists on walking behind us, in case we swipe one of the institute's antiques, I suppose. I'm struck by the elegance and the opulence of the eighteenth-century circular stair that Anthony climbs to his private apartment every day. Our orders from Hollis are to go softly, softly, lest Anthony has a change of heart and decides to run to Moscow. Wright has absolutely no intention of obeying Hollis's orders. Brian leads us across a drawing room in which the first man is tempting the first woman with an apple. For some reason, the painting reminds me that Guy said his friend Anthony preferred to play the woman's part. There was no love lost between us in those Bentinck Street years. I wonder, Will Blunt try to turn the tables on me with some reference to that time?

'How are you, Harry?' he says, as if it were only yesterday. He must be surprised to see me, but his years of secret life as a homosexual and a Russian spy have made him even more expert than the rest of us at hiding his true feelings. While Wright talks, he glances at me coyly, like one of my teenage daughter's friends. His face is long, lined and drawn with what may be care, and his tweed suit looks a little baggy. But he's always been as tall and thin as a teasel, with so little flesh on his frame, it's a miracle he doesn't rattle. He's mid-fifties, perhaps fifty-seven (I remember a birthday party in Bentinck Street). Rees used to say he was sly, Guy that he was 'sensitive and shy', and no man could hope for a truer friend. I don't know Anthony well but I imagine there has been very little love and laughter in his life.

We sit at his fireside and I compliment him on his study, which is just what I expected it to be, with fine furniture and old-master paintings, and his own Poussin over the chimney-piece; he tells me with pride that his students were responsible for gilding the elaborate plaster cornicing and friezes.

Wright isn't interested in art, it seems. 'We've heard what

you've had to say, Anthony,' he says, switching on a tape recorder. 'I don't think you've been telling Arthur the truth.'

Blunt's shoulders tense. 'I answered all his questions,' he says petulantly.

'That's n-nonsense, and you know it is too. We've kept our side of the bargain, like gentlemen. You aren't keeping yours.'

'I don't know what you mean.' A nerve is jumping at the corner of Anthony's right eye.

'You must know the name of your successor at Five. You will have briefed him.'

'I've told you already—'

'You know.'

'How do you know I know?'

'Because it's how Moscow works!'

Anthony crosses his long legs, then flicks a speck of dust from the knee of his trousers. He knows how Moscow works, and he knows Wright is telling a fat lie. 'I've told you, there was nobody else.'

Wright barks at him, 'Come on! What about your c-c-conscience? Have you thought about the agents who were executed because of you?'

'There were no deaths.'

'MI6's spy inside the Kremlin? Tortured and executed – and there were others.'

Blunt sighs impatiently. 'Did we have a spy in the Kremlin? I didn't know. I didn't put anyone's life at risk.'

'But Kim did,' I say. 'Thirty, forty of our agents?'

'M-more,' Wright chips in. 'Many more.'

'And you knew, didn't you, Anthony?'

'No one died because of me,' he says again.

'Well, that's a comfort, I'm sure.'

Blunt closes his eyes for a moment and I lean forward to stop the recorder. 'Okay. Perhaps a drink?'

He smiles weakly. 'Is it still whisky?'

As he rises, I'm reminded of the delicate spindly sort of spider you see clinging to the bricks in autumn cellars. 'I have some sandwiches in the kitchen, too,' he says. 'Ham and egg, I think.'

The moment the door closes behind him Wright is up on his feet. 'K-keep an ear open, will you?' And, taking a tape measure from his pocket, he makes a note of the height and width of the chimneypiece. 'What do you think? About six inches from the right side and, say, two feet from the floor? It's going to be tricky, but . . .'

Oh, the light in his eyes. He's going to ask the rags at A2 to drill through the wall and embed a probe microphone. The timing couldn't be better because the builders are in the house next door.

'The telephone can't p-p-pick up what he says in here because he's moved it to the end of the hall . . . He's n-no fool.'

'No,' I say. 'Anthony's no fool.'

The sandwiches are perfect white triangles. Blunt drinks gin; we – his tormentors – drink whisky. The tape recorder stays off and either this or the gin makes a difference because Anthony seems more at ease.

'Sorry I can't help you, Peter,' he says, once, twice, thrice, as we turn on a roundabout to the question of the mole at the top of MI5. What about his controller, 'Otto'? Did he ever mention . . .? He was talent-spotting at Oxford as well as Cambridge, wasn't he? And Burgess . . . can you remember? He may have let the name of someone slip? But Blunt drops his bat on that one, too.

'You won't believe this,' he says, 'but I can tell you, Guy loved this country.'

Wright snorts derisively. 'He wanted Britain to be Communist.'

Anthony can't quite suppress the flicker of a smile. 'Harry, you knew Guy, you were his friend . . .'

'Guy was working for the Soviet Union,' I say.

'And *you* were helping the R-Russians too, Anthony,' says Wright, 'not this country – R-Russia.'

Blunt closes his eyes and shakes his head with exasperation. 'You have to have lived through it, Peter. You can't understand—'

'Oh, I understand all right, Anthony,' he says angrily. 'I know all about the thirties. We were poor. I had to leave school, and my world fell apart. My father lost his job, and took to the bottle. Oh, I remember the thirties!'

The colour rises to Anthony's cheeks and he mumbles, 'Sorry.' Embarrassing to be reminded beneath your Poussin that it all comes down to class, especially if you've been a doughty champion of the proletariat. I imagine this is like the silence in my lord's drawing room when the footman announces he has the daughter of the house in the family way. Wright is shifting awkwardly in the chair beside me. 'Rees knew you were w-w-working for the other side, didn't he?' he says, perhaps to embarrass us both.

'It was foolish of Guy to trust him.'

'Was R-Rees a member of the Communist Party, too?'

Blunt hesitates.

'Come on, Anthony . . .'

'Yes.'

'And it was B-Burgess who approached him?'

'Actually, Rees *asked* Guy if he could join the Party.'

'You're sure?'

'Guy said so. Guy wanted Rees to stay outside, work for peace in a different way.'

'As a Soviet agent?'

'Yes.'

I hear the tinkle of ice and glass beside me. Wright is drinking, and I drink too, for the seconds I need to think.

'Rees denies he was a member of the Party,' I say.

'Well, he would . . .'

Blunt offers us his cigarette case, and I take one, and as I lean forward for a light I lift my eyes to his face. 'There's no love lost between you and Goronwy Rees, is there, Anthony?'

'He wrote some unforgivable things about Guy,' he says evenly. 'You know how close they were. I expect he was afraid of this' – and he gestures to the two of us – 'or worse.'

'And does Rees have reason to be afraid?' Wright asks.

'Rees was going to talent-spot for us at Oxford. Help Guy persuade students to do something useful for the Party – the Foreign Office, civil service. But before you ask, I don't know if he managed to persuade anyone. And he left us in 'thirty-nine . . .'

'But you stayed . . .'

'You know I did,' he replies. 'Look, it's late . . .' He draws on his cigarette and folds the butt into an ashtray. 'Can we leave this for another day?'

But Wright is like a hound with a bone. 'Do you know a woman called Jenifer Hart?' he asks. 'Maiden name Fischer Williams.'

Blunt places his hands on his knees to rise. 'Not really. A little.'

'You d-do know her, then.'

'A little. Through a mutual friend.'

'Who?'

'Someone here at the Courtauld Institute. I say, can we . . .?' and he looks at me pleadingly.

I say, 'We can,' at once, and I stand up, too. 'Enough for tonight, I think.'

Wright is furious, naturally, and tells me so on the pavement outside. We stand and argue beneath a street light, like a couple of old tarts who have had more than one over the eight, while cabbies circle Portman Square in the hope of our fare. I meet his anger with 'I'm Mr Nice, remember?' and argue we won't bully the truth from Anthony; and what about the mole in MI5, what about ELLI, and when did we decide to go fishing for fry?

'You're thinking of Rees,' he says, and it sounds like an accusation.

'And the rest, Peter. Look, Blunt is looking after Blunt. He's been blowing smoke up our arses for years. Ask Arthur.'

'Maybe,' he says coolly, 'but you heard him. Oxford had – has – its Communists, too. ELLI may belong to an Oxford ring. Graham Mitchell was there, and others.'

'Right,' I say impatiently, 'so I'll tell Dick White we're now on a trawl for anyone who used to be a member of the Party, not just in the Service but wherever we can find them. Is this Angleton's idea, by the way?'

Wright puts down his case to use both hands to trim his trilby. 'I'm head of D3 now. This *is* my business, my bread and butter – mine.' Before I can reply he steps into the gutter with his arm out to flag down a passing cab. 'Do you m-mind if I take this one?' It comes to a halt a few feet from him.

'Go ahead,' I say, with as much ice in my voice as I can manage.

The cab door's open and Wright is on the point of climbing inside when he turns back to me. 'Are you afraid of something, Harry? Is that what it is?'

And he's gone before I can think of something to draw his sting.

## 22

## 23 May 1964

Elsa sleeps. I have no wish to. To sleep would be to lose the perfect stillness and contentment of this hour. She lies in my arms and I am careful not to move a muscle lest I wake her, only rejoice in the pulse of her breathing, in the heat and perfume of her skin, her hair about my pillow. Her old teddy bear stares back at me from the wicker chair to the right of the door. On the mahogany chest of drawers there's a photograph of her mother, and she has hung the Picasso lithograph she bought last week in a Cork Street gallery on the wall opposite, next to a watercolour of the girls. The wardrobe is ajar. Her black silk evening dress has slipped from a hanger and pours on to the floor. Her shoes. My shoes. Her Victorian jewellery box on the dressing-table. My dad's old Davy lamp on the mantelpiece ('Really, Harry? In the bedroom?'). In these things I rejoice. Call me to the chapel rail to own the wasted years. For the love I mumbled to others, I beg your forgiveness. *Cariad*, I have travelled the road, and now I see. Fifty is too late (did you want children?), but this I know: I love you more than life – yes, this liar, this old Service cynic – and I will let no man put us asunder.

'Harry?' She turns suddenly to face me, and I realise she was awake all the time.

'I love you,' I say, and I kiss her hair.

'Harry . . . have you spoken to Blunt?'

'Yes.' And I know it's unwise and we should wait until morning, but I ask her all the same. 'You've not mentioned this business to anyone have you, *cariad*?'

She rises to an elbow and reaches for the bedside light. 'What are you accusing me of?'

'I'm not accusing you, I'm asking.'

'That's not what it sounds like.'

I try to caress her cheek and she brushes my hand roughly aside. 'I ask because I love you,' I say, 'and I don't want someone to hurt you – to hurt us.'

'But you know I wouldn't talk to—'

'Please, darling,' I cut across her, 'when was your last contact with Jenifer Hart?'

The trendy beatnik people in berets and turtlenecks who float up and down the King's Road most weekends have been driven from the White Hart by a dog-racing crowd. The public bar is full of men who still wear caps and speak proper London. First race at Stamford Bridge begins in an hour, and I gather from the young enthusiast at my side that the favourite is called The Pimpernel, and if I fancy a flutter he would be happy to take my money.

In the mirror behind the bar I watch Rees with his newspapers and a pint, a cigarette dangling from his bottom lip like a Welsh Popeye. Eight years since we last met and even at opposite ends of a smoky bar I can see those years have not been kind to him. *Nefoedd wen.* In truth I'm a little shocked. 'A short life but a gay one,' he used to say, and those years of raising hell are catching up with him now. For all that, he is still a beautiful man: Henry Fonda in *Twelve Angry Men* perhaps, or Burt Lancaster in *The Leopard*. His hair has turned white but it keeps an unruly curl, and his thick eyebrows are as dark and expressive as they were on the day I first met him thirty years ago, and if his face is creased and mottled by hard living it has not lost its shape. The man to his right rises with an empty glass. Rees removes the fag from the corner of his mouth and smiles, and I see a flash of the green-eyed impish charm that has broken many hearts. Clever women – the writers Elizabeth Bowen and Rosamond Lehmann to name but two – have thrown themselves at his feet, and many men would have liked to. He was, and doubtless remains, a brilliantly gifted child, spoiled and dangerous.

The barman rings his bell, the pub doors open, and the dog punters rise almost as one. I leave with them and wait on the opposite side of the street for Rees to reel out in his own time. He will make his way to the barge, just as he did yesterday and the day before. I follow his reflection in a shop window as he glances anxiously up and down the pavements. Someone must have rattled his cage and it doesn't take much effort to deduce who that someone might be. But you're all right, Goronwy, no one else is following you today. Off he goes, limping along the crowded pavement, and in a hundred yards or so he will turn left on to Old Church Street then right on to Chelsea Embankment, where he will cross to the riverside.

The Reeses are struggling. Hand to mouth since he was forced from his post at Aberystwyth University for writing his scurrilous pieces for the *People*. Berlin gave me an address in Kensington, but that flat's gone, the car too. They're just one step ahead of the taxman. Poor Margie. She was quite the innocent when she fell in love with Rees. As I listened to them promise to forsake all others, I knew she could have no real inkling of the unstable, undependable, pleasure-loving ego-maniac and philanderer she was promising to love and honour and obey for a lifetime. 'Extremely unwise,' I remember Burgess observing, 'a foolish step,' and now Margie is living in a leaky houseboat just a few yards from Battersea Bridge, and if the Revenue comes calling they may have to slip the mooring and drift out to sea.

'You!' she says, when she sees me at the bottom of the gangway.

'Hello, Margie.'

She's so shocked she covers her mouth. I don't hear what she says next, only her frustration.

'You look well,' I say. (Margie is an English rose.)

'He isn't here.'

'I know he is' – and to prove me right and his poor Margie wrong the cussed man calls from the cabin of the tub, 'What have you done with *Encounter*?'

Margie takes a step closer and almost loses her footing on the mildewed deck. 'Steady!' I shout, more for his benefit than hers.

'You people. Why don't you leave us alone?'

Too late. A deck hatch thuds open and Rees's head, with its tangle of white hair, pops up, like a dummy from a ventriloquist's box. 'Who is it, darling?'

'Vaughan,' she says. 'Harry Vaughan.'

His head disappears at once, and a few seconds later I hear him clumping up to the deck. Margie refuses to look at me. I am Oxford and Bentinck Street, I am other girls and Guy, I am the Service, above all I am a Welshman – *Cymro ydw I* – and she has no love for us, excepting Goronwy. 'Darling' – she takes his arm – 'you don't have to speak to him.'

'We need to talk about old friends, Goronwy.'

'Who?' she says.

'I'm afraid this isn't the place.' I gesture to the neighbouring barges and the stationary traffic on the bridge above us.

Margie squeezes his arm. 'Darling, you don't have to.'

Margie, you're wrong, and it's on the tip of my tongue to

tell you so. But Rees knows: after so much bad blood I would only break the silence if it was necessary.

'I'll get my coat,' he says.

Margie protests and he tries to calm her, and I'm struck by how Oxford and smoky his voice has become, with only the faintest echo of home. Do I sound the same? After thirty years we are as metropolitan smooth as wave-tossed shingle.

I walk him across the bridge to Battersea Park and choose a bench a safe distance from the crowd at the festival funfair. He doesn't say much, perhaps because there's too much to say. We're like old lovers who have rehearsed their grievances for years, and when the time comes, they are at a loss to know where to begin.

'You heard about Wright, then?' he says at last.

'I guessed.'

'He made all sorts of threats. Margie was very upset – accused him of behaving like the Gestapo. I suppose our telephone's tapped?'

'But you spoke to him.'

Rees draws deeply on his cigarette, then flicks the butt on to the gravel path. 'Yes, I spoke to him. I didn't have much choice.' He turns to face me. 'Eight years, Harry. Eight years. Was it such a crime?'

'You hurt a lot of people.' There was always the devil in Rees. I used to make excuses for him, until he betrayed his best friend in a newspaper and there were no more excuses to make. 'No one trusts you.'

He doesn't argue. He knows he hurt us, and I want him to feel how much. The threat of prosecution, the whispers, names removed from civil-service commissions, the early retirements, friends who served their country for years reduced to tears by false allegations.

'I didn't write about you,' he ventures.

I gaze into his green eyes. 'Because you couldn't.'

He turns away. 'What do you want to know?'

'What you told Wright?'

'Don't worry, I'm not a fool. I know you can hurt me too.' He reaches into his coat for a packet of cigarettes only to realise he's smoked the last one.

'Here.' I offer him mine.

'Bit of a prig, isn't he?' He pauses to look for a light. 'Don't imagine he's much fun. He started with Burgess, of course. Why didn't I tell MI5 he was a spy? And I said what I always say: Guy tried to recruit me in 'thirty-seven, but I wasn't interested. I didn't tell anyone because it wasn't a crime to be a Communist in those days, and later . . . Well, I assumed the Service knew he was working for the Russians.'

'And he said?'

'He said I should be in prison.'

'What else?'

'I'm cold. Can we walk?' He gets to his feet and pulls his sheepskin coat tighter. 'Can't we do this somewhere warmer? The Prince Albert's five minutes away.'

'Too public, and let's keep our minds clear, shall we?'

Rees rolls his eyes. 'Burgess used to say, everyone must believe in something: I believe I'll have another beer.'

'I remember. He loved Marx.'

We set off slowly along the river in the direction of the power station. Through the London plane trees that line the terrace, I can see columns of steam and smoke rising from the chimneys, and the breeze carries coal dust to us, the taste of the Valleys.

'Blunt was next,' he says. 'Wright wanted to know *all* about Blunt. I said I warned Dick White thirteen years ago but he wouldn't believe me. Old friends, see, Dick and Sir An-tho-ny.' He launches into a bone-shaking cough.

'*Arglwydd!*' Instinctively, I reach over and slap his back. 'Are you all right?'

'Thank you,' he rasps, gazing up at me with watery eyes. 'Margie has made a doctor's appointment for me.'

I nod and look away, a little embarrassed that I've touched him. 'Take your time.'

A string of flat barges is forming in the river for the journey from the power station back to the coal yards downstream, and a bargeman is shouting instructions to the tug at the head of the line. I can't make sense of what he says but I hear the anxiety in his voice. *Brother, I know how you feel.*

'It was rank hypocrisy,' says Rees, when he can. 'You and the others turned on me because I told the truth about Guy. Bad form to tell the truth. The establishment closing ranks – all very English. But you, Harry . . .'

'Come on! You were Guy's talent-spotter. You were afraid someone would point the finger at *you*.'

'I gave him nothing.'

'So you say,' I snap, 'so you say. What about Wright? There's more, isn't there?'

'He showed me some names.'

'Who?'

'Oxford people: Hampshire, Zaehner, Bowra, the Harts, Isaiah Berlin – Berlin! Imagine. A man who escaped from Soviet persecution – I told him it was ridiculous.'

'Jenifer Hart?'

'Yes. Jenifer Hart. I said, "I barely know her," which is true.'

'Did Guy know her?'

'He may have.'

'Who else?'

'You know how it works. Guy warned me to keep away from other Party members or I would come to the attention of Five. I kept my distance.'

'Pool? Did he mention Phoebe Pool?'

'Yes.'

'Elsa?'

He pulls a face. 'Yes. I told him that was nonsense. Absolute nonsense.'

'Did he ask you about me?'

'And I said that was rubbish, too, that you were amazed when it all came out that Guy was spying for the Russians.'

'Sure?'

'Yes, Harry. Yes. That's what I said . . . Look, do you have another cigarette?'

'With that cough?' I offer him my packet. 'Keep them all, if you like' – and he lifts his chin in a small gesture of thanks, the fag already tight to the corner of his mouth.

'Tell me what he wanted to know about Elsa.'

'Did I know her at Oxford, who were her friends, did I see her at Party meetings. I told him, "I didn't go to them." That sort of thing . . .'

'And Hampshire, Zaehner, what about the others?'

'Well, I couldn't retract my earlier statements.' He hesitates. 'I *did* mention a couple of names again.'

I groan.

'But not Elsa's,' he says hurriedly. 'Of course not.'

'Listen to me!' I reach for his arm. 'Listen. Wright will be back, and when he does contact you, say you can't help him with anything else. You hear? Not just for friends, for *your* sake, and Margie's.'

'I hear you, yes.' Our eyes meet as I search for the truth in his face. 'I'm sick of all this,' he says. 'I was in hospital, you know. Broke down at the table in front of the children. Couldn't stop crying. I want it to go away. You, too. I want *you* to go away.'

'*Gwnaf, wrth gwrs.*' I feel suddenly sorry for him and squeeze his arm, because it won't go away, no matter how many anti-Communist pieces he writes for *Encounter* magazine. 'Listen to me. You remember this proverb? *Po callaf y dyn, anamlaf ei eiriau.'*

He smiles. 'The wiser the man, the fewer his words. Do *you* remember those evenings at the Gargoyle with Dylan? The words that were spoken there.'

We walk back to the park gates and, because I must have some faith in him again, I agree to buy him a drink at the Prince Albert. For an hour I listen to his opinions on everything from the war in Vietnam to contemporary poetry, and he expresses them with his usual passion and colour. But I can't be sure he holds any of them with great sincerity, except perhaps when he turns the conversation to his latest piece on the evils of Soviet socialism for *Encounter.* Then he speaks with the zeal of the convert and I am reminded of something Isaiah Berlin said many years ago, at one of the public meetings Rees used to address or at one of his All Souls soirées. 'Goronwy,' Berlin whispered, leaning close to my ear, 'is a man who lets things happen to him.'

It's eight o'clock in the evening when I deliver him at the barge. I watch him struggling to keep his balance on the pontoon, straighten his back and take a last few delicate steps to the gangway. Ever-vigilant Margie must have heard him approach because she appears in an elegant evening dress and I hear her say, 'Oh, Gony, we were supposed to be at Freddie's an hour ago.'

And I leave him to make peace with his wife and walk home to mine.

# 23

# 25 May 1964

POSH GILLY IN the D Branch pool takes pity and brings me a cup of tea with two aspirin. I'm at my desk with my head in my hands when Wright walks in with the news that Pest Control has found fifty bugs in the walls of the American Embassy in Moscow. The Russians built the place – 'With our compliments, Comrade' – and now the CIA will have to take it apart. Peter Wright has spoken to Angleton. 'He gave me his sermon about the constant n-n-need for vigilance,' he says. He makes no mention of our clash on the doorstep of the Courtauld, and I'm in no mood for a resumption of hostilities. We simply leave it hanging in the air, like a smell we're too polite to mention.

The following day he meets Blunt alone, and twice more over the next week. I listen to the tapes and hear nothing of importance, but Blunt's fancy French clock strikes nine at one of their sessions and ten just five minutes later. What passes between them in the missing hours when the machine is switched off I can only imagine.

Arthur Martin returns on the glorious first of June to resume the lead role in the investigation. A fortnight with Mrs Martin has done nothing to improve his temper. I listen to him bullying Blunt for some detail that might identify the mole at the top of MI5 without success. Either he doesn't know or he isn't going to tell, and short of pulling his nails out we're unlikely to discover which is the case. Martin is close to acknowledging it, I think, because he talks of stripping the bones of his other carcasses. His chief suspects remain the same. Mitchell must be brought back for interrogation at once, he says, and now his feud with Hollis is out in the open he isn't afraid to discuss him with the inquiry team too. 'But we can't touch him,' he says, 'not just yet.'

Martin flies to Paris to have another crack at Cairncross on the fifteenth, and I take the opportunity his absence presents to join my erstwhile companions at Six in exile across the river. My stuff is in boxes in a sweaty little office ten floors below our chief, our Moses, and it is there that Elliott finds me, gazing out of the window at the trains rattling into Waterloo.

'The spycatcher,' he says. 'Spycatcher, you couldn't have timed your visit to us better!'

He means he has tickets for the Test at Lord's, and in the spirit of the 'good old days' he would like me to escape with him. 'Kim would never miss a Test if he was in town,' he says in the cab. 'I suppose you've heard? He's persuaded his wife to join him in Moscow. She's gone. Flown east. Just like that.'

Nick's still in mourning; perhaps he always will be.

Trueman takes his fifth wicket, the Australians are in trouble at 88 for 6, and for once the cricket is genuinely exciting, when Nick leans so close he catches my head with the frame of his glasses. 'Anthony Blunt . . . Is it true?'

I ignore him.

'That's an affirmative,' he says.

Australia are out for 176, but Dexter falls second ball of the England innings. When the umpires call stumps we retreat to the members' bar for drinks with old 'friends'. But Nick wants to go somewhere quieter, and after half an hour we take a cab to his club. White's is a club for proper gentlemen, and every time I visit I feel an urge to do something that marks me out as quite the opposite. Elliott guides me to a discreet corner. One whisky, two whiskies, and he tries to pump me for the Blunt story and the latest on the PETERS investigation. By number three he is doing all the talking, and everything is bad. 'We're all to pieces,' he says. 'Thank God Maurice Oldfield is coming home.' Fourth whisky, and finally I learn that Dick is putting Nick out to pasture: director of paperclips and telling lies to Whitehall.

'How's the wife, old boy?' he slurs. 'By Jove, you're lucky.'

'Fine, Nick.'

The head porter doesn't bat an eye when I deliver Nick to a rout chair in the hall. 'Leave him with me, sir,' he says, and I'm glad to: I'm struggling to walk a straight line too.

Umbrellas in Piccadilly, the pavements are glistening, but it was only a shower, and the air is fresh and pleasantly cool for June in the city. Lights burning brightly in the mansions at the edge of the park draw the eye. The staff of a well-known weekly have moved into Spencer House, which is very grand, and I wonder if I can persuade its editor to give me a desk beneath a crystal chandelier and an account for business lunches at Rules or the Ritz. I stop to light a cigarette, and am leaning towards the flame when a nasty tingle shoots down my spine. Is someone following me? But it may be the booze. I walk on, and only pause again when I reach The Mall. The quickest way home is by St James's Park and the footbridge across the lake. Determined to wage war on my own imagination, I take it, soberer with every step, the chill of apprehension clearing the whisky from my mind, like smoke in a gale. Middle-aged adulterers canoodle on a wet bench, and I pass a couple in evening dress, who are quite as drunk as me, but no one with a broad

Slavic face, no one with special-forces shoulders, or even a shadow on a parallel path through the trees.

I stop just short of the bridge to grind my cigarette underfoot, and that's when I catch sight of him, edging along the path as if he's distracted by more than me. Something of his silhouette, the way he moves . . . Our paths have crossed before, only I don't have time to concentrate on anything more than finding a well-lit street, and then the next. Birdcage Walk, cut through to Queen Anne's Gate. Almost closing time at the Old Star, and 54 Broadway Buildings is just around the corner, but the magic, the old protective circle, has moved south of the river. My best bet is New Scotland Yard, where I can flash my card at a constable and complain of inappropriate advances: 'A Russian gentleman? Are you sure, sir?'

Not sure enough, which is why I walk on to busy Victoria Street. 'Come on! Remember Vienna?' I say to myself, and because I'm a silly sod who's spent a lifetime taking risks I take this one, too.

No one in close-shuttered Westminster would lift a hand to help me, and I must assume he knows where I live and will try to intercept me before I can shut the door in his face. So I quicken my pace, turning from Great Smith to Little Smith, to Great Peter, until I'm almost in sight of the house. Then he comes slapping towards me. I glance over my shoulder and know it's too late. Time only to slip between cars, make it harder for him to use his superior reach and weight. But he darts forward too, catches me while I'm turning to confront him and grips my arm: 'Sir! It's me. Clive.'

'Clive!' For it is he. '*Uffar gwirion*! Christ, Clive, I'm fifty.'

Clive from Stoke, the head of my old watch team. Clive with the chipped face, who was in the forces, then Special Branch, and has shoulders the width of a sports car. Clive, as charmless as a Staffordshire Bull Terrier, but revoltingly successful with women, boasts of losing his virginity at fourteen and is sleeping with the pretty girl who works in admin at Five's garage in Battersea. The Clive who will kick down my door one day, sit on me, then ask me to come quietly.

'Sorry,' he whispers.

'Bloody hell, boy, you scared the life out of me.'

He looks puzzled.

'Doesn't matter,' I snap at him. 'What do you want?'

'Is there somewhere we can talk?'

It's after eleven o'clock and I'm drunk. A cold fear sweat is pricking my body and all I want to do is sleep, so can it wait? Clive doesn't think so. He whispers, 'Urgent,' and 'Trouble.' He doesn't know what to do. I'm not sure he'll get any sense from me, but I agree to listen, and am on the point of inviting him into my home when I come to my senses. I must keep him away from Elsa. Clive and men like him are Vienna in the forties and SUBALTERN. Memories would spiral through our nice little drawing room, like threads of autumn leaves on an icy breeze.

We walk instead to the gardens near Parliament and gaze across the river. Clive flicks his cigarette butt into its waters and rumples his hair. 'I'm tired of being a pavement artist,' he explains. 'It was a chance to improve my technical knowledge.' Clive is doing dirty tricks for Five now. Only yesterday he was on a job at an art institute in Portman Square. He says he put a couple of bugs into the wall of a bloke called Blunt. Big pat on the back from Peter Wright, appreciation, respect, and here's something else you can do. Clive bites his lip, still uncertain whether he should say. Tell a man like Clive some old nonsense is a secret and he'll promise to take it to his grave.

'Whatever it is, I'm against it,' I say.

He looks perplexed.

'A joke. Marx – Groucho Marx.'

'Ah.'

'Come on, then, spit it out. It isn't anything to do with bugging my house, is it?'

He thinks I'm joking and tries to smile. 'It's difficult. Peter says C has given him clearance. But you'd know, wouldn't you?'

I drop my cigarette. 'Know what?'

'It's like this . . . Peter wants me to break into the director general's personal office. Sir Roger Hollis's office! Sod it, Harry, what do I do?'

Poor Clive. For his benefit I frown; a smile would confuse him even more. Clive, you have stumbled into the wilderness of mirrors. Before I do this to you, my sympathy.

'What do you do?' I gaze down at the dark river, swirling, eddying, at the turn of the tide. 'You've told me, that's enough. Just do as he says, Clive.'

# 24

# 16 June 1964

W RIGHT PUTS HIS head round my door at a little after seven the following evening. 'Leo Long . . . D-d-do you remember when he left the Commission in Berlin?'

'I'm afraid I don't. Try Evelyn.'

He nods. 'Queen of the Files!' Then he asks me if I'm working late. Why? Because there is something he would like to share with me. Only on reflection it can wait until morning.

'All right, Peter,' I say, lifting my jacket from the chair. 'First thing tomorrow.'

A few minutes later I walk out of the building and into a shower of rain. One of the older Registry ladies is struggling to open an umbrella. 'Not much of a summer,' I say, and she smiles, pleased that someone above the ground floor has taken the trouble to notice her. I expect you're watching, Peter, and I hope you applaud my gallantry as I take her umbrella and escort her a little way along my usual route home.

I have an hour to waste and I decide to spend it in a comfortable little boozer around the corner in Shepherd Market, where regular Mayfair shopkeepers rub shoulders with some expensive Bo Peeps and their sharp-suited clients. I watch them touch, and listen to their brittle laughter, and I'm reminded of Vienna after the fall, where in the rubble of defeat there was no shame in a mother lifting her skirt to feed her children, and where we played our first cold-war games. Elsa, you were kind to everyone. I was in love with adventure; I was in love with myself; I was in love with you and too stupid to own it, but now I have you I will do anything to keep you.

At just after eight the duty copper in the entrance hall of Leconfield House slides back the glass in his box to check my pass.

'Working late, Mr Vaughan?'

'I am, Bobby.' (That is his name.)

The lifts to the fifth floor are monitored so I take one to the fourth and slip through the nearest emergency door on to a stair.

I have cooked up an excuse but I don't need to serve it. The lights in the director general's Secretariat are off, the desks have been cleared, and all I can hear is the ticking of an electric clock and the rumble of traffic in the streets below. Hollis is probably at his secretary's home, his new deputy may be at his own, and good old clubbable Cumming, the head of D Branch, will be on his third at the Naval and Military. The DG's personal office is at the end of the room so there's time to fire an automatic lock if an intruder with a weapon tries to burst inside. But the right man armed with the right tools could have his door open in a jiffy.

There's a walk-in cupboard in the outer office and I settle on the floor there with an ashtray, rising only occasionally to free my aching muscles. I've smoked half a packet of cigarettes and lived my life twice by the time they put in an appearance. I hear Clive's flat Potteries voice approaching first; he sounds anxious. P-P-Peter is making a great effort to be easy, as if breaking into the director general of MI5's office is quite routine. I hear the tinkle of Clive's instruments, like percussion tuning up for a symphony. They're a hair's breadth away and if they took the trouble to look around they might wonder if the stationery cupboard was on fire. Click. Click. Pause. Click. Clive has it open and in they go. I creep out of my hole.

Wright is sitting at the DG's antique desk, its top drawer open. 'Hello, Peter,' I say, before he can close it. 'Anything interesting?'

'Ch-Christ.' He places a hand on his heart. 'Harry!'

'Your colleague, Harry, yes.'

He wets his lips – 'How on earth. . .?' – and looks pointedly at Clive. Poor Clive. His bag of tricks is open on the polished mahogany conference table. For a moment he looks bewildered, then plain furious. I feel obliged to say, 'Nothing to do with Clive,' even though we all know it's a lie.

'Bloody stupid, Peter. You'll kiss goodbye to your pension if this comes out.'

'C-come on, Harry. R-R-Roger's one of our chief suspects. We have evidence . . .'

'What evidence?' The drawer in front of him is completely empty.

'M-M-Mitchell's office . . .' he says, struggling to overcome his stutter. 'R-Roger had time to clear it – remove the copy camera from the bottom drawer.'

I laugh, because he's talking about those bloody marks in the dust again.

'R-Roger has questions to answer,' he says defiantly, 'and I'm happy to discuss them, only this isn't the place.'

Clive is packing away his instruments. 'Lock up and go home,' I say. 'This isn't going to blow back on you, is it, Peter?' Wright glares at me over his glasses. He would toss me from the window if he could but he's a technician so no one taught him how to. Clive, on the other hand . . . We leave him to spring-clean the DG's office and make our way in silence to D3. I refuse a drink and a chair. No bonhomie, Peter, no insidious attempt to rope me into your conspiracy, please.

'You always define a man by his friends, Harry,' he says, as if counter-intelligence was his life's work, not bugs and batteries. 'R-Roger is trying to kill this investigation, cover it all up. Why?'

I don't know if he has more than dust in a drawer. I *do* know I don't want to debate it with him now. 'Does Dick White know?'

He hesitates. 'Of our concerns, yes.'

'Our concerns' means that Arthur Martin has carried them across the Atlantic.

'You've broken into the DG's office, Peter. How can I be sure you're not the mole?' He opens his mouth to protest but I don't give him a chance. 'I'll talk to Dick in the morning.'

He twitches nervously – 'If you must' – but his expression is one of 'damn you' insolence. An end to pretence, we can't stand each other.

'Good night,' I say. He doesn't reply.

Tonight I run through the security routine in my own office with just a little more care. When I'm satisfied I've battened everything tightly I ring the duty officer at MI6 on the scrambler phone and write myself into Dick's diary. Elsa was expecting me an hour ago, but my head is so thick with third-floor intrigue I walk home across the parks. Quicker, slower, stopping to light a cigarette, I take no notice of the time or if I have company. From St James's to Birdcage Walk, then into the lane that cuts up to Queen Anne's Gate – and it's there he comes at me, jumping out of the shadow beneath a scaffolding rig to catch me one on the temple with a piece of wood. Down I go and roll, just quick enough to avoid a flying kick in the ribs. He's in a black balaclava and mac but was in too much of a hurry to change his shoes. Such a basic mistake. The tradecraft instructors at the Fort would crucify you, Clive, and I would like to tell you so, only this time you manage to plant your shoe in my stomach and I'm gasping, and the pavement cracks are spinning. Driven only by instinct, I grab his ankle and try to haul him down. But he has twenty years on me, he's stronger, and he lifts me by the collar and swings a fist into my face.

Now I'm conscious of my cheek against the kerb and something splashing my neck and head. The lights must have gone out for a moment because he has me pinned to the floor with his foot, and – *cachgi!* – he is pissing on me. Flailing at his leg with my fist I throw him off balance and roll a few feet away. I expect him to boot me again, but he doesn't. A young couple are cowering at the railings on Birdcage Walk, too shocked to come to my aid. Nevertheless, their presence is enough. 'Yes, that's enough.' I have to spit blood from my mouth before I can shout it again. 'Enough, Clive! Sod off!'

He flinches but says nothing, only turns and walks quickly away.

'My God!' Elsa clamps her hand across her mouth. Then she holds me very gently and steers me to the drawing-room couch. 'Oh, Harry.' Her hands are trembling and she chinks the whisky bottle on the rim of the glass. 'You must see a doctor.'

'No, *cariad,* no real damage.' (Except to my pride.)

'What's that smell?' she says, and I am obliged to own my humiliation. She wants to know more besides and is angry when I refuse to tell her. 'Nothing or lies,' I say, 'to protect you.'

'No lies,' she says.

By the morning everything aches. In the taxi across the river to Six, I consider what I should do with Clive. He's a hood, Clive, and always will be. Only he came to me with a confidence and I broke it because it was too important to keep, and now Wright will kick him back on to the street. That will be punishment enough.

'What happened to you?' the friends say, when they see my face.

'Fell among thieves,' my reply, and they know better than to ask me more.

Dora Edwards brings me tea with an extra sugar. 'He knows you're here,' she says.

I take a seat in Dick's outer office and dream of cool green places. Half an hour later, I'm still waiting.

'*You* still love me, don't you, Dora? I *wasn't* drunk. These bruises will fade.'

'All right, I'll remind him.'

But first she applies more lipstick, checks her hair, smoothes imaginary creases from her skirt. Only then does she knock lightly at his door and enter.

*Dora and Dick*: it's Mills & Boon. No sex, of course: that's too preposterous to contemplate. She returns just a minute later with a sweet smile of success.

Dick doesn't look at me, only gestures at a chair. I watch him scratching away with his pen and remember Burgess and the barons called him 'the Schoolmaster' long before he took over the running of the school. Hands folded demurely in my lap like a Goody Two Shoes, I wait for some sympathy. When will he deign to acknowledge me?

'I suppose you were drunk,' he says, with disgust.

'What a suggestion.'

He gives me a level blue stare, and the sun that was pouring through the many windows of his new office slips behind a cloud.

'This I suffered in the line of duty,' I say.

He puts down his pen. 'All right, let's hear it.'

So I tell him: an officer of Her Majesty's Security Service tried to burgle its director general and he used Dick's name to persuade a grunt in A Branch to help him with the necessaries. That man was Peter Wright. And I tell him that Martin and Wright are a law unto themselves. No one else knows where the PETERS investigation is going, except Angleton, because they're his followers and they would tear the bloody place apart for him. I don't tell Dick how I got the bruises; he doesn't seem curious to know. Pushing his chair away he steps over to the window and gazes out across the slate, perhaps to blue remembered hills. It's something he does when you bring him trouble.

'If you knew Peter was going to burgle Roger, why didn't you stop him?' he says at last. 'Why didn't you speak to Arthur?'

'I'm speaking to you, sir.'

'No, Harry, you wanted to catch him out.'

'Does it matter how I went about it?'

Dick turns and stands with his hands resting on the high back of his chair. 'Peter overstepped the mark,' he says coolly, 'but taking it any further than a reprimand will serve no purpose.'

My turn to stare. 'Further' means to Hollis. 'Further' means he wants to bury it. Why? He's no rule-breaker, he has no time for the robber barons, and Hollis was his choice to take the helm at Five. I watch him pick up a piece of paper from his desk and pretend to scrutinise it. Then his gaze lifts furtively over the top of it to me. 'Anything else?'

Oh yes there is, Lord, yes. I once was blind but now I see. 'You've spoken to Martin.'

He drops the paper back on his desk. 'Arthur rang me last night. Told me Peter had made a grave error of judgement but it won't happen again, and that he needs Peter on his investigation team.'

'Bloody hell! I expect it was Martin's idea to break into the DG's office in the first place.'

Dick ignores me. 'Roger should have let Arthur interrogate Mitchell. It was a mistake to shelter him.'

I laugh.

'There are questions,' he says defensively. 'The Americans want us to consider *all* the possibilities.'

'Are you going to tell Sir Roger he's a suspect?'

'No, and he isn't. This is as far as it goes – for now. Is that clear? Not a word.'

'Perfectly,' I snap at him. 'Couldn't be clearer.'

Dick drops back into his chair and plants his elbows on the desk, his hands clasped in a big fist. 'You've dragged your feet on this since the start, Harry.'

'That's from Martin.'

'It's from me!'

'Really?' I drawl.

'Who the hell do you think you're talking to?' he says, and he bangs that big fist on the table so hard a cloud rises from the ashtray and settles like fallout on his papers and the sleeve of his blue linen jacket. 'Roger's a suspect because we all are.'

'You asked me to be a small voice of calm, and to keep an eye on Arthur. He's obsessive – you said so yourself.'

'I remember what I said!' There's a very un-Dick-like bubble of saliva at the corner of his mouth and he clears it with a knuckle. 'All right, you've said your piece. Get out.'

*Cer i grafu.* I *haven't* said my piece yet. It's quite simple, just one word. I catch him with it as he's rising to show me the door: 'OATSHEAF.' He closes his eyes and inclines his head as if I've caught him very low: I have.

'You're prepared to let them investigate the leader of the Labour Party?'

'Who told you?'

'Angleton.'

'I see.' He eases back into his seat a second time. 'It seems preposterous, I know, but we have to consider the Russians have agents of influence everywhere.'

'Golitsyn says so.'

'And others. I know a bit more about this than you do,' he declares tartly. 'Let me put it this way . . . Gaitskell's death was suspicious. I don't say more than that. It's facts I'm interested in. Harold Wilson became leader of the Labour Party on the death of his predecessor. Fact. A highly placed KGB defector . . .'

'Golitsyn.'

'Christ, yes. Golitsyn says Wilson's a Russian agent. Fact. So we keep an open mind.'

An open mind? 'Have you seen the opinion polls?'

'Of course I have!' He looks nervous and he should be. Turning politicians over is something they do in Moscow and in banana republics. 'We're checking to satisfy the Americans,' he says, as if the order has come from the president, when the only person he must satisfy is Angleton.

'Roger knows about OATSHEAF. It's for his people to sort out,' Dick says – a little desperately, I think.

'Right.' I frown and touch my lip to demonstrate to him how bewildering it seems to be. 'But isn't Roger a suspect, too? DG *and* prime-minister-to-be . . . We've lost the cold war already.'

I shut the door quietly with his parting shot ringing in my ears: 'Not a word to anyone.' Anyone means anyone but especially Elsa. If OATSHEAF goes off in Whitehall we'll have to scrape Dick and Roger off the walls. Half an hour later, I'm still in the building talking expenses with the personnel people when one of the girls from the top floor sidles up to me with a message from Dick: he wants to see me again. This time Dora Edwards barely lifts her eyes from her typewriter. (How does she know?) I'm to go straight in, she says. Half an hour later I step out on a one-way ticket back to Vienna. Just a few months, he says, to bring home a Hungarian colonel. Someone who knows the lie of the land there, he says. What he doesn't say but we both know to be true is that he doesn't trust me any more. I'm out in the cold.

# 25

## 20 August 1964

Lukas, the corporal in Watchtower 9 near Čížov, was surprised when a portly colonel of the border guard appeared at dusk on the longest day. The colonel was alone and on foot when colonels generally like to travel in big cars and with an entourage. He was even more astonished when the colonel pulled a gun on him.

Towers are manned by two guards: a conscript who can never be relied upon, and a regular with a machine gun who must be. Lukas was a regular, but not a good comrade. An informer overheard him complaining about the 'Party Hitlers' who refused his wife treatment for cancer in Brno – now she was dead. That was why the colonel had chosen number 9. The field police were coming to arrest Lukas, he said, if not tomorrow, some time soon. The choice was simple: through the wire to the West or a secret policeman's cell. Lukas didn't hesitate. What was more, he persuaded the conscript who was on duty with him to come too.

From the last dark fringe of trees in Austria I watched them march along the guard road. Beyond it there's a control strip lit by arc lights, a ditch and anti-personnel mines suspended on a wire fence. But my reception party had prepared everything. The colonel came to a halt directly opposite the hole we had cut for him and began to lecture Lukas on security. To make his point he stepped over the tripwire into the control strip.

The guards in the adjoining watchtowers will have slipped the catches on their automatic weapons. A sudden movement and BANG. I've seen it happen twice: one wounded and hanging on the wire, one dead. But I had a good feeling about the colonel. He walked across the control strip with the proprietorial air of a country squire at a pheasant shoot, trailing Lukas and the conscript after him, like faithful retainers. Shots were fired at the last to be sure, but well wide of their marks, and I guess they were meant to be.

And now Colonel Buky is living in a safe house in a smart district of Vienna. He wants to get drunk, he wants to get laid, he wants *schillings*, lots of them, and a home in the country, but he has only snippets of intelligence that might be of use to the military to offer in exchange: just the location of a few tanks here, a few planes there, a new piece of kit. We processed hundreds of men like the colonel after the rising in Hungary in '56. The border was a simple wire fence in those days – so the Commies could roll through the rest of Europe, the hawks in Washington said. We're still preparing for that invasion, even though we know they're not coming.

When the girls visit I'll take them to the border and name the spirals of smoke rising from the villages on the other side: 'Girls, this is a quiet part of the line.' Here, our agents and their agents go about the routine business of sowing mistrust, and the only casualty is truth. The real battle is fought in places like Vietnam, where people run around paddy fields with Kalashnikovs. Forget historical materialism and dialectical materialism: those people are fighting for freedom from poverty. One day freedom may have its day, but for now Eastern Europe belongs to Russia, and Western Europe is marking time, and all we can do is hope the ideologues on both sides who want to win the war tomorrow don't turn the world into a nuclear desert.

Tonight I will take Colonel Buky to a bar near the Stephansplatz U-Bahn station that I used to frequent when the war was a great deal hotter. It's glitzy and expensive and it will be full of summer tourists, but that's the sort of freedom he craves. Back in the day, the floor of the Casa Nova was so packed with couples it was impossible to do more than wiggle. The jazz was decadent, the hot licks sung in German, and when the power was cut we would kiss by candlelight. A CIA officer I liked told me it was the best jive joint he knew, and he was from Chicago. From time to time its proprietor let me join the band to play my version of 'St Louis Blues', and if the KGB was in the house the musicians would warn me by striking up 'Hold That Tiger'.

In those days Vienna was divided into zones of occupation, but the KGB was everywhere. I was on nodding terms with a few of its officers. Angleton says Golitsyn was here; I don't remember his name. My job, as always, was to recruit and run agents, and the challenge in a city full of charlatans and hucksters was knowing whom to trust. Real or fool's gold? SUBALTERN was genuine 22-carat. Elsa talent-spotted its members in the city's refugee camps, home to hundreds of thousands of Hungarians, Poles, Czechs, Ukrainians and Russian exiles. Later, we worked together, and we met our contacts in the corners of the Casa Nova.

I have booked the Park Hotel near the Schönbrunn Palace because I made love to Elsa for the first time in Room 52. Once they've dumped their luggage it's out in the car for the 'This is Vienna' tour. Elsa tries to paint a picture of the city after the Nazis, but the girls are only interested in the best places to shop, and can they see the horses at the Spanish Riding School? 'You're hoping to go to Oxford,' I shout over my shoulder to Bethan. 'Students were more curious in my day.' We drive past the vast Gothic town hall that escaped the wartime bombing, and the Parliament building that didn't, the university, palaces, museums, squares so complete Elsa is struggling to find her bearings. Her city was a dark shell. At the Prater we ride the giant ferris wheel, and I tell the girls about the making of a film called *The Third Man*.

We don't talk properly until Bethan and Mary have gone to bed. I want to make love; Elsa wants to walk. Late-summer sultry at ten o'clock, the streets are deserted this far from the city centre. A prosperous district of parks and villas, popular with rich Jewish families before the Nazis took control of the state. After the war the British Control Commission ran its sector from a bleak grey barracks building just up the road from the hotel. I had an office overlooking the courtyard; Elsa was on the floor above. The place reeked of cabbage and disinfectant. Senior army officers had rooms in the Schönbrunn, and there were refugees in the gardens. That was where Elsa met Béla Bajomi.

We did a lot of business with émigré groups in those days. Nazis and their collaborators, pimps and cheats, we soon discovered a good many of them were working with the Russians. Anything we got in the way of intelligence was treated as suspect and classified Mauve. But Béla Bajomi was one of the good guys, and as we walk away from the old barracks buildings I'm sure he's in Elsa's thoughts.

Béla was a Hungarian businessman, a former naval officer, and a devout anti-Communist who managed to escape to Vienna beneath a train. Elsa was a familiar face in émigré circles; it didn't take Béla long to find her. 1947. The countries behind the new Iron Curtain were becoming Communist satellite states. Vienna station was preparing for war. We were working with our contacts to bury arms caches for a resistance movement to fight Uncle Joe Stalin if he decided to seize the country. There were some crazy ideas kicking around at that time.

The Russians controlled all the roads into Vienna and they were turning the screw. The KGB kidnapped opponents from the streets and drove them to a firing squad. Béla Bajomi wanted to fight back. The Americans offered him more money but Béla wanted to work with Elsa. They began to build the network we called SUBALTERN. Men like Paul Lovas who worked for one of the new Communist ministries in Budapest and could travel for us on an official pass. He would note down the size and disposition of the Soviet forces he saw on white chemical carbon paper, write something to his imaginary girlfriend in regular ink over the top, and post it to one of our letterboxes in Vienna. SUBALTERN grew and grew. Béla and Elsa were running couriers in and out of Hungary every day. London was impressed and pushed us for more.

'Enough walking?' I say, when we reach the gates of Meidling Cemetery. It's after eleven and we're a long way from the hotel. 'We could catch the last tram?'

'I'm forty-six,' she says.

'And as beautiful as you've ever been.' I squeeze her tightly.

'But what do I have to show for the years, Harry?'

'A career. A husband – a poor one, I grant you. The love of two girls – Bethan's devoted to you. I am. We all are.'

She tries to smile. 'This city makes me sad.'

We catch the tram to the hotel and we make love, and when it's over and her head is resting on my arm we talk about the future. 'Leave the Service,' she says again. 'It's enough. Take the job on the *Economist*.'

'If Dick doesn't call me back, I will,' I say.

'No, Harry, *now*. The girls need you at home,' she says. 'I need you.'

I wake in the early hours aware that she's stirring, rise to my elbow and sweep a strand of hair from her cheek. Is she crying?

'Of course not,' she says. She turns her head and I kiss her. 'I'm fine,' she whispers. 'Go back to sleep.'

The next day we visit more palaces and churches, and watch the horses prancing at the riding school, and for lunch we take a picnic to a wood south-west of the city. I tell the girls I buried treasure there, only I've forgotten precisely where. 'You don't believe me? Ask Elsa, she never lies.'

'Didn't you dig it up?' She remembers we were caching a wireless and weapons to fight the Russians.

'I don't think we did.'

On the way into the city we pass the Hotel Imperial, freshly painted yellow and white, and quite as magnificent as it must have looked in the last days of the Habsburg Empire when Hitler was employed to shovel the snow from the pavement in front of its entrance. It was KGB headquarters after the war. I glance at Elsa in the passenger seat beside me, and I know she is thinking of Paul Lovas too.

Everyone assumes we were betrayed by a double. Someone local, we said. Elsa got a call from Béla Bajomi: one of his men had been lured to a rendezvous and bundled into a car with Russian plates. Elsa put everyone on notice: no blind dates, two people to every meet, new safe houses, and what we now call Moscow Rules. The following day, two more sub-agents went missing and there was no sign of the courier from Budapest. We met Béla at the Casa Nova. Elsa held his hand and pleaded with him not to do anything foolish. But later that evening he received a tip-off that the Russians were holding his men in the American Zone. The anonymous caller proposed meeting to organise a rescue. Béla left us a note: *Es muß sein.* It must be. By the time we received the note he was in the hands of the KGB.

Many months later we heard from someone who had spoken

to him in prison. Béla arrived at the rendezvous at a little before eleven o'clock. The street was badly knocked about in the fighting before the fall of the city and only a block from the Russian Zone. First rule of Moscow Rules: pick the time and the place. Second rule: don't ignore your instinct, because if it feels wrong, it is wrong. Everything about the meeting was screaming, 'Trap.' Béla heard Russian voices in the apartment but it was too late. They burst through the door and from the one behind him too. A KGB thug punched him in the face, another tried to gag him with a cloth, and he heard someone say, 'Now we have you as well. You're the real prize.'

They rounded up the entire network – and the brothers, sisters, friends and girlfriends of its members – at least a hundred people. Elsa had done her best to train our agents, but it was never going to be good enough. They were postmen, bakers, doctors, civil servants, and we exploited them because that's what we do. They were tortured, and they suffered until they could suffer no more. Then they sang.

'Tell them we were betrayed by someone in the British Intelligence Service,' Béla Bajomi said to a comrade before he died. It took years for the message to reach me. Elsa was at the War Office, and our relationship that had seemed so necessary was no longer necessary. She couldn't forgive herself or the Service, and I belonged to the Service. We have been great users of people.

'Your father says he's coming home soon, girls,' she declares at dinner.

'As soon as I can.'

'Which will be *very* soon, won't it?' she says.

The girls don't appear to care one way or the other. Mary wants a cigarette. I tell her she's too young, and Elsa dips into her handbag for a packet. Bethan presses me for an increase in her allowance; Elsa urges me to pay more. The dinner table is a battlefield. The girls are veterans of marriage break-up and show great flair in playing us off against each other.

'Can we talk about it?' I say.

'Why?' she replies. 'There's nothing more to say.'

Sunday morning at six, and I wake to find her lacing a pair of flat walking shoes. 'I've ordered a taxi.'

I feel a sudden chill. 'To the airport?'

'The airport?' She laughs and leans over the bed to kiss me. 'No, Harry, not yet,' she says, 'but if you don't leave the Service . . .'

I ask her to wait for me, but she slips out of the room while I'm having a pee. The young lad at the front desk says the taxi is taking her to the Zentralfriedhof on the other side of the city. It's the largest cemetery in Austria, a place of pilgrimage for music lovers who pay homage with flowers to Beethoven and Brahms and Schubert and at least a dozen other composers. A great-uncle of Elsa's is buried beneath a wall of ivy, not far from Johannes Brahms. At this hour on a Sunday it will take me twenty-five minutes. The graves of those the state wishes to honour are to the right of the main gate, the Jews and the Evangelicals to the left. I will turn left through a choir of marble angels and obelisks, following signs for burial group 64, where the cheap stones are lost in a sea of long grass.

The KGB dumped Paul Lovas's body in the ruins of the old Westbahnhof because the station was on our doorstep. It was covered with welts and bruises from many hours of excruciating pain. I expect he told them everything he knew in the first few minutes, but torturers never hear the truth if it comes easily. They wanted him to suffer and they wanted us to know he suffered. Paul was just eighteen. An official from the local Communist Party broke the news to his mother in Budapest. She was refused permission to attend her son's funeral. Punish 'the traitor', punish his family: that's the Russian way. *Sippenhaftung* in German: the family must pay. His comrades in the network were dead or in jail so we were left to dispose of his body.

I park in front of the monumental mason's yard where I ordered Paul's stone all those years ago. There's nobody about at this hour but the keepers have opened the cemetery gates. A low sun catches beads of late-summer dew and it glistens, like a dragon's hoard, in the grass. White-stone lovers cling to each other in a perpetual embrace, a small child cries over the corpse of a dove, and I wonder that the Austrians are more imaginative in death than I find them to be in life. At the junction of grave groups 25 and 26, I turn right at a Greek temple tomb, pockmarked in the last days of fighting, and follow the wall of the Evangelicals' cemetery.

Elsa is bent over the stone. Where did she find the dark blue headscarf? The pink carnations are from the vase at hotel Reception. Too late to turn back now, or ever, and where better to reflect upon that than a necropolis, among stained stone images of a saviour who watched impassively as the Jews of Vienna were sent to the gas chambers and the city burned in the Blitz, and where a good Catholic boy screamed for mercy but found none.

She's busy clearing ivy from the small cross we set upon his grave and doesn't hear me approach.

'I would have driven you.'

She doesn't flinch or turn, just tears at the ropes of ivy, and as it comes away it leaves welts upon the white marble. She brought lilies to Paul's funeral and a priest to say prayers. I remember how the nuggets of frozen earth bounced and rattled the lid of his coffin.

'The guilt, the shame of it . . . It will never leave me.' She places a hand on the cross as she rises.

'I know.'

She turns to me at last. 'Do you?'

'They knew the risks, even Paul.'

'They couldn't imagine they would be betrayed by someone in the British Secret Service.'

'If that's true. The network grew so quickly, some of them were careless . . .'

'That isn't what happened.'

She seems very certain. I don't know why, and I don't care to ask. Instead I say the first anodyne thing that comes into my head: 'It was a tragedy.'

She sighs with exasperation. 'Harry Vaughan, you don't believe in anyone or anything. That's what the Service has done to you.'

'I believe in us.'

'Then leave it, leave it for me.'

'Look at you, *cariad*, here with the dead before breakfast. You never leave.'

Elsa has a way of gazing down at me from five feet four when she's angry, as if she is occupying our old chapel pulpit. When she's sure I know how she feels she lays the carnations on the grave and walks away. I catch her arm, but she wrenches free and shoves me in the chest. Not hard enough, because I'm close enough to put my arms around her. The next thing I know I'm bent double in pain and gasping for breath. Bitch: she's kneed me in the groin. It's enough because she's suddenly sorry and solicitous, yet trying not to laugh. When I catch my breath, I kiss her. 'Look you, I'll tell Dick White I'm going, that it's over,' I say, even though I know it isn't, that it can't be, that I will stay to protect us both, and I'm telling her another lie.

## 26

## *16 September 1964*

T HE DAY AFTER a general election is called I'm summoned to an audience with C. Folk in the corridors of Century House are full of it, naturally. 'Too close to call,' says Tubby Powell in P Section (Eastern Europe).

'The Labour Party by a whisker': McKay in Accounts, gloomy at the prospect.

No one seems happy about it except me.

'So, Mr Wilson may be on his way to Number 10,' I say, so Dick knows I haven't forgotten why I'm in exile.

'Oh, there's still hope': his terse reply.

Only not that much, it seems, or Dick wouldn't be ready to consider returning me to the fold so swiftly.

'Just a few weeks more,' he says, pushing a file across the table to me.

I imagine his few weeks will be the length of the election campaign. 'Elsa wants me to leave the Service,' I say.

'Oh, really?' he drawls, then taps his finger on the file he's just given me. 'Do that first, would you?'

'I told Dick: "I'm ready to renounce my vocation,"' I say to Elsa at dinner later. 'See how much I love you.'

She laughs and leans across the table to kiss me. 'Your vocation for lying. But never mind promises, when, darling, when?'

'Soon.'

The following morning I'm on the flight to Vienna.

Head of Vienna station is a young redbrick Roundhead, schooled to take no risk that will jeopardise his career in the Service. He resents my presence at the embassy greatly. 'I don't know why London wants you to handle this,' he says, 'not after the mess your generation has made of things.' Our great cause is history to him now, we should have faded away, yet here I am with the file C gave me, and responsibility for the station's most promising prospect in years.

His name is Hoffmann and he's a clerk in the security section at the Czech embassy in the city. He approached a British businessman two weeks ago with the usual trade of secrets for asylum, and now the analysts in London have pored over his first offering they're hungry for more. 'Keep him in play,' was Dick's instruction. 'Then you can come home in triumph.'

Our postbox is a Protestant church in the old town. There's a Saturday market outside and its doors are open for stallholders and shoppers to rest and thank their maker. I observe comings and goings in the reflection of a shoe-shop window for a while, then turn with a most pious face to follow an old lady inside. The interior resembles a whitewashed barn with none of the exuberance of the city's famous baroque churches. Hoffmann leaves his messages between the pages of a Luther Bible, five pews from the main altar. He wants a face-to-face and he proposes Friday, 9 October, among the fountains and parterres of the Belvedere palaces.

On the Wednesday before I take my old flame, Nina, to dinner at a cool jazz club in the city. Nina is an honest friend, and a very fine pianist, and I love her for her earnestness because it reminds me of how we were in the thirties. Sometimes when she's serious an evening can drag. I'm not surprised when, after a few drinks, she produces an article on nuclear proliferation that she's cut from the *Süddeutsche Zeitung* and informs me that after much heartache she has decided it would be immoral to conceive children when the world may be obliterated in an apocalypse.

'Oh,' I say. 'Are you going to tell me why?'

Yes, Nina's itching to convince me – and while she talks I watch the thug at the bar who's watching me. I guess he's in his thirties, and very well built, and he's wearing a brown suit, because brown, not red, is the true colour of Communism.

'You see,' she says. 'How can I?'

Poor Nina must bear the war guilt of the nation on her slight shoulders.

The next morning there's a pavement artist outside my flat. He may be Russian, he may be Czech or German. It's a long time since this sort of attention was routine, and the timing is troubling, just as we're preparing to reel in an asset. Outside the embassy, two more goons in a blue Citroën, and there's a clumsy shift change at four o'clock, from which I conclude they're either very poor actors or they want me to be aware of their presence. I consider discussing them with the young station chief but only for a moment. As Marx (Groucho) said, 'He may look like an idiot and talk like an idiot, but don't let that fool you: he really *is* an idiot.' I take a gun home instead, and check my bolts and locks, and when it's time to leave for the rendezvous with Hoffmann I use the fire escape at the rear.

The air is thick with the rich beer of autumn decay. A Friday morning in October, and there are very few visitors to the gardens, only a work gang clearing leaves from the gravel. I wander between knee-high hedges and parterres with my guidebook, pretending to read about the palace, painted fresh cream and white, the nymphs and cherubs and sphinxes restored to their plinths after the ravages of war. From the first formal garden, I turn on to a path between high hedges and walk into the woods on the fringe of the park. Hoffmann has chosen to meet me beside an ornamental pond with fat Muscovy ducks preening at its edge. It's a poor place for a rendezvous and I wonder for the first time if the clerk is being used as bait to lure someone from the Service into a trap – me. This isn't the old Austria of kidnappings and killings that I remember from the forties, but every now and then it happens.

An elderly man – late sixties or seventies – is walking towards the water's edge with the air of someone who is familiar with this place. He has a thin face and a grey Lenin beard, and his clothes, brown suit and fawn cardigan, have seen much better days. From a string bag he takes some crusts and struggles with arthritic fingers to crumble them into pieces. I amble closer and he raises his chin and stares across the slime at me. With a jolt I realise he isn't here for the ducks but for me.

'Hoffmann can't come, Herr Vaughan.' His voice is military and from somewhere in the east. 'But I have come.'

My fingers close round the gun in my coat pocket. 'And who are you?'

He slides his palms together to dust off the breadcrumbs – 'Now I will sit' – and, turning his back to me, he walks over to a bench. 'Join me, please. I have something for you,' and he reaches into his jacket.

'Steady!'

'You are quite safe. A letter. May I?' And he pinches an envelope from his pocket. 'From Otto.'

'Yah, of course. How is Otto?'

'He's worried about you.'

'Good old Otto.'

My new friend leans forward to offer the envelope. 'Please.'

But I've written dozens of captions for pictures of men exchanging packages in parks, and I'm quite sure his photographer is waiting with a lens the length of my arm to snap another. 'You read it to me.'

He raises a thin grey eyebrow. 'If you insist.'

'Oh, I do.'

I watch him slit the envelope with a tobacco-stained nail, then adjust his gold-framed glasses. 'Otto writes: *I send this with an old comrade, Erich* – I am Erich. *Herr Vaughan, your friend Guy spoke of you often. He believed you to be a socialist and a man of peace, and that you would understand the choice he made. It has been so many years, but the struggle is not over, nor your part in it, Comrade.*'

Erich raises his gaze from the letter to study my face.

'Is that all?'

'No, Herr Vaughan. Otto wants to meet you, here in Vienna.' His eyes run down the letter. Then he slips it back inside his jacket. 'The investigation in London . . . he is concerned for your safety.'

That makes me smile. 'Otto who recruited Guy and our other Cambridge comrades, yes? He was good, wasn't he?'

Erich frowns. 'Herr Vaughan . . .'

'But Otto's dead.' I get to my feet. 'Purged. Consumed by his revolution. An enemy of the people in the end.'

'Otto doesn't matter,' he says.

'You're quite right. A bourgeois individualist. So was Guy, by the way.'

'Please sit, Herr Vaughan, we must talk.'

'And, Comrade, your research . . . I never met or spoke to Otto. Be sure to tell whoever sent you that.'

'Please' – he's on his feet too – 'please take this telephone number.'

But I'm walking away, escaping, Muscovy ducks croaking and flapping from my path. Erich isn't KGB. Erich's a fraud – that really does frighten me.

Nevertheless, it's the KGB story I report to London: HOFFMANN BURNED. KGB SEDUCTION. ADVANCES REJECTED.

And London acknowledges. In more enterprising times it would have turned me into a fake defector and 'dangled' me at the KGB – only it wasn't the KGB. Perhaps, Dick, you knew.

By the evening the pavement artists have gone from my street, from the Casa Nova, too. All the same, I keep the gun.

Harold Wilson promises 'fresh and virile leadership', more houses, better health, better education, that everything will be better in a 'new Britain'. 'But it's too close to call,' Elsa says, when I ring her on the eve of the vote, 'and never mind Wilson – what about you? What about us? When are you are coming home?'

The ambassador throws a party for embassy staff on election night and snap reports from the constituencies are run from the communications room to the ballroom. There should be excitement, but it is an entirely dreary affair. The crystal chandeliers are too magnificent, diplomats too careful. The evening is the usual painful waltz from group to group: 'You have a daughter at Cheltenham Ladies? How nice!'

At midnight the ambassador announces he's retiring to his bed to be fresh enough to wrestle with the diplomatic implications of the result, and the embassy sheep stampede after him. I manage to shut the gate on a couple of the livelier third secretaries. 'You can't go before we know it,' I say, taking the seat at the ballroom grand, 'and a party isn't over until I sing.'

'Do you know anything by the Kinks?' someone says.

'Hum a tune, and I'll improvise.'

But the station duty officer closes the lid on my fingers before I have a chance. 'You'd better look at this, Harry,' he says, and hands me a wire from Moscow. The leader of the Soviet Union has 'asked to be relieved of his duties'. Nikita

Khrushchev has gone. Pushed. Because first secretaries of the Communist Party don't walk away from power.

'Will the world be safer?'

'I don't know,' I say.

'Where were you when the balloon nearly went up in Cuba, Harry?'

I send the duty officer to the ambassador and the head of station and order another bottle of wine, because the man who took us to the brink of nuclear annihilation in the missile crisis of '62 is leaving the world stage.

The ambassador appears as I'm entertaining the last of the party people with my sleazy version of the Soviet national anthem. He declares it to be in 'very poor taste'. We are still discussing the implications of the Kremlin coup when we learn of white smoke in London: it's Wilson! Harold has sneaked into Number 10 with a four-seat majority.

The ambassador asks me why I'm laughing, and I would love to tell him just for the expression on his face: *Your Excellency, CIA Counter-intelligence believes a Soviet spy is now running the country.*

Late afternoon, and Friday traffic is bumper to bumper in the street outside the embassy. I'm writing a note for the ambassador on the situation in the Kremlin when the young station chief puts his head around the door. 'What do we know about this new chap, Brezhnev?'

'Ukrainian. A political commissar with the Red Army during the war, and a protégé of Khrushchev: this is a stab in the back.'

'Ah,' he says.

'It's all in my note to the ambassador.'

'Right.'

Half in, half out of my tiny office, he blinks at me through tortoiseshell-framed spectacles, apparently lost for words. My friend, I want to tell you this: it isn't too late to look for an honest job in the civil service or business, or as ambassador to a small African republic – only if I say so you are certain to take offence. 'Well, is there anything else?'

'Oh, yes, there's something from London,' and he passes me a coded wire.

'Do I need to get the book out or are you going to tell me?'

'I don't suppose you do,' he says, with a sixth-form smirk. 'They want you home *tout de suite*.'

# 27

# 24 October 1964

A BEAUTIFUL WOMAN in an emerald green dress and matching shoes is waiting for me in Arrivals. She has changed her hair to a thick shoulder-length curl, like Elizabeth Taylor's, and when she removes her dark glasses I see she's done something with her eyebrows too.

'You look ravishing.'

She smiles mischievously and reaches for the lapel of my jacket. 'No ravishing at the airport.'

'But I can kiss you.' I'm too delirious with happiness to care that we're creating a scene. 'I love you.'

We motor into London in her Sprite and Elsa shouts across the noise of its engine, 'Well, how did you manage it?'

'Change of thinking, *cariad*. You can thank Mr Wilson.'

I can see she isn't inclined to thank anyone. 'You promised to take the job at the *Economist*.'

'I will. Soon.'

'What's wrong with now?'

'Loose ends. Something they need me to do.'

She glances at me. 'Is that true? I think you're afraid to leave.'

I lean sideways and try to kiss her cheek, and she pushes me away. 'Harry! We're going to crash.'

The following day – Sunday – Maurice Oldfield rings me at home and proposes we meet at his club.

'It's your first day back,' says Elsa. 'What about your girls? They're only here for a few hours.'

'I won't be long.'

'What's so important it can't wait for Monday morning?' She sounds anxious.

'Don't worry, it's just how Maurice likes to do things.'

A chat with whisky in convivial surroundings is how my life in the Service began, and I imagine it will end the same way. I'm glad it's with Moulders because he's a civilised man with secrets of his own. Dick has called him from Washington to make him his deputy, which is just about the only sensible thing Dick's done since Philby set us chasing our tails.

The Athenaeum Club is a shining white neoclassical temple dedicated to gentlemen of learning and those with good connections who pretend to it. Lest anyone doubt the serious intent of its founders, there is a gold statue of the goddess of wisdom over the portico, and beneath the cornice, a blue and white frieze of the marbles stolen from the Parthenon by a disreputable member of a less worthy London club. Moulders is a farm-boy scholar, quite comfortable with clever people, but silver-spoon Kim was a member of the Athenaeum too, and even his friends say he's a philistine.

Maurice is waiting on the staircase beneath a marble statue of the naked Apollo. I'm sure no one in the club enjoys a finer appreciation of his divine physique. He greets me warmly but awkwardly, like a teenager on a first date, then leads me into the Morning Room where we sit by a Sunday-in-autumn fire. The steward brings us whisky, and only when we've finished our first and the usual pleasantries does Maurice lean over his broad thighs and say, 'Dick wants you to know the file's closed. There's to be no mention of OATSHEAF.'

'That's understood.'

To be sure it is, he stares at me through his large black-framed glasses, like one of the club's illustrious scientists inspecting a specimen. 'So,' he says, when he's satisfied, 'welcome back to the fold. How long has it been? Three months?'

'Longer. I'm not counting paperclips, Maurice. I want a proper job, my old job.'

'PETERS?'

'It needs someone like me.'

'Oh, you think so?' Maurice strokes the roll of fat beneath his chin where his neck used to be. 'Then you should know there have been changes. There's a new working party, FLUENCY, and Peter Wright's in charge. I don't suppose you consider that a change for the better.'

'What happened to Arthur Martin?'

'Sacked for insubordination. He just about accused the director general of working for the Russians.' He pauses. 'I imagine you think ransacking Roger's desk is an act of insubordination too . . . I advise you to forget it.'

'Does Roger know?'

'No.'

'Dick wants me to forget a lot.'

'Those are his terms. Martin's gone, he doesn't want to lose them both – Jim Angleton won't wear it. You're back because I persuaded Dick you should be – not just me, by the way, Roger wants you inside the investigation, too.' He smirks and leans forward to poke my knee with a forefinger. 'Surprise you?'

I admit it does.

'Roger knows you aren't impressed by the case against Mitchell.'

'Are you?'

He ignores me. 'We need clear thinking, because Dick wants to turn the Service inside out – investigate *every* discrepancy, no matter how small, every lead, every half-baked supposition, every suspicious incident in the history of Soviet intelligence in this country.'

'Sounds like a purge?'

'I wouldn't call it that . . . yet. But it is a troubling time.'

'With a paranoiac in charge here and on the other side of the Atlantic.'

'Those are C's orders. That's what he wants.' Maurice takes off his glasses and pinches the corners of his eyes. 'How's Elsa?'

'Fine, Maurice. Fine. Thank you.'

'Still in Whitehall?'

He knows she is. 'Yes. What are you trying to . . .?'

'C doesn't want this in Whitehall.'

'Of course, of course,' I say, doing my best to sound aggrieved at the suggestion. 'Or the politicians – the prime minister to know . . .'

Slipping his glasses back, he leans over his knees and gazes at me. 'Well, Harry, that isn't your concern.'

For the first time in twenty years I feel a need to dress my office with things that will take me from the corners and corridors of the Service. I arrive in Curzon Street with a box of photographs of Elsa and the girls, pebbles I've collected over the years from mountains and beaches, and the miner's lamp from our bedroom.

'N-n-nest-building?'

'Something like that, Peter.' I've been at my desk five minutes when he appears at the door.

'T-to get things straight before the FLUENCY meeting,' he says. 'Well, after that nastiness . . . We have to be able to trust each other, Harry.'

'That's understood.'

'We're going to get to the bottom of this, Harry, even if we have to vet a generation.'

'Right, Peter.'

He looks at me in his corner-of-the-eye way. 'You know, FLUENCY is going to be painful for some of us. P-p-people we've known for years have some tough questions to answer. But we can't shy away from that, Harry.'

I nod philosophically. Wright is Dick's new man now: what can his old one do?


There are seven of us at the FLUENCY committee table. Evelyn sits on Wright's left, pulling a loose thread from her shawl; to her right, young Alice Shepherd, and Patrick Stewart, the new head of investigations at MI5 – he's in a wheelchair. On my side of the table, Terence Lecky from Counter-espionage at MI6, and his deputy, Hinton. Wright has just told us this is a solemn moment, and we're all wearing our Sunday chapel faces, the ones we will offer to you, Lord, at the Day of Judgment. And he begins with a homily: FLUENCY will investigate anyone who so much as gave the Cambridge spies the time of day. FLUENCY will trawl the files for old Communists who might lead us to agents still active. FLUENCY will examine the testimony of defectors again for clues that might help us identify the mole at the top of Counter-intelligence, code name ELLI. Lecky interrupts him: 'Mitchell is still chief suspect?'

'One of them . . .' says Wright.

'Who are the others?'

'Well, we'll c-c-come to that, Terence.'

Wright isn't ready to name the DG at our first meeting. I'm sure he likes a white rabbit as much as the rest of us but he's careful too. He'll take his time, raise the possibility as an impossibility that must be investigated, then work on us in a series of smoke-filled one-to-ones.

'We know a R-R-Ring of Five was at the centre of everything, and that it recruited other rings. I would like to make a little prediction,' says Wright smugly. 'Half the spies we catch are hiding in our files, we just n-need to look at them more closely.' He touches a pen to his lips. 'We have a lead: a woman called Pool acted as Blunt's courier in the thirties, not only to his pals in C-Cambridge but to Party members in Oxford, too.'

I gaze across the table at Evelyn, who is careful not to catch my eye but raises a hand to the purple birthmark on her face. And just that gesture tells me she knows Pool is a connection to my wife.

'I don't need to r-r-remind you,' says Wright, 'that we proceed with caution. Strict protocols. We don't want to offer government an excuse to interfere. L-let's keep this out of the hands of the politicians . . . the socialists.'

'Hear, hear,' says Stewart, and the others nod like fairground ducks poked by a stick.

The first chance I get I step out for air. I feel an enervating sense of foreboding. FLUENCY is going to be just what I expected it to be. Protect and Survive is what the civil-defence bods urge us to do if they drop a bomb – it seems apposite. I want to crawl under the kitchen table until it's over and drag my wife with me.

Lecky and I are handling the MI6 files. Departments keep their own archives but there *is* a small registry and we have an office on the same corridor. It's the only truly dark corner in our new twenty-two-storey glass and concrete headquarters. A dark corner is the worst place to keep a secret in a building full of spies, and within hours we're welcoming snoopers from the floors above. They pretend to believe our cover story – it's polite to – but not Elliott. 'Harry, old boy,' he says, 'you and Lecky are spycatching and everyone knows it. That's all anyone seems to do these days. Work of vital national importance, I'm sure, only when was the last time we did something brave?'

In my first two days I read forty files and smoke a hundred cigarettes, and soon our office resembles Angleton's own, with files stacked high on a row of tables. I wonder if the dust that has gathered on them over many years is some sort of hallucinogen, and if you inhale too much of it you begin to suffer from extreme paranoia. Stuck here in the bowels of Dick's folly, all I'll learn of the larger FLUENCY investigation will be what Wright chooses to share with me. It's clear from our first meeting that he will make the hunt for the mole an excuse to open all the files, and he'll turn back pages, without understanding, to a time when young men and women who wanted to overcome Fascism and poverty and the exploitation of the weak chose to become Communists. A few gave themselves body and soul to the Party but for most it was a student affair that ended with the coming of war, then the fall of the Iron Curtain. Now they are loyal servants of the establishment they wished to sweep away, and the only crime they committed all those years ago was to care more about poverty and politics than was wise. I don't know, but I'm afraid for Elsa. Because in these times, now we are nice to the Jews, we seem ready to send to the stake anyone who carried a Party card.

On my third day I tell Lecky I'm moving back to Five and the files will have to be transferred to me by courier. 'I'll let the tenth floor know now,' I say, and I back out of the door straight into a secretary carrying two cups of tea. I'm still dabbing the wet patches on my trousers when a man wearing grey slacks and onyx cufflinks in his shirtsleeves, steps into the lift beside me.

'Hello, Arthur.'

'Harry.'

As always, Martin has the present and correct air of a colonial policeman, and the tight, polite smile of sufferance he reserves for people he doesn't much care for, like me.

'An accident?' He nods at my trousers.

'You, too, I hear.'

He grunts. 'You mean Hollis?'

Ping. The lift doors open on the tenth floor and we step out in tandem. 'Well, I'm here now,' he says. 'C has asked me to act as a consultant to FLUENCY. I hope that won't prove too difficult for you. Goodbye, Harry, always a pleasure.'

I watch him walk towards C's office and wonder at the folly of appointing a man with a Kremlin-size grudge against his old boss as consultant to the new working party. Dick has made another awful decision. Roger was his deputy and chosen successor at Five, and in rescuing Arthur, he may as well have daubed a board 'SUSPECTED TRAITOR' and hung it around Roger's neck.

That's what I tell Maurice when I see him in his office a few minutes later, and to judge from the silence he agrees.

# 28

# 5 November 1964

'I'M GOING TO review the VENONA,' I say.

'Why?'

'"It's all in the files,"' you said. I think we've missed something.'

Wright frowns and touches the end of his nose. 'It's not your area.'

'No, but I have an idea . . .' Do I really need his permission?

The VENONA signals are held in a secure room on the fifth floor at MI5. I can't go through them all, and happily I don't have to, because men like Arthur Martin have been poring over them for a decade. I have only a field agent's knowledge of codes, but I know the Soviets. I know how agents and their controllers think and, Guy, I remember your lies, your evasions, your gallows humour. So I read, and I pace the room with a cigarette and I THINK. I search a fog of memories, wander back to New College Lane, and on into Bentinck Street, pass the sex shops in Soho, climb the steps of the Reform Club, where Guy leans over the balcony with a naughty-boy smile: 'Are you looking for me, Harry?'

For one week only in September 1945 we managed to harvest radio traffic between Moscow Centre and London. The signals revealed an inner circle of five KGB agents working in British intelligence. We know the code names of three of the five: Guy Burgess was HICKS, Donald Maclean was HOMER, and Kim

Philby was KGB agent STANLEY. And there is something else: the CIA's favourite defector – Golitsyn – says the KGB's 'magnificent five' were at university together. Burgess, Maclean and Philby were students at Cambridge, and so was their friend Anthony Blunt. Martin and Wright won't accept that Blunt is the *fourth* man because Moscow let him leave the ring after the war, but in a wilderness of mirrors it is sometimes impossible to see what's staring you in the face. I remember Blunt in Bentinck Street. I can see him sitting on the couch, protective, sober, watchful, especially when Guy was talking about politics or sex. No, the only mystery to me is the identity of the *fifth* member of the ring.

Two of Wright's candidates I rule out straight away. I met James Klugmann at a politics evening in Oxford, and remember him as a podgy, myopic, softly spoken ideologue, who made no secret of his sympathies. And Long . . . well, there is nothing *magnificent* about poor Leo Long. The one who fits is Cairncross. Clever, committed and Cambridge, he admits passing our most important code secrets to the Russians.

'I've written something for you,' I say to Maurice.

His apartment is on my way home, a stone's throw from our old headquarters on Broadway. His dinner guests have left and I find him practising hymns on the piano for the service at St Matthew's on the morrow. Bells and smells C of E, he says. He plays the organ there because he likes 'a bit of theatre', and because the curate's wife is 'one of us', by which he means she's a spy. 'Sit. Sit. You look shattered. A glass of wine?'

'Maurice, we can stop this investigation now. We know the Ring of Five . . . Blunt is the fourth man, and I'm convinced John Cairncross is the fifth.'

Maurice drops his chins to his chest, adjusts his glasses and runs his fingers through his auburn hair, showering dandruff on the collar of his charcoal grey cardigan. On the shelf behind his head, a book on dairy farming and another on medieval stained glass. Maurice is as subtle as a fugue by Bach, but with the smell of the Derbyshire crew yard on his boots, and that is his singular charm.

'Your analysis of the evidence is compelling,' he says, when he has listened to my explanation. 'Yes, you may be right.' Then he clutches the arms of his chair and leans forward to peer at me through his thick glasses. 'Is this personal, Harry?'

'Personal?'

'What I mean . . . Do you have something to hide, Harry?'

'We all have something, Maurice. And we're bloody good at hiding it. But that isn't the point.'

'Isn't it?'

'Look, we know the names of the five.'

'That may be,' he says, easing back in his chair, 'but it's too soon. FLUENCY will have to run its course. Why? Because there have been too many mistakes – reputations are at stake. And, thanks to Philby, some of our *friends* – you know their names – are convinced the Russians have agents everywhere. They seem to think the enemy has special powers. So, like the old witch trials, FLUENCY will roll on until energy and passion are spent. But . . .' he purses his lips for a moment '. . . *Post tenebras spero lucem*. Let's hope that after darkness there will be light.'

Fine. But who will the darkness take, Maurice?

The following morning I'm in the kitchen making tea and toast for Elsa when the bell at St Matthew's tolls to summon the faithful. I imagine Maurice hunched at his organ, fat fingers stroking a prelude as members of the congregation gather for mass and the clergy robe in the vestry. His parting shot to me was, 'if you can lay your hands on the Gouzenko file . . . The defectors are the only other reliable source we have for an agent ELLI.'

But for the next couple of days I'm too preoccupied with a stack of dusty files from Six, which on close inspection prove to be of no consequence. It is the librarian's life, but without even the frisson of an occasional quiet encounter with a woman, when eyes meet across shelves on a dull day and it's possible to imagine she's hungry for sex on no acquaintance at all.

I expect to have to go on hands and knees to Wright for the Gouzenko files but, as luck would have it, Lecky has the ones I need in our little basement office at Six.

'What are you looking for?' he enquires.

'Philby,' I say, which is an acceptable answer to almost any question at the moment. 'Cross-checking his movements in September 'forty-five.' Because September 1945 is key. In the first week of September Igor Gouzenko walked away from the Soviet Embassy in Ottawa with a briefcase full of secrets and a story about a double agent at the top of British intelligence. By a remarkable coincidence another defector on the other side of the globe – Volkov – was preparing to do the same. According to Gouzenko, the identity of agent ELLI was known to only a few but he worked in 'Five of MI'. Volkov didn't live long enough to tell his story – Philby betrayed him to his controller – but he was able to warn us of a double agent, the 'acting head of a department of British Counter-espionage (or Counter-intelligence) Directorate'. Volkov was KGB, Gouzenko one of the Soviet military's creatures. But put the evidence from the two defectors together and you have a highly placed Soviet agent, code name ELLI, working for 'Five of MI,' who was 'acting head' of a counter-espionage department in London.

Ten floors above me at Century House the director of Requirements is sitting at a desk sturdy enough to bear the ton of briefing notes he releases to Whitehall every week and wide enough to reassure him that it is still a noble and worthy task for a robber baron.

I ring Elliott and say, 'Have you a moment?'

'Far too many,' he replies.

A few minutes later his secretary, Marjorie, shows me into his office, and from his grand desk he takes whisky and two thick crystal tumblers. He has made space in the room for a number of pieces of fine furniture – a serpentine-fronted walnut chest, Dutch floral marquetry chairs, a burgundy club couch. He says they are an act of defiance, a rejection of our brutal concrete and glass home and the 'modern' Secret Service Dick would like it to represent. 'Modern' means an end to the buccaneering spirit of the past, 'modern' is 'clear lines of reporting', and 'value for money', and 'internal reviews', as the last of the barons are eased out to be replaced by milksops, who would rather do nothing than risk a mistake. 'Modern' is spending time and energy investigating ourselves. Thanks to Dick White, we are becoming the sort of Communist institution we were working to destroy. Is it any wonder that a man like Wright is king of our dunghill?

Elliott pushes a glass towards me. 'Is this just a social?'

'No. I need your encyclopaedic knowledge of the Russian Secret Service.'

'Ask away.'

'Gouzenko – remember him? How likely is it that military intelligence in Moscow knows the identity of the KGB's agents and illegals in London?'

He considers his hands, spread on the desk in front of him, then considers me. 'Not Philby, if that's who you mean. The KGB and GRU are not good neighbours. Oil and water.'

I nod slowly.

'Want to tell me what this is about, old boy?'

'No, old boy, I don't, but there's one more thing. Philby – what was he doing in September 'forty-five?'

'Don't you have access to his file? Section V – Counter-intelligence – here at SIS in London.'

'Confirmed head?'

'Acting, if I recall . . . Is that all?'

'For now,' I say, lifting the whisky to my lips to hide a smile.

In only a few weeks my colleagues on the FLUENCY working party have compiled a list of two hundred allegations, dating back to the First World War. Twenty-eight are category C, which means they're credible. In the language of counter-intelligence they're deemed to be 'true bills'. It is truly remarkable what people can find when they're desperate to find something. I'm reminded of the chapel in Maerdy again, where the minister used to preach Mark 5:36: *Be not afraid, only believe.* Well, my colleagues believe. We meet in Wright's office to bat their 'true bills' back and forth across the table. Their faces are tense with excitement and perhaps a little guilt, because secretly they relish the prospect of calling senior officers to the judgment seat. I hear Patrick Stewart opine that Gouzenko's 'Five of MI' must mean MI5, and I bite my tongue. Then Evelyn points out Hollis was head of MI5's F Division – Counter-intelligence – in 1945, and glances are exchanged around the table. No one mentions Section V at MI6 and the obvious candidate – Philby – and I follow Maurice's advice and say nothing: this investigation has a long way to go.

Wright does raise the subject in a roundabout way. 'You've been l-l-looking at the VENONA, Harry?'

'Yes,' I say, 'and I have some thoughts. Perhaps I can bring them to our next meeting.'

'G-g-good, good,' he says, with a note in his voice that suggests the contrary. 'Evelyn's been working on VENONA too.'

'Two cryptonyms in particular,' she says. 'If we leave the question of the missing members of the Ring of Five for a moment . . .' Opening the file in front of her, she takes out a signal and slides it into the middle of the table. 'From Moscow Centre to the KGB resident in London.'

**TOP SECRET**

From: MOSCOW
To: LONDON
20 September 1945

To Bob.
Your no. 1436. JACK and ROSA should not, repeat, not be
met in public.
No. 6869 VIKTOR

'That's our old friend General Pavel Mikhailovich Fitin. Code
name, VIKTOR. Head of Foreign Intelligence at the KGB at the
tender age of thirty-one. Clever boy. He was on the point of
being executed in one of Uncle Joe's purges when his talent
for preying on his fellow man was recognised at the last minute.
VIKTOR was responsible for stealing all those precious atomic
secrets from the Americans. If JACK and ROSA were working
directly to VIKTOR, their intelligence must have been prized.'

'They m-may still be active,' says Wright.

Evelyn's shoulders pivot forward and back, like a hen ruffling
her feathers before settling on an egg. 'All we can say with certainty
is that they *were* active in London in September 'forty-five, and
their names always appear in the VENONA signals *together.*'

She has a mad twinkle in her eye. Old ham: she's challenging
us to work it out. 'They're a couple, dears,' she says, with
faux-exasperation. 'A couple! We're looking for a husband-and-
wife team.'

Hilton whistles through his teeth. 'Like the Rosenbergs in
America.'

'Are they our problem or yours?' says Lecky.

'Ours. They were able to access Security Service files,' says
Evelyn, 'but they may have left Five some time ago. They could
be with you at Six, or in Whitehall.'

Wright is glowing with excitement. 'You remember S-SNIPER? The CIA's man in the Polish Secret Service? Came in from the cold in 'sixty-one. He claims the Russians have a middle grade in British intelligence.'

Lecky laughs – 'Oh, come on, Peter' – and slaps the edge of the table. 'SNIPER's as mad as a hatter. Convinced he's the last Tsar of Russia, or is the tsarevich . . .'

'But a g-good memory for intelligence. Jim A-A-Angleton's sure SNIPER's allegation is a true bill.'

Evelyn ruffles her shoulders. 'What Peter is trying to say is, we can't lose sight of the ones who didn't make the top floor, the middle-rankers, the sub-agents, the agents of influence.'

'The JACKs and the ROSAs.'

'Precisely.'

Evelyn takes two photographs from her file and turns them towards us. One is of a young woman in her twenties, with fine dark hair swept short behind her ears, slightly sunken eyes, delicate features and a rectangular smile. The second picture is of the same woman but nearer to me in age. Then Evelyn sweeps a third photograph round, and this time the woman is arm in arm with Herbert Hart. Clever Herbert, Rees used to call him. He was at New College before us. A lawyer, a philosopher, and best buddies with Professors Isaiah Berlin and Stuart Hampshire. Clever Herbert worked at this place – at MI5 – during the war.

Wright plonks his forefinger on the photograph. 'Herbert Hart, f-formerly of this parish. You must know him, Harry?'

'A little. Sir Dick White knows him better. They were in B Division together during the war.'

Wright can smirk like no one else I've met. 'Hart served with B-B-Blunt, too. Now he's professor of jurisprudence at Oxford. And the woman in the photographs is his wife, Jenifer, with one *n*. Not a good wife, because she sleeps with his friends.' He pauses. 'I'm s-s-sorry, does anyone here know her?'

. I resist the urge to dry my palms on my trousers. 'She's a friend of my wife,' I say, which of course he knows.

'Is she?' says Wright. 'Well, Mrs Hart is an Oxford don, like Herbert now. In fact, they met at Oxford and married in . . .?'

Evelyn obliges: ''Forty-one. Jenifer was working at the Home Office.'

'Where, of course, she would have had access to intelligence.'

'Herbert, Agent JACK?' Patrick Stewart pushes his wheelchair from the table. 'Oh, no. Really, Peter, I'd be astonished.'

'We know his wife is a C-Communist. They were both privy to grade-one intelligence.'

'How do you know she's a Communist?' I ask.

'Blunt's assistant, Harry. Phoebe Pool was a courier for Blunt and our old friend Otto. I think we can assume Otto recruited Jenif-f-er and probably Herbert too.'

I have a malicious urge to remind him there's just one *f* in 'Jenifer'.

'There are other candidates,' Wright observes, 'but for now the Harts must be our number-one suspects. J-JACK and ROSA may be at the centre of a new ring – an Oxford ring.'

Elsa's in our drawing room – she calls it that – feet on the couch, a glass of gin on an arm, but she's still in the black coat and light blue scarf she wore for work. She has set a fire to take the edge off the room, but it's stuttering as badly as Peter Wright. It's the sort of thing she should leave for someone familiar with life below stairs (me).

'If I get it going, will you make love to me?'

Her smile is its own season. 'If you promise to keep me warm. Shall I pour you a drink?'

'No, stay where you are.'

I take off my jacket, crouch in front of the grate and begin to build again, and as I work she tells me of her day and her new minister, Mr Healey, who is a funny and civilised man. 'He reads,' she says. 'His favourite poets are Yeats and Auden. I told him my husband was a friend of Dylan Thomas, and he launched into a poem. I can only remember a phrase – *mercy of his means*?'

'From Fern Hill. *Oh, as I was young and easy in the mercy of his means,/ Time held me green and dying,/ Though I sang in my chains like the sea.*' I shuffle across to her on my knees and place a sooty finger on her nose. 'My love.'

# 29

THE GIRLS ARE with their mother and the golfer at Christmas. We do what we must with Elsa's family in Oxfordshire, where the mahogany is polished to the surface of a mirror, and so is the silver, the Christmas tree from the estate is decked with real candles, the parish choir sings in the hall, and generations of the Spears family look down from the walls at me.

'My son-in-law is something in the Foreign Office' is how old man Spears introduces me to his guests. Twenty at table on Christmas Day: two lords a-leaping, a Conservative MP banging on about the socialists in the BBC, tipsy ladies dancing and falling ('A bit rum,' someone says), and the maids serve goose and partridge. Elsa says, 'Be good,' so even when all agree the country is going to the dogs under Labour, I sip Daddy's fine wine and say nothing to provoke, only imagine serving them a generous helping of Burgess at his mischievous best.

When we're alone I grumble, and Elsa says I'm tribal, that her father and his friends have a point. Labour has slapped 15 per cent on all imported goods, except food; it can't make up its mind whether to join the Common Market or how to meet the challenge of colour television, Concorde, rocket development, and defence. It says it wants to keep the country in the economic big league but doesn't seem to have any idea how to do so. 'You sound like a civil servant,' I say.

'Because I respect people who get things done,' she replies belligerently.

We drive to the Black Mountains for New Year and stay in the guesthouse at Llanthony Priory. It was recommended by one of Elsa's friends as a place of pilgrimage for poets and walkers, but the gale whistles into our room in the west tower, the mattress is shot, the dressing-table mirror cracked, and there's bugger-all to do but imagine the view of the hillside. 'When the mist lifts we'll walk,' she says on the first day, then again on the next. But the rain keeps rolling over the Vale of Ewyas, and by New Year's Eve she is coughing like a horse and feels too rotten to move to somewhere cheerier. Turning the sheet under her chin, I ask, 'Which of your friends do we have to thank for this recommendation, *cariad*? I'll send them a postcard.'

'Jenifer came here before the war.'

'Jenifer with one *n*?'

'Harry?' Elsa has caught a note of concern in my voice. 'What is it?'

'Here. Drink this,' and I reach for the hot toddy I've prescribed from the bar.

'Now, what is it?'

I put my hand on her brow to check her temperature. 'You must rest.'

'Don't fob me off!' She's exhausted and close to tears. 'Come on!'

I should say, 'I can't tell you,' but she knows I break the rules when I want to. I'm tired too, and my only resolution for the new year is to hold on to the best of my life lying here beside me; and the light has gone, the rain rattles the window, and I'm trapped in this cell with only steak pie and beer for supper, which I'll have to eat alone. I roll on to my side and look down into her dark eyes and say, 'Peter Wright seems to think Jenifer and Herbert are spies.'

'No!' Struggling to her elbow sets her coughing again.

'Take it easy,' I say, rubbing her back. But she won't listen. She won't rest until she learns more, and when I tell her the intelligence came from Phoebe Pool she begins coughing again with a vengeance. I settle her on a mountain of pillows and insist she drink a little more of the toddy. When she's able, she says Phoebe doesn't have a political bone in her body, and that Blunt must have put her up to it. 'Art and books, that's all she cares about, Harry. She isn't a Communist.'

'And Jenifer-one-*n*?'

Elsa frowns. 'Political with a small *p*. We all were. She went on a summer camp for unemployed workers and had an affair with a milkman there. I remember laughing because he was the camp cook with a tent to himself, so disappearing for sex was easy.' She smiles and reaches out to stroke my face. 'Perhaps she was a Communist, but not a spy.'

I take her hand from my cheek and kiss the palm. We should be candid with each other about the past. This is the time. But there have been many times in the seventeen years we've been lovers, and even now as it threatens to catch up with us both I can't bring myself to ask her. And perhaps it's right to let another opportunity pass, and it's too late for that sort of conversation. Instead I say, 'You see the problem?'

She laughs, but not in a nice way. 'My two best friends at university are suspected of being traitors?'

'So, you say nothing, you know nothing,' and I place my finger on her lips.

'I know,' she says, brushing it away, 'but I don't believe it. What is the point of this investigation? I thought you were trying to find out if someone tipped off Philby. The Harts are academics and have been for years.'

'I'm afraid we're way beyond that, *cariad*.'

New Year's Day: I leave her sleeping and drive into the Valleys. I don't know what I'm hoping to find there. I feel like a city sightseer in Elsa's toy car, the sort of person who might describe the rows of sooty two-ups-two-downs, the chapels, pit heads and slag heaps as 'rum'. I came to Merthyr Tydfil as a student one summer to help run a workers' education course. The iron and steel works had closed a decade before, the furnace fires that gave birth to the town were cold, and the men had nothing to do but drink and fight, and if the slum they used to call 'Little Hell' was history, you didn't have to look hard for bare-foot coal-hole poverty. I had enough empathy to be angry, and enough hope to believe I would be one of those who would change things for the better. I took that anger and hope back to Oxford, where a few weeks later I met Rees and his friends and listened to their vision of a caring society, and I answered the call to the barricades to fight capitalism and Fascism.

Driving on to Maerdy, I park the car opposite number 72 Oxford Street, where forty years ago the breadwinner, the rent-payer, was my father *Jack Vaughan, 30, coal miner-hewer*. Where's Oxford, Tada? I asked him once.

He laughed. 'A long way from here, boy.' Gazing at our grey-stone home in the middle of a row of grey stone homes, I wonder if the mine owners were having a joke at our expense, or if they chose to name our street after the city of dreaming spires because we could barely imagine such a place – like the city of God – *Seion* in Welsh – which was the name the elders chose for the barren barnlike chapel Mum took me to on Sundays. Yes, Oxford Street, a reminder to us all that there was – is – an order to things on earth too, a shining city in England for the elect, where an entitled few learn to govern the many. I was a small miracle, because it was easier for a miner's son to pass through the eye of a needle than go to Oxford.

Word is getting about and kids are gathering to run their

fingers along the bodywork of the car and ask me questions I can't answer about the engine. I lift the smallest behind the wheel and while he plays – 'Dwylo! *Leave the gear stick, will you!'* – I gaze up the valley at the drams in the sidings and the colliery winding gear and the slag mountain that has grown fifty feet in the years that have passed since I left my first home. Tada's down the valley beside Mum in Ferndale cemetery, not far from the graves of the men who perished in the pit explosion of 1885. Tad used to tell me how his father, my grandfather, helped to dig out the bodies and that one of them was his own brother. It was my grandfather who took me to my first political meeting in the working-men's hall just around the corner from our house. I was about ten and the main speaker was Arthur Horner, the miners' leader and one of the founder members of the Communist Party of Great Britain.

Aunt Brenda is still in North Terrace, as close to Maerdy colliery as it's possible to be without drawing a wage. I'm the university nephew she boasts about but doesn't want to see. I knock on her door all the same, and she welcomes me with a peck on the cheek and shows me into the front room, because I'm too smart in my Jermyn Street shoes and shirt and my brown suede car coat for the kitchen table – that's for proper family. We drink tea and I listen to her stories. Cousin Ivo is still at the pit, Cousin Frank has moved to another. 'How is Frank?' I say, struggling to put a face and facts to the name. There are more cousins further down the valley and in Cardiff, and one called Jean is working in a branch of Woolworths in London. Brenda knows they're nothing more than names to me, and because this is Maerdy and not 'polite' Chelsea, she says so. 'It was a pit-tee you left us, 'Arry,' she says, her voice the sing-song of the Valleys. 'Your Anti Elen did her best, I suppose – wasn't what your mother would have want-ed, though.' She pauses. 'You weren't at Elen's fu-ner-al, were you?'

Brenda isn't curious about my kids, my wife, or my work, so when she has said all she wants to say I take my leave. Only before I go she shows me into her back room, crowded with cheap furniture and photographs of babies, and against one of the walls is my mum's old piano. The brass candle fittings have gone, the corners and edges are chipped white, the lid has split and there are heat rings in the varnish, because for twenty years it has served as a sideboard. I sit and play 'Cwm Rhondda' but there are so many loose and broken strings the tune is unrecognisable. Mum taught me the notes and she would accompany my father, who was a decent baritone, and now this wreck that was once their pride and joy is all that's left of that time. Brenda wants rid of it and she says that if I would like it for sentiment's sake it's mine. I thank her, but it is beyond saving.

I drive back in the grey dusk and climb the spiral staircase to our room in the monastery tower, where Sister Elsa is still in bed but feeling better, and I tell her of my visit to the village and Brenda and Mum's old piano, and she strokes my cheek with the back of her hand and kisses me sweetly. 'It's upset you. Don't let it,' she says. 'You've changed. We all have.'

1965

# 30

## *6 March 1965*

M AURICE RINGS TO warn me that Angleton is in town to
offer advice and assistance. 'And he's booked a table at
Wheeler's to celebrate your birthday,' he says.

I wonder whether Angleton has the date from Maurice or
from a file he keeps on me. In any case, I'm obliged to ring
Elsa and postpone our champagne evening.

'But not the sex,' I say. 'I'll be home in time for that.'

'No champagne, no music, *nooo* sex,' she says, her tongue in
her cheek. 'But there's always tomorrow.'

Wheeler's is a bohemian sort of place. We are obliged to sit as
tight as sardines round two square tables pushed together. My
birthday, but Angleton's party, so Martin is there, nipping at a
whisky, and Wright. I watch him smooth the scruffy fringe of
grey hair round his bald pate then wipe a bead of sweat from
his upper lip with a forefinger. Maurice is straining over his
belly to lean close enough to hear our host's quiet voice. And
Angleton sits in a tub chair on my right, his face pinched and
raddled by booze and cigarettes, insomnia and paranoia, yet
handsome in a tired intense way. As always, he's immaculately
dressed in a black wool three-piece, white shirt and college tie.

We start with pleasantries, even a toast to me. I'm on my
third glass of wine and our main course has just arrived when
he introduces the 'trouble with your Service' conversation,

which is the real purpose of our dinner. Morale is low, you're struggling for direction, he says, and it's the fault of those at the top. 'It's two years now since Philby tripped off to Moscow and the mole who tipped him off is still in place.'

'We don't know that, Jim,' says Maurice.

'Maurice, we do. I'm meeting your boss tomorrow. I'm gonna warn him that failure to deal with the penetration of both your Services is compromising the security of my country too.' He sips his drink, and I'm suddenly conscious of the sound of people genuinely enjoying themselves. 'I'm going to ask Dick to make this a joint operation. You boys don't have the resources you need for your FLUENCY investigation. We have a good man at our station in London and I want him to work with you. What do you say?'

Wright is nodding, and Martin mutters, 'I agree,' because they cooked this up with Angleton days ago – I don't doubt it – and they're here to persuade the deputy chief of the Secret Intelligence Service to support it too.

Everyone is looking at Maurice, who has a forkful of fish hovering inches from his mouth. I know he won't be happy but he's a politician, and I'm not surprised when he passes the buck to me. 'Harry?'

I think it's a bloody disastrous idea. Angleton's man in London would be just the first through the door, followed by God knows how many, until we belong to the CIA. But I say, 'Help is always welcome. Have you discussed this with the director general of the Security Service, Jim?'

He gazes at me impassively, then picks up his cigarettes. 'We must try harder to recruit a KGB officer, perhaps here in London, but it doesn't matter where, just as long as he is able to identify the mole in British intelligence.'

'Then I can take it that no one has raised the possibility with Sir Roger.'

Because it's plain from his evasion that Hollis doesn't have a clue, and our dinner and Angleton's meeting with Dick tomorrow are an attempt to sew up a new role for the CIA in the service before the DG has a chance to call, 'Foul.' I try to catch Maurice's eye, but he is still concentrating intently on stripping his fish. He clearly has no intention of committing himself to anything at Wheeler's. 'Will you excuse me?' I say, rising from the table.

I'm standing at the urinal when the door opens and Angleton steps up to the stall to my left. He doesn't speak or look at me, only does what he's supposed to do. But I make a point of staring. 'Hello, Jim.'

'Harry,' he replies, his gaze fixed on the bright white tiles a few inches from his face.

'You've certainly got it in for Roger.'

'No, Harry.'

'Trying to sew this up behind his back? I suppose you recognise our confusion as an opportunity to take control. Turn us into an outpost of Washington.'

'Don't you think Sir Roger has some questions to answer? Why has he refused to authorise the interrogation of Graham Mitchell?'

'Because he hasn't seen a shred of credible evidence against him.' I turn to wash my hands. 'Tell me, Jim, do you have it in for me too?'

He takes his time. I watch him in the mirror as he finishes his pee, then steps up to the basin next to mine. 'Really, Harry, is this necessary?' he says at last. 'It's your birthday.'

'Yes. You arranged that stunt in Vienna. "OTTO sends his regards." OTTO the Soviet illegal. Burgess's friend. Philby's controller.'

I try to make eye contact in the mirror, but he is concentrating very hard on soaping his bony hands. 'That was your message, Jim.'

'I don't know what you're talking about. Did they make a pass at you?'

'No. *You* did. Comrade Erich was working for *you*. You were testing me. I want to know why you?'

'You're paranoid, Harry,' he says, dropping a hand towel into the laundry bin.

I laugh. 'That's rich.'

'You need a holiday. Perhaps with your wife. Elsa, isn't it? I understand she works at your defence ministry.' He wants to leave but I'm standing in his way. 'We should get back to the others,' he says, glancing at his watch and shuffling towards me.

'Did you plan your game in Vienna with Peter?'

The door opens and we're no longer alone.

'Guilty conscience?' he whispers, and his shoulder brushes mine. 'See you back up there.'

The following afternoon Maurice rings me to arrange a meeting at his club, and in a corner of its smoking room he warns me Angleton is through the gate. No minutes were taken of the meeting because Dick doesn't want anyone to see it in black and white, but giving the CIA access to FLUENCY has set us on a slippery slope: he is sacrificing the independence of the Service.

'The chief doesn't know Jim like I do,' says Maurice. 'I tell you, Harry, we are going to regret this piece of business for a long time.'

Angleton meets his disciples twice more before he returns to Washington. I know because Wright tells me with the satisfied smile of a one-time technician who knows he's now running the largest mole hunt in the history of the Service. Colleagues pass him in the corridor with a wary glance: they know something's afoot. FLUENCY is supposed to be secret, but it's impossible to hide the new desks and bodies in D3. And the names of those my colleagues deem to be 'worthy of further investigation' roll in by the day. There's a little list. I even offer a name or two of my own: Maurice says I must or Dick will find an excuse to replace me.

Dylan Thomas used to say he held a beast, an angel and a madman inside. Dylan was a great poetic soul. I hold the mad-man at bay because Maurice trusts me, because I'm a member of the investigation team, because Elsa loves me, and my children are ready to give me a second chance. But Rees is never far from my mind. Rees, who has more of the beast and the madman than the angel. Rees is on the FLUENCY list. The Harts are on the list, and some Oxford professors, Berlin and Hampshire, Zaehner and Bowra. The members of the Communist Party's historians group – Hill at Oxford, Hobsbawm and Thompson at Cambridge – are on the list. Civil servants – thirty so far – including the permanent secretary at Fuel and Power ('Classic Cambridge Communist,' says Wright). A couple of soldiers, a sailor, and rich men like Burgess's friend Rothschild are on the list. Scientists and art historians – Phoebe Pool – are on the list. Trade-union leaders, of course, and, most sensitive of all, the politicians. No one dares talk of Wilson, but his cabinet . . . There are six ministers including the man charged with responsibility for the defence of the realm, Denis Healey, and Members of Parliament, like Tom Driberg and Bernard Floud, who was at university with my wife.

There are two types of fear. There's the fear that paralyses and there's the fear that mobilises. The first dulls the senses; the second sharpens perception. While the first may drive a man mad, it is possible to live a lifetime with the second. That was how it was in the war, and I imagine it was the same in Stalin's Russia in the thirties, when a careless word might mean a death sentence for a family.

Elsa still asks me, 'When, Harry? You promised.'

And I say, 'Soon,' when I mean 'It's too late.'

For now, the first concern of the FLUENCY working party remains the hunt for a master spy upon whom it will be possible to hang the mistakes of my generation. They sometimes call him the Fourth Man, sometimes the Fifth, sometimes ELLI. We meet in the last week of May to consider a draft of our report for the heads of Service. Hollis should be at the meeting – his office is just along the corridor – but he's too busy planning his retirement to realise the last six months have been a paper chase for evidence of his guilt. And Wright and Angleton won't be denied. I expect they wrote the findings of the FLUENCY report before our first meeting. In short, 'we' – the FLUENCY committee – believe the chief custodian of our country's secrets, Sir Roger Hollis, should be investigated as a double agent.

Martin, 'our consultant', is back inside the building, and Angleton's man, Bright, is invited to hear our conclusions too. No one cares that the director of the CIA will now be told before the man at the big desk along the corridor. The DG will learn tomorrow when his mistress, Val, brings him his first coffee and a Rich Tea biscuit, and our Most Secret report. He'll choke on that biscuit.

# 31

## 7 June 1965

Elsa says, 'Jack Ellis is in town. What have you done to upset him?'

We're standing beneath the white-stone portico on the north side of the Ministry of Defence with the rain bouncing on the steps below us. Across the road, Whitehall Court, an apartment building in the French renaissance style that was home in its heyday to the first incarnation of the Secret Intelligence Service. I have come from a FLUENCY meeting to whisk my best friend and lover off to the York Minster to get filthy drunk on wine and memories.

'You used to be so close,' she says.

Jack was my CIA contact in Vienna, and I was best man when he married Michelle, but the last time I saw him was in a Georgetown park at dusk, and he made me feel about as welcome as a wet shoe. Angleton's people were over him like a rash, and in the months after Philby, acknowledging a friend in the British Secret Service wasn't much safer than owning to a chum in the KGB. And now he's in London. Elsa saw him at an American Embassy lunch, a big man trying to appear small. 'He isn't going to see you, I'm afraid. Full of excuses . . . Sorry, Harry. No honour among thieves.' She steps forward with her arm out and hand open and the rain splashes on her palm. 'Wait here,' she says. 'I'll go inside and phone for a taxi.'

'Hang on.' I catch her arm. 'What was he doing at the embassy?'

'He's over with Gordon Gray, the former national security adviser to the president. Fact-finding, Jack says. I imagine it has more to do with you people than with us at Defence.'

'Gray's more than a *former*, he's a very current adviser on foreign intelligence matters. Did Jack tell you where he's staying?'

Elsa takes a step away and stares at me. 'Harry. No.'

I would like to tell her she's wrong and kiss her frown away. 'There's a reason why he's avoiding me.'

'I don't doubt it. Perhaps he's heard how you treat your wife.'

'Sorry.'

'You know you're taking *us* for granted, don't you?'

I watch her run down the steps to hail a passing cab, and as it pulls away I remember Jack observing in his folksy Texan way that Elsa is pretty enough to make a fella plough through a stump. He's right. I wish I could explain that I have to see Jack precisely because I won't take *us* for granted. Maybe I'm chasing my tail, but I think he's avoiding me because he's in trouble, or I'm in trouble, or the whole bloody Service is in trouble.

I call our liaison officer at Special Branch from a telephone box near Charing Cross station and ask him to run a check: Gray and his entourage are at the Connaught in Mayfair. At half past seven, a cab drops me in front of the Jesuit church we used for dead-drop messages during the war, and I splash across Mount Street into the shelter of the hotel porch. The Connaught is a late-Victorian red-brick affair, smart but not flashy. The dark-panelled décor of the lobby reminds me of pictures I've seen of first class on the *Titanic*. A receptionist has a map of London open on the front desk and is trying to show an elderly American lady where she will find the statue of Eros at Piccadilly Circus.

'Would Madam like a taxi?'

As he lifts a telephone my gaze is drawn to the theatre mirror behind him just as Angleton's man, Bright, walks through the frame. He's close enough to slap me on the back. *Er mwyn duw.* I don't need Sherlock Holmes to tell me he's here to see Gray.

The CIA party is in the hotel restaurant, seated at one of the tables furthest from the door. Jack has his back to me, facing a broad man in his mid-fifties with a deep furrow between his lip and his nose and the sort of straight mouth a small child draws on its first picture. I can tell from his manner that he's the focus of the conversation, and that this must be Gray. His other table companions – one of them will be Bright – are hidden by a fat pillar and a fern. The head waiter asks me if I'm going to dine and I decline, but I ask him for the name of the bar beyond the glass doors on the far side of the restaurant. 'The Coburg, sir,' he says.

And what a handsome art-deco watering hole it turns out to be. I order a Scotch and settle opposite a mirror that offers an oblique reflection of Gray. I could be in the bar all evening and leave none the wiser, and I'm in two minds as to whether to wait for an opportunity to catch Jack alone or scribble a note and come back later. *Dear Jack, if the mountain won't come to Mohammed* . . .

Then Gray eases his chair from the table and with a start I recognise the broad brown-checked jacket that Martin has made his summer uniform. A few seconds later he reaches for his coffee cup and his head bobs into view. Bloody Arthur Martin is briefing Gray on how things stand in the Service. That means FLUENCY and Hollis, and there's no question now: I must see Jack tonight.

I watch the receptionist dial Jack's room and make a mental note of the number. No, I wouldn't like to leave a message, thank you. But a few minutes later, when the front desk is busy with another elderly American, I slip into one of the lifts – it's much easier than it should be. Jack's sloppy too. There's nothing to suggest he has taken precautions with his door. A wire coat hanger will do the trick, and I find one just along the corridor: Room 520 has left a pink blouse on the door for Laundry to collect.

Jack's room is plush enough, I'm sure. Like most of London's expensive hotels, it is furnished with fake antiques and sporting prints to encourage the visitor to imagine he's a guest at an English country house. There's a small bottle of whisky and three dirty glasses on the table. By the bed, a picture of his wife, Michelle, and their daughter, Eleanor. I assume anything secret is in the safe but I search his things to be sure. Then I turn off the light and settle in an armchair with his whisky.

There isn't much left by the time I hear him approaching along the corridor. His voice is husky and I know of old that he's with a woman he wants, and that he's drunk even more than I have. It takes him a while to find his keys, and when he does he says, 'After you, darlin',' which sounds so sleazy it makes me smile. His companion is wearing a grey suit and glasses; penny for a pound she's a secretary at the embassy.

'Hello,' I say, and she squeals.

Jack spins round too quickly and cracks his elbow on the wall. 'What the hell! Git yer ass—'.

'Don't shout. You're frightening the lady.'

Who is clever enough to realise it's time to leave. She doesn't seem the slightest bit sorry about it.

'How dare you?' he says, when she's gone.

'How dare *you*, Jack?'

He takes out a handkerchief and mops his brow, then steps unsteadily towards the wardrobe. 'Son of a bitch! You've been through my things.'

'Must have been the maid.'

'And *she* drank my Scotch, too?' He helps himself to the little that's left, then lowers his heavy frame into the other armchair. 'Don't get the wrong idea . . . Merle's a good girl,' he says. 'She works at the embassy.'

'Merle? Is that her name? How's Michelle?'

'Harry, I swear you're lower than a snake's belly.'

'And you've always known it.'

The room's warm and close but not like a Texas summer, yet Jack is sweating like a pig. I watch him turn his glass on the arm of the chair, scratch his cheek, his nose, his knee, and contrive to look anywhere but at me. He's afraid. And I feel a surge of sadness because in the next few minutes we will lose for ever the laughter and the sympathy we used to share.

'What's Gordon Gray doing here, Jack?'

'Is that it?' He puts down his glass and leans over his broad knees to rise. ''Cause you know I got nothin' to say.'

'This thing with Gray . . . Is it something to do with Angleton, with us, the British?'

He gets to his feet and sways towards me.

'What are you doing, Jack? Planning to have me ejected? Come on! Why don't you sit down? I saw you with Arthur Martin this evening. Was Wright there too?' I see the answer in his face. 'No Wright. OK. But tell me, why is a security adviser to the president involved in all this?'

Jack is saying 'nothin''. Well, fine! Then the answer *is* the obvious one. 'This has gone to the president. Gordon Gray is here because the president has asked him to be.'

'Jeezus.' He steps back, a hand to his lips. 'Git outta here!'

'Shall I ring for another bottle of Scotch?'

'Go on, git!'

'*You* ring. Best no one knows I'm here chewing the fat with you, especially Bright because he'll tell Angleton.'

Jack opens his mouth but my meaning penetrates the whisky fog in his brain before he can tell me to 'git' again. He closes his eyes and holds his head. 'You're jumpin' on me with all four feet, ain'tcha?'

'Jack, we're friends, right?'

'You bastard!'

'You can trust me.'

He snorts with disgust, as well he might in the circumstances. No need to spell it out. He picks up the bottle, realises he emptied it and drops back in the armchair with a long face. What happened to the brawling scratchy cowboy I used to know? Age has wearied him; it condemns us all.

'I want to make it easy for you,' I say. 'I'm going to talk and you're going to look me in the eye, and if I go astray, touch your ear, your face, stroke your moustache, something like that, all right?'

Angleton or someone else, Deputy Director Helms perhaps, has taken the Agency's concerns about the penetration of British intelligence to the White House. True. Gordon Gray is working for the president. True. Angleton is hoping to scalp Roger Hollis. All true. Jack's fingers are squirming in his lap but that's where they stay.

'And it's all part of a grand plan for the CIA to run things around here,' I say.

'Jeezus. Can you blame us?' he blurts. 'The mess you folks have made of things.'

'That's funny because it was you who told me Angleton was as crazy as a bullbat, Jack. I guess he's finished investigating you.'

'That guy is never finished.'

'See? You *do* understand.'

Jack leans close and peers at me. 'Are you hollerin' about MI6 or is this about you?'

'Both.'

'Which is why I don't trust you.'

'Well, you should because we're friends – or we were.'

He offers a tight smile but it's gone in a flash. 'You know Jim Angleton's a Chicano, right? Injun blood. I'm tellin' you for old times' sake, Harry: Roger Hollis's scalp ain't the only one he's fixin' to take.'

Elsa is sitting in bed with her work spread across the counterpane. 'All right, tell me,' she says, and it's an order not a request. I obey. I shouldn't, it's another weak moment, but I've lost an old friend and I risk losing more besides. I push her papers aside and drop on to the bed in my suit and tie, kick off my shoes, and talk of Jack and Angleton and Gray and Hollis and me, and when I've finished she says, 'You should have resigned months ago.'

'Maybe,' I say, which I don't mean, and 'Kiss me,' which I do. She ignores me because her mind is busy with the rest of my life.

'The *Observer*. You know the foreign editor.'

'After they took on Philby?'

'*The Times*.'

'He worked for that, too.'

'Then it has to be the *Economist*.'

'Twenty-five years in the Service. I owe it something – *and* the country.' She sighs. '*Das kannst du deiner Oma erzählen*,' she says – tell it to your grandmother – and she bends over me, and beneath the curtain of her hair we kiss.

Jack says Maurice is no poker player and perhaps that's so, but he's a fine actor nonetheless, one of the Firm's best. I believe I could arrive at the Athenaeum with news of a nuclear strike and he would frown or raise an eyebrow, perhaps offer me a last cigarette, and that's about all. At one of our meetings he told me he didn't think much of lie-detector tests because he took the CIA's and passed with flying colours. But we meet the evening after my conversation with Jack and for once he is quite open about his feelings. 'Dick has lost his grip,' he says. 'He's ready to accept the FLUENCY report without question and is urging Roger to widen the scope of the inquiry. What's more, he'll get his way. You realise what that means for Roger?'

Of course I do: for the first time in history the head of a secret security service will authorise his officers to investigate him for treason.

'Incredible, isn't it?' Maurice draws deeply on his cigarette. 'Incredible.'

He pauses while the smoking-room steward serves us another drink. This has become our corner on Tuesdays and Thursdays, and any other day I have something to report. The steward has four fingers of whisky poured before our backsides touch the leather chairs. Maurice leans over his knees. 'Angleton has discussed the FLUENCY report with "our friend", who is now sure Hollis is a traitor.'

'"Our friend"?'

'That's what Jim calls Golitsyn. Funny. I read somewhere that the tsar called his mad monk Rasputin "our friend", and look what happened to him. *Our* friend Golitsyn is convinced *his* old friends in the KGB want to bump him off too, and I tell you, Harry, I'm sorely tempted to help them.'

I laugh, and we pick up our drinks. As I sip mine I wonder if this is the time to speak to Maurice about Gray and the CIA investigation. But instead I ask him if anyone in *our* government knows the head of its Security Service is accused of betraying his country. He gazes at me over the edge of his glass and says nothing, which is to say everything, because a man who has beaten the CIA lie-detector test would have no difficulty convincing me with a lie. So he wants me to know we're hiding FLUENCY from the prime minister. His eyes are almost shut, one hand open on the arm of his chair, the other pinching his cigarette in a circle – the Derbyshire Buddha. I wonder if he's giving me time to imagine doing something rash. A word in a Labour MP's ear, perhaps. But I don't have faith in his silences. I should tell him the White House knows all our troubles, that a joint CIA-FBI inquiry has the British Secret Service in its sights, and that Jim Angleton is going to crunch us up and spit us out. I should tell him, but I don't, because he's to blame too. He's let things go too far already. He's decent and sincere but he's a Service politician, and he'll do all he can to keep it in-house.

'You'll stay for dinner?'

'Sorry, Maurice, I can't.'

'Until Tuesday, then,' he says, and shakes my hand warmly, no doubt confident that he can trust me not to break our little contract.

The warmth, the smell and the roar of the big city evening are a release after the perpetual autumn of the club. As I walk along Horse Guards Road my gaze is drawn to the lights burning in the state drawing room at the back of Downing Street. Wilson may be working on his plans for a peace conference to end the war in Vietnam. Proof, I'm sure, that our prime minister is a Soviet stooge. We live in mad times. The question is, Harry Vaughan, what do you intend to do about it?

There's a bench beside the keeper's cottage in St James's Park where the secretaries at the Foreign Office feed the pelicans in their lunch hour. Jack Ellis asked, 'Is it for you or the Service?' and I said, 'Both,' which was more candid than wise. I'm looking out for myself, yes, but I belong to the Service. I've lied, cheated and killed someone for the Service. I finish my cigarette and flick the butt into the water. A young man in a boat-club blazer ambles past me but only as far as the low rail around the lake. I wait for him to turn and give me the eye, which he does very brazenly. What would you think of that, Guy Burgess? I'm old enough to be his father, and more. When I shake my head, he smiles and wanders off without a word.

I light another cigarette and rise. What the hell are we doing? Dick, my friend, this is your fault for trusting a sensitive investigation to Angleton's creatures. Vietnam to Billericay, the Reds are everywhere. If they bring Hollis down none of us are safe. My mum was a good Christian woman and she liked to say, what goes around comes around; there's a balance in the order of things. Most people believe something of the sort and have done since we ran around in skins. They have faith in a great system of cosmic justice. I don't share that faith. Too many men get away with murder. In the Service you must learn to make peace with your conscience, but I can only consider the lines on my face with equanimity if I'm able to tell the mirror they are the cares of one who fights for liberty and decency and democracy. And I'll fight this coup, this witch-hunt, inside the circle and, yes, outside it too, if necessary.

The shutters are open and there are no lights on in the house, so I assume Elsa is still dining with her senior civil-service colleagues. But her black wool coat and silver grey scarf are draped over a chair in the hall. I call to her and she doesn't reply, so I sit at the piano in our little drawing room and play, and I'm too caught up in the music and the memories it evokes to hear her enter. 'More nostalgia,' she says, because she knows 'Let's Sing Again' reminds me of my mother.

'I was thinking of her.'

She kisses my neck and I reach up to stroke her hair. 'Pleasant evening?'

'Not really,' she says. 'You?'

'No, but things are clearer.'

She leans back to look at me carefully. 'Hum. That sounds, well, ominous. Is it something Maurice said?'

'Something he didn't say.'

'Are you going to explain?'

'I don't think so.' I give her a reassuring smile. 'Don't worry. *Hawdd yw hi, I ifod yn ddewr out ôl i fur.*'

She laughs, then kisses my forehead. 'All right, Merlin, and what does that mean?'

'That it is easy to be brave behind a wall. But sometimes one has to step out from it.'

# 32

## 21 June 1965

THE LAST OF the Service Cavaliers are at Lord's for the Test against New Zealand, the family men at boarding-school prize days and the regatta at Henley, and the smart young ladies who fetch and carry in the Registry are planning their holidays in the country or on the Riviera, and if they meet the right chap on the tennis court or by the pool they may never return. End of the summer term with just the headmaster's report on FLUENCY to come, and while Dick considers how far he is going to push the knife into Roger's back, Wright and his wife are sailing off the coast near their home in Essex. Evelyn is still at her desk, of course, and will be all summer, her tatty shawl about her shoulders even as the temperature touches ninety in the office. She is playing with a corner of it, like a small child with a comfort blanket.

'Change your mind about him?' she asks.

'No, *cariad*. Have you?'

Her hand strays from the shawl to the birthmark on her face. 'I think Hollis is *more* likely to be ELLI.'

'You were certain it was Mitchell a year ago.'

'Counter-intelligence isn't a science,' she snaps. 'Besides, Mitchell may be working to Hollis.'

'On the golf course?'

No one I've met can scowl like Evelyn. I am tempted to duck her to see if she floats. Her eyes bore into me as I open the safe and choose the most recent of the dozen files that are the collected days of Graham Mitchell, code name PETERS. They are the record of his mutterings in the mirror and copies of his correspondence intercepted in our flap-and-seals operation at the post office, transcripts of his telephone conversations, a log of his movements, and the chicken-feed intelligence Martin offered him in the hope he would leak it to a Russian controller. *Graham Mitchell, former deputy director general of MI5: this is your life.* And there isn't a shred of evidence in those hundreds of pieces that proves he's working for the enemy. Still we persist. Special facilities are in place at his home, with bugs in the telephone, the drawing room and the master bedroom, and there are watchers at the house on Tuesdays, Wednesdays and Fridays. A4 doesn't have enough men to offer round-the-clock surveillance. That anyone would think three days a week worthwhile only serves to demonstrate how sclerotic and fearful MI5 has become as it turns upon itself – and it's the same across the river.

Mitchell lives with the stockbroker set in Surrey in a mock-Tudor house on a private road of houses built at the turn of the century. His home is comfortable but unremarkable, which I am sure was his intention when he bought the place. There's a large garden with brick terraces and a tennis court, a stream and several acres of open woodland and pasture. The common where we spent the summer of '63 waiting for him to meet the KGB is a couple of miles away.

To be sure I catch him I'll telephone him from Victoria but hang up when he answers. The traffic is terrible on the A316 and I don't manage to reach Chobham until half past seven. I park Elsa's little sports car a good way from his home and approach through the wood to be sure Monday is still a day of rest for the boys from A4 and no one has eyes on the house. Mitchell is on his hands and knees digging something into a bed with a trowel.

Andrew Williams

'Hello, Graham.'

'For God's sake, man!' He almost jumps out of his skin. He looks tanned or windblown from sailing, and he's put on weight, which is a good sign, because the last time I saw him he looked like a corpse. But his face is scored with deep lines that I don't remember two years ago and I wonder if the cloud of suspicion that hangs over him has taken its toll.

'Why are you here?' He's struggling to rise but I don't offer my hand because he's sensitive about his disability and would hate me to notice.

'Unofficial.'

'Of course. You would have rung the bell like a decent human being otherwise.'

'Do you mind if we sit there?' I say, pointing to a bench overlooking his pond.

'So no one can see you from the house? Look, say what you want to say quickly and go.'

'I'm afraid it's going to take a little time.' I walk over to the bench and Mitchell follows, and when we're sitting side by side he removes his gardening gloves and throws them on the grass at my feet as if he's issuing a challenge.

'Well?'

'How's Pat?'

'What do you want, Vaughan?'

'There's still SF in your home.'

'You haven't come here to tell me that?'

'No. No, I haven't.' I offer him a cigarette and he refuses. I think he'd happily choke me with the packet – the last time we spoke he asked for help and, like the Levite, I passed by on the other side. 'There's a Welsh saying: *Mae chwarae'n troi'n chwerw wrth chwarae 'da tân*. Things turn bad when you play with fire. Well, C's fire is burning out of control.'

'Ha!' he barks at me. 'Are you worried about your own skin? Any idea what we're going through here?'

'I'm sorry.'

'You're not the first uninvited guest in my garden, you know. They don't care to hide any more.'

I try to look sympathetic but I remember the relish with which he used to send the same goons from A Branch to burgle members of the British Communist Party. He used to say it was his finest hour.

'I know you'll help me, Graham, because we fought together and won, and that means something, and we knew what we were fighting for, but there are people in the Service now who don't know.'

Mitchell leans forward with his elbows on his knees and gazes at the shimmering surface of the pond where the fish are rising in concentric circles.

'I don't owe the Service *anything*,' he says, but with a note of resignation in his voice, 'and what can I do now anyway?'

'I'm not sure yet. Perhaps just listen.'

And he does, his hands clasped in a pious fist, thumbs to his lips, as he did on those rare occasions he was stumped by a crossword in the *Listener*. I tell him his old colleague Blunt is a traitor, and the CIA is plotting a coup; the President of the United States knows everything and our prime minister nothing. Dick seems ready to throw Roger under a bus, and FLUENCY is collecting names for a great British purge.

'Can I have that cigarette now?' he says. 'Roger Hollis is no more a traitor than I am, but I suppose you know that or you wouldn't be here.' He accepts a cigarette and a light from me and inhales deeply. 'That's better, yes. I've promised not to, but . . . The thing is, Roger was the first to suspect Blunt. "He's the mole," he said to me. "Blunt's ELLI." That was years ago, just after the war. He confronted Blunt, accused him to his face: "You're ELLI." Blunt denied it, of course. Do you think Angleton and Wright know that?'

'I'm not sure they would care to. Wright despises Roger.'

'And me?'

'I think so. And you know how things stand between the DG and Arthur Martin. That wouldn't amount to a row of beans if Dick wasn't bending over backwards to please the CIA.'

Mitchell examines his cigarette, then puts it out on the bench even though he's smoked only a fraction of it. 'This CIA inquiry, Gray's inquiry . . .'

'My source says its conclusions were written before Gray set foot in the country. The American ambassador or Deputy Director Helms will take them to the prime minister and demand the head of Hollis as the price of future co-operation. That's just the beginning. They want to reduce the Service to a CIA satellite.'

'Harold Wilson won't stand for that.'

'And if they bring him down?'

Mitchell pulls a face. 'I say, steady, Vaughan.'

'Just a thought.'

'It's the sort of thing the Americans do in banana republics, not here.'

'Of course you're right. We have a special relationship, don't we?'

Someone is calling from the house. 'Hello. That's Pat,' he says.

'I'd rather she didn't see me, Graham.'

'All right.' With a hand to the bench he rises and limps towards the house. I light another cigarette and try to concentrate for a moment on the warmth and the song of a robin, and evening gold on the water. One day Elsa and I may move to a cottage and become thoroughly English, like Pat and

Graham. Elsa will have a cuttings garden and I will . . . I will write a thriller.

'You haven't told me what you want me to do?' Mitchell is back with two bottles of pale ale.

'You're still a member of the Royal Thames? Mr Duff will leave you a message.' I take a slip of paper from my pocket. 'When you hear from him, ring this number, seven o'clock sharp. Use the phone box at Chobham station.'

Mitchell passes a hand across his brow. 'I don't know what you're planning . . . Will it sort things? Will they leave us alone?'

I don't have the heart to say, 'No.'

At our regular Thursday FLUENCY meeting we agree priorities. Now it's official, Lecky and I are to concentrate on Hollis's time in China in the thirties. Wright and the others will review his student days at Oxford and his career in the Service. As soon as the meeting's over Wright catches a flight to Washington. I cross the river to speak to Maurice and, for the first time in months, he invites me to brief C in person. Keep it short and factual, is his advice, and I follow it to a T. No mention is made of our differences. He's full of the boyish bonhomie that has served him so well. I imagine he's the same with Hollis, and that he makes the same meaningless excuse for FLUENCY: 'an unfortunate necessity'. I tell him 'Peter' is on his way to Langley, and he just nods. I could tell him a lot he doesn't know about our transatlantic cousins and the report they're writing for their president but I don't want to spoil the surprise.

At home, Elsa hands me a postcard of a lovely thing in a pink bathing suit on the balcony of a Holiday Inn. She knows it's a piece of 'mischief', and that 'love Kathy' is nobody and means nothing, but the message 'looking forward to the party on 12 July' means something, and so does the Washington postmark. 'You're not going to explain?'

'No.'

'Jack?'

'No.'

'Careless. Here, catch!' She throws me some matches. 'Jack should have sent you a cable.'

The following morning, Mr Duff leaves the message at Mitchell's club.

# 33

## *10 July 1965*

WE DRIVE TO Oxford for lunch with Bethan and a friend, who may be more than a friend, who went to Eton. 'Her choice, not yours,' Elsa says on the way home, 'and all that talk of the South Wales Valleys . . . Why don't you stop pretending? You were at a boarding school too.'

'It should have been the county grammar.'

'Poor Harry.' She laughs and takes a hand off the wheel to push me. 'What a desperate fellow you are.'

On Sunday evening I walk round the corner to the telephone box outside Labour Party headquarters in Smith Square to take Mitchell's call and we arrange to meet the following day.

'You're sure about this, Vaughan?'

'Dead certain,' I say (which is nonsense).

The frosted-glass partition in the alcove slides back and I show my pass to Roberts, the duty policeman. On the other side of the Pond, young men in sharp suits, with urgent expressions, hurry about the lobby of the CIA on all days and at all hours. Here at MI5 there's just Bob the Bobby flicking through a Sunday paper. I take the lift to the third floor, show my face in D3, then open my own office. There's something I must do before tomorrow and I need to pinch a typewriter to do it, only before I have a chance to do so Evelyn pushes her way into my room. I anticipated her presence but not the speed with which she pounces or her state of agitation. She's trembling like a teenager on a first date.

'*Cariad*, were you waiting for me? How sweet.'

She lifts a protective hand to her face. 'What are you doing here?'

'In *my* office? SIS business. What are *you* doing here?'

'The defector, Volkov,' she says. 'We've missed something.'

That's a lie. So I ask, 'What?'

'Well, I don't know yet,' she snaps.

'Heard from Peter?'

'Just to say he's spoken to Jim and he was pleased with the FLUENCY report.'

'Of course. Did Peter say anything else?'

'Only that he'll brief us at the next meeting'.

She has scratched the birthmark on her face, which is something she does when she's feeling anxious.

'Don't work late,' she says.

'I won't.'

When she's gone I take the Scotch from my desk drawer and settle down to wait awhile. Thank you, dear Evelyn, your face may not have launched a thousand ships but it tells a good story nonetheless. I wager she has just learned about the CIA plot to remove Hollis. Wright will have briefed her on the phone and warned her 'to tell no one'. Then the last person she expects to see on a Sunday evening, the last person she wants to see, turns up: me. She's in a state because she knows it's her duty to inform Hollis at once, but Wright has persuaded her to let events run their course. She's making a mistake: Angleton is as reliable as a three-jump cowboy, to borrow from my old friend Jack. I raise my glass to salute Jack and his post-card of the girl in the pink bathing costume.

*

At four o'clock the following afternoon I park a pool Rover on the opposite side of Pall Mall from the Travellers Club. Mitchell is in the passenger seat beside me, a cigarette between his fingers. 'Just for today,' he says. The Travellers is the gentleman's palazzo between Maurice's club and mine. Popular over the years with royalty, politicians and explorers, its members are generally less erudite than members of the Athenaeum and less liberal than those of us who belong to the Reform. Sir Roger Hollis is a member of the Travellers, and if he has the sense to realise that the 'PERSONAL' typewritten note I left for him yesterday is from someone with his best interests at heart he will arrive there in a few minutes' time.

Mitchell asks, 'What will happen after this?'

'He won't be able to stop the FLUENCY investigation, not while it has Dick's support.'

'Remember the fuss after Burgess and Maclean defected?'

'I was in Vienna.'

'White was deputy DG of Five then, of course – "No turning in upon ourselves," he said, "because that's what the bloody Russians want."' Mitchell folds the butt of his cigarette into the dashboard ashtray. 'One has to investigate these things. It's all about who one trusts to do it. Never liked Arthur Martin. A bit unstable, don't you think? At least he has some experience. This fellow Wright . . . perfectly competent technician, but what was Roger thinking making him the chairman of a working party as sensitive as this one?'

'This is your chance to ask him.'

A traffic warden taps on the driver's side window and I show him my police identification and ever so politely tell him to sod off.

'I suppose Wright was White's choice,' says Mitchell.

'Or Angleton's.' I touch his arm. 'Look.' The director general's black Bentley turns right across the traffic on to Pall Mall and draws up at the Travellers. I sink in my seat and reach across to stay Mitchell's hand as he reaches for the door. 'Not yet. Not with me in the car.'

Hollis executes a little pirouette on the pavement, then climbs the steps of the Travellers where a porter is waiting to tip his hat.

'Give him a minute,' I say, 'and remember, nothing about our source.'

'I'm not an idiot, Vaughan.'

Maybe not, but too civil service to be a decent field agent. And yet, after the isolation and the ignominy of the last couple of years, this is a task he seems to relish. I sense he has recovered some of his old Winchester College confidence. There will be no further contact between us, so I wish him luck and watch him in the rear-view mirror as he walks to the club with a pronounced spring in his step.

# 34

## 13 July 1965

A N INSTRUCTOR AT the Fort taught me that once you've pulled the pin on a standard British grenade you have four seconds' grace.

To be sure I'm clear of the blast, I spend Tuesday with Lecky in the basement at Century House. I catch him leaping at the furniture, like a dog agitating for a bone.

'Hollis was on good terms with a hack in China called Smedley,' he says, 'female of the species and an American.'

'Where's this come from all of a sudden?'

'Bright at CIA London station.'

'Ah.'

'Seems Smedley found time in her busy newspaper schedule to do a bit of moonlighting for the Communist International.'

'So Roger was friendly with a Communist in the thirties?' I say, throwing my hands into the air. 'Well, that's it. Will you ring Special Branch, Terence, or shall I?'

'All right. We all know where you stand on this, Vaughan.'

'I stand before you with an open mind.'

'Peter doesn't think so.'

'Don't fall for that "Counter-intelligence feeds off scraps" bullshit, Lecky. You know Wright and Hollis have history, don't you?'

He protests he's capable of making his own assessment, and he's reserving his judgement too. I'm not sure. He has inhaled

Andrew Williams

deeply, and now sees things the same way as Peter Wright, which is back to front. Merely countenance the possibility for long enough and nothing becomes something. As the great Tom Paine observed, 'Time makes more converts than reason.' Peter is teaching Terence to know and not to know, to search for the good facts and ignore the inconvenient ones. In the wilderness of mirrors you see only what you want to see. Funny, because it is the way the Party goes about things, too, the way Guy and Kim went about their business.

Late in the afternoon, Moulders rings me from his office many floors above. 'All sorts of trouble on the other side of the river.'

'Oh?'

'Meet me at eight tonight. Usual place.'

'Not tonight.'

The line crackles. 'Does this have anything to do with you?' he says at last.

'No idea what you're talking about, Maurice.'

'Never mind. Tomorrow. Eleven. My office.'

But the following day – the Wednesday – I return to Leconfield House and ring Maurice's secretary with an excuse. She says something tart I don't catch, because my room is full of the noise of the street. The windows are open in the hope of some small breeze on a sweltering high-summer day in central London, where the sky is filthy white and my throat feels sharp and dry with exhaust fumes. For a moment I allow my imagination to carry me to a glade by a stream, where an attractive little Jewess, who happens to be my wife, is lying on a rug, the sun through the trees dappling the skin of her legs.

I'm watching her roll on to her side and reach for the Chablis when I am catapulted back to my desk by a car horn in the street below, my shirt clinging to my back, the Smedley file open in front of me. Agnes Smedley. War reporter. Champion

of independence for India in the twenties, of the Chinese
Communist Party in the thirties. Judged by the same to be 'too
independent of thought' but a loyal supporter nonetheless, and
an agent for the Communist International. There's a picture
on file of her in combat fatigues and a Mao hat. Died 1950.
Ashes buried at a cemetery for heroes of the revolution in
Peking. Lecky has run a trace through the Passport Office for
the dates of Hollis's arrivals and departures from London, and
there's the address of a bank in Peking that he was using for
his post. There's a note from Wright, too. He's spoken to an
old soldier who remembers Hollis out there. Hollis was 'thick'
with another Communist called Arthur Ewert, a talent-spotter
for Moscow. Wright has scribbled a note on a cover sheet,
'Every man is defined by his friends.'

I wait an hour, then saunter down the corridor to the D3
Secretariat where members of the team are sweating over their
files. Wright's sitting at his desk with a cigarette between his
fingers, Evelyn hovering at its edge.

'Things t-t-took an awkward turn,' he says. 'I expect you
h-heard about it?'

'Of course he did, darling,' says Evelyn, gazing at me from
the corner of her eye.

'I *did* hear that Roy Rogers's horse, Trigger, has "passed away",'
I say, 'and that the Russians are sending a couple of thousand
military advisers to help the Communists in Vietnam.'

Evelyn snorts; most unattractive.

'I was r-referring to a more local difficulty,' says Wright. 'The
Americans have conducted a secret review of our intelligence
and found it wanting in every way. Jim Angleton was b-bursting
to tell me. Cornered me, at one of his all-night drinking sessions.
He – they w-want rid of Roger and their own people inside
MI5. They were planning to meet the prime minister to tell
him so.'

I whistle. 'Landing their ships on our beaches?'

Wright's gaze drifts from me to his desktop and then to Evelyn. 'Jim briefed me in confidence' – he leans forward to extinguish his cigarette – 'b-b-but I was duty-bound to warn Roger. I flew home last night. He's shocked, of course.'

'Dick will be, too, I'm sure.'

Evelyn has a hand to her birthmark. They both knew and chose to say nothing until the cat was out of the bag, and now they're putting on a fine show of sympathy and quiet indignation, just as you might with a friend who confides to you that his wife is sleeping with someone else and he has no idea the someone is you. Wright left just enough space to back away. I could expose him as the second-rate conspirator he is, but not without risking the identity of my source, and I don't believe it would make a bit of difference to the FLUENCY investigation if I did.

'Roger's b-been humiliated,' says Wright. 'He's refusing point blank to see the American ambassador. He's asked the Foreign Office to tell members of the CIA's London office they're persona non grata, kick them out. That's r-really not in our interests, of course, and I'm sure Dick will tell him so.' He sighs, as one with unnatural cares. 'Jim wants to help us. He's just gone about it the wrong way.'

I say, 'I see,' when I mean, 'You shit.'  /

The phone on Wright's desk rings and he answers. 'Yes, sir,' and raises his eyebrows to warn us it's Hollis on the line. 'I'll c-come right up, sir.'

But Wright hasn't done with me for the day. Vicky, one of the D Branch secretaries, has found me a small fan, but the breeze is barely enough to lift the papers on the desk in front of me. In desperation I've used the silk tie Elsa's mum bought me for Christmas to hold the window wide open. At half past four Wright barges into my office. There's no pretence when we're alone, no courtesy. He must be a cold-blooded creature because he's still wearing his tie and jacket, the sort of dark blue blazer I associate with clubhouse bores.

'I w-wanted a word in private,' he says, closing my door with his arse.

'Keeping secrets from Evelyn?'

He smiles his sideways smile. 'Of course not.'

'Does she know you broke into the DG's office?'

'It's about Jim,' he says. 'He thinks you m-may be working for the other side.'

A frisson of anxiety courses through me, and to disguise it I grunt and push my chair away. 'And what do you think?'

'Jim thinks you're obstructing the investigation. And there's your friendship with Burgess, of course.'

'Oh, really?' I laugh loudly. 'Pot calling the kettle. All those liquid lunches Angleton enjoyed with Philby at Harvey's restaurant – he was one of Kim's best sources. You know that.'

'And Operation SUBALTERN.'

'What the hell does that mean?'

'And now this b-business with the DG.'

'What business?'

'Jim thinks you warned R-Roger that the CIA was moving against him.'

'*You* told Roger. You were duty-bound to, you said.'

'Well, that isn't quite true.'

'Oh?'

Cool as you like he pushes the papers on my filing cabinet to one side so he can lean against it with his arm on the top. 'I was g-going to speak to Roger, naturally, only someone b-beat me to it. *Was* it you, by the way?'

'Well, if I did know, I'd have been duty-bound to say, wouldn't I?'

'Did you?'

'No, Peter.' I feel my shirt peel from the chair as I lean forward to look him in the eye. 'Who told Roger what and when doesn't matter. Accusing me of being a spy . . . well, that's crazy. Mad. A wild allegation.'

Wright licks his bottom lip as if he's tasting his reply. 'You *have* gone out of your way to be difficult, Vaughan.'

'Not true.'

'You told Jim you didn't consider me fit to run the investigation – a technician—'

'Science officer. He asked me and I told him you wouldn't be my first choice.'

'Well . . .' he stands up straight and reaches behind his back for the door handle '. . . we'll see, won't we?'

'Here,' I say, getting to my feet. 'Here's something for you.' I scoop up the Smedley file and offer it to him. 'A friend of Hollis in China – an agent for the Communist International. Worth looking into.'

He's smiling, but not in a pleasant way.

'Yes. Lecky told me about Smedley. "Bullshit", you called it, didn't you?'

'Bullshit to think you know a man just by the company he keeps. Accuse Dick, accuse Angleton, then you can accuse me.'

'You can't accuse me,' he says, opening the door. 'I've always be v-very careful about the company I keep. Thank you for this.' He flaps the Smedley file at me. 'I'll let Terence know I have it from you.' Then he closes the door oh-so-quietly behind him, and I close my eyes. '*Cachu* . . .' I say it very quickly three times, four times, six and seven times, then kick the bottom drawer of a filing cabinet.

Rush hour in Piccadilly, people hurrying to the tube at Green Park, everyone impatient to be home, except me. I stop and gaze in art-shop windows, step into Hatchards to inspect the

'must buy' books, then Fortnum's for some fancy chocolates. I
carry my little package through 'Honey and Preserves' to the
exit on Jermyn Street, and on Pall Mall I collect my post from
the Reform, pausing at the bottom of York Steps to tie a shoe-
lace. In Horse Guards a crowd is listening to 'Beating the Retreat',
and even with my heart pounding trumpets and cymbals, I
smile at the recollection of another Marx quip, that military
justice is to justice what military music is to music. Time to
calm down, Harry. No one is following you home today. Only
remember, it's Vienna Rules now.

Mrs Howard's help is polishing the brass door fittings at
number 21, and scaffolding is going up opposite at number
11, just across the street from home. Should I splint the front
door? Those fine upstanding chaps in A Branch may come
calling, or someone from the CIA. Elsa will want to know why.

The house is empty, the post still on the mat. An image of
Jesus stares up at me. 'Hymn practice 19.30,' Maurice writes.
Turning his card over again, I note it's a fresco of Judas's
betrayal of Christ by the late medieval painter Giotto. I expect
he picked it up on his holiday last summer. Well, Maurice, I
suppose we still need each other. But the first thing to do is
fling open the drawing-room windows for some air. Then I
change my shirt and carry a cup of tea and an ashtray to the
couch. In our dark little hall the grandfather clock strikes half
past six.

I find Maurice playing with the organ stops out. ('Bach is best,'
Dylan Thomas used to say.) The air is charged with the rich
scent of sandalwood, and as the bass pipes rumble, dust motes
dance in the rainbow light pouring through the stained glass
on to the chairs and terracotta tiles of the nave: a modest
neo-Gothic church of grey Kentish ragstone on the outside,
colourful and idolatrous within. In the threads of Maurice's

Prelude (in C major, I think) I can almost imagine there is such a thing as a divine order. The trouble with the chapel Sundays of childhood was that we relied too much on the spoken word of the minister for inspiration, and he was a competent actor but we knew his lines too well. There was no moment on the road from Maerdy, only a growing conviction, like the swell of a mighty organ, that we walk through the shadow of the valley alone. Marx (Karl) was a companion for a mile or so, until I realised he was a terrible bore, and that he had kept bad company.

The last chord of the Prelude blossoms and dies in the corners of the church, and for a few precious seconds of silence my nerves tingle with feeling, just as they do after sex, or when someone walks over my grave. Maurice coughs and turns a page of his music book and the spell is broken. I begin to clap and he turns, right hand to his large spectacles. 'You're early.'

'I'm glad, because I came in time for your performance.'

'Practising for next Sunday.' Swinging his legs round and over the pedals, he shuffles along the bench and perches at its edge. 'Sanctuary from the sinful world.'

'Music or this place?'

'Inseparable,' I hear him say, his head between his knees. 'Excuse me, will you?' He was playing the pedals of the organ in his stockinged feet and with all the confidence and agility of a Highland dancer tiptoeing round a sword, but leaning over his stomach to lace his shoes is proving to be much more of a challenge. Rising at last, flushed with the effort, he asks, 'You're not a believer, Harry, are you?'

'I'm not religious.'

'What do you believe in?'

I puff out my cheeks. 'Things,' I say, 'things. But *if I had a world of my own, everything would be nonsense.* Perhaps it is already. Now, why am I here, Maurice?'

'You *do* believe in something?'

'Must we do this now? I thought this was urgent.'

'You look uncomfortable,' he says, gesturing to the seat nearest the bench. The organ is on a dais above the floor of the nave so when I do what he wants I find myself looking up at him, like a servant on his knees before his master. 'That's better,' he says. 'Now, tell me, why did you keep the CIA investigation of the Service from me?'

'I didn't.'

'Angleton thinks you told Roger because you knew he would kick up a fuss – that you were throwing up a smokescreen.'

'I heard that from Wright, yes.'

Maurice leans closer, forearms across his broad knees. 'Well?'

'And if I did know, wasn't it my duty to notify Roger?'

'To tell me first – or the chief,' he remembers to say.

'Angleton thinks I'm a traitor. Did he tell you that too?'

Maurice stares at me. Solomon, on his bench, and *no one who utters unrighteous things will escape his notice.* I meet his gaze, motionless, unblinking, until he says at last, 'Well, are you a spy, Harry?'

'All right, Maurice. I'm ELLI.' I glare at him. 'I confess.'

His left hand moves to the keyboard and the organ booms, like a ship's foghorn. 'Good try. You're not important enough, and you know it, but, if we're to believe your FLUENCY colleagues, ELLI may be one of many spies in the Service.' The corner of his mouth twitches with just the suggestion of a smile. 'Let me ask you again . . .'

'Oh, come on.' I roll my eyes to where Heaven should be. 'All right . . . We're in your church, I'll tell you something. Obeying orders . . . it isn't an unconditional pact. No matter how many promises you make, how many oaths you take, not if you're a proper human being. The war taught us that, didn't it? Remember the camps?'

'I remember. And I remember you were at one – the liberation of Belsen, wasn't it?'

'Yes.'

He reflects upon this a moment. 'We choose sides to protect our values, then set about compromising them. Sometimes we have no choice. That's why I come here' – he opens his arms to the church – 'to remember who I am. But don't keep things from me, Harry. Hollis retires in December and he'll be replaced by his deputy, Furnival Jones, and I understand FJ thinks very highly of Wright and Martin.'

'That's true.'

'He'll push forward with the investigation. Don't give him any cause to doubt you. And, Harry,' he clasps fat hands together as if in prayer, 'lie to me and I'll cut you loose.'

I protest – 'Maurice!' – even though it's a piece of nonsense. When the time comes he'll cut me adrift in any case. He'll have to. It's only a question of when.

# 35

## *29 July 1965*

S ERVICE PEOPLE ARE familiar with many shades of secret. They recognise the difference between official secrets and a secret to save the reputation of an official. The best efforts of the management to bury the rift with the CIA are not enough to prevent it seeping through the building. Someone called Peter may have spoken to someone, and that someone is busy telling colleagues at Five that the Americans are trying to shove the director general out of the door. Hollis will limp on to retirement, but his reputation will never recover.

Our working party meets to assess the situation on the last Thursday in July. For the first time in a while Arthur Martin joins us, although his manner is so changed it would be easy to take him for an imposter. I swear this business has hurt him more than Blunt. The anger, the arrogance, the fire has gone out. Well, it's Wright's show now, and he is calm and reasonable as if the hunt for a mole is a simple technical matter, like the wiring of a listening device. The perfect white-coat voice and manner. As I listen to him remind us of the need for total secrecy an image comes to mind of a snake-oil salesman selling his dodgy potions from the back of a wagon. 'It's imperative knowledge of our work is restricted to the smallest circle,' he says, and Stewart taps the arm of his wheelchair in agreement. The investigation falls into three sections now and Evelyn has prepared a summary of our progress.

Section 1: ELLI. Section 2: 'Middle-grade agent' inside the Service. Section 3: the list of politicians, professors, Service old boys and girls that I filched from a D3 safe to show Maurice. And her recommendation is that we return to the evidence from the defectors for a new season.

'What does this deep history have to do with the real purpose of FLUENCY?' I ask, lifting the Section 3 list.

Martin glares at me; Lecky fiddles with his cigarettes; Stewart brushes dust from his sleeve. How dare I?

'Well, H-Harry,' says Wright, 'we will only find the mole if we go back to the thirties when the enemy built his networks, and these people . . .' he places his hand lightly on the Section 3 list '. . . these p-people may have a connection with ELLI. They remain a security threat.'

'Do we have the resources to investigate so many?'

'We will have,' Wright replies, with obvious satisfaction, 'when the new director general takes charge.'

The front door opens and I walk out of the drawing room into the hall to greet Elsa. 'We're going away for two weeks in September,' she says. 'I've spoken to Fiona and we can have the house in France.'

I help her with her coat, then hold and kiss her. 'Good evening?' It's after eleven o'clock.

'As these things go.' Her face is flushed with drink. 'I met Tom Driberg.'

'At the Ministry of Defence?'

'Denis Healey's trying to be nice to the Labour left – beer and sandwiches and those silly grapefruits with sticks of cheese and pineapple. Standards are slipping.'

'You're so bourgeois.'

'Well, that's true, but I can tell you, I felt very at home with the left wing of the Labour Party.'

'Say that a little louder for the microphone, would you?'

She laughs. 'That had better be a joke, Harry.'

'Tell me, what did Driberg have to say?'

'Tea first,' she says, breaking from my embrace.

I rescue my whisky from the top of the piano and follow her into the kitchen where she's spooning Earl Grey into the pot.

'Sure?' She waves the spoon. 'You should. You drink too much Scotch.'

'Hypocrite. You've been drinking too.'

'Tonight, not every night.'

'Never mind that,' I say, pulling a chair from the table. 'How do you know Tom Driberg?'

'I don't, but he knew I was married to you.'

'Oh?'

'He says he wants to talk to you about Burgess.'

'What more is there to say?'

'Well, I don't know, do I?' She picks up her teacup and walks round the table to stand beside me – 'Come on, then' – and I push my chair back a little more so she can sit on my knee.

'He's going to invite us to his home in Essex,' she says, stroking the hair from my forehead. 'He's amusing. Very rude about his parliamentary colleagues, and about you, but in a nicer way. Homosexual?'

I roll my eyes.

'Well, how was I supposed to know?'

Lifting my chin I invite her to kiss me, and it's wine, not beer, I taste.

'Wine for the ladies,' she says, 'which means me because I was the only woman there. The Honourable Member for Liverpool Walton asked me to fetch him a bottle of beer. "I'm not here to serve the drinks, Comrade," I said. "Ask me about the defence estimates."'

'Marx said, *Social progress can be measured by the social position of the female sex.*'

She kisses me again. 'That one sounds like Karl.'

I kiss her – 'It's Karl' – then kiss her again. I kiss her face, the nape of her neck. I kiss her hair, and the little notch above her breastbone. I kiss her until she holds me away and rises. 'Come on, then.' And she takes my hand to pull me from the chair. I check her. '*Cariad*, a word of warning. That nice Mr Driberg, don't tell him anything you don't want the world to know.'

I'm lying, eyes open, wondering whether I can free my arm from beneath Elsa's pillow and close the gap in the curtains. I sleep badly these days. Tonight it's Driberg, and the first thing I always think of is the time he reached over to touch my cock. 'You've got a pretty one,' he said. I thanked him for the compliment and zipped it away at once. That was in the lavatory at the Gargoyle in Soho. Burgess was a member, Driberg too, I think. The artist Matisse was a member and some of his work used to hang in the club. I remember the décor was Moorish and mirrored, as places that come alive in the soft smoky yellow of evening often are. It was the sort of place where an Honourable Member like Tom could touch my cock confident that no one would summon the police and have him arrested for gross indecency. On that night Driberg was in the company of MP Michael Foot, and the artists Bacon and Freud, the writer and Communist Toynbee, little boy Burgess and Donald Maclean, and Dylan Thomas read poetry to us until six in the morning.

Elsa stirs and I slip free, and when she settles I peel the sheet back and step over to the curtains. There's no one in a car or twitching at a curtain, no glow of a cigarette in a doorway. The street's empty, and that's how it should be at one o'clock on a Friday morning. That there might be someone bores and frightens me. Driberg thinks espionage is a great game. He came to see me when he was writing his book on Guy. 'You know, they accuse Burgess and Maclean of being "split men" and leading double lives,' he said, 'but in a world divided East–West, Communism–capitalism, anyone who cares about his fellow man must have doubts and conflicting impulses.'

'Split men' touched a nerve with Tom because he was wrestling with the compromises and contradictions of his own life. A Cavalier Communist for a time, public school and Oxbridge like the others, now he's a Labour MP who lives in a stately home in Essex, where he hides his wife. Ena knew he was a homosexual roué but married him all the same. That was in '51, the year Burgess and Maclean dropped their friends in the shit by running off to Moscow. I hear Ena has tried to do a flit of her own but the Labour Party has discouraged her because an Honourable Member should have a wife. Driberg belongs to the class of socialist who cares for the working class in general but none of its representatives in particular, yet he's a member of Labour's ruling executive and he speaks from the heart (wherever it's buried) on everything from modern poesy and the Rolling Stones to peace in our time.

Elsa mumbles something in her sleep and her voice draws me back to the room and away from the window. I slip into bed beside her again but am no closer to sleep. The thing is, Driberg has been on my mind for a while. His name is near the top of the D3 'further investigation' list I copied for Maurice. It's still there and was tabled at yesterday's FLUENCY meeting. I'm suspicious of coincidences but they happen in small circles. I give up on sleep and pad through to the kitchen for a cigarette and some tea. Three spoons of ordinary that I count out as Tom, Guy and Harry, like the escape tunnels dug by prisoners during the war. Driberg has Burgess's wicked sense of humour and the same urge to be naughty. I know he would jump at a chance to kick up a fuss about the secret state, take a swing at the establishment he belongs to. He's a liar (he's a journalist and a politician, of course he is) and yet, in his way, a sincere champion of the people. Dylan Thomas had it from the owner of the Gargoyle, who was told by the writer Evelyn Waugh, who heard it from Driberg himself, that his mother's dying words were, 'Tom, you're a liar. You're a liar and all men are liars.'

Well, if *all* men are liars, Mrs Driberg, your son is no worse than the rest of us, no worse than me. I will talk to Tom.

# 36

## 16 August 1965

THE POSTMAN BRINGS an invitation from Mr and Mrs Driberg to lunch at their stately home in Essex. I don't show Elsa, and decline with a line. The St Paul's postal unit will be intercepting Tom's correspondence, and I don't want our names to crop up in its weekly bulletin. I expect there's a phone tap on his home and his parliamentary office too.

I decide to make my approach ten days later, at a meeting of Labour's governing executive committee in Smith Square. The press is there in force because its members are debating the American bombing campaign in Vietnam. Michael Foot arrives, Barbara Castle arrives, everyone arrives before Tom. The reporters have gone to a local café for tea and a bacon roll by the time Tom turns up. There's only the representative of the *Daily Express.*

'Is that you, Vaughan?'

'The same.'

It's six years since we last met, and those years have been cruel to Tom.

'What are you going to tell the prime minister?' shouts the hack from the *Express.*

'Stop supporting the Americans,' he fires back.

The reporter is ready with a supplementary but I coax Tom back to his seat in the cab and shut the door before he's able to answer it.

'Trying to pick me up? That's flattering. I must say, you're wearing very well, Vaughan. Marriage must suit you. I met your charming wife. I'm sorry . . .?'

'Elsa.'

'Yes, Elsa. Well, my invitation still stands. Come to lunch, or we can meet in Soho, for old times' sake. But . . .' he glances at his watch '. . . you'll have to let me go,' and he reaches over my legs for the door. 'Ring me.'

I have the handle – 'This isn't a social, Tom' – and, leaning closer, I whisper, 'You know what I do for a living?'

He smiles. 'Of course.'

'This is about you.' Our eyes meet, and his are very bloodshot. 'It's about the Labour Party – the Labour government.'

'Then ring my secretary and we can—'

'No.' I take a scrap of paper from my jacket pocket and hand it to him. 'Tonight. Eight o'clock. Change cabs on the way.'

Those bloodshot eyes are twinkling with mischief now, and I know he'll be there even if he has to make excuses to the prime minister or, more likely, the next young man he's going to spoil.

'Hey, are you going somewhere? If not . . .' The cabbie is watching us in his mirror.

Driberg snaps at him, 'Just wait.' But our business is done and I sit back to let him pass. Hand on my knee he rises and looks sideways at me. 'Do you remember when I touched . . .?'

'How can I forget?'

He chuckles. 'Such a lovely one.'

I watch him grandstanding as he walks through the protesters outside Transport House and wonder whether I'm making a terrible mistake. But he has proved a fearless champion of civil rights and I know the moment he takes his place at Labour's table he will condemn the bombing in Vietnam with colour and passion. Tom is just the sort of posh socialist Roundheads like Wright hate most of all.

'Piccadilly,' I say to the cabbie.

'Right you are,' he replies. 'That was Tom Driberg, wasn't it?'

The short taxi ride from Driberg's apartment in Kensington to the Wheatsheaf pub will take him from society's inner circle to its outer, from white villas and garden squares to yellow brick terraces and the estates of the working classes he champions in Parliament. Perhaps he knows the pub because the landlord welcomes homosexuals, and the police in this part of west London are too busy chasing real criminals to care what consenting adults get up to in the bar at the back of a local boozer. But Driberg is more familiar with the East End, where he's thick with a couple of gangsters who run clubs and a protection racket. One of them is a homosexual who serves lads to guests like canapés.

Driberg's late, naturally. I watch him pay his cabbie and enter the pub, and when I'm sure no one is tailing him I follow. I find him at the bar with a gin and tonic, and for the second time today I'm struck by how he's gone to seed. I remember in the Gargoyle years he was tanned and fit with a natural wave in his hair, and supremely confident – he might have been taken for a middle-aged maharajah. He's in his mid-sixties now, his face creased like an old boxer's, and what's left of his hair is grey. Time and indulgence have caught up with him, as they are bound to with us all.

'The landlord recognised me,' he says, lifting his glass with pride. There are about a dozen people in the pub, a couple of Irish labourers in dungarees standing at the bar, a party of the young around a table against the wall. 'A malt whisky, please, George.' Driberg beckons his new friend over. 'George is from Glasgow.'

'When you're ready, Tom.' I nod at a table in a dark-wood alcove with a view of the door and the bar.

'I was going to Mick Jagger's party and I might still, if you hurry,' he says, flumping on to the burgundy plush bench beside me. 'Ginsberg introduced us a few weeks ago – Allen Ginsberg, the poet, do you know him? Well, we were talking poetry and Jagger was sitting on the couch in these tight trousers. One couldn't fail to notice. "Oh, Mick," I said, "*what* a basket you have."'

I snort with laughter.

'Mick has invited me to his party, so he must have forgiven me,' he says, with a sly smile.

I reach into my jacket and take out a newspaper cutting from ten years ago. I have kept it between the pages of Driberg's book about Burgess. 'Recognise this?'

'By me?' He reaches into the breast pocket of his suit for his spectacles: 'For *Reynolds News*.'

I take the cutting back. '*The Burgess-Maclean witch-hunt is now being transformed into a government witch-hunt.*'

'That's right,' he says. 'When they surfaced in Moscow, Fleet Street had one of its fits of moral outrage. Is there anything more ridiculous, I ask you? Every few days a new story of Communist plots in the civil service, Parliament, the universities, and the *Daily Express* was the worst. It was getting very silly, actually, dangerous, and I think I say so.' He gestures to the cutting.

'You do. "*It is better that there should be a few Burgess-Maclean cases than that our nation, should be like a McCarthyite police state, with elaborate checks on people's movements and associations and with power for security officers to detain and question suspects.*"'

He picks up his glass. 'To the point, I think.'

'Yes, and it made me think of you.'

'And my hand on your cock?' he says, patting my knee.

I ignore him. 'We're in the middle of a proper witch-hunt, Tom, not one cooked up by a few greasy newspaper hacks.'

'Go on.'

'A cabal of counter-intelligence officers have used Philby as an excuse to turn us upside down in search of a mole at the top of MI5. At the *very* top of Five.'

'How close to the top?'

I pick up my glass; it's almost empty. 'Another?' This is my story and I must be careful how I tell it. 'Same again?' I raise my glass and gesture to George at the bar. Driberg glances at his watch impatiently. 'You said this was about me and the government?'

'The CIA is driving the whole thing.' I know the letters CIA will be like a red rag to a bull. 'It's a power grab, Tom. The Agency has tried to remove Roger Hollis and place its own people inside MI5. And it's just the beginning. There's a list of socialists and former Communists: MPs, civil servants, academics. And Number 10 knows nothing.'

'I'm on the list?'

'Of course.'

'Oh, good. Who else?'

'Some of your friends and some of mine,' I say, rising to collect our drinks from George.

'Evidence, Harry,' he says, when I return. 'Names. Dates. Pieces of paper.'

'All in good time. A little parliamentary pressure . . . A question or two to the home secretary would be helpful.'

'How far can I take this?'

'Well, it's a matter of trust, Tom. The conversation we're having now is enough to put me in prison.'

'You know me, I'm used to keeping secrets,' he says ('*And* breaking them,' is on the tip of my tongue).

We talk of keeping in touch and agree some simple rules. I'll make contact when the time's right, but in an emergency he can ring me from a phone box or write, but hand-write the address so the envelope can't be replaced, and seal the corners with sticky tape to prevent MI5's post-office unit sliding a knitting needle beneath the flap to curl and extract the letter. And commit *nothing* of importance to paper.

By the time we rise to leave there's a crowd in the bar. 'Lot of poofs,' he observes.

'There's a room through there.' I nod towards a door.

'Well, why didn't you say so, old boy?'

I wonder if Tom is the only member of the Labour Party who uses that expression?

While we wait for a cab he talks of Guy in Moscow, of his flat in a Stalinist block surrounded by soldiers and Party apparatchiks. Isolated, lonely, drunk as often as he could be, tears rolling down his cheeks as he picked out hymn tunes he learned at Eton on an old upright piano.

'He often spoke of you, Harry.'

'Did he?' I step into the road to flag a cab. 'You take this, Tom.'

'We can share.'

'Best not.'

Driberg nods. 'They'll use the press against us, you know. That awful fellow Pincher on the *Express* writes whatever MI5 tells him. Accused me of being a KGB stooge. And Goronwy Rees – you're still in touch with him?'

'No.'

'Guy was surprised and hurt by his newspaper pieces – all that tittle-tattle about orgies in Bentinck Street.' He pauses. 'He was surprised you weren't mentioned in any of them, old boy.'

'Was he? Well, it's a lesson.' I open the cab door for him. 'We'll have to be careful, won't we, old boy?'

# 37

## 30 August 1965

THE FLUENCY INVESTIGATION wallows in the heat. Files on persons of interest rise and fall from the Registry, Evelyn still haunts the corridors after dark, and we meet on Thursdays to go over the same ground in ever-decreasing circles, like survivors of a desert crash driven mad by thirst and the sun. Most of the intelligence is held at MI5 and Wright is pushing anything like a lead at his own people. So I leave Lecky and his deputy, Hinton, to their own devices at Century House and walk across the park to my desk at Leconfield House every morning. Files from the Registry at Six are delivered to me by the courier and I speak to my colleagues on the scrambler phone for just long enough to be sure they have nothing of importance to share. No one expects FLUENCY to report again before Roger Hollis retires. Because it's bucket-and-spade weather and normal people are on holiday, I stroll back to St James's Park a couple of times a week to meet Elsa for lunch, and when she returns to her defence cuts and ministerial briefings I sit alone with my eyes closed and consider what has to be done.

The anxiety I feel in the pit of my stomach reminds me of the summer of '39 when we knew war was coming with Hitler. I was young enough then to manage on only a few hours' sleep. Beer and sunshine with friends in the afternoon, night shift at the *Daily Mirror*, where one of the paper's old boys tapped me on the shoulder and asked if I would be interested in special work. The day before the declaration of war I was invited for a little chat with Marjorie at the St Ermin's Hotel on Broadway, and after a routine background check I became a spy. I learned later that Guy had put in a good word for me.

On the anniversary of that day twenty-six years ago I walk to St James's Underground station and buy a ticket for a Circle Line train to Temple. I'm dressed for meetings with people who care about these things in a light summer jacket and open-neck shirt, and I'm carrying the battered leather briefcase that used to belong to my bank manager uncle. Poor old Rhodri wanted me to be 'a steady fellow'. I remember him saying so the day my father left me in his sister's care.

Mr James Simpson is by reputation a radical, or what passes for one among the barristers of the Inner Temple. I guess he's in his early thirties but he exudes the cast-iron confidence of one who has followed a straight path from boarding-school cloister to Oxbridge and the Bar.

'The House?' I say, nodding to his print of Christ Church College, Oxford.

'Yes. You?'

'New College.'

'Before my time, I suppose,' he observes, with a cruel smile.

'So, Mr Simpson,' I say, 'I have a friend who works in the Foreign Office, and my friend is going to break the law.' He sits a little straighter. 'Perhaps we should have some coffee.'

I tell Mr Simpson my friend's story, and clever Mr Simpson isn't fooled for a minute. George Blake represents the worse scenario, he says, because he was sentenced to forty-two years for spying. Politicians and newspapers turn cases like these into a circus, and in those circumstances justice isn't as blind to public opinion as it is supposed be. There's a sherry-party rumour that the judge in the Blake trial telephoned Number 10 Downing Street for advice before passing sentence.

'Blake was a Soviet spy,' I say, 'and my friend would be acting in the national interest.'

'That's as may be,' he says, 'but Blake was convicted of breaking the Official Secrets Act – and your *friend* would be too.'

From Temple I walk into the City, and in a banking hall on Poultry I purchase a security box. An assistant manager shows me into the vault and from Uncle's briefcase I take two rolls of film and some handwritten notes. As the manager slides my box back I wonder at the wealth hidden in those stainless-steel walls and how many of the other key-holders are breaking the law. The assistant manager leads me back to the main banking hall where the green marble pillars and grey marble floor, the footfall echo and hushed voices put me in mind of a great church. Uncle Rhodri wouldn't have credited such a place. Uncle Rhodri was chapel.

Roger Hollis worked for a bank in China and then a tobacco company. There's a note from Martin in the papers in front of me: *Recruited to the Security Service 1938. Assessment carried out by Dick White and Jane Archer.* Jane Archer retired to a thatched cottage in Dorset years ago and is almost seventy, but her name is spoken with awe by those who encountered her in the Service. She was Five's first female officer, some say its most able, and, in the years she spent with us at MI6, our leading expert on Communist counter-intelligence.

'I know why you've rung,' she says, 'and I've spoken to Arthur Martin already.'

'All the same, can I come down to see you?'

'No need. John and I are in London. Seven o'clock tomorrow?'

'Fine. And, Jane, keep this to yourself.'

The telephone crackles and hisses and I picture her holding

it away from her face. 'All right, Harry,' she says at last. 'For now.'

Wright takes the Thursday meeting up two floors again, so we can discuss the director general along the corridor from his office. Today's *Times* tells me Pakistani jets have attempted a raid on New Delhi, and the Indian Army is pushing towards Karachi. Thousands of men are engaged: thousands may die in the hours the members of our committee spend in conclave, considering the mistakes of the past. Terence Lecky has something new to offer us: Hollis took the Trans-Siberian railway home from China in 1936 and might have broken the journey in the Soviet Union. I ask how long he was there for, and what we know of his stay, but Lecky cannot say. So, for now this new piece floats in the corner of our great jigsaw: we don't know where it goes or even if it belongs, but my colleagues seem confident it will fit a picture of Roger, the master spy ELLI. Only we're not to call him Roger any more. The small office in B Branch responsible for allocating MI5's cover names has given us DRAT. Philby is our PEACH, Mitchell is PETERS, and now the director general of the Security Service is DRAT, which makes him as good as guilty.

I point out again that Roger's an Oxford man, and the profile we have from Jim's favourite defector – Golitsyn – suggests the Ring of Five were at Cambridge.

'Well, H-H-Harry, Oxford is not above suspicion,' says Wright. 'ELLI may have belonged to another circle – an Oxford circle.'

'Sorry to be a bore, but can I ask for some evidence?'

'Well, you know, H-H-Harry, from Blunt and Pool.'

I want to press him but he's pushed his chair away and is rising from the table. The meeting is to break early so he can catch a flight to Washington. 'Jim's arranged for me to have a word with SNIPER,' he says. 'I'm hoping SNIPER will offer us more on the middle-grade agent in the Service . . . if he isn't too sick.'

'Really?' I push my chair away too. 'Bloody marvellous, I'm sure.'

'H-Harry's against, of course.' Wright inspects his fingernails. 'Anyone else?'

Lecky turns to me. 'It's worth a try, Harry. Why not?'

'You've changed your tune, Terence. Why not? Because SNIPER's convinced he's the last Tsar of Russia. He's mad. You said so yourself.'

My colleagues look uncomfortable but they won't speak against Wright. I swear we're lost in a dark forest with madmen, holy men, crooks and tsars for our guides.

I watch from my office window as Wright climbs into a cab, and ten minutes later I do the same. I go in search of quiet reason.

Jane Archer greets me on the doorstep of her friend's house in Chelsea and shows me into a dark sitting room. 'We have half an hour alone,' she says. 'Is that enough?' She's dressed in sensible shoes and a thick tweed skirt, as if she's just returned from arranging the flowers in her village church. She reminds me of Margaret Rutherford in the Miss Marple story *Murder, She Said*, only younger and with finer features, and if it's possible to judge superior intellect in a face, that's what I see.

'Is this official?' she asks.

'Unofficial.'

'You want to ask me about Hollis.'

'That's right.'

'Well, I can only tell you what I told Arthur.'

'You helped to recruit him.'

'In 'thirty-eight. The director general – it was still Vernon Kell – was impressed by Roger but he wanted another opinion.

287

"Meet him, Jane. Is he for us?" he said. So I arranged a tennis match – mixed doubles. Dick White was my partner. I remember Hollis didn't cut much of a figure at first – shy, awkward, he had a hopeless backhand – but as the game progressed, well, he fought hard, demonstrated grit and a cool head under pressure. He lost the match to us but he impressed, and that was that. He was as good as in.'

Jane looks down at her hands, resting neatly in a nest of tweed. 'That's how things were done in those days.'

'I remember.'

She raises her head slowly. 'Well, are you going to ask me?'

'I'm not sure . . .'

'You want to know if I think he's a spy.'

'Did Arthur ask you?'

'No, the science boffin.'

'Peter Wright's spoken to you?'

'Obviously. He asked me: Mitchell or Hollis, or both? I said, "Neither." I don't think either of them is capable enough, but if there is one, Hollis is the more likely.'

I nod slowly. 'Difficult question – difficult times.'

'Of course, I may be wrong,' she says, rising smartly. 'I have been before.'

She must be thinking of Philby, whom she worked with after the war.

'Not often, Jane,' I observe with feeling.

'Harry?'

'In here,' I shout to Elsa. 'Come and make love to me.' I hear the thump of her bag on the tiles in the hall and the clicking of her heels. She must be wearing the black slingbacks she bought last weekend.

'Drink?' I swing my feet off the couch before she can complain that I'm wearing my shoes. 'I've just seen Jane Archer . . .'

288

No reply.

'. . . and she sends her regards to you.'

Still no reply.

'Elsa? Where are you?'

'I'm here.' She's standing in the shadow beneath the door frame, as perfect as a painting by Vermeer in her grey satin dress and short black cardigan, but I can see that she's tense, and something is wrong.

'What? Is it something at work?'

'No.'

'You're cross. With me?'

'It doesn't always have to be you, Harry,' she says, stepping into the room.

'Right.' I try to rise but she pushes me back on to the couch.

'Aaagh! You're all so stupid,' she shouts in frustration. 'Playing your silly games.' A strand of hair falls in front of her face and she whips it back behind her ear. God, I love her, although it isn't the time to say so. She spins away to the drinks cabinet and pours four fingers of gin. The tonic's warm and flat; she doesn't care. 'It's Wright,' she says, her back still turned to me.

'Peter Wright?'

'For God's sake, Harry, how many others do you know?' She turns to face me. 'Sorry.'

'Come here, will you?' I take her hand with the gold band I gave her when I promised to love and protect her. 'Tell me.'

'Jenifer Hart came to see me. Just turned up at the ministry. That bloody man is making their lives a misery. He's accused her of giving secrets to the Russians when she was a civil servant and he's grilled poor Herbert, too: "Did you know your wife was a Communist? Did you tell her about your work with MI5?" She left the Party before the war, Harry, but Wright won't let it go.' She takes a swig of gin. 'They've dropped her from her post on the Civil Service Selection Board, and there's trouble at the university now – rumours. A journalist called Pincher turned up at her college. She's strong, she can cope, but she's worried about Phoebe, because Wright and his chum . . .'

'Who?'

'Someone from Special Branch.'

'Go on.'

'Phoebe's in a terrible state. You know how fragile she is, and this pressure . . .'

'Where?'

'She's in the psychiatric wing at the Middlesex.' Elsa squeezes my hand and turns to look at me. I want to comfort her, kiss her, but she breaks away as soon as our lips touch. 'There's something else. Wright showed Jenifer a list of suspects – the old crowd. I don't know what she was thinking. She picked out Sir Andy Cohen at the Foreign Office, Arthur Wynn at Technology, Dennis Proctor, permanent secretary at the Ministry of Power, and Floud – Bernard Floud MP. And, Harry . . . me. She picked out me.'

'She picked out *you*. How bloody stupid. Why, *annwyl*?'

'I don't know,' she says, a little too vehemently. 'Harry, I've nothing to hide, you know that, don't you? But it's Phoebe. Jenifer says this may tip her over the edge.' She squeezes my hand hard, her ring against the knuckle of my little finger. 'Harry, it might kill her. Can't you stop it?'

'Jenifer should have kept her mouth shut.'

'I know. She knows.'

I kiss her again and stroke her hair. 'Look, don't worry.' I should wait, leave it until the morning. I should leave it altogether. 'I have to go out. Don't wait for me. Have a hot bath, then go to bed. We'll talk again in the morning.'

'What are you going to do?'

'There's someone I must see.'

*

Anthony Blunt's assistant tells me he's at dinner and isn't expected home before eleven, so I unlock the gates to the Portman Square garden with a piece of wire and a pen, select a bench and sink into my coat. My mind is buzzing like a swarm of bees and I'm soaked before I realise it's raining and have the sense to shelter.

At last a cab draws up in front of the institute and I watch Anthony disappear beneath its porch. I imagine him climbing its fine classical staircase – the finest in London, some say – then kicking off his Italian shoes to sprawl like a spider on his walnut and satin chaise longue. A commissionaire opens the door and tells me it's too late to disturb the director. I show my police calling card and 'No, I won't wait on the step.'

Anthony pads down in his slippers. He looks exhausted, gaunt. The lines that fall in an arch from his nose to his jaw are deeper, as if the year since we last met was closer to ten. 'Can't this wait, Harry?' He glances at his watch.

'I'm afraid it can't, Anthony.'

'But Peter was here only yesterday' – he passes a hand across his brow – 'for *three* hours!'

'Yes, well, I want to talk to you about that.'

'All right.' He sighs. 'You'd better come up to the flat, then.'

'Hang on.' I catch his arm. 'Is there somewhere else?'

He hesitates. 'Why on earth . . .?' then smiles his effete smile. 'Oh, but they're your colleagues, Harry.'

'That's right,' I say, 'but this is between you and me.'

So he leads me down to the basement and through swing doors into the kitchen and I wait in the darkness while he fumbles for a light switch. At last he finds it and I'm momentarily dazzled by the gleaming stainless-steel surfaces. 'I do believe this is the first time I've set foot in here,' he says.

'Spoken like a true socialist.'

'That's the sort of snide remark Peter likes to make.' He leans against a worktop and I hoist myself on to the one opposite. The kitchen's small but expensively equipped with racks of French knives and top-of-the-range cooking implements. Bright and clinical, like an operating theatre when the blood of the last patient has been washed away.

'Does Peter talk to you about me?' He lifts a trembling hand to his temple. 'I've told him all I know but he does insist on coming back. I think he enjoys it, that it's some sort of therapy for him.'

'You may be right, Anthony. I expect you know him better than I do.'

'He can't understand why we made the choices we did all those years ago. He says we knew nothing of the working class, and he keeps returning to his own life – the time he spent as a farm boy in Scotland. He wants sympathy, and all I want is for him to leave me alone. He can be very mean, you know.'

'I believe you. But it's Phoebe Pool I want to talk about, not you.'

Blunt's misty green eyes drift away from me. 'Poor Phoebe.'

'Wright says you used her as a courier. Is that true?'

'Oh dear.'

'Is it true?'

'Not really. She's never shown any interest in politics. I didn't get to know her properly until 'forty-seven or 'forty-eight and I'd left MI5 by then.'

'That's not what Wright says.'

'I may have implied she helped out every now and then – the odd message.'

'Why?'

'Because Peter kept pressing me.'

'Looking after number one, were you? You selfish bastard.'

He flinches. 'Once Peter has an idea about something . . .'

'And Proctor? Dennis Proctor, the permanent secretary at Power?'

'No.'

'Proctor was your friend, Guy's friend. Wright says you told him Proctor was a spy.'

'I said I didn't think so but I didn't know.'

'Phoebe Pool gave Wright Jenifer Hart's name.'

'I know.'

'Who else?'

'Sir Andrew Cohen.'

'Who else?'

'The Floud brothers – the MP, Bernard, and Peter. Peter was a curator at the Victoria and Albert Museum, but he's dead.'

I slip from the work surface. 'That's all?' I step towards him. 'No one else from the Courtauld, for instance, or from Pool's student days at Oxford?'

'Harry, please.' He looks at me imploringly. 'I told him Phoebe wasn't well, that he should leave her alone.'

'No one else?'

'Nothing about you, if that's—'

'Shut up – this doesn't concern me. Friends before country, you said. Well, I don't want innocent people dragged into this and, Christ, Blunt, nor should you.'

'Your wife? I'll do all I can—'

'You've done plenty already,' I say. 'Too much.'

He covers his face with his bony hands. 'Because it's intolerable,' I hear him mutter. 'Wright won't leave me alone.'

I grab his wrist and pull his hands away. 'Stop it, Anthony. Stop playing. Stop it! Tell me, who else have you dropped in the shit?'

# 38

## 1 November 1965

WRIGHT PUTS HIS head round the door. 'Roger wants to see us both.'

'When?'

'Now.'

I put out my cigarette and reach for my jacket. 'Any idea?'

'No.'

Since the CIA's coup attempt in the summer I've spent no more than a few frosty minutes alone with Wright. We have become expert at dancing around each other. I expect he's heard a report of the kitchen conference with Blunt, who has no reason to keep it secret. Clever Sir Anthony has probably sown as much discord as he can, hoping perhaps that we'll be too busy scrapping with each other to care about him. But he has done the harm he can do, and it's the beast and the madman in Rees that concerns me now. I know Wright has visited and tested him again because Isaiah Berlin wrote to tell me so. *And not just Rees, Harry, your Mr Wright is trying to bully us all.* In particular, he has the Service's Oxford old boys in his sights, good people like Professors Hampshire and Hart and Zaehner, *and, Harry Vaughan, he asked about you, too.*

Hollis greets us with a limp handshake and a broad smile. 'Glad of this opportunity,' he says. Wright catches my eye and raises an eyebrow, and I admit I'm surprised too. This must be a new Roger, clubhouse Roger, who's retiring in a few weeks, because the Roger we used to know was cool and reserved with almost everyone.

'Coffee? Would you arrange it, Val?' he says to his secretary.

He shows us to his sofa and sits opposite in a small magenta easy chair that wasn't here on my last visit. My gaze is drawn over his shoulder to the desk, and not for the first time I feel a pang of regret that I was persuaded not to tell him I'd caught Wright rummaging through its drawers.

'This business of independence for Rhodesia,' he says, 'the prime minister's spinning like a top. I saw him at the opening of the Post Office Tower. Rhodesia's for the other side of the Service, prime minister,' I said. 'There isn't much we can do.'

I sense Wright bristling beside me and, shameful though it is to own, I'm relieved that, for however long this interview lasts, Hollis will be the focus of his malevolence.

'What are you and Mrs Hollis going to do, sir?' I ask, a little cruelly.

'Oh, the usual things people do in the country,' he replies. 'Yes. Hard to grasp, but not long now before I'm hanging in the rogues' gallery.'

We turn to look at the pictures of his predecessors on the wall to the right of his new chair and my gaze is drawn to the portrait of Dick, whose inability to say 'no' to Americans has landed us in this mess.

'Well,' Hollis slaps his knees, 'you're probably wondering why I've asked you up. Simply, I have a question – for you, Peter. Why do you think I'm a spy?'

We must look uncomfortable, and he's trying not to smile. Wright finds his voice at last. 'The disappointments of recent years, sir. So many f-f-failures.' He runs the tip of his tongue along his bottom lip. 'The old fears. I think it's important to rule out all the possibilities.'

'Oh? But you *must* have been looking at new possibilities?'

No pretence of bonhomie now. Roger wants answers; Roger wants facts. The son of the bishop has turned the other cheek for months. Not today. This is his last chance to fight before the Roundheads take over. Wright looks sideways at me, perhaps for some support: *Oh, no, boy, you're on your own.*

'Well, we've been going back through the files, sir,' he says, 'and there's Anatoli G-Golitsyn's evidence.'

'Tell me,' says Hollis, 'tell me it all,' and Wright does: all the crazy code names, half-truths, suppositions and downright lies. And Roger? He has the patience of Job, which is too much patience. I watch his quiet anger dissipate and his broad smile return, and I know he's thinking it's too comical, too ridiculous, and with only a few weeks to go, it's not worth worrying about such a feeble case.

'Well, Peter,' he says, with a laugh, 'I can see you're ready to hang, draw and quarter me.'

'If there's anything you can h-help—'

'Please don't interrupt, Peter.' Hollis raises both hands, like a policeman in front of an approaching truck. 'Thank you for your frankness, but I am afraid you are wasting your time: I am *not* a spy.'

'B-but c-can you offer any proof, sir?' Wright's colour is up. 'Can you help our investigation?'

'With more bits of paper? I can probably find some notes.' He sighs. 'Honestly, I don't remember. And I wonder: is this FLUENCY business more than a waste of time?' He addresses the question to me, but Wright jumps in to answer. 'We sh-should have been through this process years ago, sir.'

'I was asking for Harry's opinion, Peter.'

'Well, after Philby some sort of investigation was inevitable, wasn't it, sir?'

'Some sort, yes, but has it gone too far, and—'

Wright interrupts again. 'It's a c-complicated business, sir. You r-receive our b-briefs, you know how—'

'Riveting, I'm sure. Riveting. *All* that history, *all* those files.' He smiles as if he's practising. 'Yes. Well, thank you for your time, gentlemen,' he rises, 'don't let me keep you from your . . . researches.'

I assume Hollis wanted me to witness their exchange because he wants me to include it in a report to C.

'What happened to the coffee?' I mutter, as we leave.

'Typical of R-Roger,' Wright replies.

Val is bent over her desk in the DG's outer office but she glances up as we pass and I can see from the spark in her eye that she knows our business and despises us. That woman has steel in her soul. I expect she would have made a firmer director general than her lover.

'No doubt about it,' says Wright, the second the lift gate clangs shut. 'The way he c-c-clicked his teeth with his pencil when I mentioned ELLI, and drumming the edge of his seat. Hollis is the one. He's our mole.'

'Not now, Peter. Not here.'

He ignores me. 'I expect he wanted you there because you're on his side.'

'Are you accusing *me* of being a spy, too?'

He smiles. 'Not yet.'

I watch the lift light fall from five to four and say nothing, but Wright is too excited to let it go. 'If Hollis thinks we're going to drop this . . .'

'I'm sure he knows you better than that, Peter.'

'Good,' he says emphatically. 'I've spoken to Jane Archer. She says it could be Mitchell or Hollis or both – she thinks Hollis.'

'Either or neither?' I turn to face him, the length of my arm away. 'She said neither to me, Peter, neither of them, and she seemed pretty certain.'

The corner of Wright's left eye twitches. 'You visited her?'

*Ting* goes the lift bell to signal we're back on the third floor and I reach for the brass handle to open the gate, but he's closer and grabs it before me, holding it shut.

'You're d-d-determined to protect him.' His voice trembles a little.

I roll my eyes. 'Reds everywhere. Trying to save the country from the DG and his deputy, and the prime minister?'

'Not just me. We've b-been investigating Harold W-W-Wilson for years – at least ten years.'

'*And* our old Oxford soldiers, some of our finest minds, after the service they gave this country during the war.'

The lift protests as someone tries to summon it to another floor. It feels very small and warm. I want to ask Wright why Elsa is on his list and warn him to keep away, but he'll blame Pool or Hart or both, and it's better he doesn't know I'm on to him.

'Our enemy's w-winning,' he says. 'He was cl-cleverer than us in the thirties and we've been p-playing catch-up ever since.'

'That's Jim Angleton speaking. People made bad choices in the thirties for good reasons. That's all. Carry on like this, we're going to become just like our enemy.'

'If you feel like that you should resign from the w-working party.'

'And leave this to you and Angleton?'

'I could ask Dick to r-r-replace you.'

I sigh. 'You could try. Now, are you going to let me out of here?'

He stares at me belligerently for a few seconds, then turns to draw back the gate. I slip past without a word, but as I approach the swing doors into the corridor he calls to me – 'V-Vaughan'

– and I have to suppress the urge to keep walking. We're teetering at the edge of a precipice and it's time to retreat a little.

'Peter?' I turn. 'What now?'

A secretary is crossing the landing and we must shift from foot to foot together, as if we're performing an Aboriginal dance, until she disappears through the doors behind me. Then Wright raises his gaze from his shoes to my face. 'J-J-Jim Angleton's conducting his own enquiries into Russian penetration at the Agency, I'm sure you've heard.'

'Ever vigilant.'

'Are you sneering?'

'Not on this occasion. It's his job. I would rather he was hunting moles on his patch than crashing about on ours.'

Wright smiles, but not in a pleasant way. 'Then you'll be pleased to hear he's made more arrests. Jack Ellis is an old friend of yours, isn't he?'

'A good man,' I say coolly. 'A big-hearted Texan patriot.'

'J-Jim will be the judge of that.'

All those years young Peter spent shovelling shit on a Scottish farm: behold the man. I watch him push through the doors and wonder how much this is about me. Jack Ellis doesn't have the imagination to be anything but a red-blooded American patriot so I guess he's being punished for talking to me, and the worst of it is that I always knew there was a chance he would be. I feel shame and afraid for my friend: friend no more. In that smoke-filled office in Langley, the blinds shut to the morning, Angleton sits with a cigarette between his yellow fingers, his head buzzing with wild imaginings, quite incapable now of recognising the difference between loyalty to him and to his country. Stalin was the same, they say. And Kim Philby, these seeds you managed to sow, this fear and confusion is your legacy: you're still winning.

*

The Langley switchboard puts me on hold while it rings through to the Soviet Division. Then the Agency operator comes back to me: 'Sorry, sir, Special Agent Ellis is out of the office.' The operator can put me through to the deputy chief of the division, Mr Bagley.

'No, that won't be necessary,' I say.

I know I shouldn't share it with Elsa but guilty secrets are the hardest to keep, and Jack and Michelle are her friends, too. She has tickets for a new play at the Royal Court theatre in Sloane Square. The liberal press says it's thoughtful and unsentimental, the conservative press degenerate filth. For the entertainment and education of bourgeois London, a play about their young working-class neighbours, with no money, no hope, bugger-all to do on their estate but stone an abandoned baby. I'm not in the mood for that sort of lesson and I tell Elsa so. She protests: 'These tickets are hard to come by.'

'Sorry. I'll explain, but not here on the street – there,' and I point to the White Hart at the corner of the square.

There's a flock of canaries in the lounge bar, young folk in bright clothes chatting noisily about the play I've decided to skip. 'Want a ticket?' I ask a girl in a Mary Quant mini and a peaked sailor's cap like the one Lenin wore during the revolution.

'Oh, no,' she snips at me. 'I have friends. I'm going with them.'

Elsa laughs when I tell her. 'Come on, you're in your fifties.'

'You know it was perfectly innocent. I'm much more innocent than you think.'

'All right. I believe you.' She smiles and touches my face. 'Now what's so important it can't wait until after the performance?'

'Jack's in trouble,' I say, and I tell her why, and my excuses. I sound about as innocent as Anthony Blunt.

'Resign, Harry,' she says, 'for God's sake.'

'And let him win? And what about you?'

She sighs and lifts my hand from her knee. 'What are you saying? Don't make me the excuse. You're not doing anything worthwhile – you said so yourself.'

I shrug. 'Still trying to fight the good fight.'

'That's rubbish,' she whispers fiercely at me. 'You love the intrigue and the lies. You love it and hate it, too, and you despise Wright but you see his shadow when you look in your mirror.'

'That's unfair. Plain wrong.'

'You think so?' She pushes away the gin she's barely touched and rises. 'I've had enough. I'll telephone Jack and Michelle.'

I think of Jack with the secretary from the embassy and wonder if he would have let me wheedle the truth from him if I hadn't caught him at a weak moment. He loves his wife, Michelle; we all love our wives, I'm sure. 'They'll be monitoring Jack's calls,' I say. 'Best leave alone.'

We weave our way through the young people round the bar, with their educated London accents and their talk of change, and I hear an echo of my own student days. Pub nights after public meetings, Goronwy Rees's eyes still shining with zeal for a real revolution: now just a Sloane Square fashion accessory. Elsa tugs my sleeve. 'You've been here before. Look behind the bar.' Beneath the wall-mounted whisky bottles, there's a photograph of the actor Dirk Bogarde. 'They must have filmed some of *The Servant* here.'

'You're right,' I say. 'My God, what a bastard I was in that movie.'

1966

# 39

## 3 January 1966

THERE'S A GREEN Bedford van in the street on the first working day after New Year's Day and it's still there at half past six in the evening. No sign of the workmen but the door to the block at number 12 is wedged open with a toolbox. They're parked on double yellow lines with passenger side wheels on the pavement. I squeeze past with my bag of groceries and make a mental note of the name: Hardy Jones Electricians, in trust-me gold letters. The splint is still in place in the frame of our front door, there's no sign of entry, and when I check the directory I find a company of the same name in Kennington. I ring but it's late and no one answers. That's the Monday. On Thursday, a couple of decorators arrive in a yellow van and carry their stepladders, buckets and brushes into our neighbour's house. This lot are Leigh and Sons and they promise *High Quality Work and a Friendly Service*, which means nothing, because they teach painting and plastering to the A2 goons at Five, and I'm sure they're encouraged to take pride in their work.

The Beatles have grown from wannabes to international popular music stars, prime ministers and presidents have come and gone, yet the hunt for a deep-penetration agent and his sub-agents in the Service rolls on into a third year. In many small ways it's polluting my life. Elsa's right: I'm drinking too much and carrying more on my hips. We laugh less than we used to, and she says she loves me just a little less every time

I tell her now is not the right time to leave the Service. But she keeps asking, 'What must you see through, Harry? You're not making sense!'

She left the house without a word an hour ago and I'm glad because I don't want her to see me twitching at a curtain.

I'm still getting out of my coat when Evelyn steps into my office. 'Happy New Year!' I say.

'This is your copy,' she replies, dropping the latest FLUENCY report on my desk. 'We meet the new DG at nineteen hundred tonight.'

'Right you are.'

No one is sad to see the back of Hollis but no one I respect is jumping for joy over his successor: Martin Furnival Jones, FJ to everyone, Highgate School and Cambridge University, where he studied languages and law. Two years older than me – he's fifty-three – but he joined the Service the year after, in '41. He's even shyer than his predecessor. A birdwatcher, I hear. As far as I can tell the only truly remarkable thing about FJ is the size of his ears, which are as large as dinner plates. As for his judgement, well, Arthur Martin has been bending those ears for years.

'Monstrous,' FJ says, when we gather in his office later that evening. 'You want me to accept these?'

Wright says, 'We do,' and launches into a long tendentious defence of the FLUENCY working party's conclusions. I watch FJ prowling round the room in shirtsleeves and braces, a pipe clenched between his teeth, and I know he's thinking, Oh, Lord. Wright drones on, too excited to keep it simple. What he's trying to describe are three circles of penetration. Outer circle: the Communist 'agents of influence' in government, in Parliament, in the civil service, in the universities, in trade unions, in pressure groups and charities. Four hundred names so far, the names of men FJ might meet at his club, names an educated man in the street might recognise. Middle circle, the 'true bills' unearthed from the service archives that point to a 'middling-grade agent' in MI5. The report names eight possible candidates before settling on the 'perfect match': Michael Hanley, the director of C Branch at MI5. Finally, the nub, the kernel, the crux, the heart of the conspiracy, the master spy ELLI, stripped of all his influence now: Sir Roger Hollis.

'Monstrous,' Furnival Jones says again. 'You understand what this means?' A corner of Wright's mouth lifts just a little – the hint of a smile – but I guess FJ's too upset to notice. 'Hollis and Hanley! Really, Peter?' He smacks his copy of the report on the table in front of us. 'You're accusing not only my prede-cessor of being a spy, but the man most likely to be my successor too!' FJ glares at all of us. 'It's ludicrous.' Turning to his desk he snatches up his tobacco pouch and begins packing a fresh pipe. Wright glances at Michael Stewart, who understands he is to speak in our defence. Is FJ listening? He's working on the pipe, tamping, sucking, a tongue of flame in front of his face, which is more expressive than I can ever remember it, his eyebrows lifting and collapsing into a web of frown lines.

'Enough!' He hasn't the patience to listen to more. 'Do you *all* agree on these conclusions?'

Wright looks at me. 'Almost all of us, sir.'

'Who?'

I hold up my hand. 'Me, sir.' The dunce from across the water.

He glares at me and pulls hard on his pipe. 'All right, explain why not.'

Where to begin? With the VENONA first and the identifi-cation of the agent code named JOHNSON. My analysis points to Blunt, not Hollis. And the evidence for ELLI points to Kim. Philby was one of the KGB's 'Magnificent Five', and at Cambridge with the other members of the ring. We know their names now, but my colleagues are too determined to ruin Hollis to recognise it. Philby is agent ELLI and he left us in '63, never to return. Then I speak for Hollis who was the first to suspect Blunt and the first to press for files to be kept on every Communist in Britain. What about the successful operations that were run against the Party in his time at the top? And on I go while the temperature in the room rises. Because it's impossible not to be personal when *foul whisp'rings are abroad* – I shake the report at FJ – *infected minds*, and if I have a criticism of Sir Roger it's that he let the poison spread.

Wright protests, naturally. They all do. But to my FLUENCY colleagues I say, 'This conspiracy only makes sense to you because you feed off each other. Step out of the bunker and breathe.' And to FJ I say, 'This is Jim Angleton's doing, and if it's more than madness, it's a means to control both his Service and ours.' And for a final flourish, well, I want to talk of the other list, the unofficial list, the one with the prime minister's name at the top, but I hesitate. It's so 'monstrous' it's easy to deny. I debate it at the back of my mind, and before I reach a decision my chance has gone. FJ has heard enough of me: it's a wonder he hasn't chewed through the stem of his pipe.

'Christ. This is an unholy mess,' he says. 'How much do the Americans know?'

'We've kept J-J-Jim Angleton up to date,' says Wright, 'of course we have. H-Harry's the sort of old-school Service liberal who likes to forget how much we owe the Americans.'

'No, Harry!' FJ raises his hand to shut me up. 'This is my decision. I want FLUENCY to concentrate on the middling-grade agent. Top priority because he's still in the building – if he exists. Understood? I want Hanley and the other candidates investigated first, then your outer circle – the people in government. In the meantime, I'll consider what to do about Roger.' He steps back to the conference table and places his fingertips on the FLUENCY report. 'And this' – he lifts a corner – 'under lock and key, every copy.'

'The c-combination safe in my office,' says Wright.

'Every copy. Ladies and gentlemen, we are going to run this down to the ends of the earth – to the ends of the earth, you hear?' And he walks away again.

We collect our papers in silence. No one looks at me. Perhaps they're wondering whether we'll be able to close the fissure that's opened so publicly between us. Sod them. Let's have an end to pretence. Wright lingers at the table while the rest of us file towards the door, Stewart's wheelchair at our head. I'm carrying my copy of the report and concentrating hard on finding a way to keep it when FJ calls me: 'A word, Harry.'

Wright's shoulder brushes mine as he passes.

'Sit,' says FJ, waving me to a chair. 'Scotch?'

'Thank you, sir.'

There's a bottle on the conference table. It's an aggressive bottom-shelf whisky of the sort that leaves you with a foul mouth in the morning, and a more moderate man would refuse.

'What a mess! And it's becoming personal, isn't it?' He pours me a generous measure, then carries his own to the other side of Hollis's old desk. 'You've spoken to C?'

'Not yet, sir.'

'Well, *I have*. Sir Dick supports the FLUENCY recommendations. Press on, he says, and I agree. But you . . .' He raises his chin belligerently. 'Peter wants me to ask C to drop you from the committee, so tell me why I shouldn't.'

'If you've made up your mind he's right, you should.'

'I haven't,' he snaps, 'but you're the odd one out and I want to know why.'

'Why? You trained as a lawyer, sir. Show me the proof.'

'It isn't clear-cut. It never is in these cases.'

I whistle through my teeth sceptically. 'People are thinking like priests, not lawyers. We're afraid because Jim Angleton and his friends in the Service keep telling us we should be, that the Russians are much better than us, that there are hundreds of Kim Philbys out there. We're dancing to the CIA's tune. It's a bloody power grab – that's what all witch-hunts turn out to be.'

FJ picks up his glass but lowers it again. 'What about you, Harry? Above it all, are you? Peter thinks you're hiding something from us.'

I laugh. 'Of course he does.'

He stares at me. 'We'll see.' Then his gaze drifts down to the FLUENCY report on the desk in front of him. 'Give me a note. Put your reservations on paper and I'll consider them.'

On my way to the door I notice that a portrait is missing from the photographic gallery of FJ's predecessors. There's a hook but the picture has gone long before it was able to leave a tobacco tidemark on the wall. Poor old Roger. He wasn't a vain man but I hear he was as pleased as Punch when it went up and made a point of showing it to all those who visited him in his final days. But now, well, FJ's secretary will have it in the bottom drawer of her desk. I smile sweetly as I pass her in the DG's outer office and think almost wistfully of Val and her unshakeable faith in her lover.

If I return to the third floor for my coat and briefcase there's a chance Wright will ask for my copy of the FLUENCY report. So I take the lift down to the Registry where one of the queens gives me a cardboard file. A wet winter night in the city at turning-out time and I must compete with theatregoers on Piccadilly for a cab to take me home.

Elsa is in bed with a Mary Stewart novel and doesn't raise her gaze from the page. 'There's something in the oven.'

'Sorry, darling, really I am.' I drop the file at the bottom of the bed and take off my jacket. 'The new DG kept us late.'

I'm not hungry but don't want to say so. I burn my hand badly removing the casserole from the oven and have to hold it under the kitchen tap. When the rawness eases I kick off my shoes, hang my wet jacket on a chair and pad back through to our bedroom. Elsa has thrown back the covers and is on all fours reading the FLUENCY report. 'You shouldn't!' I slap my hand on it. 'It's dangerous.'

'Shouldn't I?' She grabs my wrist with one hand and snatches up the report with the other. 'The case for the prosecution? Jenifer Hart's here, I suppose?'

'And other bad people. Give it to me, please.'

'You're very careless with secrets, Harry.'

'Sometimes with my wife. The wife I'm trying to shelter from this mess because I love her so much.'

She lifts her eyes from the paper to mine. 'That's the first time you've said you love me in a long time.'

I reach out to tidy a strand of loose hair behind her ear. 'You know it's true, don't you? I *do* love you very much.'

At last an affectionate smile. 'Blimey, you *are* desperate. Here,' and she hands me the report.

'There you go, girl, cheapening my feelings.'

'Let me be the judge of your feelings,' she says, scrambling back under the covers, '*when* you come to bed.'

I laugh and start on my buttons. '*Wildfire at Midnight*?' Her Mary Stewart novel is face down on the bedspread. 'Let's see!'

I keep my sub-miniature camera under a floorboard in the box room upstairs. A smart black Minox B, not much more than the length of my index finger with a chain to measure the focal point necessary for copying papers: the full twenty-four inches for a good A4 image. It was a gift from Jack Ellis. The box room is at the back of the house so I can close the shutters and light the report with a table lamp without arousing suspicion. By half past eight in the morning Elsa is at her desk in the ministry, by nine I've finished. Just the list of names, the analysis and the case against DRAT. Half past nine: opening time at the bank on Poultry. The same young assistant manager takes me to the vault where I deposit a single roll of film and a few more pages of notes.

Ten fifteen: across the river to Century House to show my face to Lecky in the basement. Then I pop my head round Maurice's door on the twelfth and arrange to meet him at his flat in the evening. Eleven o'clock, and I'm on my way to MI5 in Curzon Street.

Someone in D3 must see me paying off the cabbie because a reception committee greets me the minute I set foot in my office. To discuss 'my role as MI6 liaison', they say. No hard feelings about yesterday, only for the next few weeks the FLUENCY working party will be investigating the middle-grade mole in MI5 and will have no need of my assistance. Or, to put it more succinctly than Peter Wright is ever able to: bugger off, Harry Vaughan.

'Where's the report?' says Evelyn. 'Did you take it home?'

'To the Registry,' I say, waving the new file.

'You were supposed to hand it to Peter.'

'Did we agree that?'

'Yes, we did,' she says.

'Right-ho. As for my role as Six liaison, the new DG wants me to write a paper outlining my concerns. I guess I'm on board for as long he says so.'

Wright tries to smile; Evelyn doesn't. 'Then we must keep you informed,' he says. 'We *do* all want the same thing, don't we?'


The interrogation of those who fit the profile of a 'middling-grade' agent begins at once.

Michael Hanley's the first. He's senior suspect, 'a perfect fit', according to Wright. Head of C Branch, a future DG, they say – or they used to. He's a huge florid fellow and the corners of his mouth turn down as if he's always in a temper. Monday morning at nine o'clock his secretary takes him morning coffee, but would he please leave it on his desk and report to the director general's office.

'An accusation has been made against you,' says Furnival Jones. 'You must submit to an interrogation, Michael.' Hanley protests it's a lie but he has no choice. He must surrender to the wild indignity of an interrogation by his boss. Two floors below, his accusers listen on headphones in the D1 operations room as FJ tries to get under Hanley's skin. Troubled public-school boy (tick); Oxford leftie (tick); studied Russian at a language college visited by a KGB talent-spotter (tick); and Angleton's man Golitsyn says he fits the profile (tick). Best of all, Wright has spoken to a psychiatrist who treated Hanley for a time. FJ asks him: 'Guilty feelings you had to share with someone, Michael?'

'No,' says Hanley, 'the burden of *keeping* secrets and telling lies, even to those I'm close to. You must have felt the weight of that burden too, sir?'

There's no rough stuff this time but he is required to speak of his wife and his life at home, mistakes and intimate secrets, in the full knowledge that two floors below his colleagues are listening. It hurts; there *will* be scars. By five o'clock on Wednesday it's over and the FLUENCY working party gathers in the D1 operations room to discuss the evidence.

'Well?' FJ is shell-shocked. 'You should have seen the look on Michael's face.'

'He's not our man,' says Wright, and all of us agree.

'Then you'd better start looking for someone else,' he says – and that's what happens.

# 40

# 17 January 1966

A TAP ON an office door, and would you please report to
523 on the fifth immediately. Wright sits there with a D
Branch interrogator, while Evelyn and Stewart listen to a feed
in Operations and note anything suspicious. I don't know the
suspects, it would take me days to master their files, so I step
back from it to write my paper for FJ. At the end of each day
I return my copy of the FLUENCY report to the safe in Wright's
office and try to gauge whether my comrades are closer to 'a
success'. If Evelyn isn't knitting over a basket with a head in
it then I know 'enquiries are continuing'.

The interrogations are meant to be secret, but by the end of
the first week there isn't a soul in the building who doesn't
know Wright and his cronies are grilling the middle grades.
On Friday, I make a rare visit to the canteen at lunchtime to
grab a cheese and tomato sandwich, and the moment I join
the queue the chatter and laughter stop. As far as the junior
desk officers in front of me are concerned, I'm a member of
Wright's gang. They've heard about the nine o'clock knock and
the interrogation that follows. Five suspects so far? Six?
Colleagues above a certain rank are asking, 'Will it be me next?'
I guess they're calling it a witch-hunt already. The trouble is,
Hanley was 'the perfect fit' until he wasn't, and in search of
another, FLUENCY is casting its net far and wide. Is it necessary? I don't know. Is there some evidence of a recent leak?

No one has said so. This may be a piece of our history too, and those of us fortunate to study it as a subject at university know how simple it is to manipulate.

I deliver my paper on the FLUENCY report to FJ on the last Monday in January. In the evening I meet Driberg in the draughty saloon bar of the Wheatsheaf. I'm late and Tom isn't happy. 'You promised me proof,' he bellows across the bar, 'and it's been weeks!' Heads turn to look for the man with the fruity upper-class voice.

'Keep it down,' I say, drawing a chair to the table. 'These things take time – and I've been away.'

'You read about my speech in the House? Page lead in *The Times*.'

'Sorry, no, I didn't.'

Tom frowns. 'I'm trying to push parliamentary scrutiny of the intelligence services up the political agenda.'

'Good.'

'Names? Papers? Where are they?'

'On the way,' I say. 'Patience, Tom, please.'

'I don't have any – never have. When?'

'I can't tell you.'

'Then why did you drag me out here?'

'To reassure you, and to arrange a secure channel,' I say. 'If you hear from Mr Green, you should ring this number' – I've written it on a piece of paper for him – 'seven in the evening sharp.'

That makes him feel better. Like Burgess, he has a school-dormitory passion for secrets but he isn't very good at keeping them. I want him to be indiscreet, but not about me. That's why he's still waiting for something to make the front pages.

We don't talk for long because a young man at the bar has caught his eye. 'Tight little arse,' he says, picking up his drink. 'Time to turn on the charm.'

*

Great excitement the following morning. I'm shuffling back to my office with a cup of tea balanced on two files when I hear clapping in the operations room at the end of the corridor. It can only mean one thing. 'We *have* him,' says Stewart. 'We bloody well do!' He's sitting with the sound feed from the fifth floor, Evelyn and a D Branch interrogator called James at his side.

'Who do we have?'

'Gregory Stevens,' he says, 'the acting head of the Polish Section. Peter said he was next best fit after Hanley and he was right. He just came out with it. Confessed. "Me," he said, "all true. I confess."'

'Where is he now?'

'Still up there. The DG's security man is on the phone to Special Branch. They'll want to interview him under caution.'

'Right.' I put down my files and lift the saucer from my cup. 'Quite a turn-up for the books.' Stewart is smiling, which I suppose is reasonable in the circumstances.

'Is there anything else in his background?'

'Half Polish. Bit of a fantasist, his psychiatrist says.' He pushes a file towards me. 'Do you have a psychiatrist? Am I the only person in this building who doesn't? The shrink says we can't rely on Stevens to tell the truth.'

'Oh? Does he know his patient works for MI5?'

'Shush!' Evelyn is gesturing furiously at us, one half of a headset pressed to her ear.

'Look at page six,' Stewart whispers. 'He visits Poland regularly – with permission, of course – but as you see,' he taps a passage halfway down a page of the transcript, 'his uncle is active in the Polish Communist Party.'

'And he's been open about it?'

Stewart doesn't reply because we're both watching Evelyn, whose face is contorted as if she's in pain. 'He's laughing,' she says, pressing fingers to the birthmark on her cheek.

I snatch the other set of headphones from the table before Stewart has a chance and, yes, he *is* laughing. He must be falling off his chair.

I hear Wright say, 'Are you all right, Stevens?'

And I hear Stevens say, 'Perfectly all right,' and laugh a little more.

Then Wright's voice again: 'I'm n-n-not sure I understand you? What is it?'

I exchange glances with Evelyn. 'How hard has Peter pushed him?' I ask. Stevens speaks before she's able to.

'Well, you were determined to find a spy, Wright, weren't you?' he says, his voice trembling. 'I'm giving you what you want. I knew you would get excited about my Polish family.'

I hear the rustle of papers being gathered together, then Wright says, 'We'll end it there, Stevens,' and his chair screeches as he gets to his feet. 'The director general will want to speak to you.'

I drop the headphones on the table and Stewart grabs them. 'What was that about?'

'You tell him, *cariad*,' I say to Evelyn. There's a nasty red weal on her neck. 'He's unstable,' she says, 'and after this . . . he's going to have to go!'

Stewart has no idea what we're talking about.

'It was all a joke – he was joking,' I explain. 'Stevens is innocent.'

'What?'

'Well, it was more of a protest than a joke.'

'Shit,' he says.

'Yes,' I say. 'Sorry, and all that.'

Oh, the look on Evelyn's face. Vaughan or Stevens? Given an opportunity she would choose to guillotine me first. One day she may have a chance.

Evelyn is right about one thing: Stevens has gone from the building within an hour, never to return. 'Terrible waste. He was very able,' Stewart admits to me a short time later. A number of Stevens's colleagues in D Branch feel the same. Over the next few days the temperature on the third floor and in the Registry drops to freezing. One of the interrogators tells me there are whispers in the building of 'the special unit' in D Branch using Gestapo-style tactics.

I haven't seen Arthur Martin in the last few weeks, but we meet by chance on the pavement outside Six's headquarters. I am to talk to recruits about field work in Berlin and Vienna, and Martin has just left a meeting on the crisis in Rhodesia. But all he wants to discuss is FLUENCY and 'that nasty little affair' with Stevens. And, to my surprise, he declares, 'This whole business is poisoning us all.'

I nod and say nothing in the faint hope of witnessing a Damascene conversion to my point of view.

'We may have been looking at this the wrong way,' he says. 'The Russians may not have a middle-grade agent in the Service. It's possible SNIPER was given a piece of deliberate disinformation – something the KGB knew would sow confusion in the Service. Perhaps the Russians are disguising their agents as defectors and we can't trust any of them.'

Only a week ago he was quite certain he could see a clear image of a middle-grade mole, and now we are in the wilderness of mirrors again.

'What about Golitsyn?' I say.

Martin bristles. 'Oh, Anatoli is on the level,' he says, edging away from me, 'Anatoli is completely trustworthy.'

*1 February 1966*

Wright has persuaded FJ to cast the net further and wider. I arrive at Leconfield House at a little after nine to find the corridor outside my office choked with furniture. Half a dozen officers from A and D are joining the four interrogators seconded to the investigation last summer. FJ's secretary says he's still considering my report, which is sweet of her. Plainly, he's spiked it already.

We meet in the fifth-floor conference room on the Thursday and Wright presents us with a revised list of people, in and outside the Service, whose loyalty it is our duty to question. There are names a competent Fleet Street reporter would recognise – cabinet ministers, a High Court judge, the Oxbridge professors, senior civil servants – and there are old friends, and friends of Elsa he wouldn't, like Rees and Hart and Pool. The discussion turns to who will handle what and when, and it is soon apparent they don't want to involve me, that I am to be eased out of the circle. Then Lecky asks Wright about Jenifer Hart.

'C-condescending,' he says, 'an unrepentant Communist, and she dr-dresses like a tart. The sort of Oxford academic who thinks she's too clever to live by the same code as the rest of us, and that investigating people's politics is no better than looking up a lady's skirt. But I showed her some names, and she picked out a few.'

'Who?' I ask. 'Can we see that list too?'

'J-just the people we've spoken about,' he says, flicking lazily through the file on the table in front of him. 'S-sorry, I don't have it with me.'

He's lying, and I know why he's lying, and he knows I know because he launches into a sermon on 'conflicts of interest' that 'test our loyalties', and while he speaks Evelyn gives me the evil eye. I listen with my head tilted sideways, drawing on a cigarette, like Noël Coward, a picture of composure, even though I know what this amounts to. It's a simple chain equation, really, where $x$ is Blunt and $y$ is Pool and $h$ is Hart and $z$ is me, and the answer can only be Elsa. Wright – the committee – has begun to investigate Elsa. Change the factors, make Elsa $z$, and the answer turns out to be me. Angleton is already after me and his reach is long. That's why measures are necessary.

At half past five I stroll out of the building with my briefcase, like any other government servant. But the moment I turn off Curzon Street my pace quickens. Am I foolish? Perhaps. It isn't Moscow: they won't lift her off the street. There are telephone boxes at Green Park station – I can ring her. But one of the boxes is out of order and there's a queue for the other. So I join the snake of people hurrying home across St James's Park with hats low and collars turned up against the rain. In the dark little cut that runs between Birdcage Walk and Queen Anne's Gate I think of Clive, who broke my head on his boot and pissed all over me. Well done, Clive. I'll always remember you in this place. Is our story over? It's been a while, I know, but I look for you and your pals everywhere. I'm like an old man with a *fear of fear and frenzy*.

My neighbour, the Tory MP, is working at his dining-table, and across the street at the door of number 11 Mrs Holland is hunting in her bag for her keys. 'Hello,' she says, and raises her hand in greeting. 'Filthy evening.'

'Yes,' I say, 'a filthy day.'

Her front door closes and I kneel before my own as if I'm praying to a house god. The splint I wedged in the hinge is in place but not quite the right place. I open the door carefully and leave my briefcase on the console table. The drawing-room door is open too far, and the newspaper on Elsa's desk has been moved just a little. I check the phone, I check the lampshades, I check our pictures, the hairbrushes in front of her vanity mirror, the music on top of the piano. The house doesn't feel the same.

Then I hear Elsa's key in the door and I hurry along the hall to greet her.

'*Cariad*!' And we're back on the street before she has time to ask me why.

'For God's sake, Harry,' she says, rubbing her wrist. 'What's wrong with you?'

'Sorry, darling, but there's something I have to tell you.'

# 41

## 3 February 1966

I WATCH MARGARET Rees struggling with her shopping and a bit of my heart goes out to her, though she's never cared for me. I hear she's being treated for cancer, and it can't be easy keeping body and soul together on the little Rees earns from his journalism. But somehow they've found the money to come ashore and are renting a top-floor flat on this leafy street in Holland Park. At least, it's where the postman delivers his bills. The neighbours say she's living alone, that Rees hasn't been near the place for weeks.

'Where is he, Margie?'

She flinches at my voice and her step falters, but only for a moment. There's only the width of a parked car between us but she doesn't even glance in my direction. Head bowed, she ploughs on with her heavy bags, no doubt hoping she can cover the fifty yards to her front door in time to shut it in my face. Early evening on a quiet residential street, and people are hurrying home from work under their umbrellas, so I don't want to risk a scene: she's quite capable of orchestrating one. We're almost in step now, so close her bag bumps against my shin.

'He's going to have to talk to me,' I say. 'He's in danger, Margie.' I touch her elbow and she jerks it from me. 'Margie, *is* he up there?'

Her pace quickens and, spreading the bags like wings, she steps in front of me to block the last few yards to her garden gate. But they're too heavy to carry like that for more than a few seconds, and the bag in her right hand falls open, a bottle of milk shatters on the pavement. With a will she might push me aside and skip the last few yards to the door, but her resistance has broken too. She stands passively, arms and bags at her side, like a thrush with broken wings.

'Let me clear this,' I say, bending to pick up the glass. The milk has splashed her stockings and the hem of her grey woollen skirt. Then I hear her whimper and rise with the broken glass to face her. 'I startled you, Margie, I'm sorry.'

Her cheeks are glistening with tears of frustration. 'Leave him alone.'

'Where is he?'

'You're despicable.' She wipes her face with the back of her hand. 'Despicable bullies. All of you.'

'Peter Wright's been here.'

She presses fingers to her forehead. 'Hateful man. He won't leave us alone. Barging into our lives whenever it suits him. Worse than the Gestapo. He treats Gony like a criminal. Aagh! It makes me so angry. He's the reason Gony is as he is.'

'I'm the only person who can stop this, but I need your help, Margie. Where is he?'

'You? You would make it worse.' She looks at me defiantly. 'I don't know what you want but leave us alone. Leave him alone. Leave the past alone. Now, get out of my way.'

I watch her unfasten the iron gate and struggle up the little flagstone path to the house with her shopping.

'Sorry, Margie,' I shout after her. 'Sorry. I didn't want any of this.' Then I turn away in search of a bin, my hands sticky with cream from the broken bottle.

The following day I telephone Rees's friend Freddie Ayer. 'Goronwy didn't tell me that you were speaking again,' he says. 'Unwell? Yes. He's suffered another breakdown, I'm afraid.'

The old Colney Hatch 'lunatic asylum' was once the largest in Europe. I used to pass it on my way through north London to the military's wartime interrogation centre. Six miles of corridors, they say. But Goronwy is being treated in its grounds, in a new self-contained hospital for patients with neuroses of one kind or another. Ayer called it a 'patients like us' hospital for Hampstead housewives, artists, musicians, poets and people from the BBC.

'Depression, they say.'

'Have you seen him, Freddie?' I ask.

'Only family at this stage,' his reply.

But I make excuses to the D3 secretary, who is supposed to keep my diary, and drive out the same day.

The cab drops me in front of the old hospital's wrought-iron gates, and I walk up the drive, round the silent fountain towards the reception hall in front of the chapel. Once again I'm struck not only by the confidence and ambition of the buildings but also their brutal scale. It's a Victorian civic palace in the Italianate style with a dome and towers and loggia, and yellow brick wings that stretch almost as far as the eye can see. Built to impress, built for numbers, it would serve just as well as a prison, and for many who are committed here that is what it becomes. The brick is beginning to crumble as if our decline from imperial power, through two world wars, can be traced in its decaying fabric. Why am I here? Is it another piece of madness? Rees can be in no fit state to speak to me, yet speak he must, because I know Wright will have no qualms about pressing him in a fragile state.

I push through the doors into the entrance hall and am almost bowled over by a nurse making for freedom.

'Excuse me, the Halliwick? Can you tell me . . .?'

'Just keep walking,' she shouts over her shoulder, and that's what I do. Corridor to corridor, to the confused, the mind-numbing echo of many footfalls and distant voices, as if the ghosts of the place walk with me. Until at last a white coat directs me to a door that leads back to the sun, and a path across a well-mown lawn to a new red-brick and glass unit, with more of the human scale.

'You're not on the visitors list,' says the nurse at Reception.

'Because no one in the family expected me to visit,' I say. 'I'm Goronwy's brother, Geraint, from Wales.'

'All right, I'll ask,' she says truculently.

She's back after just a few minutes. 'End of the corridor, through the doors on the left.'

The ward sister is waiting for me and leads me along a carpeted corridor into a recreation area where about a dozen patients are taking part in an art class, most of them women in their forties.

'How is my brother?' I ask.

'Still very depressed, I'm afraid.' She points to the far end of the room where Rees is sitting with his back to us, staring out at grass and bare earth beds. He's wearing a white shirt and khaki trousers, as if he were on holiday in Italy – it's high summer on the ward – but also brown leather slippers of the sort you wear at home. The slippers are affecting because they belong to someone more vulnerable than I remember. I put my hand on his shoulder.

'Geraint?'

'No, it's Harry.' I step to the side so he can register my presence, which he does without a flicker of emotion. 'How are you?'

He doesn't reply, only turns back to stare at the garden. I take the seat to his right. The other patients are busy with their paintings or reading or sleeping: no one is interested in us.

'I'm sorry to see you here,' I say (it sounds trite), 'and I wouldn't have come but you should know that Peter Wright will visit you too.' I lean forward in an effort to capture his attention. 'Are you listening, Goronwy?'

His shoulders shrink as if he's expecting a blow.

'It's all right. Look at me,' I say. 'Goronwy, look at me.' But he shrinks a little more, his face in his hands now, as if he's preparing to curl into a ball.

'Goronwy. He'll ask you about Elsa again. He'll ask you if she joined the Party. And he'll ask you about me. Do you understand?'

He understands. Does he care? Does he care about anything? I touch him again and feel his body stiffen. I can't see his face but a fat teardrop plops on to the floor between those slippers. They're welling through his fingers. Is it instinct, or what we once meant to each other? I stand and put my arm around his shoulders. 'Hey, *mae'n iawn*,' I say, to say something.

Someone is approaching. A chair is dragged away, and a nurse with a generous ruddy face bobs in front of him. 'What's the matter?' Rees says nothing and she looks up at me in search of an explanation. I could say, 'Disappointment,' and 'Regret,' and 'Fear,' I could mention Guy – does his psychiatrist know? – but instead I look hopeless.

'I think you'd better go,' she says. 'Can you come again tomorrow?'

I don't reply, but bend and kiss the back of his grey head. Then I walk away.

Sister catches me in the corridor near the nurses' station. She's a no-nonsense young woman with large hands and thick calves. 'What a shame,' she says, 'you've come so far,' and she wants to know if my 'brother' mentioned the policeman to me because he hasn't been the same since his visit. He said his name was

Inspector Jamison. Grey tonsure. Glasses. Large nose. Fawn jacket. And a stutter. 'Mr Rees was very distressed,' she says, 'and now this today.'

'Yes, I'm sorry,' I say.

'You're his brother,' she says. 'It isn't your fault.'

I smile ruefully. 'I shouldn't have come.'

As I walk back along the echoing corridors of the old lunatic asylum I feel only pity for Rees and disgust that a tug of war over the past has brought him to this place. Did Wright wring it from him? I hardly care.

I eat and drink alone at the Reform for the first time in weeks, and by the time I reach home it is late evening. Elsa has left a note on the silver tray that her father gave us for calling cards and letters. I joked at the time that it was a secret dig at his daughter for marrying the footman, and she laughed and threatened to give me the sack if my service didn't improve. Goodness knows what she thinks of it now things are so tense. *Your daughter Bethan rang to speak to you – remember her?* she writes. *She'll ring again tomorrow. Don't wait up for me, Elsa.* She doesn't say where she's gone or how long she'll be. She's worked late every evening this week but one, when she went to bed with a migraine. Next week she flies to West Germany with Mr Healey.

I'm used to finding companionship and solace in music but I haven't played the piano for a fortnight and have no appetite for it now. Stripping the cover from our bed, I wrap it round me, like a cocoon, and stretch out on the drawing-room couch, cigarettes and an ashtray on the polished parquet floor beside me. I just about manage to resist the urge to pour another drink because it would certainly make my mood worse.

The telephone drags me from sleep at five past ten, and rolling out of the eiderdown cover I stumble into the hall.

'It's me,' she says, and I know she's upset. 'Harry?'

'Here, darling.'

'Harry, something terrible has happened. . .' She has to pause.

'Elsa, what is it? Where are you?'

'I'm at Jenifer Hart's.'

'I'll come.'

'Harry . . . it's Phoebe. Phoebe Pool.' She takes a shaky breath. 'She's dead.'

# 42

ELSA CRIES AND the only comfort I can offer her is to coo, 'Darling.' She refuses to let me go to her. 'I'm staying with Jenifer tonight. I think that's best.' How can it be best? I want her to be with me.

'Harry, she's afraid.' She repeats it slowly: '*Afraid.*' She won't say more on the phone.

'Tell her not to be,' I say, 'and, Elsa, please come home as soon as you can.'

She hangs up but I stay on the line for a click, and even though I don't hear one I whisper, 'You bastards,' into the mouthpiece.

Late on Sunday morning I hear the key in the lock and step into the hall to greet her. She looks exhausted and angry. Hand on my chest she wriggles free from my embrace and steps back to the open door. 'Let's go for a walk.'

In this drab season, we amble the streets, feeling as grey as the weather.

'The police *told* us Phoebe threw herself in front of a train,' she says.

'You don't believe them?'

'Jenifer says she was pushed.'

'Was she there?'

'No.'

'Then how the hell does she know?'

'She doesn't, but she's afraid.'

I reassure her Jenifer has no reason to be, and if the police say suicide that's what it is, but all the time I'm thinking, *Wright, you bastard, you did this.* Of course the coroner will record that she took her own life. No one will testify that she was hounded by a member of MI5; neither will her friend Anthony Blunt confess that she was one of the *useful idiots* he offered to the Service to seal a deal to save his own skin.

'This is madness, Harry,' says Elsa. 'It's poisoning our lives. Perhaps I'll move out for a while, until you can put it behind you.'

'Please wait until after your trip to Germany. You may feel different.'

'*Why*, Harry? Why are they doing this?'

I make the mistake of shrugging my shoulders as if she's asking me if England can win the World Cup this year. Christ! Our lives together, her work, our happiness is at stake. And she tugs her arm free and turns to reproach me. 'Who will be next?'

I ambush Furnival Jones at his office door first thing on Monday morning. 'It's about the reputation of the Service,' I say, because fear of a scandal carries more weight with management than an appeal for natural justice. 'And Phoebe Pool knew some important people . . . If the press gets hold of this it will accuse us of driving her to her death.'

That's enough to get the wind up FJ and he summons Wright to his office. 'Is this going to blow up in our faces, Peter?'

'I d-d-don't think so, sir,' he says. 'Actually, I'm inclined to view her suicide as an admission of guilt.'

I protest: 'Oh, come on! Phoebe Pool wasn't a spy, she was a patient in a mental hospital in great distress – I hear she could hardly speak. She had no idea what she was doing, but you coaxed her into naming her friends as Communists.'

'N-n-not true.'

'Blunt told you Pool was his courier? Blunt was lying. He threw you a bone. You'd know that if you'd gone about this properly. Pool cared nothing about politics. She was a sad, disturbed creature. Blunt gave you her name because he thought no one sensible would believe her capable of being an agent.'

'Well, Peter?' says FJ.

'The O-O-Oxford circle may be as important as Cambridge, sir, and Pool was one of our sources. If I m-may say so, Vaughan isn't being honest with you.' Wright turns to look at me. 'You're on g-good terms with some of our suspects. And his wife was at Oxford with Pool and Hart, sir. They're old friends.'

FJ glares at me. 'Is that true?'

I shake my head in frustration. 'That's a smokescreen.'

'You deny it?'

'No.'

'Then you should step away from the investigation.' FJ picks up his pen and starts to write. 'I'll suggest Sir Dick appoints someone else from SIS.'

'Well, sir, I should warn you, the chief knows as many of the FLUENCY suspects as I do – more. Professor Sir Stuart Hampshire.'

FJ puts down his pen. 'Hampshire?'

'Goronwy R-R-Rees gave us his name,' says Wright.

'The chief and Sir Stuart are very close,' I say. 'It was the chief who recommended Sir Stuart to the government as a suitable person to review our signals intelligence.'

FJ closes his eyes and groans. 'Did you know that?'

Wright says, 'We're w-w-waiting until he's finished the review before we speak to him, sir.'

'When?'

'In a year's time.'

'Bloody hell, Peter!' FJ slumps back in his chair. 'It will be too late by then.'

'I have no doubt Stuart Hampshire is an honourable and decent man,' I say. 'The point is, I'm not the only one who knows some of the many suspects on Peter's lists. Actually, you know them too, sir. FLUENCY should only be interested in evidence.'

FJ nods. 'All right, Vaughan, you've made your point. And let's have no more deaths. Christ, did you read that damn fool Driberg's speech in the Commons? He wants a committee of *politicians* to oversee our work. So let's not give the socialists a stick to beat us with.' He spreads his palms on the desk. 'Now, gentlemen, excuse me, I have to prepare for a meeting at Number 10. So if there's nothing else?'

I would like to say, 'Stop *him* bugging my home,' but I can't risk the small amount of credit I have with FJ. Oh, the pleasure Wright would have in accusing me of being paranoid, after all the things I've said about Angleton. There will be no justice for Phoebe Pool. Furnival Jones would have to have seen all I've seen during this investigation to recognise a filthy little stitch-up. Wright and Blunt, parasite and host, teasing each other, a little in love with each other, meddling in other people's lives, careless of the consequences.

'You're a liar, Peter,' I say, as we walk towards the lifts.

'Just d-doing my job, Harry,' he says mildly. 'What about you?'

'No one does a proper job here any more.' I pull back the lift gate. 'You take this one. I'll wait.'

Wright steps inside and reaches for the handle. 'You know we're g-going to have to speak to your wife.'

'My wife?'

The gate clunks into place, the lift whirs, and through the

brass grille he says, 'Well, Elsa's name keeps cropping up.' Then the lift falls – to hell as far as I'm concerned.

Maurice Oldfield urges me to keep my cool. I creep into Century House at one o'clock when I can be sure the new head of Counter-intelligence at MI6 is lunching at his club. I've spent no more than a few minutes with Christopher Phillpotts and I pray and will offer sacrifice to whatever God there may be that it remains that way. He was doing Maurice's old job in Washington, and has come home with baggage. I'm supposed to be carrying out 'special duties' for C, but I fear our new head of Counter-intelligence will try to claim me.

I stand at Maurice's window and gaze out at a grey-blue iridescent mass of cloud tumbling along the Thames. Century House will soon be under siege.

'Do nothing for goodness' sake,' I hear him say. 'I'm trying to keep you out of this.'

I laugh.

'I know, I know.' He holds up his hand. 'What I mean is, our new head of Counter-intelligence has drunk deeply of Angleton's cup, and he's come home to root out Communists from our side of the Service. We're all under suspicion, of course, but you . . . you have your own *special* relationship with Jim Angleton.' He adjusts his large glasses with his right hand. 'So, watch it!'

Nicholas Elliott says more. 'It's a fucking disease. Crackpots' – he means Phillpotts – 'has brought it home from Washington. Back here five minutes and he's turning the place upside down.'

By the time I find Nick's new corner office on the sixth floor the rain is lashing his windows.

'Another purge, Harry! It does Dick no credit that this is happening on his watch. Have you heard? Andrew King's gone.'

King was station chief in Vienna after me in the fifties and a decent one, too.

'Why?'

'Because he was a Communist at Cambridge in the thirties. For a few months only, and he told his board all about it when he joined the Service twenty years ago. But now it's once a sinner, always a sinner. He was judged by Crackpots and found wanting. Donald Prater has been called back from Stockholm for the same reason. Warner is leaving Geneva because he has too many Russian acquaintances. I keep fielding calls from our station chiefs asking me how the hell they're expected to do their jobs if they can't make contacts with potential defectors.'

'How many?'

'Have gone? Eight so far. Collins, Paulson, but there'll be more. Do you know Don Bailey? He's resigned in protest. Brave man.' Elliott reaches into his desk drawer and takes out a bottle and two glasses. 'You see? It's driving me to drink.'

'To *more* drink, Nick.'

'But you'll have one, won't you, old boy?' He pushes a generous measure of whisky towards me. 'I'm thinking of a job in the City and some decent money.'

I gaze over the rim of my glass at him. The City? Perhaps. I've never seen Nick in anything but a suit, always immaculate, always expensive, a natural clothes-horse because he's as thin as a rake. 'You've been threatening the City for years.'

'And now they're pushing me out!'

'Dick's just made you controller of Western Europe.'

'Dick who? Seriously. Your old friend Arthur Martin is going to "interview me" – that's what he calls it – for the third time! He's made it his life's work to prove I knew Philby was a spy, that I'm guilty.' Elliott rolls his eyes. 'Honestly, Maurice Oldfield has to step up – he is the bloody deputy chief. He should speak to Dick. Put the Service before his own ambition. What about you? You're part of all this.'

I pick up my empty glass and raise it to my eye, and now there are at least half a dozen Elliotts twinkling in the crystal, all of them different in some small way.

'What on earth are you doing?' he says.

'This is how Jim sees things.' I place the glass back on his desk and rise. '*I aros yn ddiogel*, Nick. Don't give up. It's too soon for the City.'

He just grunts.

Foolishly, I stay at Century House for a special showing of a documentary film about a nuclear attack on our country called *The War Game*. There are thirty of us in the briefing room and for an hour or so we sit and watch the end of the world as we know it in black and white. The film has been shot like archive, as if the sky has fallen in already. Between reels I close my eyes and think what it would be like to be a survivor in a room like this with twenty-eight middle-aged men in suits, one woman and three plates of Rich Tea biscuits. The BBC has decided to pull the film because the public can't bear too much reality, but the new controller of the Soviet bloc has a copy. Just as the air-raid sirens go off I notice Phillpotts four to the right of me, black brogues on the back of the chair in front. Minutes later the Soviet missile explodes, causing instant flash blindness and a firestorm. Then our bombers reach the borders of Russia and mutually assured destruction is complete. At this point I consider escaping but decide it might send the wrong signal, and sit through the grisly aftermath, the rationing, the looting, the corpse-burning and a declaration of martial law.

The moment the lights go on Phillpotts hails me. 'Did you enjoy that?'

'Oh, lots of laughs.'

I watch him edge round other people's knees with the obvious intention of collaring me. He is Laurence Olivier playing Heathcliff in *Wuthering Heights*, tall and with a matinee-idol smile that he can turn on and off. Flash! It's on, and he shakes my hand warmly.

'Clever of Shergold to arrange this,' he says. 'Good to remind people why we do what we do. Look, Vaughan . . .' he takes my arm and steers me towards the door '. . . have you a minute?'

'Not really.'

His grip tightens a fraction. 'I've been in touch with Peter Wright. He's happy for me to speak to you.'

'Is he?' I pull my elbow free. 'Oh, good. But Wright isn't my keeper. If you want to speak to me, ring and arrange a time.'

'All right, Vaughan,' he says frostily, 'I will,' and he turns and stalks away.

My appointment with Sir John Nicolson is at five o'clock but there's a signal fault on the Underground, then a traffic jam on North End Road, and by the time the cab drops me at the entrance to his hospital I'm fifteen minutes late. The Manor House is an uninspiring red-brick building in a style commonly encountered in the twenties suburbs at the edge of the city. From newspaper cuttings I know it has a link with the trade unions, which may be why Hugh Gaitskell chose to come here when he became ill in the December of '62.

Reception rings Nicolson's office and there's no reply, so I persuade an orderly to show me the way. We meet the director on a long corridor between Chest and Orthopaedics, coat draped over his arm, his day at the hospital done. Can we speak somewhere private? Reluctantly Nicolson agrees. His office is in Administration, half a mile of corridors away, so he steers me into a ward and, with a proprietorial air, asks a nurse to find him a side room. There's still a name on the door, but Mr Ken

Jones has taken residence in the mortuary. Nicolson stands on the other side of an unmade bed with his back to the window. On a bedside locker, a vase of rotting red carnations and a well-thumbed paperback. Maybe it's the flowers or the smell of stale urine, but the sickly-sweet smell of decay reminds me of Belsen concentration camp. Perhaps they left poor Jones in this hot little room longer than they should have done.

I ask Sir John about Gaitskell and he rumbles through a mental note of the Labour leader's case. He was admitted to Manor House Hospital suffering from flu-like symptoms, which he said he'd picked up on a visit to Paris. His symptoms became more acute and he was moved to the Middlesex Hospital. The antibodies in his blood were attacking his organs, and tests seemed to indicate an immunological disease, *Lupus erythematosus*. Nicolson concedes that the medical team should have realised sooner, but Gaitskell was fifty-six, and the disease is most common in women under forty. His end was swift and unpleasant. 'We did all we could in the circumstances.' Nicolson clears his throat to disguise his feelings. 'Hugh was a great friend of mine, you know.'

I ask him if he is a hundred per cent sure it was lupus. He says the post-mortem wasn't that conclusive, and if I want more information I should speak to Dr Somerville at the Middlesex. 'Hugh was just terribly, terribly unlucky, Mr Vaughan, and so were his countrymen. One of your colleagues came here with a wild story . . . Hugh wasn't murdered. But if you'd like another opinion, speak to Somerville.'

Elsa is home early, packing for Germany. She flies tomorrow. 'Mary wants to stay here on Wednesday and Thursday.'

'You told her you'd be away?'

She lifts her gaze from the blouse she's folding. 'She's your daughter!'

'Just to manage her expectations,' I say. 'It's you they want to see most.'

I ask her if she's seen *The War Game* and she says she has and is going to recommend it to all the military men she meets.

'And when you get back?'

'You mean us? I've asked a friend if I can stay for a while. Just to be away from this place.'

'Who?'

'It's only a possibility – while you sort things out here.' She's leaning over her case as she packs one of the navy skirts she wears to the ministry, then the white silk blouse from Bazaar that I bought her for Christmas. A lock of hair falls in front of her face and she sweeps it behind her ear without thinking. She does it several times a day and always with grace, as natural as the bubble and sun sparkle of a fast-flowing stream, as natural as the high cry of the curlew in wild places.

'I love you,' I say, and put my arms about her, frozen over the bed with my chest against her back.

The tension drains from her at last and she turns to face me. 'I don't want to leave home, Harry,' she whispers.

'I'm working things out,' I say. 'It's just I'm afraid there'll be hell to pay when I do.'

'Stop the riddles,' she says. 'Tell me why.'

I don't want to – 'Not now, not here, darling' – and I push her gently away. Then I close the suitcase and lift it from our bed. 'I can be quiet – can you?'

# 43

On your first day at the Fort, they teach you that the enemy is always listening and sometimes your friends too. That's how it was in Vienna and Berlin and Washington. Men I'll never meet have heard me groan with pleasure and whisper love to women I shouldn't have. You never get used to sharing your life with a stranger. Elsa thought to escape it when she resigned from the Service. She's sleeping peacefully beside me now, but in a few hours she'll fly away, and in the course of her journey she'll reflect on what is happening to us, and hovering in her thoughts will be questions about the past that we've never asked each other.

Was Elsa a member of the Party?

She seemed to strain every fibre of her being to make a success of SUBALTERN. I know that's what I thought at the time. Her people were the ordinary men and women of the refugee camps, patriots like Béla Bajomi who turned down CIA money to work with her. When SUBALTERN collapsed her record and connections were good enough to secure her a senior role at the War Office. And now she is under investigation. Sooner or later Peter Wright is going to ask her, *Are you a member or have you ever been a member of the Communist Party?* If the answer is 'Yes,' she'll be forced to resign, and in Moscow Philby notches up another.

## 9 *February 1966*

I read in my paper at breakfast that West Germany has agreed to give East Germany twenty-four million dollars of consumer goods – coffee and butter and fruit – in return for the release of nearly three thousand political prisoners. By my calculations, that's a ransom of eight thousand dollars per prisoner, proving once again that Soviet-style Communism is bankrupt in every way. You wonder what we fear when a political system is struggling to feed its people. The answer must be the wild men on both sides. Angleton. Wright.

We meet in his new office a few hours later. Someone in B Branch has decided his status entitles him to three windows and a glass conference table. From the science room in the basement, with no windows, he has risen in three years to the third floor with three, and he looks smug about it. As further proof of his ascendancy he has called us together to announce he has persuaded FJ to reopen PETERS and DRAT. This time Graham Mitchell will be interrogated, while enquiries continue into Roger Hollis's past. My colleagues on the FLUENCY working party are delighted, of course. And there's more 'good news' because Wright's D3 team has come up with a fresh list of senior civil servants who may or may not be members of the Party. His favourite has just stepped down as permanent secretary at the Ministry of Power.

'You know, Burgess's friend, Proctor,' he says. 'Classic KGB fodder.'

Sir Dennis Proctor is living in a farmhouse in the South of France on his fat civil-service pension; Wright is intent on blowing into his life like the mistral. He flies there tomorrow. 'And I've spoken to Christopher Phillpotts,' he says to me, at the end of the meeting. 'He wants you back in Six's fold.'

'Then he will have to speak to my shepherd,' I reply.

On my way home I stop at a phone box and telephone Chobham. Ring once, ring twice, ring off. And to be sure Mitchell understands, I send a postcard of the Tower of London too. We shot a German spy there during the war. Twenty-five years ago, almost to the day. The poor sod landed by parachute and broke his leg, but because we're a civilised nation we waited for it to heal before we executed him.

## 10 February 1966

On Thursday mornings, renowned cardiac specialist Dr Walter Somerville sees private patients at a clinic in Harley Street. His waiting room smells of lavender and the walls are hung with competent oil paintings of cow pastures and calm seas. His secretary is dressed immaculately in baby pink Chanel – 'Ordinary tea or China?' – and she is very attentive. Surgery is almost over and Dr Somerville has only a fat man in his forties to see. Just the effort of breathing is making him sweat. The doctor's door opens as I'm blowing the steam from the rim of my cup. He looks at me intently, as if he's trying to diagnose my condition or marry me to one of his files. Then the penny drops. 'The policeman? I'll be with you in a minute,' he says.

Somerville has met dozens of 'policemen' like me. From his file in the MI5 Registry I know the following: he's Irish, he's fifty-two, he worked as a doctor in Dublin but volunteered for military service at the outbreak of war. He was seconded to the chemical-warfare establishment at Porton Down and then to the US War Department, in the service of which he was badly burned preparing weapons for the invasion of Japan. It didn't spoil his good looks, and he was approached by one of the big Hollywood studios to do a screen test. But since 1952 he has worked at the Middlesex Hospital, and on a number of chemical-warfare committees.

Like all senior doctors he's a terrible time-keeper, and his 'with you in a minute' becomes thirty. I have strolled through the landscapes on the walls of the waiting room many times before he's ready to see me. At last he shows me to a comfortable leather chair and flumps wearily into his own. His face is big and square and he has a pronounced under-bite that makes him appear pugnacious. Hollywood may have been hoping to cast him as a cowboy.

He apologises for keeping me, especially when he's sure there's nothing more to say. 'I told your Mr Wright everything.'

I tell him I'm carrying out a confidential audit of the investigation, just to be sure my colleague has considered all the possibilities.

'I see.' His eyes narrow a little. 'You mean you don't trust him?'

'My colleague says one of Mr Gaitskell's doctors contacted MI5. It wasn't Sir John . . .'

Somerville leans forward earnestly. 'And it wasn't me.'

'My colleague seems to think . . .'

'I know perfectly well what he thinks. You're aware of my connection with Porton Down?'

I say that I am.

'Well, your Mr Wright brought me an article from a Russian medical journal about a drug called hydralazine that causes similar symptoms to *Lupus erythematosus*. Proof, according to your Wright, that Mr Gaitskell was poisoned. "Don't be ridiculous," I told him and am happy to tell you now. "We use hydralazine to treat hypertension and, by the way, we've known about its side effects for years!"

'I see. So you're ruling out the possibility that someone slipped a pill into his coffee?'

'Absolutely. Mr Gaitskell would have had to take many pills over many weeks for it to have an effect. I tried to tell your colleague.'

'Is it possible KGB scientists have found a way to produce a single-shot dose of hydralazine?'

'We would have to try to develop our own to be sure.' He touches the corners of his mouth for a moment. 'I hesitate to say – perhaps you know . . .'

'Go on.'

'Mr Wright asked Porton Down to try. But I understand its chief doctor has refused on the ground that there isn't any proof Gaitskell was murdered so time spent researching the efficacy of hydralazine as a single-shot weapon would be a great waste of money. I concur wholeheartedly. Now, is there anything else?'

Anything else? Oh, yes. Plenty.

### 11 February 1966

The flood of intelligence material that used to cross my desk in Leconfield House has slowed to a trickle. While Wright's away in France the D3-FLUENCY empire is governed by his satraps, McBarnet and Stewart, and they have become very secretive. But late on Friday afternoon I'm sitting with my feet on the desk, smoking, thinking how best to use the short time left to me, when Evelyn steps into my office with two files.

'Run a check on these, will you,' she says, handing them to me, 'especially with Moscow and Berlin.'

'What are we looking for?'

'Links to people of interest.'

'And why are we looking?'

She frowns and her hand creeps up to her face. 'It's in the files.'

'In these?' I hold them up between a thumb and a forefinger. 'That's all there is?'

'That's why we're asking SIS to help us. Now be a good boy. *Tout de suite*, if you please.'

Maybe she thinks I'm too bored to care, and I'll push the papers through to Berlin and Moscow stations without question. She's wrong. I recognise the names straight away: Kagan and Sternberg are rich industrialist friends of the prime minister. Evelyn will have picked their files clean of concrete intelligence before she handed them to me, but I've been doing this long enough now to recognise a piece of CIA work. She's fishing for anything that might suggest Kagan and Sternberg are on the payroll of the Kremlin. Why? Both men earn more than a small country from their ordinary business interests every year. My sense is this is something to do with Wilson.

I ring Tom Driberg at home.

'I'm going to a party,' he says. 'You can have five minutes, that's all.'

We meet outside the Marquis of Granby on Romney Street, because it's only a stone's throw from Parliament and from home. Driberg is in a filthy mood and curses me roundly when I refuse to talk in front of his driver.

'Tell me what you know about Kagan and Sternberg,' I say.

'Why do you want to know?'

'I thought you were in a hurry.'

'I *am*, old boy, but you're supposed to be giving *me* information.'

'This will help.'

He rolls his dark eyes. 'I can't tell you much. Jewish refugees from the Nazis who have made good here. Sternberg in plastics, and Kagan has made a fortune from his Gannex raincoats – you must have seen Harold in one. They're his capitalist friends, and I hear they make a hefty contribution to the cost of his private office. What else? Kagan told me he has family in the Soviet Union – in Lithuania, I think. Is that why you want to know? Are they spies?'

'I don't expect so.'

'If you don't think they're spies, why are you asking?'

'Any idea how much money they give Wilson?'

'Haven't a clue. Sorry. There,' he says, with an extravagant flourish. 'Not much use, I'm afraid.'

'You have been.'

'Really? Then when are you going to be of use to *me*?'

'Soon.'

'Good!' He's in too much of a hurry to join the party to argue. Drinks at his gangster friend's flat in Soho, he says, and he'd like to invite me but he can't guarantee I would receive a warm welcome. I walk him to his chauffeur-driven car and open the door, just as I would for the Queen. 'By the way, Harold's going to the country,' he says, patting my hand as it rests on the door. 'There's going to be an election. Don't tell anyone I told you so.'

There's always a table at the Marquis. I could drink at home, but this is Friday and pub noise helps me think. Whisky and smoke, and my imagination wanders back to the wilderness of mirrors, where I consider every possible side of Elsa, our time together, and the years before she met me. And when I know I'm lost, beset by *horrible imaginings*, I stop, and reflect instead on what Tom has told me of the prime minister's business pals. Are they dipping into their own pockets to fund his campaigns, or acting as a channel for KGB money? Angleton and Wright conjured up a plot to murder Gaitskell in the First Act of their conspiracy drama, the election of a Soviet agent as prime minister in their Second, and now they have conceived a Third in which two of the country's foremost industrialists risk their fortunes and reputations to keep a Kremlin puppet in power. Too fantastic! But I can think of no other explanation for the information Evelyn is seeking from our stations in Berlin and Moscow. One thing I'm sure of: OATSHEAF is alive.

The madness didn't end, and why would it? They're convinced the prime minister of Great Britain is a Soviet agent of influence.

## 12 February 1966

I take two wrong turns in search of the car park by the fish ponds. Chobham Common is furled in dense fog and Graham Mitchell is late arriving too. He pulls up beside me in a comfortable Rover and invites me to join him. Parked a short distance away but barely visible in the mist are two more cars. There's no sign of their drivers and it's safe to assume at this early hour their owners are either fishermen or walking with their dogs. Mitchell is unhappy, nevertheless, and grumbles that Elsa's little blue sports car is too conspicuous. 'Calm down, Graham,' I say. (I won't take lectures on security from a career desk officer.)

We sit shoulder to shoulder in our coats as the little we can see through the windscreen disappears behind a film of condensation.

'Cigarette?' He hasn't shaved and, with white stubble and slack cheeks, he appears older in the morning light than his sixty years. 'How's Pat?'

'We agreed no more contact,' he says wearily.

'Circumstances change.'

'You know, it will be three years this year since I left the Service.'

'You never leave, you should know that. What can you tell me about OATSHEAF?'

He shuffles sideways to look me in the eye. 'Is this a fishing expedition?'

'In a way, yes.'

'Then I can't help you. OATSHEAF means nothing to me.'

'It's the CIA code name for the file on the prime minister.'

'Is it? Well, that's none of my business.'

'Come on, Graham.'

'Or any of yours, Vaughan. Strictly Security Service business.'

'I'm making it mine, and so should you, if your working life has any meaning. We're better than the Russians – that's what we've always told ourselves. That's how we've learned to live with ourselves.'

Mitchell closes his eyes and holds the bridge of his nose. He would love to slip away to Pat and *The Times* crossword, perhaps an early-morning round of golf.

'By the way, Graham,' I say, 'Wright has permission to bring you in for interrogation.'

His hand drops so he can stare at me again. I don't think I've ever seen the colour drain from someone's face so quickly. Did he really believe that it was over?

'When?'

'I don't know. Soon.'

'Christ. What is Dick White thinking?' he says, fumbling with the door handle. 'Christ. I want some air. Can we walk?'

Pulling his coat tighter, he limps towards the edge of the car park as if he's carrying the weight of suspicion on his back. I follow a few paces behind. He knows I'm going to press him to fight, urge him to rescue his reputation. Does he have the guts? On we walk through the winter scrub, our coats beaded with dew. The mist appears to leach the little colour left in this season from the heather and cottongrass and birches, and there is a strange stillness, as if we are walking through a dream landscape. After about ten minutes we come to a plank bridge across a stream.

'I won't ask you what you're going to do,' Mitchell says, turning at last, 'and I don't want you to tell me.'

'Wright says the Security Service has been investigating Wilson for years.'

Mitchell shakes his head. 'I know nothing about OATSHEAF. Look in the Central Index under WORTHINGTON. Norman John Worthington.'

'That's Wilson?'

'A pseudonym to safeguard the file.'

'Can you tell me what's in it?'

'No, Vaughan, I can't.' He takes a step towards me. 'I don't know why I've told you that much.'

'You do.'

We stand an arm's length apart, staring at each other. 'Christ,' he says, at last. 'Can I have a cigarette?'

'Calm down. Here.' I offer him my packet and take one too. 'Look, my lips are sealed.'

'Are they?' he says, grabbing my hand to steady the lighter flame. 'Are they?'

'*Er mwyn duw!* Yes, they are.'

He nods, then draws deeply on his cigarette.

We finish them in silence, then turn back along the track. The mist has cleared just a little. As we approach the car park I touch his arm to check our pace to a few shambling steps. 'Just one more thing: why did Five open a file?'

He hesitates. 'Let's just say Wilson's loyalty was a matter for speculation. You know how it is – once we've opened a file it's on a shelf for ever.'

'Marked by the apparat.'

There's the grinding of gravel as he comes to a halt abruptly with his hands on his hips. 'Honestly, Vaughan, whatever your scheme is, don't go outside the Service. Keep it in-house. Do you hear me? Don't start a crusade. And don't involve me.'

# 44

## *14 February 1966*

I TELEPHONE ELSA first thing on Monday only to discover she checked out of her Bielefeld hotel a day early. No messages, and no one at nearby RAF Gütersloh knows where she has gone. By the time I've finished my fruitless search for her I'm late, and Evelyn is waiting at my door to greet me with a sour expression. She thrusts a list of supplementary questions at me. 'Be a good boy and pass these on to Berlin and Moscow.'

'Come in, take a seat,' I say, as I unlock my door. 'I want to know what this is about.'

'It isn't your concern.'

'But you want my help?'

We stare at each other, like gunslingers in a Hollywood Western, until sense prevails and – hand still on her revolver – she steps inside my office.

'Sit down,' I say, pulling a chair away from my desk.

She ignores me. 'All you need to know is that the prime minister's two business chums have very loose tongues – especially the raincoat millionaire. Kagan impresses a Lithuanian drinking pal with tales of the comings and goings at Downing Street. His pal just happens to work for Moscow Centre.'

'And you suspect Kagan might be KGB too?'

'It's possible,' she says cautiously. 'The prime minister's a bit of a Romeo – he's sleeping with a member of his staff – and

349

that makes him a good blackmail target. A word from Kagan to his pal . . .'

'And that's what this fishing trip is all about?'

'We have the necessary authority.'

'Right,' I say. 'Then leave it with me.'

She squints at me suspiciously. 'You'll get them off today?'

'Of course.'

I kick the door shut after her and light a cigarette. The radiator's leaking and I forgot to empty the bowl beneath it on Friday so there's a dirty great puddle on the floor. That's the first mess to clear up. Like a naughty schoolboy, I tip the water that's collected in the bowl out of the window into the street below, and it splashes on to the pavement and a couple of smartly dressed businessmen. Gazing down at their angry faces it occurs to me that Evelyn may be trying to do something similar. *Prime minister's friend is a KGB spy* would make a fine newspaper splash just before a general election. Perhaps Wright intends to place it with a 'friend' in Fleet Street, like Pincher on the *Express*. Well, if you're convinced the prime minister's a spy it makes perfect sense to do all you can to stop him winning.

Half past five, and secretaries and junior officers are already leaving Curzon Street at the end of the working day. Evelyn will be at her desk three floors above, and on the fifth, FJ will have begun the evening office, clearing his desk, locking files in the safe, then home to his handsome house in Hampstead for dinner with his wife and daughter. The shift's changing in the Registry: queens are slipping into or out of their coats. I recognise most of them now: who may be willing to help, who will hinder. Library rules apply most of the day with very few opportunities for conversation, but at handover queens have a little time to catch up on tasks still outstanding and share their news.

Dropping my briefcase by the duty officer's desk, I slip

through a group of them and walk towards the Central Index room. No one bats an eyelid: I'm a familiar face, one of those awkward sods in D3 who are making everyone's life a misery.

Miss Allan is the guardian of the index. I smile sweetly at her and step over to the wooden boxes that line three walls of the room.

'Can I help you, Mr Vaughan?' she says, fingering the yellow pearls at her neck. She has a voice like HM The Queen. In the past I've bowed to her knowledge of the index and let her guide me, but not on this occasion. 'No, Miss Allan, thank you.'

She's piqued. I watch her flounce back to her desk and jot my name on the visitors list.

WORTHINGTON comes after WALLIS in the index. Mr Wallis was an old Fascist who died in 1955, and to judge from the entry on his card his friends were many, and many were his scrapes with the law. There's nothing but a telephone extension on Mr Worthington's card and an instruction to 'apply to the director general'. No file number, no comrades in the same constellation, no cross references, no past, no future. Norman Worthington is a 'no trace'. Taking a biro from my pocket I push up my shirt cuff and jot the extension number on my wrist.

'Found what you were looking for, Mr Vaughan?'

'Thank you, Miss Allan.' I turn with a smile. 'May I say that is a lovely blouse? *Pert iawn*, we say in Welsh. Pink suits you.' Raising my right hand to my lips I pretend to pinch a thought. 'I wonder, do you happen to have an internal directory?'

Of course she does, and now she's been stroked a little she's willing to share it with me. Sure enough, extension 505 is one of the director general's numbers. No one's able to access Worthington without his personal authorisation. If I want to read it I must find a way to open the combination safe in his office.

*15 February 1966*

The following day I receive a postcard from Berlin. She says everything's fine, which reassures me not one whit. Why hasn't she rung? She promised to. And why has her card come through the post room at MI5? I telephone military headquarters in West Berlin: no one has seen her since the secretary of state flew home. I try the ministry main building in Whitehall and discover Mr Healey has been back at his desk for three days. Mrs Vaughan? Still in Berlin, they say. I ask for the name of a hotel and they admit they don't have a clue what she's doing or where she's staying. She's on leave, they say. A few days' leave! Guy Burgess was on leave. That's what he said: 'I'm taking a few days.' Only his leave became the rest of his life.

I sit at my desk with Elsa's postcard – the familiar image of the ruined church that Berliners call the 'hollow tooth' – and I consider the possibilities, one stop after another – subject, counter-subject, inversion, like one of Maurice's great fugues – until my head is booming. Stop! From the bottom drawer of my desk, a bottle of whisky. This is the edge of reason that Jim Angleton tiptoes all the time. How easy it would be to fall. Like the winter climber who ventures on to a wind-cut cornice at the crest of the mountain, a footstep too far, a single hysterical impulse, and crack! Over the precipice he goes. I have known days and nights of confusion and fear in the field but never been tested quite like this. Has she gone?

*17 February 1966*

The FLUENCY committee is gathered at Peter Wright's conference table to discuss his visit to France.

'P-P-Proctor's g-guilty,' he says.

'Did he say so?'

'Would you?'

'If the evidence put it beyond doubt.'

I know Sir Dennis Proctor a little because he was a friend of Guy's. He reached the top of the civil service and is now enjoying his pension and a lucrative company directorship. I bet the last week playing host to Wright in France felt like the longest of his life.

'He admits he's been l-l-left wing all his life,' says Wright, 'but claims he was *never* a Communist. One night he got pretty drunk and admitted he'd always admired Burgess.' Wright looks at me from the corner of his eye. 'I have it here,' he says, turning the pages of his notepad. '*N-no secrets from Guy, even when I was working for the prime minister. Guy only had to ask and I would tell him* . . . P-Proctor shared every secret that crossed his desk with his friend, and Burgess passed it on to his Soviet controller.'

'Well done, Peter,' says Stewart. 'How much damage? Can we prosecute?'

'*Pour encourager* the civil service,' says someone else.

And my head is a swarm of wild imagining. Where is she? I've shared so much of my work with her. *Er mwyn duw.* Too much drink and too little sleep and too many meetings in smoke-filled rooms like this one, with papers from the thirties that are so fragile they have to be pared apart with a knife; too much suspicion, too little purpose, and no reason to be joyful.

'Proctor's f-first wife committed suicide,' I hear Wright say. 'I wonder why. She spoke to Burgess just before he scuttled off to Moscow, and not long after that she took her life.'

'I'm sorry, Peter,' I say. 'Will you excuse me?'

I don't have time to be careful. I ring a travel agent I've done business with in the past from my desk: he says he can get me a flight to Berlin tomorrow. I ask him to buy an open ticket for me in the name of Morgan. Then I ring the number two at Berlin station and call in a favour: would he please check with the army and local police if Elsa Frankl Vaughan is still in the western half of the city. At six o'clock I lock my office door for what may be the last time and take the lift to the entrance hall, where the duty policeman wishes me a pleasant evening and I wish him the same.

The temperature is close to freezing and everyone is moving more quickly. I join the procession across the parks, just as I've done for the last three years, glad of the winter darkness, the prickle of the cold on my face and in my throat. I know every tree, every park bench, and the office windows that overlook Queen's Walk, where we used to say a hack at the *Economist* was keeping a seat warm for me. Too late. Tonight the air is too thick for hymns. My calmer self says I'm wrong to assume the worst; my cynical Service self can only recall that it was like this when Guy fled in '51.

I'm so full of these mad thoughts I don't check whether the splints are missing from the front door. As soon as it's open I notice a chink of light at the end of the hall. Either someone has forced their way in uninvited, or they need no invitation. I drop my briefcase on the floor and lean my back against the wall. No greeting. No word. I feel . . . I don't know . . . relief, of course. I feel foolish. I feel an overwhelming sense of sadness settle like a mist on the lake of my heart, because nothing is as it should be.

'Welcome home,' I say.

Elsa's sitting at the table in her black wool coat, a suitcase at her feet. She doesn't rise to kiss me, merely acknowledges my presence with a weak smile that lasts no longer than the beat of a crow's wing.

'I wasn't sure you were coming home,' I say.

'Why?'

'You know why: I haven't heard from you for days.'

She says nothing, and her face shows nothing – neither warmth nor remorse – and it hurts so much I lose my temper. 'Where the hell have you been?'

'Didn't you get my card?'

'Was it too much to pick up the phone? Christ. I didn't know where you were. Your minister came home days ago, girl! You left Bielefeld early on Saturday, skipped the hotel in Gütersloh – no record of you there, or in Berlin. And no one at the MoD seemed to know—'

'You contacted the ministry?' she says, rising from the table.

'I was beginning to think you weren't coming back. I was worried. Where the hell were you?'

'I was doing my job! Honestly, Harry, what's wrong with you?'

We glare at each other. I'm furious. I'm sad. I'm in love – when she's angry most of all, because her dark eyes are sparkling like a mountain lake and there's an intense frown between her perfectly arched eyebrows, and always a strand of hair on her cheek. And I want an excuse to touch her. 'So, *are* you home?' I say, nodding at the suitcase.

'For now.'

I take half a step and reach out to her, but she turns and bends to pick up the suitcase.

'Here let me,' I say.

'No, thank you.' Grabbing it with both hands she half lifts, half drags it to the kitchen door where she pauses, and without turning to look at me she says, 'I'm going to have a bath.'

'Can I bring you something? Boil the kettle? A glass of wine?'

No reply. I listen to her bumping the suitcase up the stairs and every thump makes the house seem less like a home. Burn Daddy's antique furniture. Tear the kitchen cupboards from the walls. I feel more alone than I've felt since the last time we broke up and I went back to Vienna.

The loose floorboard on the landing squeaks, the pipes groan as she turns the brass taps on full and water cascades into the bath. *From all your filthiness, all your idols, I will cleanse you,* the minister used to boom at us in chapel. Only it isn't that easy, because the filth bloody well sticks. The smell lingers. The questions remain. You're back, Elsa, but the questions haven't gone away. I hear. I see. I know you're not telling the truth. And you said, 'No lies, Harry, not to each other,' but that's how it seems to be between us now.

# 45

MRS LINDA GILL-THOMPSON would like an adventure. Mrs Gill-Thompson went out of her way to catch *my* eye. She smiled, looked away, then back in a heartbeat, and her second smile was the try-if-you-like smile of a woman in her forties who wants to be desired, is tired of being alone, and is only too conscious of time slipping to the grave. I *am* vain, it's true. I was flattered, curious, that's all. Then a day and two nights later I woke with a print of her face on my mind's eye, and as Elsa slept beside me the seed of an idea took root. Because the crowded room where our eyes first met was the DG's Secretariat, and Mrs Gill-Thompson's desk is only feet from his door.

On the Friday after our significant moment I found a reason to be in the entrance hall at half past five in the evening, and when she emerged from a lift with some of the other girls I caught her eye again, once, twice, thrice, before she followed her friends on to the street. It was no great matter to engineer some business in the Secretariat the following Monday. Since then we have spoken four more times and I have asked her to meet me for a drink.

'Mrs Gill-Thompson, did the DG receive my memo on new faces at the KGB residency here in London?' I say, for the benefit of her neighbours in the Secretariat.

'I don't think so, Mr Vaughan,' she says, reaching for the papers in her tray. 'Let me check.' As she leafs through them I

slide a note in front of her: *18.30 The York Minster. Dean Street.*
She scribbles an answer: *Fine. The usual!*

Mrs G-T presumes intimacy on a short acquaintance because
she knows I'm trusting her to keep her mouth shut. Does she
care I'm a married man? I don't think so. She's flattered, and
she enjoys the secrecy, because it's part of the flight. She's taller
than Elsa, thicker at the waist, not unattractive but not as
attractive. Her voice, her values, her clothes are just what one
would expect of a county lady, even though the worn tweed
suit and shoes she wears to work suggest money is an issue.
She has spirit and a sense of humour, and it's easy to imagine
her enjoying sex. But all I want from her is the sort of office
intelligence that will help me lay my hands on the OATSHEAF-
WORTHINGTON file.

### 6 March 1966

I'm fifty-two today. Elsa takes pity on me and we make love
for the first time since she came home from Germany. Make
love? We wrestle and bite, and when it's over, she's up and
into the bathroom straight away.

'Are you free tonight?' I shout.

'No,' she says. 'Sorry.'

'What about Ronnie Scott's?'

'I can't.'

Can't? She means 'won't'. 'Come on, girl, perhaps after your
*very* important engagement . . .?'

She steps back into our bedroom in a towel and picks up
her hairbrush. From my pillow I watch her at her toilette: hair
dryer, a little perfume, panties on under the towel, then to the
wardrobe to choose her clothes. Jesus Christ. I want to shout,
'Enough,' but I haven't the stomach for another row.

'Aren't you going to shower?' she says.

'No hurry.'

She sits on the edge of the bed with her back to me and I wonder if she's waiting for me to leave so she can dress. Just the thought saddens me so, because we've never been shy with each other before.

'Love you,' I say.

I spend my birthday in a noisy Service car on the road to the laboratories at Porton Down. Waiting at the security gate for final clearance, I experience the same sort of apprehension I always feel in a hospital only worse, because the men in white coats are busy thinking of ingenious and invisible ways to kill not cure you.

'I don't know why you bothered to come,' the chief white coat says, as we walk to his office. 'I told Peter Wright that I haven't the foggiest idea how one would infect someone with *Lupus erythematosus*.'

I ask him about the Russian paper that suggests the drug hydralazine can cause a condition like lupus if taken in large doses. 'Are you asking me if it is possible to refine it into a one-shot weapon?' he says. 'I doubt it very much. Besides, there are so many easier ways to eliminate someone, why would you bother?'

By the time I've returned the car to the Battersea garage and caught a taxi home it's close to seven o'clock. The splints have gone from the door again, but this time the house is empty. I run upstairs to check our bedroom, and the black stockings and skirt she wore to work this morning are lying in a heap in front of the chimneypiece, and she must have considered her blue silk dress for the reception she's attending this evening because she cast that on her chair. I keep my clothes in the mahogany tallboy to the left of the window, and two of the drawers are open. She's been rummaging through my things too. A photograph of the two of us in Vienna in 1948 that I keep as a reminder of a perfect day is missing from the top drawer. My first thought is to be glad she wants a souvenir of that time, but as I turn from the tallboy a shiver of doubt courses through me. Why has she gone through my things? I hurry across the landing to the box room and lift the loose floorboard where I keep my camera: it's still there, and the cymbal beat in my chest begins to slow. Sitting with my back to the box-room bed I am calm enough to reflect that it's just a photograph of the two of us and perhaps she was searching my other drawers for more. I suspect her, she suspects me, and if we don't address our mutual suspicion a few fading photos is all we're going to be.

But it's midnight when she drops into bed beside me and when I say, 'We must talk,' she is full of excuses.

### 10 March 1966

Wright chooses the first day of election campaigning to report on the Communists and 'fellow travellers' he would like to turf out of Parliament. He tells us the Security Service is bugging more than forty Labour MPs, trade unionists, even a Liberal or two. The operation has been growing in the dark, like mushrooms on a bed of cow shit. FLUENCY meetings are generally tense occasions with the MI5 contingent chary of the three of us from MI6, especially me. Wright and his cronies have usually discussed the business of the day before we meet and offer us only bones, unless we have something to trade for more. But Wright is all smiles today, and so very anxious for my views it puts me on my mettle. The reason for his faux bonhomie is soon apparent. He is going to target the Labour Member for Acton and chairman of ITV: Bernard Floud.

Evelyn leads from the file, and it's the same old story of Oxbridge activism in the thirties. Solid establishment type with a conscience and an abhorrence of Fascism led astray. Silk shirts and PJs from an expensive tailor, membership of an exclusive student drinking club, white-tie dinners and dance the night away, before a good dose of political instruction from the Communist Party in the morning. Floud served in intelligence during the war but was privy to no major secrets. Now he's a man of influence, tipped for ministerial office if Labour wins the election, as many believe it will. Only Bernard Floud and his late brother, Peter, have been named by Pool, Hart and Blunt. All the pieces are there, apparently. Floud was at school with one of the Cambridge spies and he remains on good terms with dozens of 'persons of interest'.

'What about you, Harry?' says Wright at last. 'You were at Oxford at the same time.'

'I knew him a little.'

'Anything that might help us?' he says mildly.

'The student Labour Club was full of secret Communists in those days. You've heard me say it before: youthful idealism doesn't turn you into a Philby.'

'Floud was a f-friend of yours.'

'Is that a question?' I say, drawing a cigarette from a packet. 'I met him, oh, half a dozen times. Struck me as insecure. He would have gone into the Church a hundred years ago.'

'You don't know when he left the Party?' Wright is in control of his stutter; a bad sign for me.

'Peter, I told you. I didn't know he was in it!'

He nods reflectively.

'Anything else?' I say, and regret it at once. Because it's always a mistake to sound defensive even when there's good reason to be.

'Floud was a member of the Civil Service Communists Group after the war. They used to meet at the flat of an historian called . . .' Wright looks down at his notes.

'Eric Hobsbawm,' says Evelyn. 'Another of the Cambridge Apostles.'

'We know Floud was still a C-Communist in the forties: he was blacklisted for promotion.'

'Ah. I didn't know, did you?' I wave my cigarette at Evelyn and the rest of them.

'How could I, dear?' she says acidly. '*I* wasn't a member of the Party.'

'We believe F-Floud recruited a number of the Oxford circle – Jenifer Hart, perhaps Pool, and others, and their controller was our old friend OTTO.' He touches the corners of his mouth with thumb and forefinger reflectively. 'We believe Floud spent some time in China. R-r-run a check, would you? Everything you've got in your registry – his wife, brother and sister-in-law were Communists, too. And his associates at the television company. Evelyn will give you a list.'

'Right. Terence?' I look at Lecky.

'Got it,' he says.

'Floud held a k-key role in the Oxford circle, and if we put some pressure on him . . . I don't need to remind you that Hollis and Mitchell were at the university, Hollis spent time in China, and we know Mitchell was active in left-wing politics in the thirties.'

We know nothing of the sort, but it isn't the time to say so. It's Floud and the list of his associates that concerns me. Lecky collects it from Evelyn after the meeting and lets me see it before he returns to Century House. There are fifteen names I recognise, like Hart and Pool and Rees, and Arthur Wynn, the civil servant who operated as a talent-spotter, and Sir Andy Cohen at the Foreign Office, but one name I expect to see is missing. Because I know, and they know, that Mrs Harry Vaughan was thick with Floud at university, and that they're still on good terms. Elsa's name was on a list shown to Hart, and Wright has made no secret of his wish to interview her. I don't know whether to be relieved or afraid. I *do* know Evelyn doesn't make mistakes with lists and files, and she must have omitted Elsa's name for a reason.

Back at my desk I take the Johnnie Walker from my bottom drawer and pour a stiff one. I'm almost ready. But is it too late? For the first time in twenty-five years I don't know what she feels about me. The phone rings and it's Mrs Gill-Thompson from a phone box on Piccadilly. Her sons have an exeat from their boarding school and she won't be able to meet me before Monday.

'Monday should be okay.'

'Then come to my flat for dinner, Harry,' she says.

'That's nice. Can I let you know?'

'Of course.'

I know she's disappointed I haven't jumped at the chance – she has every right to be. 'It's just that . . .'

'Your wife,' she says.

'Can I let you know on Monday morning?'

The money runs out before she can reply.

My wife. What am I doing? I slide my feet from the table and rise. I have to take better care of her. Will she be home? For form's sake, I lock the safe – it isn't secure – then slide my jacket off the back of the chair. A posse of junior desk officers and secretaries is waiting for the lift to rattle down from the fifth floor. They fall silent when they see me: I'm one of the witchfinders. We're all relieved when the lift arrives. I pull back the gate for the ladies and reveal a nasty little surprise inside. Clive is smirking at me. Clive: the old soldier who enjoys pulling the wings off butterflies and who lost his virginity at fourteen. Clive, who beat the crap out of me.

'Hello, Harry,' the cheeky bastard says.

'Mr Vaughan to you, Clive. And you are working for whom?'

'A Branch,' he says. 'Mr Wright sorted things for me.'

The lift is calling, the girls behind me impatient, and I stand aside to let them enter. We squeeze in like sardines, Clive in the corner opposite. He tries to catch my eye. He has something he wants to say, perhaps 'No hard feelings.' Well, sod that, Clive. You're a thug and always will be – it is your nature. When the lift lands, I keep walking.

A few seconds later he passes me on Curzon Street. 'Be seeing you, Harry,' he says, and he means it.

# 46

## 14 March 1966

'HARRY? IT'S MAURICE. I want you to come to C's flat – at once.'

The office door's open, I'm still in my coat, and I've sent a secretary to fetch me a cup of coffee. I haven't seen Dick White for weeks and only fleetingly then. An instruction to call on him at home is not what I expect this wet March Monday. 'Is this about me, Maurice?'

'Not everything we do concerns you, Harry,' he says. 'Jim Angleton has turned up unannounced. For some reason he doesn't want his people at the embassy to know he's here.'

'Is it the Third World War?'

'You know his mysterious ways: *plants his footsteps in the sea, /And rides upon the storm*, Don't be late, Harry – and don't tell anyone.'

C is still at the house in Queen Anne's Gate. A flat at the top of our new concrete sweatbox south of the river would be beneath his dignity, and if he sold the old place the ghosts of chiefs past would haunt him for ever. A few lucky juniors still work in the basement and the housekeeper still polishes the brass door fittings until they gleam like a mirror. I make a point of adjusting my tie in the letterbox because I did something of the sort when I visited him to hear what lay in store for me three years ago. Impossible to imagine then I would still be on this merry-go-round.

Oldfield is doorman today because Sir Dick is upstairs with his guests.

'Guests?'

Maurice ignores me. 'Here's FJ.'

The director general of the Security Service has stepped out of a cab at the bottom of the street, and a few seconds later, Wright's bald head appears at its door.

'Why am I here?' I whisper to Maurice.

'An ally,' he replies.

FJ is surprised to see me. 'What's this about, Maurice?' he says. 'I had to put off the home secretary.'

'Jim Angleton rang me this morning and asked for an urgent meeting of both our services to discuss Soviet disinformation and penetration.'

'Yes, of course he did. That's all we ever talk about these days!'

Wright's lips are twitching, as if he's suppressing a smile.

We are meeting in Dick's dining room at the back of the house. FJ is first through the door, and as we shuffle in behind him I hear Angleton's prep school voice, with just the hint of hometown Idaho, as he rises to greet us. I don't know if he's surprised to see me because he's a gentleman and when he's stone-cold sober his face gives nothing away. He offers me his hand and I feel the same strange sensation of clutching a bagful of bones that I remember from when we first met. I swear he's even gaunter. '*Bin gar keine Russin*,' he says, which means in German, 'I am not Russian at all.' A nice piece of irony.

My answer is a line from the same poem: '*I will show you fear in a handful of dust.*'

'Ha!' he says. 'I believe you're the only intelligence officer of my acquaintance who cares for Eliot's poetry. How are you, Harry?'

'Fine, Jim, fine.'

A thickset man of about forty with a certain Slavic look about the eyes is watching us closely. Can it be? *Es muss sein.* This is Angleton's pet defector, the prime minister's accuser, and Hollis's and Mitchell's and dozens more besides: Anatoli Golitsyn. For five years he's drip-fed information for money and he still has a place at the top table. Oldfield says defectors are like grapes: the first pressings are the best. Golitsyn keeps giving. Either he's rationed his information very carefully or he's making it up. To my mind, it turned to vinegar a long time ago, but I don't believe Jim Angleton cares one way or the other, as long as Golitsyn's stories suit his purpose.

Sir Dick White nods curtly to me as he takes his place at the top of the table, Angleton on his right, FJ on his left; I'm below the salt with Wright. Our meeting begins with an apology from Jim for summoning us on the wind at short notice. He says he's come with the full authority of the director of the CIA to discuss the threat to the integrity of our secret services, to the West, to our values. For years we've taken it for granted that there's a split in the Communist world: the Soviet Union and China are enemies. 'Well,' he says, 'it's a fraud, a charade, a fiction to fool us all, and the red menace is as united as it has ever been in its pursuit of world domination.'

He pauses to weigh the impact of his words on us. Dick White is frowning, and FJ is chewing the end of his pipe, and I know they're thinking, Utter bollocks, but because Jim's CIA they're too polite to say so.

Golitsyn is sitting on one of the room's fine marquetry chairs, a roll of hairy stomach peeping through his shirt. His eyes are small, furtive and bloodshot. I guess strong drink has been taken on this secret mission to save the West.

'This is the reality we must face, gentlemen,' says Angleton. 'Moscow is engaged in a campaign of disinformation and penetration on a global scale. Look at what Peter is uncovering here. While our leaders talk of peace and disarmament, Communism is spreading through the world like a plague. We need to put the Russians straight, step up the housekeeping, share more information, be more critical of our sources. We've been sweating a fake defector for a while – a KGB plant sent to mutilate the intelligence we have from Anatoli and discredit me.'

Oldfield lifts his hand like a reticent schoolboy. 'This false defector, can you tell us his name, Jim?'

'Yuri Nosenko, Maurice. He claims he was KGB, Second Chief Directorate. Anatoli saw he was a fake straight away.'

'Nosenko? Really?'

'Really, Maurice, yes.'

'With your permission, Jim . . . because not everyone will be familiar with his history. Perhaps you remember,' he says, addressing both intelligence chiefs, 'Nosenko came over in January 'sixty-four with grade-one intelligence on KGB agents in Europe and America. You told me yourself, Jim. The bugging operation at your embassy in Moscow, he gave you the precise location of fifty—'

'Fifty-two.'

'Fifty-two microphones hidden in the walls of the embassy. What's changed, Jim?'

'Anatoli predicted Moscow would try to undermine us, and that's precisely what Nosenko is attempting to do.'

Golitsyn blurts, 'KGB fuckers!' He was picking his teeth with a finger but now he wags it at Maurice. 'You not know KGB like Anatoli. KGB will do anything to destroy me. It sent Nosenko to say no moles in British intelligence, no ELLI. Bull*shiiit*.'

'Anatoli takes it very personally.' Jim pats his arm. 'He's right to, of course. They would love to rub him out.'

Dick White shakes his head. 'We all appreciate Anatoli's courage but, Jim, how can you be sure Nosenko isn't telling the truth?'

'You know how it is – the more solid the information from a defector, the more you should distrust him. We're working Nosenko. I promise you, we'll get a confession. Yes, he gave us the names of some KGB agents, but they were only throwaways. Moscow decided to burn some of its people to promote Nosenko as a fake source of intelligence. It's a clever way to protect important agents, like the mole ELLI at the top of your Security Service.'

Dick White looks down and shuffles his papers; Furnival Jones is fiddling with his pipe. Beneath the table Maurice pushes his foot against mine. Easy, he's trying to say, easy. Come on, Maurice! Angleton is trying to rewrite the rules. A defector – a first-rate source – has challenged his mad vision of Western governments and their intelligence services controlled by the KGB, and what does he do? He condemns the source as fake.

'Can I come back to the Chinese, Jim?' I say. 'Why do you think the split with Moscow is a charade? We've heard nothing from our agents or yours.'

'It goes back to 'fifty-eight, Harry,' he says, squeezing the butt of his cigarette in an ashtray. 'The KGB held a conference to decide how to win the war with the West.'

'Can you share your source for that?'

'Well, Anatoli was there.'

'I spoke to head of KGB,' Golitsyn says, with obvious pride. 'He says Soviet Union cannot win war with missiles, but we have many agents in high places in West. We use our spies. Deceive Americans. Deceive British.'

'And the KGB created a new department for planning deception and disinformation,' says Angleton. 'It came up with the idea of a split in the Communist world to lull politicians in the West into a false sense of security and encourage talk of disarmament.' He pulls his glasses down his nose and peers over the top of them at me. 'I won't bore you with the history, but it isn't the first time the Communists have tried this sort of stunt.'

'I see,' is all I can think to say without offending him in front of the management. Once again, he's asking us poor Limeys to put our faith in his Rasputin, and now I've met him I'm even less inclined to do so. I know Maurice feels the same.

'Why didn't you tell us about this before?' he says, turning to address Golitsyn directly. 'Why now, after four years? Why has it taken you so long, Anatoli?'

Golitsyn flushes and clutches the table as if to rise. 'You think Anatoli lying?'

Angleton places a hand on his arm. 'It's a fair question. Anatoli said nothing because he thought people would laugh at him.'

FJ takes the pipe from his mouth and examines it carefully; Dick closes his eyes.

'Do you know how ridiculous that sounds?' I say. 'With respect, Jim, you don't think you're putting too much faith in one source?'

Golitsyn leans forward and stares at me menacingly.

'I don't care how it sounds,' says Angleton, addressing Dick and FJ at the top of the table. 'I don't have to remind anyone how much we owe Anatoli, I'm sure.'

Maurice's foot finds mine again: *Shut up, Harry.*

'Jim, I confess I'm not inclined to go all the way with you and Anatoli on this one,' says FJ.

Dick nods, like a fairground duck, beside him. 'We should agree to differ on the Sino-Soviet split. I'm sure we agree on everything else. Perhaps we should consider what we can do to counter the enemy's fake intelligence. Jim, you might like to outline your proposal for a committee to investigate our sources.'

Angleton reaches for another cigarette. 'Certainly.'

There's something like a collective sigh round the table: the captain of our boat has taken us clear of the rocks. Let's forget we're dealing with a crisis that may only exist in the wild imaginings of a paranoiac and a self-seeking chancer. Jim talks about his committee and we listen in respectful silence. And when we break for coffee Dick asks me to go. 'It would be best,' he says coolly. 'Your objections were noted.'

He's right. They have been noted: before I'm able to leave, Golitsyn jogs my elbow. 'You don't believe me?' He's holding a delicate china cup in his fat fingers, and above his hairy wrist, double cuffs, diamond cufflinks, a blue made-to-measure suit. The money we've paid him over the years.

'It's not that I don't believe you,' I say diplomatically. 'I don't agree with your assessment.'

'The KGB want to kill me,' he replies. 'I risk my life, and your Queen make me Commander of Order of British Empire.'

I offer him my congratulations and thanks. Perhaps he thinks me less than sincere because his eyes narrow and he takes a step closer. 'You were in Vienna. I was in Vienna: Colony Department of KGB. I remember you, remember your wife. We catch fifty, a hundred British agents.'

'Yes.'

'KGB mole in MI6.'

'That was never proved.'

'I know.'

'There was talk of Kim Philby.'

'Not Philby,' he barks at me. 'KGB agent was in Vienna station.'

I hear the tinkle of a cup marrying a saucer and the shuffling of feet: there's a hush in the room. Everyone is listening to

Golitsyn, which is what he wanted to happen. I put my cup on the table then turn back to look him in the eye. 'If you have reliable intelligence, Anatoli, I hope you will share it with us. I hope you shared it with us four years ago, or were you afraid someone would laugh at you?'

He stands and stares at me, his mouth open like a stage dummy at rest. Who am I to question? This time it's Wright who comes to his rescue.

'I b-b-believe it was something we m-may have missed at the time,' he says. 'Anatoli has done so much. He has given us a hundred and fifty-three serials to investigate.'

'I'm sure we're all grateful, Peter,' I say to be polite, even though I'm bloody furious. Golitsyn is the excuse for everything Angleton has done and hopes to do, and now he's threatening my wife and threatening me, and he can because he's untouchable. 'The serials – a hundred and fifty-three, you say – how many have amounted to anything at all?'

Dick answers: 'What the hell are you talking about, Harry? What's the matter with you? Apologise to Anatoli.'

'It's a simple question,' I say. 'Isn't anyone able to answer it?'

Wright is ready to try, but Dick doesn't give him a chance. 'I think we should continue with our meeting,' he says icily, 'and we can say goodbye to Harry.'

# 47

'GOODBYE' MEANS STOP rocking the boat with the Americans and one American in particular. Angleton is more to us than the President of the United States. What does the president know that the CIA doesn't tell him? Jim is intelligence and resources; Jim makes us feel we matter, that we enjoy a special relationship. We must humour Jim, make excuses for Jim, even take his part against our elected representatives. These thoughts I carry around the corner to the Old Star and, in quick order, down a Scotch, then another, and after a damp sandwich and two cigarettes, I'm calm enough to hail a cab outside our old office in Broadway and return to the fray.

The first thing I do is telephone Mrs Gill-Thompson at her desk in the Secretariat. 'Sorry, Linda,' I say, 'emergency meeting. I can't make it tonight, what about Tuesday?'

'That will be fine,' she says, in the business voice she has for the office eavesdroppers.

'Seven thirty?'

The line crackles as if she's switching the receiver to her other ear. 'Come to mine,' she whispers, and it isn't a question, it's a command, and I hear myself say, 'Yes, I would love to.'

A few seconds after she's hung up, and before I have time to feel a proper heel, Maurice telephones, and he's furious in his quiet way. 'Yes, Jim is a little mad,' he says, 'so we handle him carefully. Intelligence is knowing people, and not just the other side, our people, too.' Bloody fool Harry forgot there was a job to do: bloody fool Harry has another chance. Dinner tonight with Jim and Anatoli, and the menu choice for me must be humble pie. I protest I'm the last person they want to get drunk with, but Maurice says I'm wrong and, by the way, it's an order!

At five o'clock I ring Elsa to tell her I have a working dinner, and that I will be out tomorrow, too. 'All right,' she says, as if it's a matter of no importance.

'We keep missing each other. Ships in the night. What about the weekend?'

'Perhaps,' she says flatly. 'Look, I'm going into a meeting, let's talk about it later.'

'Why can't we decide now?'

'Well, you're the one who's going out tonight,' she snaps, and the next thing I hear is the drone of the empty line.

Dinner is around the corner at Maurice's in Marsham Street. Five of us at a coffin-shaped table. 'Better here,' our host explains, as he pours the wine, 'because we can talk freely.' Caterers who can be trusted not to bug the room serve us steak with a béarnaise sauce. On my right Golitsyn is broad shoulders and elbows, and I struggle for space to use my knife, while opposite me Angleton picks at his food and Wright beams with sly pleasure. To clear the air, I offer an apology for my tone at our Queen Anne's Gate conference, and because they're still sober they accept it graciously – or they pretend to. Jim and Maurice ensure the conversation is convivial until we shut the front door on the caterers. Then we shuffle through to our host's study-drawing room for brandy and the business of the night.

'It was the timing, Moulders,' says Angleton, turning to fake defectors at once. 'Nosenko just plopped into our laps a few months after the assassination of President Kennedy. His mission was to sow confusion, deny KGB involvement in Kennedy's murder, undermine our work. Anatoli realised he was a fake straight away.'

Golitsyn's gaze settles on me, perhaps to gauge the sincerity of my repentance. He can rest easy. Angleton has brought an excellent brandy and I am going to give it my undivided attention. The room's hot and smoky and Angleton is the only one in a jacket, his tie as tight as a hangman's noose, long legs crossed, like a calendar girl's. He must have ice in his veins. Maurice is quite the opposite. They sit side by side on a battered leather couch, the rest of us on hard chairs facing them, and dominating the room between us, a coffee-table covered with glasses and bottles and ashtrays.

Angleton leans forward lazily to flick the ash from his cigarette. 'You're not alone. We're still dealing with penetration at Langley. Leaks from the Agency's Soviet Division.'

I can't see his dark eyes behind his glasses because the room is so full of smoke they appear almost opaque, but I know he's conscious of me watching him, and he knows why, too.

'You've probably heard,' he says. 'We've arrested some senior officers – Jack Ellis.'

'No!' Maurice wriggles to the edge of the couch to stare at him incredulously.

'I'm afraid so. I had my suspicions, then Anatoli examined his file. His profile fits.'

'KGB,' says Golitsyn, definitively.

Maurice glances at me. I concentrate on appearing to feel nothing. 'Jack isn't KGB. He's as loyal and patriotic as they come.' I lean forward and pluck the brandy bottle from the table. 'Anyone?' They all want more. There's a hush in the room as I do the honours, because they know what's coming and want to charge their glasses before the show gets going – even you, Moulders, because wittingly or unwittingly you've helped

375

Angleton set this trap. He was so very anxious for my company, because he's going to make the evening about me.

'Well, Harry,' he says, 'you and Jack go back a long way – to Vienna.'

I want to talk about something else. 'Remember our dinner at Maurice's house in Washington? Remember what we talked about, Jim? Harold Wilson the spy. The KGB murdered Gaitskell.'

He frowns. 'We discussed the possibility.'

'You were very clear at the time. "Harold Wilson is a Soviet agent," you said. Do you still believe that? Because if you do, why the hell are you wasting time on Jack Ellis?'

He turns to look at Wright. 'I understand MI5 has some concerns about the company your prime minister keeps.'

'Yes.' Wright shifts uncomfortably in his chair. 'But it isn't a m-matter for FLUENCY.'

'Of course, you've spoken to Downing Street, Peter,' I say. 'I mean, the White House knows. That's right, isn't it, Jim?'

Angleton draws deeply on his cigarette.

'You see?' I say, addressing Wright. 'And I know it's old-fashioned to say so, but collaborating with a foreign power to undermine an elected British government, well, that's treason in my book. What about you, Maurice?'

'Bravo.' Angleton slow-claps me. 'What a performance!'

'I'm serious, Jim.'

'Oh, deadly, I'm sure. A sincere servant of democracy. He should speak to Dick White, shouldn't he, Maurice?'

'You don't deny . . .'

'Sure do. It's a matter for MI5. Peter?'

'We investigated G-G-Gaitskell's death because one of his doctors asked us to. N-no one's accusing Wilson.'

'Not the business of the evening.' Angleton flourishes his cigarette at Maurice. 'We should move on, don't you think?'

Oldfield frowns at me. 'That would be best.'

Best for whom? I wonder.

Maurice gets to his feet. 'Coffee?' No one wants coffee. 'Then I'll fetch water,' he says, 'and cheese,' and he shuffles out to the kitchen. The second the door closes Angleton turns on me. 'Did you think you'd get away with it for ever, Harry?' He leans forward to clutch the arm of my chair. His bony fingers are awkwardly jointed, like the legs of a large spider.

'Get away with what, Jim?'

'Your smokescreen.'

'Western values, Jim, rule of law, freedom of speech. You're right, they are under threat, but is it Communism or those who wish to save us from it we should fear most?'

He smiles. '*Quis custodiet* . . .? That dog won't hunt. No one is afraid of the guards when the enemy is at the gate.'

'Jack Ellis hates Communists as much as you do.'

'Never mind Ellis, it's you we're talking about, Harry.'

Maurice is back and standing with a tray of tumblers, cheese and a plate of biscuits. I catch his eye and he looks away.

'Vienna, Harry.' Wright is speaking. 'F-f-first SUBALTERN, then the wiretapping operation – you were eavesdropping on the Soviets . . .'

'Correct.'

'. . . until it was b-betrayed. How many m-men and women were lost in those operations? Eighty? Ninety?'

'Too many.'

'Anatoli remembers,' says Anatoli, poking a finger at me. 'KGB mole at Vienna station work for VIKTOR – only VIKTOR. Anatoli spoke to VIKTOR.' He sways towards me drunkenly, eyes shining with pride that he once met the murderous shit who used to run Russian foreign intelligence.

'Let's give him his proper name. General Fitin controlled the KGB's most important sources,' says Angleton.

'You're accusing me?'

He stares at me impassively through a bridge of fingers.

'I've seen this pattern,' I say.

'Harry . . .' Maurice brandishes a bottle at me. 'Gentlemen. A friendly chat. The chance to tie up a few loose ends, that's all. Here,' he says, and tries to fill my glass.

'No, Maurice.'

'V-VIKTOR's agents JACK and ROSA,' says Wright. 'We thought the Harts. Jenifer was a member of the Party and an agent – but she can't be ROSA because Herbert Hart is clean. JACK and ROSA were a couple – they may still be. We know they w-were operating in London in 1945 but it's p-possible they were posted to Europe. They may be the middle-grade agent or agents we're looking for in the Service.'

My laugh sounds brittle.

Wright's smile suggests he's thinking the same. 'And we've discovered something else about VIKTOR's mole in Vienna. Anatoli,' he says, inviting Golitsyn to speak, 'it's your secret.'

'I remember order from Moscow Centre,' he says. 'No one touch the Jewess. Close SUBALTERN, take the rest – not her.' He raises his glass with a smug smile. 'I remember VIKTOR said "not the Jewess".'

Twenty years flicker through my mind like images in a zoetrope: the two of us stand at the grave of the boy the KGB dumped on our doorstep when SUBALTERN was blown, tears, and her long goodbye to the Service, to me – she said she couldn't live with the guilt. The house came down around us and, yes, we were the only ones to escape but not without scars. 'How can I look Béla Bajomi's wife in the eye?' she said.

They're staring at me, waiting for me to speak. Stupid bastards. Look me in the eye and say it: Harry and his dear lady wife.

Maurice clears his throat. 'Housekeeping, Harry, that's all. No one's pointing the finger.'

I concentrate on Angleton. 'You're pointing it, aren't you?'

'I'll say only this.' He picks up his brandy and coaxes it round the glass. 'Seems to me JACK and ROSA ain't gone away.'

I watch him take a sip. 'Is that right?'

'Yep,' he says. 'That's right.'

Wright leans forward as if to speak but I cut him with a gesture. 'You've killed us, Jim, you know that. You've done it for them – the Russians, I mean. You're worse than Kim because you've hurt your own side. All this talk of fakes, well, you're the fake. You're Moscow Centre's creature, only you can't see it. *Listen* to me . . . Keep away from my wife, you hear! Keep right away.' I get to my feet with the neck of a bottle in my right hand. 'You, too,' I say, pointing it at Wright. 'And you, Maurice – you pusillanimous shit.' I kick a leg of his coffee-table and set the glasses tinkling. 'Here, catch!' And I toss him the bottle.

'Sit down before you fall down!' he says quietly.

'*Twll dy din di!*' I say. 'And arseholes to you.'

I know what I'm doing. Sober enough to appreciate that the clock stands at a minute to midnight.

# 48

## 22 March 1966

I HAVE SEX with Linda because there's no other way. I feel sorry but it's fine. I'm using her, she's using me, but she's hoping for more. Her head is a pleasant weight on my chest, her hand on my belly, curling hair at my groin about her forefinger. The bedroom is thick with perfume and the sweet scent of our lovemaking. I feel guilty but I learned to live with guilt a long time ago. The kissing, caressing, licking, fucking, this post-coital stupor and the kind words to come create trust.

'Are you free on Friday?' she says, and I say I'll try to be. And as I stroke her hair and cat's cradle her fingers, she talks to me of her boys and her dead husband and the routine of the office, and how much she dislikes FJ.

Then we do it again. After that it's easier than I thought it would be. Wet with sweat, garrulous with happiness, she doesn't seem to think my questions strange. 'Oh, it wouldn't be difficult during the day,' she says, 'and even at night. There's a key in the duty office. You would need the numbers for the safe, of course.'

We're face to face on the pillow, my thigh clamped between hers. 'Who knows the numbers, *annwyl*?'

'I do,' she says. 'At least I think I do.'

I put my finger on her nose. 'Really?'

'I cover for the DG's secretary,' she says. 'They're supposed to change them every few weeks but they don't.' She cranes her neck to kiss me. 'Are we planning a robbery?'

I smile. 'That's what double zeros do.'

On her doorstep she says, 'I really like you, Harry,' and I say, 'I like you, Linda,' and I mean it too. She asks me to play the piano for her next time and I promise I will, only there won't be a next time. She watches me walk away – looking back I can see her silhouette at a bedroom window – and I imagine her anger, her distress when she hears what I've done. She's a widow with sons to keep, and when it breaks she'll lose her job. Twenty years after SUBALTERN, still messing with people's lives.

Big Ben strikes half past as I'm fumbling with my keys. Elsa is sleeping. I brush my teeth, undress in the bathroom, then carry my clothes back into our bedroom and drape them on my chair. I generally sleep naked but there's a chill in the room – or is it shame? – and I rummage in a drawer for pyjamas. As I'm buttoning the top her breathing changes, and I turn to discover she's gazing at me, an unnerving reflex of streetlight in her eye.

'Sorry to wake you,' I say.

She doesn't reply, only stares at me.

'How was your evening?'

Still nothing. Do I smell of Linda's soap? I move round the bed to my side. 'What is it?'

But she continues to ignore me, only gathers the bedspread and curls into a ball, her back towards me. And I don't think I've felt more alone, not after my mother died, or at boarding school, or even when Elsa broke from me the first time. She's the only woman I've loved, and she doesn't realise it but we need each other more than ever.

*

The wheels are moving so slowly I could be persuaded no one suspects me of being a KGB spy and I dreamed the whole thing. I simply dropped into a hole, and now I'm out again. Angleton has gone, I haven't seen Wright since Monday; Evelyn McBarnet is no pricklier than usual; the phone rings; files are delivered to my trays. Only it wasn't an illusion: the wheels *are* moving, but they are proceeding with caution. Keep old Harry away from the sensitive stuff but don't spook him or he'll run, like his friend Guy. I know they're weeding files and anything that looks good is chicken feed they're hoping I'll offer a KGB controller. Standard procedure: we tried the same stunt three years ago on Graham Mitchell.

Thursday's FLUENCY meeting is cancelled because FJ is interrogating Mitchell. Wright and Evelyn are monitoring a sound feed in D Branch. I wander through the office at the end of the day and I can tell from the long faces that they don't have their ELLI.

'PETERS is over?' I ask. 'Graham's in the clear?'

Wright gives me his stoniest stare. 'A-a-an absence of evidence isn't proof of innocence. Arthur thinks someone is r-running Mitchell as a stalking horse.'

The someone he means is Hollis.

'When are you bringing him in?'

'We're pr-preparing the brief,' he says. 'I'm interviewing one of the Oxford circle tomorrow – an old friend of yours, Floud, the *Honourable* Member for Acton. You should be there.'

'If you like,' I say, knowing full well that he doesn't like, because he will coax Floud to incriminate Elsa, and perhaps me too.

Later, I receive a note from Maurice asking me to meet him in the usual place. Is he hoping for a confession, or will he apologise for offering me as a sacrifice?

'Were you followed?'

'Don't you know, Maurice?'

St Matthew's is full of shadows, just a pool of yellow light at the altar and a strip above Maurice's organ music, the last of a dull day indigo in the windows. Maurice was playing the hymn 'Hills of the North Rejoice', his thoughts roaming to Derbyshire, perhaps.

'What do you want, Maurice?' I say.

'You know it's gone too far now, Harry. I can't protect you.'

I laugh.

'It's not just you who's in the shit,' he says, craning earnestly towards me. 'I trusted you.'

'Afraid you won't make the top job after all?'

'Shut up, Harry! Shut up and listen.' He sighs. 'It's too late for regrets . . . if you're working for the Russians.'

'Want to hear me deny it?'

He frowns. 'I'm quite sure you're a consummate liar. No, I want to tell you Golitsyn is in a boarding house near Bournemouth with our files – promising to point us to KGB moles, and not just in the service. He's begun with your chum Berlin – Isaiah Berlin. As far as I can tell his much-vaunted methodology consists of accusing Jews and anyone who has ever made a mistake – which is how it works with internal investigations in Moscow. Oh, and you – he's pointed the finger at you, but you know that.'

'Why are you telling me, Maurice?'

'I didn't think it could get any worse,' he says dejectedly, 'but they seem hell bent on a secret war against anyone they suspect.'

'Wilson?'

'They'll use the prime minister's friends – the raincoat millionaire – to create a stink in the press, you know the sort of thing. And Jim will take it to the White House.'

'Why are you telling me?'

Andrew Williams

'Dick is going to summon you to a meeting at Century House. Christopher Phillpotts will be there. Arthur Martin will be there. I will be there. Expect a grilling. You'll be suspended while investigations continue.'

'But why are you telling me?'

'Doesn't matter why.' He removes his glasses and pinches the corners of his eyes. 'Three or four days, a week at most – that's what you've got.' Then he places his spectacles back and stares at me.

'I don't know why . . .'

'Do you understand, Harry?' he says, more forcefully.

I smile. I won't make him spell it out.

'Good,' he says, turning back to his music.

I walk back to the west door to the accompaniment of 'Guide Me O Thou Great Redeemer' with all the stops out. A nice joke, and one that brings a very large lump to my throat. *Mewn pob daioni y mae gwobr*, we say. There's reward in every kindness, even for the likes of you and me, Maurice.

Home is two minutes away but, just as Guy did on the eve of his flit to Moscow, I choose the Reform. Frank, the smoking-room steward, brings me a large one and some paper, and I write to Driberg, promising to deliver the material he's been badgering me for in days. Then I telephone the *Daily Mirror*'s news desk and speak to Dylan Thomas's friend, Watkins.

'We're putting the paper to bed,' he grumbles. 'What about tomorrow?'

'Do you want the story or not?'

Watkins suggests a Fleet Street pub; I insist on somewhere private. The last time we met I was a hair's breadth from taking a swing at him. He's odious; he's untrustworthy; he's a barfly. But he'll do.

*

384

By the time I've completed my business calls and paid off my fifth and final cab it's after eleven. I make a call to Elsa but she doesn't answer, and she doesn't look up when I walk into the kitchen. Today's *Times* is open on the table in front of her and a plate with scraps of toast and an apple core. She's still in her civil-service black skirt and white blouse, and the coat she must have worn to the office has slipped from a chair on to the tiled floor. Her head is resting in her right hand, and I don't need to see her face to know she has been crying. And because I feel ashamed and guilty and in love, and because I can't tell her the truth, and because I'm afraid of rejection, I don't step over to the table and hug her. I say the first trite thing that comes into my head: I ask her if she's had a good day. I regret it straight away but my tired mind is still swarming with the minutiae of my plan to expose the madness that has driven me to this place.

Elsa simply raises her gaze to my face.

'Sorry, darling,' I say automatically, and risk a step closer. But there's a stillness in her that frightens me, something close to despair. I felt it in Vienna and I feel it now.

'Are you all right? Things have been . . . It will be over soon, I promise.'

She closes her eyes and mutters something I don't hear, and I ask her to say it again. She does, and very firmly. 'It's over now!'

'What do—'

'I want a divorce.'

'For Christ's sake. Elsa . . .' Her eyes are shut. 'Look at me!'

'All right!'

'No, it isn't bloody all right. Didn't you hear me? I need time.' I take another step and she holds up both hands, her fingers open like a fan.

'Keep away from me!'

'What? Christ. Can't we talk about this?'

'No. You're a liar and I want a divorce. There's nothing more to say.'

'I want to explain—'

'It's perfectly clear,' she says. 'You're a fake. Everything about you is a lie.'

'*Er mwyn duw, Elsa.*'

'A fake!'

'You know me better than that.'

'Now I do.' Her chair screeches as she rises. 'You betrayed me.'

'Bloody hell, I'm trying to protect you.'

'Get out of my way,' she says.

'Not until you speak to me.' I reach out to her but she brushes my hand aside.

'You bastard.' And she slaps me so hard she knocks me off balance. 'Bastard,' she says again.

'Tell me why.'

This time I catch her wrist and twist her hand away.

'You want to know, you bastard,' she says, her voice ringing with quiet fury. 'Your whole life is a lie. The pain and damage you've done . . .'

'No. What have they told you? That's shit.'

'No? What do you mean, no? Only two nights ago you were fucking a secretary. Deny it!' Her lovely brown eyes are wet with tears. 'Go on!'

How can I? I can only stare at her.

'You can't!'

'I want to explain. It was nothing, believe me, darling. It was . . . work.'

'Don't call me darling,' she says. 'There *is* nothing to explain. Now, will you let me go?'

I stand as dumb and rooted as an Easter Island statue. Our

386

eyes meet and I see anger, I see pain: what do I do? I open my mouth to speak but before I can think of something to say she has gone.

That night I lie awake in the spare room, and at dawn I hear her moving round our bedroom, pulling the big suitcase from the top of the wardrobe, emptying the old chest of drawers she uses for her underwear and blouses. I could tell her to stay, that I'll leave, but I don't have the strength to look her in the eye. I know what I want to say – that I've made mistakes, I'm not a good person, but I love her, no matter what she may have done, but I can't be honest without making her an accomplice. So I lie in the little box room and listen to her bump her bags down the stairs. Too late, I skip to the landing window at the front of the house. There's a cab idling in front of the house, and a minute later it turns out of the street. I'll make it up to her, and I have to believe she'll let me. If I brood on any other ending I won't manage the next few days. I must focus all my hurt and anger. I know who's to blame, and I step away from the window with a fierce determination to raise hell.

# 49

## *30 March 1966*

CLIVE'S BOYS HAVE moved in opposite: flat 2, number 11, above old Mrs Holland. How do I know it's Clive? I feel his presence, like winter in the bone. He is the black ghost dog of the road, the *gwyllgi*. A couple of his A4 goons are there with a kettle and a camera and they will be relieved in the early hours by a couple more. By then I'll be in bed in our spare room. Yes, I'm glad Clive's there because if I manage to pull this off it'll taste sweeter. 'Don't hold grudges lest it cloud your judgement,' we were taught, but sometimes it helps you see things more clearly. My turn to piss on you, Clive.

I'm sitting in the kitchen now with cold tea and a plate of toast, a coat Elsa forgot to pack on the chair beside me. I pick it up and press the collar to my face, smell her perfume, and for a time I feel as listless as a lotus-eater, incapable of rousing myself to any purpose. She rang on Saturday: she was sending a taxi for more of her things and that was all she was willing to say. Tossing the coat back, I rise and walk to the sink for a glass of water. Tomorrow the country votes in a general election. The opinion polls suggest Wilson will win, and if he does his government will build half a million new homes in the next four years. I expect Angleton will call it Communism. First results are expected sometime in the early hours of Friday morning. By then I will be either toasting Wilson with a good malt or locked in a Special Branch cell. But everything rests on remaining free to cast my vote.

Dick took his time summoning me to Century House. A vestigial regard for me, perhaps, or a quite natural reluctance to countenance the possibility that the officer he trusted to catch spies three years ago might turn out to be one. Whatever the reason, he has allowed me to put everything in place. In the four days that passed between my meeting with Maurice and my interview with Dick I was able to rent a room near Paddington station, rescue the microfilms from my deposit box and leave copies with my lawyer, check MI5's duty roster for election night and settle on a route in and out of the building. I'll drive Elsa's little Sprite – she left the keys in the house – and I've moved the copy camera to the room in the Paddington guesthouse. Jack gave me another CIA toy in Vienna: I don't care for guns but the High Standard HD22 has a barrel silencer, like the ones you see in the movies, and it should frighten the life out of anyone who gets in my way.

A strange thing happened on the morning of the meeting with Dick. One of the D3 secretaries hissed at me in a corridor. I stopped her and demanded an explanation. To my great surprise, she said, 'You're ruining our Service.'

'Me, personally?'

'Your cabal – spreading your poison.' She said she wasn't afraid to speak her mind even if everyone else in MI5 seemed to be, and our treatment of poor Mr Stevens was a disgrace!

In the end my meeting with Dick lasted for only ten minutes. He didn't want to talk about the evidence. 'There's enough,' he said, and the chorus of senior officers he invited to my interview was in agreement. I protested hotly because they were expecting me to. Phillpotts was rude about my record and quoted 'our friend Anatoli's suspicions', and Martin accused me of keeping bad company at Oxford and of obstructing the FLUENCY investigation.

'This witch-hunt is ruining the Service,' I said, and I repeated the conversation with the secretary who accosted me in the corridor.

'That's what a Soviet mole would say,' Phillpotts sneered.

'There's one too many in this room, and I think it's you,' I said, quoting Marx (Groucho), then called him 'a twat'. Things were rowdy after that, and it ended with 'the Schoolmaster' ordering me from his office. The watchers moved into the OP point above Mrs Holland the same day.

I've made it easy for them by traipsing from pub to club for the best part of two days, only staggering home at closing time. Poor Harry must be taking it badly because he's drinking like a fish. First the wife (oh, yes, they'll know), then the Service. All he has left is his liberty, and he will lose that in due course, too. That's what I hope Wright and the rest of them are hearing from the watchers. I'm putting on a performance Dirk Bogarde would be proud of.

I sleep badly and am up early. At nine o'clock I walk around the corner for *The Times* and breakfast in my favourite greasy spoon.

'You all right, Mr Vaughan?' Toni, its Italian proprietor, enquires. 'You looking a little rough.'

One of Clive's boys has followed me in, and when he makes eye contact with me I smile. 'How's Clive?'

He can't have played the game for long because he looks thoroughly confused.

'Old lags are the hardest targets to follow,' I say. 'Remember, keep your distance.'

'Right,' he says, rising from the table, 'I'll remember,' and by the time Toni comes back with his order, he has gone.

'He didn't like the look of me, Toni,' I say. Toni thinks I'm 'a very funny man'.

I read in *The Times* that the Conservative leader, Ted Heath, was in 'a defiant mood' at his last press conference, which is surely code for 'resigned to defeat'. I'm paying the landlady at the Snowdon boarding house in Paddington an extra two pounds for a television to watch the results programme. Labour needs the BBC's big cardboard arrow to swing three per cent for something like a hundred-seat majority. That would be a historic result.

I devote the rest of the morning to burning personal papers, and to tracing Elsa's new address and telephone number. At midday I resume my quiet display of falling apart at the Old Star on Broadway, and finish it two hours later in the Reform. This time the watchers keep their distance so it's no great matter to order whiskies I don't drink. I'm carrying the gun and silencer in my coat and I have a nasty little moment at the club when the porter – my old friend Mason – insists on hanging it up in the cloakroom for me. MI5 will have a club stooge it can call on to keep an eye on me. I pretend to fall asleep in one of the gallery chairs overlooking the atrium, *The Times* like a skirt across my knees. Who knows which of the grey heads dozing in armchairs beneath the portraits of the Liberal statesmen of the last century is the one who's watching me, or even if there is anyone? It's the ghost of Guy Burgess I feel the presence of, and when I close my eyes I hear his voice echoing in the gallery again: 'You can't blame Angleton and the CIA for all this, old boy,' he says. 'The Service is there to protect the few – members of clubs like this one. It's their tool, and its fury will turn on anyone who threatens their interests.'

A memory comes to me of something the living, raging Guy once read to me in this place, and with time still to spare I

wander round the gallery to the library and hunt for an edition
of the playwright Oscar Wilde's reflections from his prison cell.
The great man was serving his sentence for gross indecency,
and twenty years ago Guy spoke his words with a tear in his
eye. As I prepare to spring my surprise on the Service, this
short passage will serve as my apologia too.

*Most of all I blame myself for the entire ethical degradation I*
*allowed you to bring on me. The basis of character is will power,*
*and my will became utterly subject to yours.*

It is spitting fat drops of rain in the street known as Pall Mall.
The young man I spoke to in Toni's café is skulking in a doorway
at the corner of Waterloo Place, while his mate is moving so
slowly on the opposite pavement that the last of the rush-hour
commuters are tripping over his feet. No hurry, chaps. I'm
going to cast my vote.

My polling station is in the parish hall at St Matthew's. I
made a point of visiting it during the service last Sunday and
listened through an open door as Maurice accompanied the
English congregation in a passionless rendition of our great
Welsh hymn 'Guide Me O Thou Great Redeemer'. A group of
party tellers with red, blue and yellow rosettes are standing at
the door this evening. My neighbour, Mrs Boycott, is there for
the Tories, and when we make eye contact she smiles a one-of-us
welcome, confident the son-in-law of Harold Spears can be
trusted to vote the right way. 'Just two hours until the polls
close, Mr Vaughan,' she says. 'You like to cut it fine.'

'Yes, Mrs Boycott, that's true,' I say, slurring my words for
the benefit of Clive's boys, skulking in doorways nearby. I hope
they've fulfilled their democratic duty. Inside the hall the
polling-station staff sit at a long trestle table ticking names and
dispensing voting slips. I carry mine to a booth. The sitting

MP is a chap called Smith: Eton and New College, Oxford (before my time); a banker with a stately home in Berkshire. Conservative, naturally. I know nothing about the Labour man but I give him my vote. Under the beady eye of the young woman who guards the ballot box I fold and post it, then turn away and make for the door. But instead of stepping on to the street I open the one in the wall to the left of it that leads into the church.

'You can't go in there,' someone shouts.

Oh yes I can, and I do, closing the door firmly behind me. By the time a young chap from the polling station finds me, I'm on my knees pretending to pray.

'I'm sorry, sir, you can't stay here.'

'Are you coming between me and my maker?'

'I'm sorry,' he says, again.

'So you should be,' I say. 'Now sod off, will you!'

I follow the sound of his footsteps as he returns to the polling station to seek advice, and the moment he's gone I'm off my knees. The door on the west side of the church opens into St Ann's Street. I know it's bolted on the inside and only bolted and that Father Turtle has lost the key. Just after eight now, and as I walk quickly up the street I try to calculate how long I've got before the alarm goes up. Has Harry scarpered like his old mate Guy, they will ask themselves, or is he just playing? From St Ann's I cut through a Peabody housing estate to Abbey Orchard Street. Then Dean's Yard, abbey precincts, and through the gatehouse to Sanctuary, where I manage to pick up a cab. It's 8.45 p.m.

'Curzon Street, please.'

My thoughts and my pulse are racing, and for a moment the sensation reminds me of Vienna in '48 when a Soviet agent fired his gun at me. The driver wants to talk about the election but is quite happy with the sound of his own voice. He drops me a few yards short so I can do what I've done for the last three years and walk into the lobby as if nothing has happened and the DG is waiting to see me.

My right hand is round the silencer in my coat pocket, the gun is over my breast, but as I approach the entrance I feel a fool for bringing it. I'm hoping to see 'Bobby' Roberts on duty behind the glass in the security alcove and I do.

'Thought you'd left us, Mr Vaughan,' he says.

'Back across the water, Bobby, just my desk to clear. Oh, here . . .' I reach into my jacket for the temporary pass I filched in my last days and slide it under the glass. 'I handed in my other one.'

This is my first big test. I can't pull the gun on him because he's just the sort of Queen-and-country chap to put duty before his life and the pursuit of future happiness. I watch him lift the pass in front of his nose.

'Come on, Bobby,' I say. 'I promised the wife I'd be home to watch the BBC. Did I tell you? Her father's a Conservative MP.' (I know Bobby's a Tory too.)

'I'd better ring the duty officer, sir.'

Someone has told him my clearance has been withdrawn, and here I am out of the usual office hours.

'Don't bother,' I say, 'I'm on my way to see the DO,' and pinching the pass from his fingers I turn towards the lifts. 'Labour by fifty seats.'

# 50

# *31 March 1966*

I SLIDE THE gate back and push the brass lever up to five, and the last thing I see as the lift begins to rise is Bobby reaching for his telephone. On any average evening the duty officer takes calls and monitors the rip-and-read on the teleprinters and not much more. Wylie is the officer on the slate. If I'm lucky he'll make his way to the lifts to meet me; if I'm not he'll telephone FJ at once. I marry the gun and silencer and wedge it into my coat pocket. No violence, please.

Young Wylie must have sprinted along the corridor to meet me because the lift judders to a halt and he's there to haul back the grille.

I don't know Wylie but he seems to know me. 'We were told you'd moved on,' he says, a tremor in his voice. He's an earnest-looking fellow, state not public school and from somewhere in the north of England. This is going to be a difficult night for young Wylie.

'Picking up my things,' I say, 'if that's all right? Check with the DDG, if you like.'

He gives me a sheepish smile. 'I'd better.'

These are the FLUENCY days when no one dares to show initiative. Wylie was always going to plump for procedure, which is what I want him to do.

We walk side by side along the teak-panelled corridor to the front of the building, passing the assistant directors' offices, banking, personnel, until the carpet runs out and is replaced by stained linoleum, and the ceiling is spotted with damp and nicotine. There's no one else on duty here: Wylie is captain, first mate and crew. I watch him fumbling with his key. 'In at last,' he says, stepping aside for me. The remains of his supper are on the desk, and on the arm of the only easy chair, a spy thriller by Len Deighton. 'Entertainment,' he says, a little embarrassed. 'I wish there was more of it around here.' He waves the paperback at me. 'It's all so bloody routine.'

Along one wall, the usual grey civil-service filing cabinets, along another, an old army camp bed for quiet nights, which are most nights. A door in the wall opposite leads to a small windowless box where a teleprinter is chuntering a message.

'That could be your adventure,' I say, with a flourish.

He laughs. 'Perhaps.'

'Best check.'

'All right, I will.' He slides round the table and into the communications room. Young Wylie, seeker after adventure, only there's something in his manner, a reticence, a diffidence, that suggests precisely the opposite. I don't expect him to give me any trouble. The teleprinter grinds to a halt and I hear him rip the signal off the roll. 'It's nothing,' he shouts through to me, and a moment later he shuffles back into the office, his gaze fixed on the slip in his hands.

'Sit down, Wylie,' I say quietly, and he looks up at me at once. His jaw drops open (yes, it happens). 'That one.' And I wave the gun at the chair on the other side of the desk. 'Sit down now!' But he's too shocked to move. 'Wake up!' I point the gun to the right of him and fire into the wall, and the percussion is no louder than the thud of a hardback book on a carpet, but I guess that only makes it more terrifying.

'Hands on the desk. Do what I say and you'll have your own thrilling story to tell. The keys to the DG's office – where are they?'

He opens his mouth to speak, and thinks better of it.

'Christ.' I step forward and press the barrel of the gun to his temple, then yank his chair from the desk. 'Do you know how long I've been doing this kind of work? I'm going to start with your kneecaps,' I point the gun at his left one, 'and it's going to make a hell of a mess. So, one more time, where are the keys to the DG's office?'

He shuts his eyes, his face wrinkled with doubt and anguish. 'No. No, no—'

I slug him with the butt of the gun before he has a chance to say it again, and he slides from the chair. Then with my foot on his chest I ram the barrel against his kneecap. 'I'm going to count to three. One. You'll never walk properly again. Two. Let me tell you, young man, it isn't worth it. Three—'

'Cupboard by the door!' He jerks his knees up to his chest and rolls on to his side with his head in his hands. 'The cupboard.'

'Key for the cupboard?'

'Top right drawer of the desk.'

'Very wise,' I say. 'You made the right choice.'

While I'm tying his hands the telephone rings and I ignore it, but a minute later it rings again. Someone seems to want to speak to Duty urgently. 'Any idea who that will be?' Wylie doesn't reply. He's ashamed; he shouldn't be.

'Never argue with a gun,' I say. 'If I was a proper bastard I wouldn't have given you any chances.'

But the telephone is unsettling. Sooner or later the caller will send a search party to the duty office.

I have the key; have I the combination? Linda was so sure. I walk back to the lifts and on into the Secretariat. Still no one. The brass hats on the fifth floor are never in at this hour; there may be juniors on the third; there are the queens on the ground, and perhaps an election knees-up in the bar, but I'm a familiar face and there's a good chance news of my fall from grace has yet to trickle from the fifth to the rest.

The light above the DG's door is red to remind me I'm not in his diary. The long walk in through rows of desks with covered typewriters is to allow time for the DG to activate the new electronic lock that turns his office into a fortress, only I've got the key. The lock slides back with a satisfying clunk. I close the door behind me and switch on the lights and it's the stern portrait of the first director general who greets me: Vernon Kell was no friend to democracy. Against the wall to the right of him, the DG's black cabinet safe, as brutally utilitarian as a cannon in the captain's cabin of a man-of-war. Inside the safe are the secrets director generals don't trust anyone to keep, and when they're shredded and burned they will be completely deniable.

Thumb and two fingers lightly on the combination dial I turn it forward and back to Linda's birthday in March – 2 and 0 and 3 – and then the years she was married to her soldier husband – 1 and 5 – and I jerk the handle down before I have time to doubt her. The lock retracts with a clunk, and in the seconds it takes me to swing the safe door open I love her.

Furnival Jones's medals and honours are in flat black display cases on the top shelf. On the other three: neat stacks of buff-coloured personal files in moisture-resistant polythene bags, and three of the Y Boxes MI5 uses for material on people it suspects of spying, like me. That's where I begin, and the first box I pull from the shelf has my name taped to the top! I haven't time to examine it and it might spoil the surprise to come, so I reach for the second of the boxes, and written in small black letters is *Norman John WORTHINGTON*. With a little shudder of pleasure I break the seal to check my friend Norman is prime minister of our glorious country. There's a thick personal file in the box and, yes, there is no doubt about it: there are reports on Harold Wilson from as far back as the forties. The OATSHEAF evidence is here too, and telephone-tap transcripts of conversations the PM has had with his business friends, Kagan and Sternberg. I want it all; I have it all, and I must leave with it at once.

I shove the empty Y Box back on the shelf, and it's only as I'm swinging the safe shut that I remember there's another. I have what I came for and there isn't a second to waste, but I'm a spy, best beloved, and my bloody insatiable curiosity always gets the better of me. Oh, and this time I'm glad. In fact, I feel a surge of joy better than sex, better than the music of Miles Davis, because the name on the third box is *Sir Richard Goldsmith WHITE*. I skip through some of the material and Dick is being treated as a suspect too – a candidate for the mole at the top of the service, the master spy ELLI. I take just enough to embarrass.

There are a couple of empty burn bags for the confidential waste in the outer office and I use one to carry the files. The telephone begins to ring as I'm emptying them into the bag: who the hell's going to answer it at this hour? Perhaps the balloon's gone up already and FJ is on his way to the office. I retrace my steps as far as the emergency stairs opposite Banking, and canter down five flights to the only other exit from the building. Until now everything has gone smoothly, but I don't have to try the doors to know they're locked and barred and I have no choice but to leave by the lobby. I can only pray that Mr Wylie is still tied to a chair. I will emerge from the boiler-room corridor with a sack over my shoulder, like a coalman, and if Bobby Roberts has his wits about him he'll ask me why I didn't take the lift, like a proper gentleman.

But Bobby's listening to his radio. I'm almost across the lobby before he sees me. 'Mr Vaughan!' The door of the security alcove opens. 'Mr Vaughan.'

I turn to him – 'In the flesh, Bobby' – and hold up the sack. 'I have what I came for.'

'Not good,' he says, walking towards me, 'not good at all.'

I grip the gun in my coat pocket. 'What isn't good, Bobby?'

'You was right, sir. The socialists are going to win a majority.' Poor Bobby looks at me like a whipped dog.

'That's the trouble with democracy,' I say, and he agrees.

'Can I shake your 'and, sir?' he says. 'It's been a pleasure.'

Good luck to you too, Bobby. I'm sorry for the trouble that's coming your way, but excuse me if the rain falling on my face has never felt softer, and London air has never tasted sweeter. You bastards, I have you.

# 51

I ARRIVE AT THE Snowdon boarding house to find the other guests gathered in the lounge watching television. Mrs Morris tries to persuade me to join them for a sherry. 'Mr Parry's a salesman like you,' she says. I thank her but decline, and would she be good enough to furnish me with a late key? 'Oh, I'll be up all night,' she says.

My room is a double on the second floor with a view over railway tracks. The walls are damp, the paper peeling in the corners, the ceiling's canary yellow with cigarette smoke and there are honeymoon stains on the bedspread. A night train rattles the glass, and when I switch on the TV for the BBC's election report, the presenter is lost in a blizzard. The ambience reminds me of the war years, when I was young and able to make sense of everything.

There's a cheap plywood desk under the window, and with both bedside lamps I'm able to create a circle of light for the camera. Then I pour a large whisky and settle on the bed with the papers. I begin at the back of the Wilson file with what I take to be the birth certificate of Mr Norman John Worthington. It was written by B1a only weeks after Wilson was elected to Parliament in 1945.

*The security interest attaching to Harold Wilson and the justifi-*
*cation for the opening of a file derives from comments made*

*about him by certain Communist members of the Civil Service*
*which suggest he has a similar political outlook.*

Wilson was negotiating a trade deal with the Soviet Union, and for good security reasons, the Service was desperate to prevent him succeeding. Our wartime ally was now our enemy but Labour was so anxious to come to a trading arrangement that it authorised the secret export of a new fighter engine and was within a hair's breadth of selling Moscow the entire plane.

Wilson was observed to be *close to Politburo Member and Trade Minister, Mikoyan,* and to indulge in *epic all-night drinking sessions with him.* Another minute raises the possibility of a blackmail plot for the first time. Wilson was believed to have become close to both a woman on his staff and a Russian national, and the KGB *may have photographs of a compromising nature.* No evidence was offered for this assertion, no names, no dates.

There was another flurry of minutes and briefing papers in 1951 when Wilson resigned from the government. The CIA was reported to be *concerned about his attitude* and suspected him of *being a fellow traveller.* And to judge from the drip, drip of rumour and conjecture that made its way into his file in the fifties the Service took the possibility seriously. Twelve visits to Russia in ten years, and meetings with top Soviet leaders: *Mr Wilson is taking the road to Moscow.* A note in Peter Wright's hand offers the view: *No one should ever be permitted to become Prime Minister after twelve trips to Moscow.*

Wilson seems to have done some work in the fifties for a company importing timber from Moscow. *Is he taking bribes for political favours?* the deputy DG enquired. And the Service started to monitor the activities of business associates, like Kagan and Sternberg, the newspaper man Robert Maxwell, and Bernstein, the chairman of Granada Television. Moscow station complained that Wilson *frequently goes off the radar in Russia,* and a joint Five and Six report concluded he was engaged in an 'improper relationship' with his political secretary, and was probably sleeping with the Labour MP Barbara Castle, too. And there's another note from Wright: *Evidence suggests Wilson was compromised on one of his visits to Moscow, between 1956 and 1959, and that the KGB has pictures and tapes of him with his secretary.* Evidence? There isn't any in the file.

That brings me to the OATSHEAF investigation. In the first few weeks of 1963, intelligence services on both sides of the Atlantic were thrown into a flat spin by the defection of Philby, then the election of a new Labour leader. Was it another great victory for Moscow? Wright and Angleton believed so, and Golitsyn confirmed their suspicions. Wright wrote a memorandum with the title 'Two Years of Soviet Victories' for the benefit of Dick and FJ.

*1963*

*January: Philby is tipped off by the mole at the top of the MI5, and Hugh Gaitskell is poisoned.*

*February: Harold Wilson becomes leader of the Labour Party.*

*June: the KGB engineers the disgrace of Minister of War, John Profumo, in an effort to precipitate the fall of the Conservative Government.*

*1964*

*October: Labour wins the British General Election and a Soviet agent of influence enters Number 10: Harold Wilson.*

*December: Wilson's failure to offer material support for American action in Vietnam is more evidence of Communist influence on British policy.*

Wright was circumspect while Hollis was in charge, but FJ had barely got his feet under the DG's desk before he came under pressure to authorise a press campaign to discredit the new prime minister. *We have a higher duty to the country and to our allies,* Wright argued, *and if we do not bring about a change the matter may be taken out of our hands.*

Only one of our allies would have the will and the means to interfere, but Wright spelt it out for Dick and FJ in any case: *Counter Intelligence Chief, CIA, has offered his full support for any action we deem necessary to ensure a satisfactory solution to this problem,* he wrote.

I've reached the front of the file. There's one more memorandum, and it is the maddest and most frightening thing I've come across in more than twenty years as a spy. Dated the day after Angleton's secret visit to London a fortnight ago, it was written by Wright and sent to the heads of both MI5 and MI6:

> *I cannot stress enough the importance of immediate action if we are to retain the special relationship with the Americans. The CIA is losing patience and it is prepared to think the unthinkable. In a private discussion after our meeting of 14 March, Jim Angleton indicated the CIA was anxious to 'relieve us of our problem'. He said, 'These things can be managed!' I did not consider it wise to enquire further at this stage, but whatever you imagine will be close to the truth! I do not have to remind you that our government's refusal to offer the United States its full backing for the war in Vietnam has left us with precious few friends in Washington.*

His cryptic little phrase 'whatever you imagine' is like a punch in the guts. Imagine? I don't need to. Rising from the bed I step across to the window and open it for some air. The draught swirls the smoke from most of a packet of cigarettes into crazy patterns that remind me of the night Angleton told me Wilson was an agent. I had no doubt then that he was capable of imagining anything. An accident, perhaps, an act of terror, or an inexplicable illness: the sort of murderous caper the CIA likes to pull in banana republics. Who can be sure of what is moving in the darkness of that man's mind?

I use two films preparing the first package, two more on the second, and I'm starting on the third when the BBC calls it for Labour, with a majority of more than fifty seats. By now the brass will know what I've done. I only have time to glance at Dick's file but I recognise the acidity of the prose. *His friendship with Anthony Blunt* and his *failure to deal with Philby* in the fifties, his *generally poor record*: Evelyn holds back nothing. Did he permit Philby to escape *to avoid embarrassment and criticism of his record*?

I slip the file into a large padded envelope with a note, *To Dick, with my compliments! Harry,* and I address it to *Sir Dick White* and mark it *Personal.*

Only the hardcore boozers are left in the Snowdon's lounge and they're too engrossed in each other and the television to notice me. Elsa's sports car is parked around the corner, and as I start it, I own to a feeling of quiet satisfaction. Bowling through empty streets with the car's roof down, that quiet satisfaction swells in me like the final movement of a great symphony. Drunk on my own audacity I open the throttle and fill the city with the roar of the engine. First package of films to the *Daily Mirror* at Holborn Circus for immediate delivery to Watkins on the night news desk. The second package I drop into a pillar box near St Paul's; the third at the Palace of Westminster. On a night such as this, I think it is safe to assume Tom Driberg was elected to serve another term, and will be back to pick up his correspondence.

Special Branch will have the make and plates of the car by now and will be searching our house for clues as to my whereabouts and intentions. But I have the last package, Dick's, to deliver – and I'm giving him the gun too. So I park the Sprite a few streets from Queen Anne's Gate and walk. The lights are blazing at number 21, Dick's driver is parked outside, and there's a policeman on the door. They will know nothing of my activities or the panicky conversations taking place inside.

'Package for the chief,' I say, and thrust it at the copper.

'You can deliver it yourself, sir,' he says, turning to knock on the door.

I drop it on the step before he has a chance to, and walk away. He calls after me, and I expect him to give chase, but it's only a few yards to the corner, and I run as fast as I can the second I'm out of sight.

The election party's over at the Snowdon and Mrs Morris is collecting the dirty glasses. She says I seem very cheerful for such an early hour, and that I must be Labour. Harold Wilson is on the television in my bedroom promising to grow the economy. I switch him off and ring Reception for an outside line.

'Elsa? Is that you?'

'They said you might.' She's upset.

'And "they" are listening, I suppose.'

She doesn't reply.

'Try to think the best of me, whatever "they" tell you.'

'What have you done, Harry?'

'I'm trying to sort this out,' I say. 'I can't tell you how – *they* know . . . Look, I just want you to know I love you and that I'm doing this for both of us, and—'

'Where are you, Harry?'

*Ych-y-fi.* That hurts.

'I mean . . . you're not going anywhere, are you?' she says quickly.

'I'm not going anywhere.'

'Are you close?'

'Yes, I'm close. But I'm going to sleep now, *cariad*. Only remember I love you and remember who I am – the person *you* know. I promised you I would arrange things. I have.'

'Harry. Wait, Harry. Where are you?'

I move the receiver slowly away from my ear and hang up. Her persistence has shaken me. It feels as if someone is pressing my chest with weights, like the ones they used to force witches to confess. The files are open on the bed, and I clear them on to the floor so I can lie back with my eyes shut. Harry Vaughan was friends with Guy Burgess: they'll tell her I'm a spy and try to pin the collapse of SUBALTERN on me. But it won't wash because there's too much in these files. And I'm here to answer for everything. Her sports car is parked on the street outside, the lodging house is called the Snowdon, and there's a Welsh salesman in Room 8 who bears more than a passing resemblance to a film star. I reach over to the bedside table and pour a very stiff whisky. The chase is over and I'm completely knackered.

I wake with the empty glass still balanced on my chest, every muscle taut, every nerve. The light of a grey morning is filtering through the muslin curtains. The door's shut, the room empty, but something has dragged me back from fathoms deep. The bedsprings groan as I roll on to my side and place the tumbler on the table, so I wait for the rattle of a passing train to swing my legs around and rise. They'll come – I've made it easy – but I hope we can do things in a civilised way. My mouth is sticky and dry, as if I've run a marathon, so I step over to the washbasin, fill my hands and splash a little water on my face, and I'm just reaching for the hand towel when crash! Someone has put a boot to the door. Again! And the frame splinters at the lock. No point in protesting there's no need for rough stuff because I can see that's the way they want it to be: six of them and Clive, with his Browning pointing at my chest. 'Take it easy,' I say, my hands in the air, but his face has an ugly expression. He's pumped up for a fight, and so are his companions.

'On the floor, on the floor!' As I'm bending forward, he catches me on the temple with the butt and down I go with stars. Knee in the small of my back, arms dragged back to cuff me, and it hurts like hell. But I laugh, and I can't stop laughing, until he rolls me on to my back. 'What the fuck do you have to laugh about, Vaughan?'

'Ffŵl Ebrill!'

He looks at me dumbly.

'April Fool's Day,' I say. 'I just remembered. It's today!'

Clive isn't amused. Clive punches me in the face.

WE'RE NOT LIKE ordinary men and women: we have secret knowledge, we have comic-book powers, the law is something we honour more in the breach than the observance. You can't stick to the rules when you're fighting a war – that's what they tell you – and it's flattering, it's glorious, what an adventure, free to, in Peter Wright's words, bug and burgle at the behest of the small circle who wield power in the name of 'the state'. Only I'm their enemy now and those powers are directed at me, and the ancient right of habeas corpus that prevents every man from being held unlawfully does not apply to this one.

They carried me from the boarding house. I remember their military-style boots, the smell of polish and a sick headache, and they wouldn't let me rise from the floor of the van until I was bundled out beneath a blanket and into a concrete barracks building of the sort we threw up everywhere during the war. There, I was searched, then dragged along a corridor of empty cells to this one, with its high window and tiny *tent of blue*. I guess that was a week ago and that they're holding me at the old camp on Ham Common where we interrogated spies during the war. My guards have no conversation. They bring me rations and take my bucket away. I have blankets and a camp bed, a table that folds down from the wall, a stool, and a copy of the Bible, which I have almost finished. Like Hess in Spandau I am their only prisoner. The concrete weeps, there are holes in the perimeter wire, and my food comes in a can from somewhere outside the facility and is always cold.

Phillpotts was my first visitor. 'I'm fire-fighting, Vaughan. I don't have to be gentle!' He wanted the copies I'd made of the files and he knew he wasn't going to coax the names of the recipients from me. People who say torture doesn't work are talking nonsense. But if you throw a prisoner to the goons you really can't be squeamish. Trust them to do it their way. I lost a tooth on my first day and might have lost some more but for Phillpotts, who called them off before they could really get going.

Lecky was my next visitor. 'Look, old boy,' he said, 'did you, or didn't you?'

'Did I do what?'

'Give the damn file to the Russians?'

'The one that proves the CIA is plotting a coup? No, Terence, I didn't.'

'I don't know what you're talking about,' he said, 'but we want them all back. How many copies did you make?'

That was five days ago and no one else on the outside has come near me since. The guards are under orders not to speak to me. Yesterday I was permitted to pace a square between the buildings. For twenty minutes the tent of blue was a bloody glorious pavilion. I have too much idle time and I've started to dream. Sometimes I'm not sure if I'm asleep or awake. I dream of you, Elsa. *Behold, you are beautiful, my love*, it says in the Song of Solomon; *your eyes are doves.*

'You're not f-f-famous, I'm afraid.' Wright reaches into his jacket for one, two, three, four films and places them on the pine table in front of me. 'No one is agitating for your release.'

We're alone together in the 'interview' room where I lost a

tooth, and after three weeks' solitary I'm genuinely pleased to see him. The strange thing is, he seems to feel the same way. He greeted me with a lop-sided smile, and commented regretfully on mine. 'Quite unnecessary to use violence,' he says. 'I c-can't imagine what Phillpotts was thinking. But Six has passed you on to us now.'

Exclusive property of MI5 and Peter Wright. I expect the room is wired and members of my FLUENCY family are on site, listening for slips in my story. It feels very personal already because the table is so narrow our feet keep touching. I can see a patch of grey stubble he missed with the razor this morning, and he will certainly be able to smell a noxious odour from me after nearly a month without bath. I look frightful but he wants me like that. Every small advantage counts. Why? Because interrogation is a battle of wills, and he knows an insider like me will see the punches coming.

'The *Mirror* chap, W-Watkins?' He shakes his head. 'Your friend W-Watkins's tax affairs are a terrible mess. He could go to prison. Well, in the circumstances, he was happy to help us.' He picks up one of the films and rolls it between his thumb and forefinger. 'And the other films? Dr-Driberg! That surprised me. Tom Driberg! Did you choose him because he was on good terms with Burgess? Doesn't matter. A liar and a queer and a shit. But our shit. Our liar. We run Driberg.'

I laugh. 'Come on!'

But he's serious. In fact, he looks as smug as I've seen him. 'T-Tom was selling intelligence to the Czechs, you see, and in return for our silence he agreed to pass us information on the L-L-Labour Party.'

I put on a brave face – that's how you play.

'But you didn't put all your faith in Driberg and Watkins, did you? How many copies are there?'

'Are you going to let me see a lawyer?'

'For your moment in court? To destroy the reputation of the Service? No.'

'Save the Service!' I bark at him. 'You want to remove the prime minister. I didn't just photograph the bloody papers, I read them too. We're the servants, not the masters of the state.'

'You're talking nonsense,' says Wright.

'Did Dick enjoy reading his file?'

That seems to touch a nerve. 'You – you h-had time to shoot more films. Did you take them to your controller?'

'My controller?' I scoff. 'I sent the information to the *Mirror*, remember?'

'B-b-because it weakens the Service and drives a wedge between us and the Americans. You're tr-trying to protect the network – protect ELLI.'

'Vaughan, the KGB agent on the inside?'

'Instructed to shut down the FLUENCY investigation.'

'I see.' I reach for his cigarettes. 'Do you mind? The guards won't let me.' Wright nods and pushes his lighter across the table.

'Where are the other films, H-Harry?'

I say, 'Oh, God, that's good,' and draw deeply on my cigarette. 'I learned a word at Oxford – yes, that place – an Old English word. *Selfæta*. It means an animal that preys on its own kind – self-eater. That's how I think of you, Peter.'


Wright leaves me to stew for almost a week. The next time I see him he's wearing fawn slacks and a hideous checked jacket that he must have bought in America. Everything in the interrogation room is as it was before, except for the table, which is new, and a couple of feet less intimate. And no pleasantries, no cigarettes, just 'Where are the other copies, Vaughan?' My silence will hurt people, he says, like the secretary who gave me the combination of the director general's safe, and the policeman who was foolish enough to allow me into the building, and young Wylie who surrendered the key. Then he talks of sending me to America. 'Jim thinks we should make you disappear,' he says, 's-so you should think of your children.'

'I do,' I say. 'I do.'

But we're just dancing round each other. The fight proper begins when he takes a big fat file from his bag, the file I saw in the DG's safe – my file. Ah, the devotion Evelyn has shown me: she is like an old and bitter lover. Without shame we begin with Harry Vaughan the boy in tackety boots, whose clothes were fine-dusted with coal every day except Sundays. Born to the chapel and the miners' union and to the spirit of socialist revolution in a village the popular papers call 'Little Moscow'.

'You couldn't leave the village, could you?' he says. 'Did you choose the VENONA code name JACK because it was your father's name?'

I deny it for the record.

'He was a m member of the Party. When did you join? Was it at Oxford?'

I pretend to consider this a moment then say, 'I'm going to give it to you on a plate, Peter.'

He looks puzzled.

'Yes, I joined the Party in Oxford.'

He looks down at my file but not before I see the triumph in his eye. 'Who r-r-recruited you?'

'I'm not going to tell you that.'

'Was it Goronwy R-Rees?'

'It was 1938. I left the following year when the Soviet Union struck a pact with the Nazis to enslave the people of Poland.'

'What did you do for the Party?'

'Nothing.'

He smiles. 'You all say that.'

I shrug.

'R-Rees says B-Burgess recruited you, that he tried to warn you.'

'Does he?'

'But he was the one, wasn't he?'

There's a patch of mould the colour of gangrene on the wall behind his right shoulder and I focus my gaze upon it. In my mind's eye I see Rees in his leather slippers, gazing through the window of the ward at a barren garden. Yes, Rees is a coward, Driberg a liar, but they're like flies in the FLUENCY web: so desperate to free themselves they're prepared to entangle another. Salem to the Soviet Union, it's the same. That's how these witch-hunts work. I could hurt Rees, but to what purpose?

'Did you know B-Burgess was a Soviet agent?' says Wright.

'I knew he was a Communist.'

'Rees says you knew he was an agent, that you told *him*.'

'That isn't true. I didn't need to tell him.'

'And w-when you joined the Service you said nothing,' he says contemptuously.

'There is a saying, Peter: *Gall pechod mawr ddyfod trwy ddrws bychan*. A great sin can enter by a small door. It was the war and the Soviet Union was our ally, remember? There were more important things to worry about – and after the war I was posted to Vienna.'

'And Philby? You knew he was a spy, too.'

'Is that a question? I knew as much about him as you did, and a good deal less than Sir Dick White.'

He looks at me sideways. 'I d-don't believe you left the Party.'

'Of course you don't.'

'You have fought us all the way.'

'Because you are as big a liar as Burgess, only he knew he was a liar.'

Three fruitless years of searching, and they are yet to discover an active agent. Wright is sure he's found dozens, scores, and I am the latest. Proof? I searched his safe, he says, and I prevented him searching Hollis's. I have protected 'the Oxford Circle' that isn't a circle, and sheltered Mitchell, and now I'm trying to leak information that would ruin the Service. 'We made a terrible m-mistake,' he says. 'We locked the chicken house with the f-fox inside.'

'And the prime minister? Just how far *are* you prepared to go? How far is Jim Angleton prepared to go?'

He doesn't answer.

'I'm trying to save the Service,' I say for the tape.

'Where are they, Vaughan?' He means the remaining copies of the files.

'They're ticking away.'

He knows if they go off they'll bring down the whole bloody FLUENCY edifice and finish Angleton once and for all. So, what now, Peter?

# 53

THE GORILLAS ARE back with their knuckle-dusters. They drag me from my cell in the early hours and prop me in a chair, and when I fall to the floor they bring me round with a bucket of water and prop me up again. I'm not brave and I'm no more capable of tolerating pain than the next man, but there are moments in every life when we find something surprising in ourselves, and this is one of those times. I don't know their names; I don't expect I'll forget their eyes. One of them has a little scar above his lip, the other a lion rampant on a very hairy forearm. They are clipped and talk in clichés, like soldiers, and I guess they believe it's their duty to give me a good hiding.

'How many films? Who has the films?' Over and over and over. For how long? I can't tell. My body is screaming to me to spit it out through my teeth; my face hurts so much they've made it easier to say nothing. But it isn't the Lefortovo in Moscow and these two are not KGB torturers. I guess it must be dawn when they take me back to my cell. One of the regular guards brings me warm water and a mug of sweet tea. A little while later – at least it seems so – he shakes me awake and offers me more tea and a packet of cigarettes.

'Five minutes, Vaughan,' he says. 'Then you're back in.'

I know he's lying when I see Wright sitting at the table. He won't witness any physical 'persuasion' because it has to be deniable.

'S-s-s-sit,' he says, and I laugh.

'Shit, did you say? Yes, it is!'

One should not mock the afflicted except in exceptional circumstances. 'How do I look?' I grip the edge of the table and lower myself on to the seat I so recently occupied for a beating. 'My wife used to think I looked like Dirk Bogarde.' I wince and touch my lip for his benefit. 'Your thugs have turned me into . . . into Ernest Borgnine.'

'I d-don't expect she cares what you l-look like, Vaughan.'

'Well, I'm sure you're her best friend.'

'Oh, we get on well enough.' He reaches into the pocket of his appalling jacket and slides a photograph across the table. 'R-recognise this?'

'Of course. Vienna, 'forty-eight.' It's the picture of the two of us in the snow that I used to keep in a drawer at home.

'L-l-let's go back to that time, shall we?'

I pick up the photograph and concentrate on the memories. Even with a split lip and a bruised face, and with Wright sitting across from me, it brings a lump to my throat.

'SUBALTERN wasn't your operation, but you'd met Miss Spears in London . . . You st-started to see her, and that gave you access to the intelligence from the SUBALTERN operation.'

I put the photo down and stare. 'That's nasty.'

'Was Otto your controller?'

'Otto was probably dead.'

'How do you know he's dead?'

'I don't know he's dead.'

'You told the agent you met in Vienna that Otto was dead.' Wright turns the pages of his notepad. 'In the garden of the Belvedere Palace two years ago – October.'

'I merely presumed that to be the case.' Leaning forward a little I prod his notebook with my forefinger. 'It should be there. Anthony Blunt said Otto was called back to Moscow during the purges. What do *you* think happened to him?'

'You said you *knew* he was dead.'

'*No*, Peter,' I say, as if correcting a child. 'Evelyn?' I know she's listening somewhere. 'Evelyn, *cariad*,' I shout, 'check the CIA transcript of the meeting, will you?'

Wright's face twitches with irritation. 'It d-d-doesn't matter. Your w-w-wife says you arranged a transfer to SUBALTERN, even though she didn't want you to.'

'*She* thought it was a mistake for us to work together. *I* thought she was taking too many risks. It was our biggest operation, and I wanted to be part of it.'

'She remembers it differently.' He glances at his notebook. '"Harry was a drag on the operation."'

I try to smile. Play wife against husband? ROSA against JACK? I would do the same.

'You don't b-believe me?'

'Peter, I don't want to be rude but your record of telling the truth . . .'

'Oh, I've spoken to her m-many times. Arthur and I thought we should have a word. Well, her n-name kept cropping up. Remember my visit to Dennis Pr-Proctor in the South of France? I went on to Berlin. We kept that from you, of course.' He pauses to let this penetrate, then says, 'Your wife, too,' just to be sure.

I try not to blink, may even manage a smile, but it grieves and hurts me more than the worst sort of pummelling from his thugs. *O fy Nuw.* I don't want to believe him but I do.

'Your w-wife's history . . . well, we have our suspicions,' he says. 'But she *has* co-operated with us – and she says you shared everything with her.'

'Not everything. I did tell her you were dangerously deluded, and you'd push your best friend in front of a train if Angleton wanted you to.'

He ignores my jibes. 'Any one of a d-d-dozen security breaches would be enough to send you to prison for a very long time.'

'You want to take me to court?' I laugh – and wince as the split opens in my lip.

'Your wife says you hate the Service and she doesn't understand why you won't leave. But your KGB controller won't let you.'

'Is that a question?'

'I told her you were – *are* a Communist – that you were recruited by Rees and Burgess, and that a former KGB officer remembers you in Vienna . . .'

I snort derisively.

'. . . that our defector says the Russians had a m-mole in the city, code name something like JACK—'

'*Something* like! Dear me.'

'Your wife could see why we were suspicious. Things began to make sense – she says you hid a l-l-letter from her. Was it from your controller?'

'From Rees.'

'He denies it. There's the matter of the visit to Anthony B-Blunt to tell him to shut up. The splints in your door. And your wife says you're always checking to see if someone is following you. Oh, the l-l-lies you told her.'

He smiles weakly and reaches for his cigarettes. 'Yes, the lies. I had to tell her about the secretary in the DG's office, and that you used her to steal s-s-secrets that could damage our country. Elsa was upset, naturally, and ready to help us prevent you running off to Moscow.'

'I made it easy for you to find me. As good as wrote you an invitation.'

'Then how do you explain the open ticket to B-Berlin?' He turns a couple of pages of his notebook. 'You purchased it under a false name last February. A place on the Cromwell Road called Golden Day Travel, under the name Morgan.'

'Flying out to meet Elsa.'

'She knew n-nothing about it.'

'A surprise.'

He looks at me sceptically, and with good reason. No word from her in days, talk of an Oxford circle, yes, I suspected her of being a spy. I don't know if I'm right. I think it's easier not to know.

'Who's ELLI?' Wright leans forward, commanding my attention. 'H-help us and we can talk about a deal.'

I sigh. 'A job in the Royal Household, like Sir Anthony? Look, it's all in the paper I wrote for FJ. The mole was the *acting* head of a department of British counter-espionage or intelligence. Philby was *acting* head of Counter-espionage at MI6. The agent with the code name STANLEY in the VENONA signals and agent ELLI are one and the same man. Christ, the code names even sound the same. Who's ELLI? Philby's ELLI, and this – this witch-hunt in the Service is his crowning glory. I know you won't change your mind, Peter, you're not big enough. You and Jim will dig for ever, until there's nothing useful left of the Service.'

'If you c-c-care so much about the Service,' he says, 'tell me where you sent the other copy of the file.'

I smile and shake my head.

'To Maurice Oldfield?'

I laugh.

'Your wife says you were working with Oldfield. Did he help you pinch the file?'

'I didn't need any help.'

'The polling station in the church hall – his idea? You knew the d-door out of the church was unlocked.'

'You haven't spent much time in the field, have you, Peter? It's the sort of thing you take care of first.'

That makes him twitch. 'Then why was M-Maurice meeting you at the church?'

'Hymn practice.'

'I don't believe you.'

'I don't care.'

He picks up his pen and puts it down again almost at once. 'We have enough to lock you up and throw away the key.'

'Conspiring with a foreign power to discredit a prime minister and overthrow an elected government: you will have to join me, and,' I raise my voice for the microphone, 'Sir Richard White too – guilty of a shocking breach of faith.'

'That's nonsense.'

'Is it?'

He rises from his chair, smoothes the creases from his slacks and walks over to the window where he stands gazing out at grey concrete beneath a grey sky. What is he thinking? Nothing good for me. He isn't able to temper the prejudice that shapes all our actions and opinions with reason. Not as clever as Angleton but just as implacable and, like Kim Philby, capable of sacrificing the lives of many people in pursuit of his convictions. Not so different from the Nazi fanatics I interrogated at a table like this one during the war.

'Did you hear me?' he barks. 'We can make you d-d-disappear.' He takes a step back towards the table. 'Or we could do a deal. You hand over the films and a full confession and we'll sweep it under the carpet.'

I nod sagely. 'Did Dick authorise you to make a deal?'

'It's from C, yes.'

My knee is bouncing under the table. Careful! My body aches from my swollen eye to the broken bones in my foot, and I'm trying to contain a spring tide of feelings.

'Well?' He stands with his hands on the back of a chair. 'Does M-Mitchell have the films?'

'No.'

'All r-right, Vaughan. What do I tell C?'

I look up at the strip light in the ceiling because I expect they've hidden the microphone there. 'What should you tell Sir Dick? Tell Sir Dick to "fuck off". Tell him he's got to go, that you've got to go – Furnival Jones too. And Angleton should never be allowed to set foot in Britain again. I want to see the home secretary or the attorney general. I want to see a lawyer. I want an apology – *and* to my wife – and I want my pension paid in full.' I lower my gaze to his face. 'Hope they got that, all right.'

The corners of his thin mouth turn down, and once again he resembles the imp that used to gaze disapprovingly at me from the wall opposite my college window.

'You've been pl-playing a game,' he says, collecting his notebook and cigarettes. 'Vaughan and Rees, naughty Welsh boys. Game's over.'

'Really?' I say. Guards or goons? That's all I care about now. If he leaves the room before me it will be to let loose the bullies again. 'G-guards!' he shouts, and relief breaks through me.

As they lead me away he has one more thing to say. 'Vaughan!' I stop and turn to look at him. 'Your wife says she'll n-n-never trust you again – a man who cheats his wife.'

'You made that up, Peter.' That may be how she feels but she would consider it too bourgeois a sentiment to share with Wright. 'It's another of your lies.'

He just stares at me.

'The truth is, you can't trust anyone,' I say. 'It's the Service, of course. Only I have the wit to know when I'm lying, and you don't.'

# 54

## 15 July 1966

I HEAR VOICES IN the corridor, then the grinding of the rusty lock and the fat mouse squeak of my cell door, but I don't get up and I don't turn to look because I know the guard called Jake is on duty and he's a surly bastard. 'Ah, the morning papers?' I say. 'Well, thank you, Jeeves.'

It's something like nine o'clock. I've dressed and eaten, pissed in one pot, washed in another and am lying on my army cot.

'Over there,' I mutter, and point in the general direction of the tray.

My visitor clears his throat, insisting on my attention. Rolling on to my side, I'm amazed to see Maurice Oldfield at the open door, brown brogues in one hand, a hanger with jacket and trousers in the other. 'Hello, Harry,' he says. Just that: 'hello'. He stands in the sunlight, which pours through the bars on bright mornings, like a portly angel or a matinee idol in the spotlight. Lord, have you sent thy instrument to set me free? And as I stare at him a lump the size of a golf ball rises in my throat. One hundred and six days I've spent in this cell: I want to shout that at Moulders! But he's holding *my* cream jacket and those are *my* blue trousers, and he's smiling with warmth and concern, so he'd better do the talking because I don't think I'm able to.

'The beard,' he says. 'I hardly recognise you.'

That makes me laugh.

He checks his watch. 'You can shave if you're quick.'

I swing my legs round and rise. 'Where am I going?'

'I'll tell you in the car.'

'Tell me now!' I snap at him.

He hesitates. 'You're going to Downing Street.'

Maurice doesn't ask how things have been for me. An astute fellow like Maurice won't poke a hole in the dam lest he's engulfed by a flood of pent-up anger and pain. He leaves me to shave and change, and I hear him talking to my guards in the corridor.

'You're bringing me back here?' I ask, as he leads me to the waiting car.

'Believe me, I hope not,' he says, 'but I think that will be up to you.' More he refuses to say in front of the goons MI5 has sent to secure my delivery.

'But have you seen her, Maurice?' I say, as we pull away. 'How is she?' He puts a chubby hand on my arm. 'Leave of absence.'

'You *have* seen her?'

'Yes.' He slips his glasses off and examines the lenses. 'She *did* ask after you. I couldn't tell her much.'

I nod. 'Does she think I'm working for the KGB?'

'I don't know what she thinks. We need to sort everything out, Harry,' he says firmly. 'Today, I hope.'

The sun is blinking through the windscreen, the car full of cigarette smoke. We turn on to the A3 into central London and our driver works his way up through the gears. I can't see the road ahead for the square head and shoulders of his companion in the seat in front of me, but tidy tree-lined streets flash past my side window, solid red-brick houses with names like The Ferns and Elm Lodge, clipped box hedges and borders of snap-dragons and dahlias. The tip of my tongue finds the gap in my front teeth – bottom incisor – then the gap at the top, and I wonder, Bloody hell, how can things be so normal, so ordinary? They just *are*, of course, they just are, and I know I should be happy that they are, and not resentful that Richmond and Putney cannot imagine what is said and done in their name.

Tired of the silence after so many days in my cell, I ask Maurice about the Union flags I see hanging from the balconies of flats and in shop windows. 'Is it war?'

'Association football,' he says. 'The World Cup.'

The officer in front of me twitches, and I guess he's thinking, Where the hell have you been, Taff?

In a bloody hole, boy, in a concrete hole.

'You missed the seamen's strike,' says Maurice. 'The prime minister declared a state of emergency. Blamed Communist agitators for stirring up trouble.' He turns to catch my eye, just to be sure the irony isn't lost on me. 'What with strikes, cuts, a credit squeeze, the country is in a bit of a mess.'

We're crossing Westminster Bridge and preparing to turn right into Whitehall when Maurice tells me the prime minister is on a visit to Moscow, and I'm foolish enough to feel disappointed he isn't in Downing Street to welcome me. Wilson is on another mission to make peace in Vietnam; no one gives him a hope. Maurice says the Americans want him to 'butt out'.

'You're sure he'll want to come back from Moscow?' I ask. Maurice isn't amused. 'Oh, come on,' I say. 'You've brought me here, but you've told me nothing.'

Leaning forward a little, he tries to peer over the shoulders of my escort. 'Here on the left,' he says to the driver, 'just in front of the Treasury – we'll walk the last few yards.'

My police escort climbs out first and stands waiting at my door. 'All right, man,' says Maurice, walking round the car to join me. 'He isn't going to run off, and if he does you can afford to give him a head start.'

A bus roars past, trailing a cloud of diesel fumes, followed by a black cab and another, and as we walk along Whitehall I struggle to hear what Maurice is saying. Taking him by the arm, I lead him from the traffic into King Charles Street where we stand beneath the white-stone portico entrance to the Foreign Office.

'We're trying to keep it from the press . . .'

'What, Maurice? What?'

'I told you. The MP Bernard Floud – he committed suicide. Gassed himself a few days ago. I'm afraid Peter Wright tipped him over the edge. Wilson was going to make him a minister.'

'I don't—'

'Wright was putting him under pressure to reveal his links to the Communist Party.'

'Were there any?'

'At one time.'

'One time,' I scoff.

Maurice puckers his lips – an expression of disapproval that makes him look quite camp. 'You should have told me the truth,' he says.

'About the Party? Christ, Maurice. I was a member for a few months before the war.'

'Dick was furious with me. Accused me of being naïve, of endangering the security of the Service.'

'Because of me?'

'And now the job is probably Phillpotts's to lose.'

'What?' It takes me a moment to realise he's fretting about the succession. 'Is Dick going?'

'As deputy, it should be me who succeeds him.'

'Sod off, Oldfield.' I point to the gap in my teeth. 'See? I don't care who crows from the top of the dungheap. If we're not here to talk about the plot against this country and its prime minister we're not here to talk about anything, and you can ask the car to take me back.'

'Where are the other films?' he says.

'You think I'm going to tell you here?'

'Well, as a favour. It would help me.' He smiles mischievously.

'No, I don't expect you to. However, if I might advise you . . . You've made C look a fool, and even a decent man like Dick finds that hard to forgive. Don't push him too hard. He knows he's made mistakes. Take my word for it, things are changing for the better.' He glances at his watch. 'Look, we must go.'

I expect him to lead me to the door of Number 10 but we pass Downing Street. 'The Cabinet Office,' he explains. 'We have an appointment with the cabinet secretary.'

Sir Burke Trend's office on Whitehall is opposite the Banqueting House where a king was beheaded by revolutionaries. Civil servants exist to snuff out revolutions. They like the state to evolve at the pace of a Galápagos tortoise. I have never met a stupid civil servant, or a bold one. I know nothing of Trend but I expect he was expensively educated and is a member of one of the more prestigious London clubs, and as I climb the stair at the Cabinet Office – modest by the Empire standards of Whitehall – I wonder if my fate was settled in the smoking room at White's or the Reform or the Civil Service Club and if I am only here so Trend can reveal it to me.

Our guide knocks and Trend bids us enter. I shuffle forward with a hand to my waistband: after three months of prison food my trousers are too large. The Nazis used to humiliate their opponents in court in the same way, before pronouncing a death sentence.

'Burke Trend,' he says, clipping his name in a business-like voice. He's fit-looking fifties – about my age – lean, even a little gangly, with a high forehead and a strong jaw, and as he shakes my hand his face is a *tabula rasa*. I am ready to believe after only a few seconds that he is a consummate man of secrets, and as the PM's principal adviser, I suppose he must be.

'No introductions necessary, I think.' He stands aside so I can see my masters seated at his table. Sir Dick White is doing his best to ignore me. Furnival Jones is gripping his chair so tightly his knuckles are white.

'Gentlemen,' Trend gestures to the conference table, 'if you please.'

I sit opposite Dick, who lifts his eyes from a file and fixes me with a hostile stare. Trend takes the seat at the head of the table; the management sits opposite. We're in a grand room in the classical style with pillars and a high ceiling, fine early-Victorian plasterwork above the picture rail, burgundy flock paper below it, and half a dozen portraits of aristocrats I don't recognise. No filing cabinets, no embarrassing secrets, except the ones we will speak at Trend's mahogany conference table – and if he runs around them in true civil-service fashion, well, there are plenty of spare chairs.

'To the matter at hand,' he says, 'which is nothing less than the special relationship with the United States. The prime minister is hoping to visit Washington this month, Mr Vaughan.' He peers at me over his tortoiseshell-framed glasses. 'Any suggestion in the press that the prime minister is the subject of an investigation by rogue elements in our intelligence services and the CIA would damage our relationship further *and* his efforts to secure peace in Vietnam. Do you understand?'

'Perfectly,' I say.

'Course you do.' He reaches into his navy suit jacket for his pipe and tobacco. 'Then if you are still in possession of . . . certain papers, perhaps you will be good enough to return them to the Security Service.'

FJ snorts at this piece of politesse; I answer him with a belligerent stare.

'Have you a copy?' Trend points his pipe at the file beneath

Dick's balled hands. 'Or have you passed it to someone else, Mr Vaughan?'

'Have you read the file?' I ask.

'I have.'

'And the prime minister?'

He hesitates. 'The prime minister knows as much as he wishes to know.'

'Does he know *rogue elements* were plotting a coup against him?'

'For God's sake!' FJ splutters. 'Bloody nonsense. I know what you're doing, Vaughan.'

'Do you?' I lean over the table, my fingers balled into a fist. 'Well, what the hell were *you* doing? The file was in *your* safe. The chief of Counter-intelligence at the CIA is – and I quote – "offering to relieve us of our problem". The problem was the prime minister of this country!'

FJ ignores me and addresses Trend directly. 'Jim Angleton was flying a kite, Sir Burke, that's all.'

'A kite?' Trend strikes a match and holds it to the bowl of his pipe. 'Really. Well, Mr Angleton has clearly exerted a good deal of influence on our intelligence services.' He pauses to puff and char the tobacco. 'And I must say, gentlemen, I am inclined to agree with Mr Vaughan that they have been led astray.'

I catch Dick's eye and he looks bloody uncomfortable.

'But, Mr Vaughan, let me be clear,' says Trend. 'The prime minister does not want this unfortunate episode to sour our relationship with the United States – which is in a delicate enough state – and you must agree he has more reason to be angry than anyone. He has been deeply affected by the death of Mr Floud. He doesn't want an American-style witch-hunt here for Communists. You sent the WORTHINGTON file to a reporter, Mr Vaughan . . .' Trend pauses to draw on his pipe again. 'Mr Oldfield believes you acted for the right reasons – not for money or a love of sensationalism. I hope he's right and we can count on your discretion, because the prime minister is adamant that none of this can appear in the press.'

I nod slowly. 'But there will be changes? Angleton is running the whole damn show. There have to be changes.'

'Mr Vaughan. Please.' Trend taps on the table. 'I understand Mr Angleton enjoys the confidence of the director of the CIA . . .' He turns to Dick, who nods curtly.

'Then we will continue to give him an audience,' Trend says, 'but that is all. I have assured the prime minister that the WORTHINGTON file will be destroyed and there will be a thorough review of the FLUENCY investigation. So, Mr Vaughan, your desperate act *has* succeeded in changing things.'

I don't know whether to believe him. There are so many loose ends: what about Wright? What about the phone taps on MPs and the civil servants who have lost their jobs? What about Blunt, who has been allowed to keep his, and what about the three months I've spent in detention without trial, and the hammering they gave me for doing my duty? What about my wife?

Trend is tapping the ash from his pipe into a glass ashtray. 'Well, that's my piece,' he says. 'The details I leave to you.' Collecting his papers, he rises with a polite smile. 'Gentlemen.' I listen to his footsteps as he approaches the doors behind me. Dick sits straighter; FJ takes a deep breath; Maurice reaches for his cigarettes. Threats and coercion are the business of the uncivil service. My old colleagues are just waiting for them to close to open hostilities.

Dick first: 'Your moral outrage doesn't convince me, Vaughan,' he says. 'This is about saving your skin. I've made mistakes, I admit, but you were certainly the biggest.'

I smile. 'Flattering, really, when you've made such a terrible mess of everything. I couldn't let it go on. Believe it or not, I have some values, and I joined during the war to protect them. One way or another the Service has been my life, and, well, I did what I did to make sense of that life.'

Dick glares at me. Nothing I say will convince him entirely of my innocence.

'If I may?' says Maurice, very calmly. 'I think the cabinet secretary was fairly clear, Harry. Wilson doesn't want to antagonise the Americans, but he *does* want changes to the Service.'

'What sort of changes?'

'He told you: our relationship with Jim Angleton, and the FLUENCY investigation will be shut down. More scrutiny of the Service by Parliament, and . . . some staffing changes.'

'There's no need to be diplomatic,' says Dick. 'I'm going.'

'What about Wright?'

'None of your damn business, Vaughan,' FJ growls at me. 'You're not holding the Security Service to ransom.'

'That's exactly what I'm doing.'

'Then you're not as clever as I thought you were. You should know it's dangerous to poke a tiger with a stick.' FJ squints at me as if he's lining the sight of a rifle. 'You're not the only one who has something to lose.'

For the first time in weeks I feel a pang of fear.

'Your wife was a member of the Party, wasn't she?' he says. 'Her associates – Pool, Hart, the recently deceased Mr Floud . . . and *you*, Vaughan, above all, *you*. JACK and ROSA.'

I shake my head. 'That's rubbish.'

FJ raises his chin belligerently. 'You will remember the meeting with Golitsyn . . . that he told us the KGB was running a female agent in Vienna. She was a Jewess, and when the order came to roll up SUBALTERN, no one was to touch her. So . . .'

'So the witch-hunt isn't over,' I say bitterly. 'You're still prepared to believe that charlatan.'

Maurice is fidgeting with his cigarette lighter, desperate not to catch my eye. Because he's the one who knows I care very deeply for someone the Service can bring low. Counter black-mail with blackmail is their – his – strategy, plain and simple.

'Elsa has never been a Communist,' I say.

Dick snorts derisively. 'She says she didn't know you were a Party member, that you lied to her. Perhaps she was lying to you.'

'Golitsyn is an anti-Semite. And what are you paying him? Ten thousand a month? He'll keep giving you names. I won't let him – you – ruin my wife.'

'You've done that already, I hear.'

That hurts.

Maurice clears his throat noisily. 'A gesture of good faith, Harry. Return the file, give us your word you'll keep this whole affair under your hat, and this other matter with your wife, it will go away. She will be free to move on, you can have your pension . . .'

'That's the deal?'

'That's the deal.'

'I see.' They watch me. Dick's face is a painful-looking red, as if he's fallen asleep on a Costa Brava beach; FJ is stroking the lobe of his elephant-size ear; Maurice is polishing his glasses on his Manchester University tie. He's trying not to smile. He's glad there are going to be changes, but he doesn't want me to tear the house down. And if he delivers old Harry he will be gathered back into the fold – the top job may still be within his grasp.

'But I don't believe you,' I say, pushing my chair from the table. 'The file is my insurance – Elsa's insurance.' And I get to my feet and begin to limp towards the door.

'Wait, Vaughan!' Dick tries to command me. 'Vaughan!'

'Don't ask the goons to stop me,' I shout over my shoulder. 'You don't want a scene in the Cabinet Office.'

# Witchfinder

The doors wouldn't look out of place in Buckingham Palace. Mahogany panels and architraves, full-grain French-polish finish: quite beautiful. I'm sure no one has had the temerity or the impertinence to slam them in the hundred years they've hung here. I'm going to, Guy. I open the right-hand one, step out and swing it back to meet the other. What a noise, really! A boom to send a shudder through the civil service, the Reform, White's and the Carlton, to reach Wilson in Moscow and wake Angleton in Washington, to lift the last dust from the corners of our old Empire and set generations of its masters revolving in their fucking graves. Fuck 'em all.

# 55

THE COPPERS WHO brought me from the camp make no effort to prevent me leaving. I imagine I cut rather a pathetic figure as I limp towards Trafalgar Square, right hand gripping the top of my trousers. Turning into Horse Guards I weave my way through the throng of tourists and World Cup football fans, who surround the troopers in their pantomime uniforms, and cross the parade ground with a vague notion of bathing in whisky at the Reform Club. I stop and rest by the white-stone memorial to the Guards Division, my mind reverberating with echoes of the last hour. I realise I can't bear to set foot in my club or anyone else's. Maurice says Elsa is on leave from the ministry. I've been away for so long, she may have made our house her home again.

I hail a cab before I remember I have no money. The driver likes my linen jacket but doesn't think it's worth the fare, so I hobble home across Broad Sanctuary and through the abbey precincts, turning left, right, then left again through the neat, narrow streets. There's a layer of dust on the beading and frame of the door and city rain has smeared grime on the windows, like tears of mascara on a woman's face. The shutters are closed but I knock and knock, a godless man praying for a small miracle.

Our elderly neighbour opposite has heard me and comes to her door in her fluffy pink little-girl slippers. 'Your wife left a key with me,' Mrs Holland says. 'Hang on just a tick.' She disappears inside, pulling the door shut behind her. Perhaps she's thinking of those nice 'policemen' who rented her house to watch me.

'Here you are!' The key is dangling on a pink ribbon. I let her keep the ribbon.

The bulb has gone in the hall, the shade, the furniture too. And it's the same in the sitting room she used to call the drawing room, except the old upright piano and a canterbury full of music. I run my forefinger along the dusty keys to bottom C. *Bong.* Then again. *Bong.* It needs tuning. My whisky tumblers are on the table we bought together, and just half a bottle of whisky. As I'm cleaning a glass at the sink there's a knock at the front door. I hear the letterbox flap open and Maurice clearing his throat. 'Harry, I want to speak to you. Please.'

He blinks at me nervously. 'Thought you'd be here.' He has taken the precaution of stepping away from my door into the street.

'It's my home, Maurice.'

'Yes.'

I turn away and back to the kitchen and he follows me. 'Do you want a drink?'

He does.

'I'm going to have to charge you for it,' I say, raising the bottle. 'This isn't going to be enough for me.'

'Of course, they still have your things.' He reaches inside his jacket for his wallet.

'I'll pay you back when I can.'

'No need,' he says, placing five pounds on the table.

'What do you want, Maurice? Did Dick send you?'

'No one sent me. I came because you deserve the truth.'

'Ah,' I reply sceptically.

I'm standing against the sink and Maurice is seated at the table a few feet away.

'You were hoping for a revolution,' he says, 'and I'm afraid you will be disappointed. Number 10 will expect Dick's successor to stop the CIA meddling – to sup with a longer spoon – but you heard Burke Trend: Jim Angleton will get his audience. Wright will keep his post – a post.' He raises his hand to stifle my protest. 'Oh, Harry! Come on. It's an American show now – if Jim wants Wright . . . We're on the slide, you know that, and Wilson knows it, too. You won't have heard the news . . .'

I laugh harshly.

'. . . for months. But the economy is on the rocks. Prices and wages are running wild, and we're relying on the Americans to prop up the pound. We've got nothing to bargain with. Our cupboard is bare. That's why Wilson wants this nastiness with Washington to go away. Turning on the CIA would be a terrible mistake.' He pauses. 'Wilson is clear . . .'

'You've spoken to him?'

'Not directly – to someone who has, and who bears you no ill will.'

'Trend?'

Maurice ignores me. 'Wilson is disgusted with Dick and FJ. He swore at them both, called it "treason". But he knows the WORTHINGTON file would hurt him – might even finish his career. The Gaitskell murder plot is absolute nonsense – fantasy – but his friendship with Kagan and Sternberg, his association with a KGB agent in London, those trips to Moscow . . . You know it's possible the KGB *does* have something of a compromising nature.'

'Christ, Maurice.'

He frowns. 'You're not thinking, Harry. Think! We don't know. Wilson doesn't know. Let's assume he's a saint – there's nothing he can't tell his wife. Well, his reputation can still be damaged – if there's enough smoke. The prime minister doesn't trust the Service not to leak the file to his enemies in the press, and we both know he's right not to. Why doesn't the prime minister clear out the Service? Why can't he start a revolution? Because he's afraid of us, and with good reason.'

'You, Maurice. *Not* me.'

'The rogue elements in the Service,' he counters. 'Afraid, and because he's a bit of a Boy Scout, he's fascinated by the Service, too. Harry, he wants us to bury that file, burn it, anything to keep it out of the press. He doesn't trust you not to leak it – nobody trusts you. I speak as your friend: hand it over or your life will be hell.'

I laugh bitterly and open my arms to the room. 'You see? Worse than this?'

'Yes. I'm sorry.'

'If I hand the file to you I become the problem, because it's all up here.' I tap my temple with a forefinger. 'Someone at the top of the Service – you, perhaps – will come up with a brilliant plan to tidy the loose ends, first me, then Elsa.'

'And if we give you some sort of guarantee?'

I laugh again.

Maurice frowns and adjusts his glasses. 'It isn't our Service that should concern you.'

'Is that a threat?'

'No, you fool, a warning. Remember, it's all about the Americans.' He leans forward, his hands spread on his broad thighs. 'Jim's very upset.'

'Anatoli, too, I hope?'

'Oh, yes, Anatoli too.' He gets to his feet and sways towards me. 'Ah. A little too much on an empty stomach, I think. Look, do you want to spend the rest of your life looking over your shoulder? That's what it will mean.'

'I've spent my life doing that, Maurice.'

'Just think about it, will you? When you're calmer, you know where to find me.'

I follow him to the front door where he stoops to pick up the post that has been collecting on the mat for weeks. The effort has him gasping. 'I'll do that, Maurice,' I say, but he refuses to let me. After a good deal of grunting and sighing he turns to present me with the bundle. 'I just want to be sure,' he says. 'Believe me, Harry, it's in your interests to let us have whatever copies you have.'

'I'll be the judge of that. It's insurance, that's all. You can tell Dick, tell Trend, I won't hand it to anyone else.'

He nods.

'And tell Dick I resign. Tell him I won't be a member of a club that accepts people like him and – and me any more.'

'Marx?'

'The same,' I say, reaching over his shoulder for the latch.


She left the bed in the spare room, a chest of drawers and the *armoire de mariage* we bought on our honeymoon in France. My suits and jackets and best shirts are crumpled in a heap where the Special Branch goons who searched the house threw them three months ago. The dressing-gown, too.

I spend the day brooding and drinking Maurice's fiver, and the following morning I nurse my hangover in Toni's café, where I discover in the bundle of post a solicitor's letter notifying me of Elsa's wish to sell the house and separate. The law recognises desertion of a spouse as grounds for divorce. Well, Elsa, I accuse you of deserting me.

I played it in my head for weeks, hurt, confused, sometimes furious, I would shout and stamp about the cell until one of my jailers beat on the door and threatened to beat me too. You betrayed *me*, Elsa. You let that snake Wright seduce you with his s-s-suspicions and lies – told him everything you knew. Why? In the terror hours of the night I saw you with your KGB controller and imagined your whole life as a performance, our lives together as a sham. You were ROSA, or someone like her, and you betrayed me to save yourself as you were schooled to do, and the tears at the grave in Vienna were crocodile tears, because you betrayed young Paul Lovas too, you betrayed SUBALTERN, you were the 'Jewess' mole in Vienna, my Jewess, my wife. And I was so shaken by my reflections I would stand with my forehead against the cell wall and concentrate on the coolness of the painted brick, the susurration of the trees beyond the fence, the cry of a blackbird startled by something in the night.

Fear will make us believe anything. I want to tell her our love is stronger. I want to say: don't let *us* be victims.

## 21 July 1966

I hear she's on holiday in the South of France, and that she's taken another flat in Dolphin Square. Number 328. I consider flying out to find her on one of the passports I cached in the bank deposit box but, after much reflection, decide to wait.

Watchers followed me everywhere for the first few days, and I rushed around London trying to do important things before they grabbed me and carried me back to Ham or to the basement of the War Office. They disappeared today. They followed me to the dentist, and when I left forty minutes later they'd gone. There is beery rejoicing in the streets, because England has beaten France in the World Cup.

The following day I ring my erstwhile employers and request a meeting to discuss my pension. A young thing in Finance and Administration tells me it's on hold and I may not be eligible, so I take a cab across the river and try to barge into

Century House. Security won't let me up and no one in Finance will come down, so I ask to speak to Maurice. Eventually, Nick Elliott arrives in Reception and leads me to an office on the ground floor. *'Persona non grata,* old boy,' he says, as if I didn't know. I tell him, pension and passport or I'll put it in the hands of my lawyer, along with the three months I was held at Her Majesty's pleasure. 'Nothing personal, Nick,' I say.

'Of course not,' he replies, with a broad smile. 'Need a recommendation?'

Parting is awkward as we pretend we're going to keep in touch: 'Perhaps at the cricket.'

Wilson is back from Moscow to tackle the crisis in the country's finances, and I read in *The Times* that his visit to Washington will not take place. I guess he's not welcome. On Monday, I visit my brief to discuss the file. Mr Simpson doesn't know the details but would very much like to. 'Release it to the press,' he says. 'Turn your imprisonment into a political *cause célèbre,*' but I'm conscious of Maurice's warning and that it will do Wilson (and Elsa) more harm than good. Simpson will find another crusade to elevate him to the bench. 'Is it safe?' he asks.

'Fort Knox safe,' I say.

'Are you safe?'

To that I have no answer.

### 26 July 1966

'Where's Elsa?' Bethan asks reproachfully. She knows 'on holiday' isn't the whole story.

She is on her way to a pop concert – a group called the Animals – and with time to spare she has dropped by in the hope of finding Elsa at home.

'Is it something you've done?' she says.

My personal history gives her the right to ask, and I try not to feel hurt by her accusatory tone. 'It's not what you think,' I say.

'Then what?' Feet square apart, hands on her broad hips, it would be easy to imagine I'm being held to account by her grandmother. Elsa and Oxford and a smart Etonian boyfriend have given her the confidence to look at the world and her father with a steady eye. 'It's complicated,' I say. 'Actually, it's to do with work.'

'The Foreign Office?'

'Elsa's angry with me because I may have to go away again.'

Bethan rolls her eyes to the kitchen ceiling in mock despair. 'Daddy, that's a lie. You're a spy! Mother told us.'

I frown. 'She shouldn't have. I hope you haven't told—'

'No,' she says scornfully, 'just what you told us to say – diplomat – and Mary says the same.'

'She knows too?' I feel guilty and ashamed that they've had to lie for me. 'I'm sorry, darling.'

I tell her I'm retiring and yesterday I had lunch with a contact on the *Economist* and there may be work for me in Vienna or Bonn. 'But I won't go if Elsa wants me to stay,' I say.

Bethan takes a determined step towards me – 'Persuade her' – and takes my hand. 'It's too sad.' When she looks up at me there are tears in her eyes. 'Please, Harry.'

I've spoken to Elsa's solicitor and have found one of my own, but I've instructed him to do nothing at this stage. I do chores, buy some clothes, walk miles about the streets of central London, morning and evening, and I feel some strength returning. England are in the final of the World Cup and will play West Germany. At breakfast Toni wants to talk about the game, the barber who cuts my hair too. The whole circus is a welcome distraction. I expect Harold Wilson's grateful too.

## *30 July 1966*

The radio sits on top of the piano, along with a bottle of pale ale, and when someone scores I stop and listen to the commentary. England are winning and I'm happy for them, but I want to make music, drink music, and after months in the desert, Fats and Basie are flowing again. Why? I don't know why, only *I wouldn't mean a thing, no, no, no, without someone to sing to.*

In the strange way of these things, that's the sad little number I'm singing when she opens the sitting-room door.

*Let music in your heart, but you must do your part . . .*

I'm not expecting her; I don't hear her in the hall; I feel her presence.

'Hello,' she says flatly.

'Hello, you,' I reply, twisting on the piano stool to look at her. She has a healthy tan and is still dressed for the Riviera in a white blouse, green linen split skirt and tennis shoes. I'm in a striped shirt with holes at the elbows, like Bogart in *The African Queen*. I'm afraid to go to her, which is bloody foolish of me, I know.

'I'm sorry about this.' She gestures to the room. 'I was angry.'

'And you're not now?'

She shrugs. 'I hear you want to talk to me.'

'I want *us* to talk.'

Elsa closes her eyes momentarily. 'Don't start.'

'Don't start what?' I snap at her.

'It's over.'

I push the stool back and rise. 'Did you believe him?'

'Wright? I didn't know what to believe. You told so many lies – you were in the Party . . .'

'For God's sake, girl, for a few months . . .'

'You should have told me! And SUBALTERN. Wright said a defector named you as the informer.'

'And you believed him?'

'And the file. I work . . . work for the Ministry of Defence. Wright asked me questions – I told him the truth. What did you expect me to do? I'm not like you.'

'I shared things with you. You must have known he would use that against me. Christ, I was trying to protect you because I love you – protect *us*. You should have trusted me!'

'Ha!' She clenches her fists like a bantamweight boxer. 'Protect us!' she shouts. 'Protect us! Stealing a file from MI5, lying to me. Sleeping with your secretary?'

'She wasn't . . . Yes. By doing all those things.'

'Protect yourself.' She's trembling now. 'You bastard!' Her voice is quiet and low. '*You*'ve done this to us.' She takes half a step as if to strike me but checks and holds up the palms of her hands. 'It's over.'

They're cheering on the radio. Another goal for England, I suppose. The dissonance here, now, in our sitting room, it's worthy of the Marx Brothers. She takes a deep breath and I do the same. 'I want my life in the Service to have meaning – it did in the war, and after, in Vienna. You remember, we were fighting to build a better country, a better world?'

'That isn't you,' she says coldly. 'I wonder if it ever was. You found the Service and you became the Service.'

'*Wfft*. You think that little of me?'

She only glares.

'Look, the file,' I say, 'you would be in danger if I gave . . .'

'I don't want to know, Harry. I don't. You *must* give it back.' She looks away furtively. No one else would notice but I know her like no one else. 'Oh, why don't you turn it off?' she says, gesturing to the radio, and in the next breath: 'Let them have it, Harry. Make a clean break.'

I laugh harshly. 'Who asked you to come here? Wright?

Maurice? *He'll listen to you, Mrs Vaughan. Tell him you'll go back to him, and . . .'*

'Don't be— No! I made my feelings quite clear about that.'

'Did you, *cariad?'*

She must hear the sadness in my voice; I hear only anger and contempt in hers. How did it come to this? I'm not sure I have any more fight in me. I have no more anger. I made such plans in my cell: leaving the Service, the job at the *Economist,* the girls – they'll blame me, and I am to blame but not just me. I could tell her . . . They were stoking the fires for you too, my love, the 'Jewess' mole in Vienna. You were in the Party, weren't you? Did you ever leave it? It has always been the forbidden question. But the file you want me to hand over, that bloody file, is your insurance, our insurance. You have seen only broken images. I would lead you from the wilderness, help you see things as they really are, but you're too full of righteous anger to listen. Now trust has gone, nothing I say will save us. This is what FLUENCY has done. We stand in an empty room in our own home with six feet of polished floor as wide as the Grand Canyon between us.

'For God's sake, Harry, are you listening? Are you going to give it back?'

I shake my head. 'No, I'm not, *cariad.* Tell Maurice, "No." He knows the reason why.'

She opens her mouth but can think of nothing else to say. The football is droning on in the background, excitement at a new pitch.

'You're staying at the ministry?'

'Why wouldn't I?'

I shrug. 'No reason.'

She bites her top lip. 'I have a meeting with the cabinet secretary next week. I'm on leave until then.'

'Burke Trend?'

'Yes.'

I nod.

'You've heard from my solicitor? We have to wait a year.'

'There'll be no trouble. And this' – I gesture to the room, the house – 'all yours.'

'Good.' Her face softens a little. 'Right. Then I'll leave you to the football.'

'I think it's almost over.'

'Ah. Well, it isn't your game, is it?'

'Twenty seconds, twenty seconds, and Hurst and Ball are charging wide,' the football man intones.

I watch her shuffle backwards and her gaze roam to every corner of the room except mine. *Cariad,* I'm not going to stop you. Then she looks at me and I see she's fighting back tears. She's sorry, yes, but not enough to save us. 'Goodbye, Harry,' she says. 'Please . . . be careful.'

Why be careful? Why does it matter? It doesn't bloody matter. That's what I think as she turns her head to leave. 'Be happy,' I say. 'Be happy, Elsa.'

There's shouting and cheering. Football man is screaming. Players are hugging each other, falling to their knees. The game's over. They've won.

1976

# Epilogue

WITNESSES HEARD THE engine roar and car tyres on the granite setts, like a small earthquake. Silver Mercedes, two passengers, accelerating south-west towards the Danube canal. Frau Weber was driving to the elementary school where she teaches. She saw the Mercedes slew right and mount the low pavement. Another witness – twelve-year-old Rudy – says the victim turned to run but it was too late: he was tossed over the bonnet like a rag doll. That it was no accident was evident from their accounts of what happened next. The big Mercedes came to a halt after only a few metres, and as the young school-mistress watched in her rear-view mirror, and Rudy cowered in the doorway of number 10, the driver changed gear and reversed at speed over the victim – just to make sure.

Detectives identified him as Mr Henry Vaughan, a journalist who sometimes played the piano at a local café and was well known and liked in the district. The café owner described him as 'honorary Viennese'. Vaughan rented a small apartment on Herminengasse in the Old Town. Neighbours said he wrote for English magazines and often went away on assignments, that his friends were journalists and musicians, his girlfriends too, and sometimes he would speak of his daughters, but they never came to visit. Yes, he was 'political', and journalists always make enemies, but no one could imagine who would want him dead.

At home the big story was the prime minister's resignation,

*The Times* was the only newspaper to find space for a hit-and-run 'accident' abroad. None of the old crowd are left at the embassy in Vienna, the station chief is in his twenties, and if he knew Vaughan used to be one of us he didn't consider it worth a mention in his rip-and-read report to London. It must have been a shock on the morning after the murder, 20 March, when Maurice Oldfield rang to say he was sending someone to investigate – me.

I joined the Secret Intelligence Service a few months after Vaughan's departure – in disgrace, they said. There were rumours he was a KGB mole, that he'd done a deal in return for his freedom, and when Dick White followed him out of the door it looked as if he was taking the blame for another embarrassing penetration of the Service. I remember our relationship with the Americans was frosty for quite some time. White's successor was a colourless civil servant dedicated to doing nothing that might embarrass the government. Those were the doldrum years, when we were frightened of our shadows, and it was only in '73 when Sir Maurice Oldfield became chief that morale began to improve. Michael Hanley was appointed director general of MI5 at about the same time, even though he was one of the officers the FLUENCY team had suspected of being a spy.

As I rose through the ranks of the Service I was briefed in general terms on the years we wasted hunting for a mole at the top, the lessons to be learned from the collapse of our operational efficiency and morale. In that mad time after Philby, the spycatchers were just about running the Service. I don't know Peter Wright – he retired two months ago – and I've only met Jim Angleton once, but he was a CIA legend: the spies he hunted down, the black-bag operations he ran. I was flattered he made time to see me. It was only after the death of Harry Vaughan that I learned the truth about his involvement with FLUENCY and the OATSHEAF investigation.

My mother's German – it's my first language – and I have spent four of the last ten years in Berlin, so I wasn't surprised when C summoned me to his office two days after the assassination and handed me Vaughan's file. I *was* surprised when he told me it was a matter of 'national importance' and that I was to tell no one in or out of the Service where I was going and why. 'Report directly to me, Cath,' he said, 'only me. You're on the next flight from Heathrow.'

My orders were to recover any material that might compromise 'the Service and the security of the country'. Had Vaughan been selling intelligence? Who was responsible for the hit?

A team of municipal workers was still scrubbing the setts in Herminengasse and someone had laid flowers on the pavement close by. Vaughan's flat was at the top of an elegant early-nineteenth-century mansion block painted sunshine yellow and white. The door was hanging off its hinges. Neighbours told the police that it was forced the day before the assassination, and that two unknown men were seen leaving the building in the middle of the afternoon. The intruders had ransacked the place. Vaughan didn't report the break-in and he hadn't found time to clear up the mess. I searched the flat too, and found bills and cuttings and sheet music, and photographs of a person of interest – his second wife, Elsa Frankl Spears. His passports were still there and in one of them there was an exit stamp dated two days before his death and the stub of a BEA airline ticket from London.

It was impossible to know if anything of value to the Service was taken. The police were connecting the break-in and the murder, and when I arrived with my story of a 'former diplomat' they shifted the focus of their investigation to the agents of 'a foreign power'. There was a sketchy description of the driver of the Mercedes – thirties, perhaps, swarthy, moustache – but Frau Weber couldn't find his face in the police files. The usual suspects were the Russians or one of their satellites, and the best guess of the officer in charge of the investigation was that the hit team had crossed the border into Hungary while Vaughan's body was still lying in the street.

The detectives were happy to see it that way, but I'd read Vaughan's file, I'd spoken to Sir Maurice, and it didn't make sense to me. Why would Vaughan offer his 'insurance' to the Russians now, after ten years? Why would they eliminate their source?

Vaughan was a journalist with a story, and the ticket stub was a clue. I asked London to check with the airline. Vaughan had bought his ticket on the morning of the seventeenth and flown direct to Heathrow on the same day. He had returned on the eighteenth when he must have discovered his apartment had been broken into. The following day, the nineteenth, he was murdered in broad daylight in the crudest manner and with no regard for local sensibilities. It was an assassination from the wild forties when the city was divided into military zones. The Russians are more careful these days.

I began to wonder if Vaughan's trip to London was connected in some way to his death. Check the newspapers who paid him for pieces, I said. What was he writing? Vaughan was sitting on a sensational front-page scoop – he had been for ten years. Had he decided it was the right time to sell it? Out of the blue – on the sixteenth – Harold Wilson announced he was going to resign as prime minister: his political career was over. The following day Vaughan flew to London. Coincidence? Sir Maurice didn't think it could be. I don't know who he spoke to after me – the director general of MI5, I imagine – but he rang me back a few hours later with the answer.

Vaughan spoke to *The Times* about the FLUENCY investigation and promised the paper proof from 'a file'. Naturally, the editor was cock-a-hoop at the prospect of a world-wide scoop.

He wanted to splash the story before Wilson left office, and commissioned a mock-up of the front page with the headline: *British and American Spies Plot Against the Prime Minister.*

Vaughan explained to the editor that he'd kept his word for ten years and would have kept it for another ten but for an article in a small-circulation British magazine that could only have come from someone close to the Service.

The piece had been dismissed by Fleet Street newspapers as fantasy, because it trotted out the old FLUENCY allegations: Harold Wilson might have been compromised on a trip to Moscow; he might have accepted money from the Kremlin; his predecessor might have been murdered by the KGB. No proof was offered to back up the story, only the word of 'a source close to MI5'. Peter Wright was the source – I know that now. Vaughan must have known straight away, and that he was flying a kite. There would be more leaks, more fake evidence. Wright is unrepentant. Obsessed. Can't let it go, and neither, perhaps, could Harry. Did he act in defence of democracy, or to expose an old enemy? FLUENCY cost him his wife, his family, his purpose. When Wilson announced he was going, he went to *The Times.* But ten years wasn't long enough, and with his death there is no story, no one to speak out, no file. It's all deniable.

Once London knew the truth it wanted me home, and Sir Maurice was suddenly too busy to speak to me. Why? He must have worked it out straight away. I wasn't sure, and I wasn't going to let it rest until I could be. On a filthy wet Sunday evening I returned to Vaughan's apartment on Herminengasse and combed the place thoroughly for some sort of covert listening or recording device, and this time I did my job properly. There was a hole two inches in diameter in the sitting-room wall that was consistent with the insertion and clumsy extraction of a probe microphone, and a wire in the telephone was disconnected rendering the handset useless. It would have been a simple repair for a man like Vaughan, with technical training, but for some reason he had decided to leave the phone inoperable.

I believe Vaughan removed two bugs from his home in the days before his death, perhaps more. My guess is that he had lived with them for some time, and his decision to remove them signalled to the agency monitoring his activities that he was preparing something. Vaughan possessed one huge secret: the intelligence from the WORTHINGTON-OATSHEAF file. Was he going to sell it? Was he going to publish it? After ten years the alarm bells were ringing, and Vaughan was a problem again. Angleton retired last year, leaving the mess he had created for someone else at the CIA to clear up – which the Agency did with great efficiency. The neatest solution was to dispose of Vaughan and blame the Russians, confident MI6 wouldn't enquire too closely.

Is there a copy of the WORTHINGTON file at Langley? I have no proof. *The Times* will send a reporter to Vienna where the criminal police will hint that it was the KGB. The reporter will seek confirmation from us through the usual channels, and we will encourage him, with a nod and a wink, to report that it was a Russian hit, and the paper will be happy because it still has a story, and we will be happy it's the one we want it to tell. The Service will sit on Wright. The cover-up will be complete. The circle intact. Another blow struck in the Cold War.

Sir Maurice says we will never know for sure. But he *knows*. *I know*.

'Vaughan didn't want to be paid for *The Times* piece,' I say.

'Clean hands to show to the world's press. They weren't, of course . . . his hands. How could they be?' Sir Maurice takes off his glasses with both of his own and pinches the bridge of his nose.

'You mean he . . .'

'That he was working for the other side? No, I don't believe so. There was some evidence his ex-wife, Elsa . . . We couldn't be sure.' He pauses. 'Where's the funeral?'

I mention the name of a municipal cemetery in south London.

'Gracious. Who chose that place?'

'One of his daughters, sir.'

'Headstone won't be up five minutes. Some spotty youth who hates the world will kick it over.' He sighs heavily and puts his glasses back on. 'Would you mind organising a wreath?'

# A Chronology

*1934* Soviet 'illegal' ARNOLD DEUTSCH, code name OTTO, arrives in Britain to recruit a network of spies. His first important recruit is KIM PHILBY, who recommends his Cambridge University friends GUY BURGESS and DONALD MACLEAN. They are inspired by an image of Russia as a worker-peasant state, and freedom from the old class system of interwar Britain.

*1935* MACLEAN is recruited to the British Foreign Office, and begins to supply his Soviet controller with intelligence.

*1936* British socialists and Communists support Spain's Republican government in the civil war against General Franco's Nationalist forces. Republican forces are supplied by the Soviet Union, the Fascists by Nazi Germany. PHILBY works behind Fascist lines for *The Times*, and uses his cover to spy for the Russians.

*1937* By the time OTTO is recalled to Moscow he has recruited more than twenty agents, of which the 'Cambridge spies' are to prove the most successful.

*1938* BURGESS joins Section D of the Secret Intelligence Service (MI6).

*1939* In the summer the Soviet Union signs a secret agreement with Nazi Germany – the Molotov–Ribbentrop Pact – delineating spheres of influence in Europe. On 1 September, the Germans invade Poland, and Britain and France declare war. Some British Communists who looked to the Soviet Union for a lead in the struggle against Fascism turn their back on the Party; the Cambridge spies remain.

*1939–45* PHILBY works for MI6, BURGESS joins MI5, and MACLEAN continues at the Foreign Office. During the course of the war the Cambridge spies pass thousands of pieces of high-grade intelligence to the Soviet Union.

*1945* The fall of Berlin in May marks the end of the war in Europe. The wartime alliance crumbles. An 'Iron Curtain' divides the Communist Eastern bloc from the countries of the West: the Cold War begins.

*1945*, July–August. At the Potsdam Conference, President Harry Truman warns Soviet leader Joseph Stalin that the United States is preparing to use 'the most powerful explosive' yet witnessed by man. Stalin pretends he knows nothing of the weapon, even though British, American and Canadian agents working for the Soviet Union have supplied his scientists with technical information on the development of the bomb. On 6 August America drops an atomic bomb on the Japanese city of Hiroshima and, three days later, another on Nagasaki.

*1945* On 5 September IGOR GOUZENKO, a cipher clerk working for Soviet military intelligence in Canada, defects with more than a hundred classified documents. GOUZENKO reveals the presence of Soviet spies inside the atomic bomb project, and a double agent, code name ELLI, in British intelligence.

*1945* On 19 September, a senior Soviet intelligence officer in Istanbul, KONSTANTIN VOLKOV, tries to do the same. VOLKOV warns that one of its most valuable assets is a mole in a British counter-intelligence section in London, but his defection is discovered and he is executed before he can reveal more.

*1948–49* In the first major crisis of the Cold War, the Soviet Union tries to enforce a blockade of West Berlin to starve it into submission. The United States and its allies supply the city from the air.

*1949–51* PHILBY serves as MI6 liaison officer in Washington, a position that offers him remarkable access to CIA intelligence. He supplements official briefings by gathering information at alcoholic lunches with his friend, senior CIA officer JAMES JESUS ANGLETON.

*1950* In March, British physicist and atom spy KLAUS FUCHS is convicted of supplying important technical intelligence on the development of the hydrogen bomb to his Soviet case officer.

*1951* PHILBY warns MACLEAN that the Americans are close to identifying him as the Soviet agent inside the British Foreign Office. In May, MACLEAN and BURGESS escape to Moscow. Senior MI5 officers believe PHILBY tipped them off, and he is recalled to London. It is the end of his career as an MI6 officer, but not the last of his contacts with the Service. His friends in Six and the CIA – NICHOLAS ELLIOTT and JAMES JESUS ANGLETON – refuse to believe he is a Soviet spy.

*1950–54* Fear of Communist spies and 'enemies within' reach a new height in the United States with the pursuit and investigation of prominent people in government, the army and the arts by the House of Representatives Un-American Activities Committee and Senator JOE MCCARTHY.

*1953* DICK WHITE becomes director general of the Security Service (MI5).

*1954* JAMES JESUS ANGLETON becomes chief of Counter-intelligence at the CIA and PETER WRIGHT joins MI5 as a scientific officer.

*1955* An MI6 investigation exonerates PHILBY of involvement in the defection of BURGESS and MACLEAN. But in America the FBI leaks information to a newspaper, naming PHILBY as a Soviet spy – 'The Third Man'. The charge is refuted in the British Parliament by Foreign Secretary HAROLD MACMILLAN.

*1956*, February. BURGESS and MACLEAN are revealed at a press conference in Moscow. In response, BURGESS's friend, GORONWY REES, writes a series of sensational and salacious articles about 'the greatest traitor of all' for the *People*. His pieces imply a ring of Communist spies in British society that 'must be rooted out'. But REES is the first casualty when he is forced to resign as principal of Aberystwyth University.

*1956* DICK WHITE is appointed chief of the Secret Intelligence Service (MI6) and is replaced as director general of the Security Service (MI5) by his deputy, ROGER HOLLIS.

*1956* In November, Soviet forces crush the Hungarian Rising.

*1961*, January. CIA agent and deputy head of Polish military counter-intelligence, MICHAEL GOLENIEWSKI – code name SNIPER – defects to the United States. He brings intelligence that leads to the arrest of five members of a spy ring at a British defence establishment. SNIPER's intelligence also helps to expose MI6 officer GEORGE BLAKE as a KGB double agent.

*1961*, August. Work begins on what will become the Berlin Wall.

*1961*, December. KGB Major ANATOLI GOLITSYN defects to the United States with evidence of Soviet penetration of both MI6 and the CIA. In the spring of 1962, MI5 officer ARTHUR MARTIN debriefs GOLITSYN in Washington. The intelligence he provides leads to the exposure of a clerk at the British Admiralty, JOHN VASSALL, as a Soviet spy, and helps to strengthen the case against PHILBY.

*1962*, June. KGB Lieutenant Colonel YURI NOSENKO becomes a CIA agent. He remains in place until February 1964.

*1962*, October. The deployment of Soviet nuclear missiles in Cuba leads to a direct confrontation with the United States. The Cuban Missile Crisis comes close to provoking full-scale nuclear war. The crisis ends when the Soviet Union agrees to remove its missiles in return for a guarantee that America will not invade Cuba.

*1963*, January. British Labour Party leader Hugh Gaitskell dies of a mysterious illness and is replaced on 14 February by Harold Wilson.

*1963*, January. MI6 officer NICHOLAS ELLIOTT is sent to Beirut to confront PHILBY with the fresh evidence of his guilt. PHILBY admits he was a spy but tries to deny working for the KGB after 1946. He agrees to return to Britain and make a full confession only to ensure he has time to arrange his escape to Moscow.

# Sources

'Your spies are here. My methodology has uncovered them,'
Anatoli Golitsyn intoned darkly, pointing his finger like the
witch-finder at two files on the table in front of him.

From *Spycatcher: The Candid Autobiography
of a Senior Intelligence Officer*, Peter Wright

R ESEARCHING *WITCHFINDER* WAS a challenge because British
intelligence services files from the sixties are not available
to the average Joe. Well groomed files will be released in due
course, no doubt, but I have drawn almost exclusively on
published histories and memoirs. They offer only a partial view
of the events and characters in my story. The task was made
more difficult because *Witchfinder* is set in Jim Angleton's
'wilderness of mirrors' where – in the words of Peter Wright
'defectors are false, lies are truth, truth lies, and the reflections
leave you dazzled and confused'.

I have charted my own course, used my imagination to fill
gaps, changed some events and omitted others, and in the interests of the story compressed an eight-year-long investigation
into penetration of the British intelligence services into three.
The FLUENCY working party was established to examine
evidence of penetration of both services; in my story it is responsible for the wider D3 investigation into suspected Communists
too. British MP Bernard Floud committed suicide in 1967;

Phoebe Pool in 1971. Graham Mitchell was questioned by Martin Furnival Jones in 1970, Roger Hollis in 1971. Sir Dick White resigned as chief of the Secret Intelligence Service in 1968. Hungarian patriot, Béla Bajomi and his network existed, and the survivors were convinced they were betrayed by a double agent in the British Secret Intelligence Service, but their operation was not given the code name SUBALTERN; that belonged to another MI6 agent operation in Vienna after the war.

For simplicity I refer throughout the book to 'the Service' to indicate both the British Security Service (MI5) and the Secret Intelligence Service (MI6).

A Soviet intelligence agency was founded just six weeks after the Bolshevik Revolution, and was known by nine different names in the forty years that followed, the last in 1954 when it became the KGB. I use the name KGB throughout the story. The cryptonyms of its agents in Britain changed regularly: Guy Burgess was known as MÄDCHEN and HICKS; Anthony Blunt, TONY and JOHNSON. I take just one name. The term 'mole' to indicate a penetration or sleeper agent was popularised in the seventies by John le Carré, and is now so well-known I chose to use it too.

In *Witchfinder*, Harry Vaughan believes the mysterious mole in British intelligence, ELLI, is a mistake, and that ELLI and STANLEY are one and the same double agent: Kim Philby. Harry was wrong. It was not until 1982 that MI6 was able to identify one of Anthony Blunt's recruits, Leo Long, as agent ELLI. The intelligence was supplied by its own greatly prized agent, ex-KGB colonel, Oleg Gordievsky. Not only was Roger Hollis finally cleared of all suspicion, but Gordievsky was also able to confirm that John Cairncross was the Fifth Man.

Labour politician Tom Driberg's contacts with MI5 and the KGB are a matter of dispute. KGB senior archivist Vasili Mitrokhin claimed the MP was working for the organisation; Peter Wright, that he gave intelligence to a Czech controller for money. There's no evidence to suggest he offered more 'intelligence' than could be found in a good newspaper.

Much has been made of the contacts between British left wingers and Eastern Bloc 'diplomats' during the Cold War. Driberg is just one of a number of Labour Party politicians and trade unionists who have been accused of acting as Soviet 'agents', 'agents of influence' or 'confidential contacts'. Gordievsky reported to his handlers in the early 1980s that there was a file in Moscow Centre on British Labour Party leader Michael Foot, code name BOOT, and that he accepted money for information. The allegations were printed in *The Sunday Times* in 1995 and Foot sued and won damages for a 'McCarthyite smear'. Nevertheless, charges against Foot and others have not gone away. Ben Macintyre claims in his excellent book, *The Spy and the Traitor*, that the KGB made payments to Foot totalling £1500, a sum equivalent to £37,000 today, and that the money was probably used to prop up the left-wing *Tribune* newspaper.

Foot believed it was his duty to understand what was happening behind the iron curtain, and, where possible, reach across it with the hand of friendship. The British intelligence services naturally viewed any approach to or from the other side with suspicion, especially if money was changing hands. But Foot did not hide his contacts with Eastern Bloc 'diplomats', he was critical of the Kremlin, he did not betray his country, leaked no state secrets, and he did not break the law.

Macintyre suggests elsewhere in his book that the KGB in London exaggerated its contacts and that much of the information it sent to Moscow in the early 1980s was 'pure invention'. London was a good posting, and to hold on to a plumb position it was important to point to successes. In fact, Gordievsky reported to his handlers at MI6 that Soviet penetration of the British establishment was 'pitiful', and that 'paper agents' were kept 'on the books' so that KGB officers in London looked busy.

The Director General of MI5 informed the Cabinet Secretary, Sir Robert Armstrong, that Michael Foot, the leader of Her Majesty's opposition, was once a KGB agent. Armstrong considered the evidence and chose very wisely not to take it to Prime Minister, Margaret Thatcher. Spies are often economical with the truth.

Wright's account of the hunt for spies and Communists in positions of influence in British society in his book *Spycatcher: The Candid Autobiography of a Senior Intelligence Officer* was my most important source. It purports to tell – in the words of its jacket – the 'devastating story of a government agency (MI5) which operated outside propriety and the law'. *Spycatcher* is a self-serving, deceitful memoir, yet it offers an extraordinary insight into the motives and actions of counter-intelligence officers on both sides of the Atlantic in the years after Kim Philby's defection. The British government's attempt to suppress its publication thirty years ago helped turn it into a bestseller and spread its author's conspiracy theories around the globe.

In his authorised history of MI5 – *The Defence of the Realm* – Christopher Andrew quotes from an internal review of the Hollis and Mitchell investigations conducted after the publication of *Spycatcher.* The review concluded there was 'a lack of intellectual rigour in some of the leading investigators,' and that Peter Wright was 'dishonest' and 'did not scruple to invent evidence where none existed'. Above all, it condemned the baleful influence of Golitsyn who realised in 1963 that 'he had told all he knew and set about developing his theory of massive and co-ordinated Soviet deception, supported by high-level penetration of all Western intelligence and security services.'

Wright, Martin and de Mowbray never stopped believing Soviet agents and Communists were at the heart of British intelligence, of British life. As Christopher Andrew observes, 'conspiracy theory of the kind contracted by all three is an incurable condition'. Angleton remained a sufferer, too. In a briefing to CIA officers in 1974 he spoke of a massive Soviet deception campaign, and of British prime minister Harold Wilson 'as a servant of the Soviet Union' – and he continued to peddle the myth that Wilson was helped to power by the murder of his predecessor, Gaitskell.

Like the witchfinders of previous centuries, Angleton and Wright, and their coterie of counter-intelligence officers, believed they possessed powers of understanding that placed them above senior colleagues, the law and the will of Parliament. 'I certainly didn't, and most people in MI5 didn't have a duty to Parliament,' Wright observed to an interviewer in 1988. 'It's up to us to stop Russians getting control of the British government.' In the last pages of *Spycatcher* he laments the retirement of the 'great mole hunts' as 'the passing' of an 'age of heroes'. Now we know those 'great' mole hunters did as much to undermine efficiency and trust in the intelligence services as Kim Philby.

I would like to acknowledge my debt to the following authors. Christopher Andrew, *The Defence of the Realm,* and *The Sword and the Shield: The Mitrokhin Archive and the Secret History of the KGB*; Tony Benn, *Out of the Wilderness, Diaries 1963–67*; Roy Berkeley, *A Spy's London*; Tom Bower, *The Perfect English Spy: Sir Dick White and the Secret War, 1935–90*; Andrew Boyle, *The Climate of Treason: Five Who Spied for Russia*; Miranda Carter, *Anthony Blunt: His Lives;* Anthony Cavendish, *Inside Intelligence*; Gordon Corera, *MI6: Life and Death in the British Secret Service*; John Costello, *Mask of Treachery*; Richard Crossman, *The Crossman Diaries: Selections from the diaries of a Cabinet Minister 1964–70*; Nicholas Elliott, *Never Judge A Man By his Umbrella*; Jenifer Hart, *Ask Me No More*; Michael Holzman, *James Jesus Angleton, the CIA, and the Craft of Counter-intelligence*; Keith Jeffery, *MI6: The History of the Secret Intelligence Service 1909–1949*; John le Carré, *The Pigeon Tunnel*; David Leigh, *The Wilson Plot*; Andrew Lownie, *Stalin's Englishman: The Lives of Guy Burgess*; Ben Macintyre, *A Spy Among Friends: Kim Philby and the Great Betrayal,* and *The Spy and the Traitor*; Tom Mangold, *Cold Warrior: James Jesus Angleton, the CIA's Master Spy Hunter*; David Martin, *Wilderness of Mirrors*; Yuri Modin, *My 5 Cambridge Friends, By Their KGB Controller*; Martin Pearce, *Spy Master: The Life of Britain's Most Decorated Cold War Spy and Head of MI6, Sir Maurice Oldfield*; Kim Philby, *My Silent War: The Autobiography of a Spy*; Roland Philipps, *A Spy Named Orphan: The Enigma of Donald Maclean*; Ben Pimlott, *Harold Wilson*; Chapman Pincher, *Their Trade is Treachery*; Goronwy Rees, *Sketches in Autobiography;* Jenny Rees, *Looking for Mr Nobody: The Secret Life of Goronwy Rees;* Stella Rimington, *Open Secret: The Autobiography of the Former Director-General of MI5*; Nigel West, *Mask: MI5's Penetration of The Communist Party of Great Britain*; Francis Wheen, *The Soul of Indiscretion: Tom Driberg, Poet, Philanderer, Legislator and Outlaw*; Peter Wright, *Spycatcher: The Candid Autobiography of a Senior Intelligence Officer;* The US National Security Agency Central Security Service (https://www.nsa/gov); Philip M. Williams, *Hugh Gaitskell.*

From Jenny Rees's moving biography – *Looking for Mr Nobody: The Secret Life of Goronwy Rees* – I drew, not only the character and colour of her father and his friends, but the quote from W. B. Yeats's *Vacillation* that appears at the front of the book. Lines from *The Collected Poems of Dylan Thomas: The Centenary Edition* are quoted with permission of The Dylan Thomas Trust, and from T.S. Eliot's *Collected Poems 1909–1962* with the permission of Faber and Faber Ltd. *Let's Sing Again*, words and music by Jimmy McHugh and Gus Kahn © 1936, is reproduced by permission of Cotton Club Publishing/EMI Music Publishing Ltd.

Finally, I would like to thank the following Party members: agent Julian Alexander, for recruiting and encouraging me; my editor-controller at Hodder, Nick Sayers, for his patience, his advice, his rigour; and my network of friends and family for everything else – especially Kate, Lachlan and Finn.